A PERFECT OBSESSION

Also by HEATHER GRAHAM

DARKEST JOURNEY

DEADLY FATE

HAUNTED DESTINY

FLAWLESS

THE HIDDEN

THE FORGOTTEN

THE SILENCED

THE DEAD PLAY ON

THE BETRAYED

THE HEXED

THE CURSED

WAKING THE DEAD

THE NIGHT IS FOREVER

THE NIGHT IS ALIVE

THE NIGHT IS WATCHING

LET THE DEAD SLEEP

THE UNINVITED

THE UNSPOKEN

THE UNHOLY

THE UNSEEN

AN ANGEL FOR CHRISTMAS

THE EVIL INSIDE

SACRED EVIL

HEART OF EVIL

PHANTOM EVIL

NIGHT OF THE VAMPIRES

THE KEEPERS

GHOST MOON

GHOST NIGHT

GHOST SHADOW

THE KILLING EDGE

NIGHT OF THE WOLVES

HOME IN TIME FOR CHRISTMAS

UNHALLOWED GROUND

DUST TO DUST

NIGHTWALKER

DEADLY GIFT

DEADLY HARVEST

DEADLY NIGHT

THE DEATH DEALER

THE LAST NOEL

THE SÉANCE

BLOOD RED

THE DEAD ROOM

KISS OF DARKNESS

THE VISION

THE ISLAND

GHOST WALK

KILLING KELLY

THE PRESENCE

DEAD ON THE DANCE FLOOR

PICTURE ME DEAD

HAUNTED

HURRICANE BAY

A SEASON OF MIRACLES

NIGHT OF THE BLACKBIRD

NEVER SLEEP WITH STRANGERS

EYES OF FIRE

SLOW BURN

NIGHT HEAT

* * * * *

Look for Heather Graham's next novel
DYING BREATH
available soon from MIRA Books.

HEATHER GRAHAM

A PERFECT OBSESSION

MIRA®

ISBN-13: 978-0-7783-1987-0

A Perfect Obsession

For questions and comments about the quality of this book, please contact us at CustomerService@Harlequin.com.

www.MIRABooks.com

Printed in U.S.A.

To Bryee-Annon Pozzessere and Joseph Hunton,
with congratulations on their marriage.
And to Ellysse and Zohe Hunton, beautiful additions to our family.

CHAPTER
ONE

"HORRIBLE! OH, GOD, HORRIBLE! TRAGIC!" **JOHN SHAW**
said, shaking his head with a dazed look as he sat on his bar
stool at Finnegan's pub.

Kieran nodded sympathetically. Construction crews had
found the old graves when they were working on the foundations at the hot new downtown venue, Le Club Vampyre.

Anthropologists found the new body among the old graves
the next day.

It wasn't just *any* body.

It was the body of supermodel Jeannette Gilbert.

Finding the old graves wasn't much of a shock—not in New
York City, and not in a building that was close to two centuries old. The structure that housed Le Club Vampyre was a
deconsecrated Episcopal Church. The church's congregation
had moved to a facility it had purchased from the Catholic
Church—whose congregation was now in a sparkling new
basilica over on Park Avenue. While many had bemoaned the
fact that such a venerable old building had been turned into

an establishment for those into sex, drugs, and rock and roll, life—and business—went on.

They were expanding the wine cellar, and so work on the foundations went on, too.

It was while investigators were still being called in following the discovery of the newly deceased body—moments before it hit the news—that Kieran Finnegan learned about it, and that was because she was helping out at their family pub, Finnegan's on Broadway. Like the old church-nightclub behind it, Finnegan's dated back to just before the Civil War, and had been a pub for most of those years. Since it was geographically the closest establishment to the church with liquor, it had apparently seemed the right place at that moment for Professor John Shaw. They'd barely opened; it was still morning and it was a Friday, and Kieran was only there at that time because her bosses had decided on a day off following their participation in a lengthy trial. She'd just been down in the basement, fetching a few bottles of a vintage chardonnay for her brother, ordered specifically for a lunch that day, when John Shaw had caught her attention, desperate to talk.

"I can't tell you how excited I was, being called in as an expert on a find like that," the professor told Kieran. "They both wanted me! By 'they,' I mean Henry Willoughby, president of Preserve Our Past, and Roger Gleason, owner and manager of the club. I was so honored. It was exciting to think of finding the *old* bodies…but then, opening a decaying coffin and finding Jeannette Gilbert!" He paused for a quick breath. "And the university was entirely behind me, allowing me the time to be at the site, giving me a chance to bring my grad students there. Oh, my God! I found her! Oh, it was…"

John Shaw was shaking as he spoke. He was a man who'd seen all kinds of antiquated horrors, an expert in the past. He fit the stereotype of an academic, with his lean physique, his thatch of wild white hair and his little gold-framed glasses. He held doctorate degrees in archaeology and anthropology, and both science and history meant everything to him.

Kieran realized that he'd been about to say once again that it was horrible, like nothing he'd ever experienced. He clearly realized that he was speaking about a recently living woman, adored by adolescent boys and heterosexual males of all ages—a woman who was going to be deeply mourned.

Jeannette Gilbert—media princess, supermodel and actress—had disappeared two weeks ago after the launch party for a new cosmetics line. Her agent and manager, Oswald Martin, had gone on the news, begging what he assumed were kidnappers for her safe return.

At that time, no one knew if she actually *had* been kidnapped. One reporter had speculated that she'd disappeared on purpose, determined to get away from the very man begging kidnappers for her release.

Kieran hadn't really paid much attention; she'd assumed that the young woman—who'd been made famous by the same Oswald Martin—had just had enough of being adored and fawned over and told what to do at every move, and decided to take a hiatus. Or it might have been some kind of publicity gig; her disappearance had certainly ruled the headlines. There were always tabloid pictures of Jeannette dating this or that man, and then speculation in the same tabloids that her manager had furiously burst into a hotel room, sending Jeannette Gilbert's latest lover—a gold digger, as Martin referred to any young man she dated—flying out the door.

In the past few weeks the celebrity magazines had run rampant with rumors of a mystery man in her life. A secret love. Kieran knew that only because her twin brother, Kevin, was an actor, struggling his way into TV, movies and theater. He read the tabloids avidly, telling Kieran that he was "reading between the lines," and that being up on what was going on was critical to his career. There were too many actors—even good ones—out there and too few roles. Any edge was a good edge, Kevin said.

While all the speculation had been going on, Kieran couldn't help wondering if Jeannette's secret lover had killed her—or if, maybe, her steel-handed manager had done so.

Or—since this was New York City with a population in the millions—it was possible that some deranged person had murdered her, perhaps even someone who wasn't clinically insane but mentally unstable. Perhaps this person felt that if she was relieved of her life, she'd be out of the misery caused by being such a beautiful, glittering star, always the focus of attention.

It was fine to speculate when you really believed that someone was just pulling a major publicity stunt.

Now Kieran felt bad, of course. From what she knew now, it was evident that the woman had indeed been murdered.

Not that she knew any of the findings. In fact, she knew only one: Jeannette had been found in the bowels of the earth in a nineteenth-century tomb. But she knew it was unlikely that the woman had crawled into a historic coffin in a lost crypt to die of natural causes.

"It was so horrible!" John Shaw repeated woefully. "When we found her, we just stared. One of my young grad students screamed, and she wasn't the only one. We called the police immediately. The club wasn't open then, of course—except to those of us who were working. I was there for hours while the police grilled me. And now…now, I need this!" His hand shook as he picked up his double shot of single malt scotch and swallowed it in a gulp.

He was usually a beer man. Ultra-lite.

It was horrible, yes, as Shaw kept saying. But, of course, he realized he'd be in the news, interviewed for dozens of papers and magazines and television, as well.

After all, he'd been the one to find Jeannette Gilbert, dead. In a coffin, in a deconsecrated church now turned into the Le Club Vampyre. Well, that was news.

The pub would soon be buzzing, especially since it was around the block from Le Club Vampyre.

The whole situation was interesting to Kieran. In her "real" job, she worked as a psychologist and therapist for psychiatrists Bentley Fuller and Allison Miro. But, like her brothers, she often filled in at the pub; it was kind of a home away from home for them all. The pub had been in the family from the mid-nineteenth century, dating back to her distant great-great-uncle. Her own parents were gone now, and that made the pub even more precious to her and her older brother, Declan, her twin, Kevin, and her "baby" brother, Daniel.

As manager, Declan was the only one who made the pub his lifework. Kevin pursued his acting career, and Danny strove to become the city's best tour guide. Yet they all spent a great deal of time at Finnegan's.

The tragic death of Jeannette Gilbert would soon have all their patrons talking about this latest outrage at Le Club Vampyre. They'd been talking about the place for the past six months, ever since the sale of the old church to Dark Doors Incorporated. The talk had become extremely glum when the club had opened a month ago. A club like that in an old church!

The club had, of course, been the main topic of conversation yesterday, when the news had come out that unknown grave sites had been found—and Professor John Shaw had been called in.

Of course, people were still talking about the old catacombs today. Not that finding graves while digging in foundations was unusual in New York. It was just creepy-cool enough to really talk about.

Creepy-cool was fine when you were talking about the earthly remains of the long dead.

Not the newly deceased.

At the moment, though, Kieran was one of the few people who knew that the body of Jeannette Gilbert had been discovered. That was because she knew Dr. John Shaw, professor of archaeology and anthropology at NYU, famed in academic circles for his work on sites from Jamestown, Virginia, to Beijing, China. He and a group of his colleagues had met at Finnegan's one night a month as long as she could remember.

When she'd seen him enter today looking so distressed, she'd ushered him into one of the small booths against the wall that divided the pub's general area from the offices. She'd gotten him his scotch, and she'd sat with him so she could try to calm him.

"Oh, my God! I can just imagine when it hits the news!" he said, looking at her with stricken eyes. And yet, she recognized a bit of awe in them.

Of course, he hadn't known Jeannette Gilbert personally. Kieran hadn't, either. She'd seen her once, on a red carpet, heading to the premiere of a new movie in a theater near Times Square.

Sadly, Jeannette hadn't been an especially talented actress. But she'd been too beautiful for most people to care.

"I'm so sorry you're the one who found her," Kieran said.

That should've been the right thing to say; usually, people didn't want to find a body. Still, John Shaw worked with the dead all the time—the long dead, at least—and he was going to be famous in the pop culture world now, as well as the academic world.

But it was obvious that he was badly shaken.

He was accustomed to studying bones and mummies—not a woman who'd been recently murdered.

"I was—I am—very excited about the project. I don't understand how the church could have lost all those graves. Can you imagine? Okay, so, you know how they built Saint Paul's to accommodate folks farther north of Trinity back in the day? Well, they built Saint Augustine's for those a little north of Saint Paul's. And, according to my research so far, the church was fine until about 1860, when way too many people went off to fight in the Civil War. It wasn't deconsecrated—just more or less abandoned because the congregations were so much smaller. Then, according to records, Father O'Hara passed away, and it took the church forever to send out a new priest. Apparently, there was structural damage by then, which closed off that section of the catacombs. You see, until about seventy-five years ago, there was an entrance to the catacombs from the street, and I suppose everyone— church officials, city organizers, engineers, what have you— believed all the graves had been removed. Of course, most of the dead were buried then in wooden coffins, and in the ground outside, so most of those became dirt and bone. But there'd been underground catacombs, too. Coffins set upon shelves. Some of the dead were just shrouded, but some were in old wooden coffins, and they were decaying and falling apart, and I had workers taking them down so carefully— and then, there she was!"

He sipped his scotch again and looked at Kieran intently. "You're not to say a word, not yet. The police…they asked me not to speak about this until…until someone was notified. I don't think either of her parents is living, but she must have family…" His voice trailed off. "My God. It was ghastly!" he said a moment later. "Gruesome!"

Once again he picked up his glass and swallowed the scotch in a gulp.

Kieran wasn't sure why she turned to look at the front door when she did; it was always opening and closing. Maybe she wanted to look anywhere except at John Shaw. She was a working psychologist, and yet she wasn't sure what to say to the man.

She glanced up just in time to see Craig Frasier come in, blink, adjust to the light and walk toward the two of them.

She wasn't surprised Craig was there; they were seeing each other and had been since the affair over the "flawless" Capeletti diamond. It had all started as they danced around each other following a diamond heist. They were both assigned to the case, but Kieran's involvement had been more than a little complicated. They'd progressed to each having a dresser drawer at the other's apartment, and were now talking about moving in together.

While she had truly fallen in love with Craig, she was a little hesitant—and a little worried that the man she believed to be her soul mate also happened to be a special agent with the FBI. Her family was striving to be legitimate now, but that hadn't always been the case. Growing up, her brothers had had a few brushes with the law.

And trusting her beloved brothers to behave wasn't easy. They were never malicious; however, their ways of helping friends out of bad situations weren't always the best.

Then again, she'd met Craig because of the Capeletti diamond and Danny's determination to do the right thing...

And because of some criminal clientele.

"Excuse me," she murmured to John, assuming that Craig had come to see her.

The door was still open; he stood in a pool of light, and her heart leaped as she saw him. Craig was, in her mind, entirely impressive, tall and broad-shouldered, with extraordinary eyes that seemed to take in everything.

But he had not, apparently, come to see her.

He greeted Kieran with a nod, held her shoulders for a minute—and then offered her a grim smile as he gently set her aside so he could move past her.

Something was up. Craig spent his free time here with her and her family. Her friends, coworkers and the usual clientele all knew that Craig and Kieran were a couple.

Today, however, there wasn't even a quick kiss. Craig was being very official.

He was heading straight to the booth where John Shaw was seated.

Kieran stood there for a minute, perplexed.

Jeannette Gilbert had been killed, but as a local woman her death should've remained a matter for the New York City Police Department, not the FBI. And John Shaw had left the body less than an hour ago.

Why would Craig be here so quickly? And more to the point, why was the FBI involved?

She didn't get a chance to slide back into the booth and find out what was going on; she felt a tap on her shoulder and turned.

Her brother Kevin was next to her. He was a striking man—in *anyone's* opinion, she thought. He was tall and fit, with fine features, dark red hair and deep blue eyes. They were twins, and it showed.

"I have to talk to you," he said urgently.

"Sure," she said.

"Not here. In the office," he told her. To her surprise, he glanced uneasily at Craig, whom he liked and with whom he was pretty good friends.

Kevin whirled her and headed her down the entry aisle toward the bar, and then to the left and down the hallway to the business office. He peered in, as if afraid their older brother might be there, since it was, basically, Declan's office.

He closed the door behind them.

"She's dead, Kieran! She's dead!" Kevin said, looking at her and shaking his head with dismay and anxiety.

She stared at him for a moment. He couldn't be talking about Jeannette Gilbert—no one knew that she'd been found at the church yet, not according to John Shaw.

Her heart quaked with fear. She was afraid he was talking about an old friend, or a longtime customer of the pub.

Someone he cared about deeply.

"Kevin, *who*?" she asked.

"Jeannette."

She frowned. "Jeannette Gilbert?"

He nodded.

"Okay," she said slowly. "I know that, because John Shaw just told me. But he only found her body a few hours ago. The police asked him not to say anything."

Kevin took a deep breath. "Well, John Shaw might not have said anything, but one of the workers down there—a grunt, a student, I don't know—came out and told people on the street, and the story was picked up, and there are already media crews there."

She studied her brother. "Kevin, it's terrible. A beautiful young woman has—I'm assuming—been murdered. But, Kevin, I'm afraid that terrible things do happen. But...we didn't know Jeannette Gilbert. Not personally."

"Yes," he said. "We did."

"We did?"

"*I* did," he corrected. "Kieran, I was the so-called 'mystery man' she was dating! I might have been the last one to see her alive."

The NYPD had been called in first; that was proper protocol, since New York City was where the body had been found.

She'd last been seen by her doorman entering her apartment; she was a longtime Manhattan resident. She had, in fact, grown up in Harlem, a little girl who'd lost both parents and gone on to live in a household filled with children and an aunt who hadn't wanted another mouth to feed.

By the age of seventeen, however, she'd had an affair with a rock star.

While the rock star denied any kind of intimate relationship with her at the time, he'd gone on to put her in one of his music videos soon after.

An agent had picked her up and it had been a classic tale— little girl lost had become a megastar. By twenty-five, she was gracing runways all over the world and, because of her modeling, doing cameo spots on television shows and even appearing in small roles in several movies. She was considered a true supernova.

Jeannette's physical appearance had been called *perfect* by every critic out there.

She could walk a runway.

She had beautiful skin, luscious hair, long legs and a body that didn't quit.

Craig Frasier had learned all this about Jeannette in the last few hours. Before that, she'd only been a face he might have recognized on a magazine cover.

But he'd made it his business to read up on her quickly.

Because her death had suddenly become the focus of his life.

He'd been in his office, reading statements from witnesses about the murder of a known pimp, when he'd been summoned, along with his partner, Mike Dalton, to Assistant Director Richard Egan's office.

Craig and Mike had been partners for years. Craig had been assigned a young, new agent when Mike was laid up on medical leave—a shot to the buttocks—about a year ago. He'd learned then how much he appreciated his partner; they knew each other's minds. They naturally fell into a division of labor when it came to pounding the pavement and getting the inevitable paperwork done.

And there was no one Craig trusted more to have his back, especially in a shoot-out.

Egan, a good man himself, was hard-core Bureau. His personal life had suffered for it, but he never brought his personal life into the office. He was the best kind of authority figure, as well—dignified, fair, compassionate. And efficient. He never wasted time. There were two chairs in front of his desk, but he hadn't waited for Craig and Mike to sit down. He'd started talking right away.

"I had a back-burner situation going on here," he'd told them. "We'd been given information, but the local police down in Fredericksburg, Virginia, were handling the case. A girl—a perfect-looking girl, an artist's model—disappeared about six months ago. A few weeks later, her body was found in a historic cemetery outside Fredericksburg, in a mausoleum. She'd been stabbed in the heart, then cleaned up, dressed up and laid out in a family mausoleum. She was discovered when the family's matriarch died, since she'd been put in the matriarch's space. As I said, it seemed to be a local matter, and the Fredericksburg PD and Virginia State Police had the murder. We were informed because of the unusual aspects."

Egan had paused, running his hands through his hair. Then he'd resumed speaking. "We're all aware of the high-profile disappearance of Jeannette Gilbert."

Mike had nodded. "Yeah, we were briefed with the cops about her disappearance when she went missing. We weren't really in on it, as you know. But we were on the lookout."

"Ms. Gilbert's been found. An archaeological dig at old Saint Augustine's."

"You mean—" Mike began.

But Egan had cut him off. Yeah, he meant the new nightclub. Egan wasn't a fan. He'd gone on and ranted for a full minute about the destruction of old historic places. In his opinion, that suggested New York City had no real respect for the past.

Craig knew Mike hadn't been asking his question because of the club; he'd been trying to ascertain if she'd been found dead.

Mike had glanced over at Craig, who shrugged.

They'd both just let Egan rant, figuring it was obvious. The poor girl was dead.

Egan had ended by saying, "Yes, she's dead. And it is bizarre—as bizarre as that Fredericksburg case, maybe even more so. Because in this case, the perp had to know she'd be found quickly. He placed her in a historical site where anthropologists and archaeologists were expected to arrive imminently. Later, you can go over the info on the Virginia case, do some comparisons. We're part of the task force on this, but we're taking the lead, and you two are up for our division. Because, gentlemen, I believe we have a serial killer on our hands."

They'd asked about the security tapes at the club.

Techs were going over those now, Egan had said.

"That's a bitch!" Egan had exclaimed. "Try looking for something out of the ordinary when every damned customer in the place looks like an escapee from a B Goth flick or worse! Not to mention that the club closed down when the crypt was discovered. There's no club security overnight other than the cameras, but cops have been patrolling the place since the historic folks stepped in."

From the office, he and Mike had gone straight to the church. The ME on duty was Anthony Andrews, a fine and detail-oriented doctor, but he hadn't really started his examination of the body yet.

Photographers were still taking pictures, trying to maintain the scene just as it had been after Professor Shaw had opened the first coffin and seen Jeannette Gilbert.

A half-dozen members of a forensic team were moving around, but Dr. Andrews delicately stopped the photo session to show Craig and Mike what he'd discovered. Gilbert had been killed in another location, stabbed through the heart, and then bathed and dressed and prepared before being placed in the old coffin.

Seeing her was heartbreaking. Craig hadn't known the woman or really anything about her until today, but she'd been young and beautiful, and her life had been brutally taken. She lay in the old coffin, dressed in shimmering white, a wilted rose in her hands. With her eyes closed, it looked as if she slept.

Except, of course, she'd never wake again.

"Defensive wounds?" he'd asked Andrews.

"Not a one. She was taken by surprise. Whoever killed her stood close by—had to be someone who seemed trustworthy. Maybe someone she knew," the ME had speculated. "Or she could've had some kind of opiate in her system. Anyway, she didn't expect what was coming."

"Time of death?" Mike had asked. "She's been missing about two weeks."

"I'm thinking one to two weeks," Andrews replied. "And I don't believe she's been embalmed—but she was somehow preserved. Maybe in a freezer while he worked on her or made arrangements or..." He sighed. "I need to get her on the table."

Two patrol officers, the first on the scene, had closed off the area. Luckily, the club had been closed, pending the investigation of the newly discovered crypt. Detective Larry McBride, with the major crimes division, had been the first to arrive. Craig and Mike had worked with him before. He was particularly mild mannered, but he had a brilliant mind and nothing deterred his focus.

"Glad you guys are lead on this," McBride had told them. "This is... Well, I believe we have a real psychopath on our hands. Bizarre! Wherever he killed her, he bathed away the blood. I've got officers who'll be doing rounds with pictures of the dress. Pending notification of the so-called aunt who raised the girl, they'll be asking all her friends if she owned the dress. It's possible the killer obtained it."

"Checked the label," Andrews had said. "It's from Saks."

McBride had nodded. "Nice dress. She looks like a princess." He paused. "I have a daughter her age… So, anyway, no inside security by night—but cops watching on the street. The men on duty swore no one went in until Roger Gleason opened up to wait for the archaeologists. Gleason says he comes in every day, even though the club's closed for a few days. I interviewed him personally, and he seems to be on the up-and-up. Says he's personally not that interested in the historical stuff, but seeing that the work goes well will actually make his club more famous. Still, he's not one of those guys who lets his own property go unattended. He was working up here—and heard Shaw's screams. Shaw swears there was no one down there at the time but him, an associate professor and a few grad students. I have names and numbers, which I've emailed to you already. They were all questioned. I don't think they had anything to do with Ms. Gilbert's death. The mystery here is, how the hell did the bastard get in with the body? Anyway, the security footage is down at your office now. And, of course, we're hoping Forensics can come up with something. This killer…well, they're calling in shrinks. You know, profilers. The murder was cold, swift and brutal. But then, the killer takes all this time with her. He comes in like a shadow, and then leaves her on display, waiting to be found. I talked with Egan, and I've been hanging in for you guys. Actually, I'm almost afraid to leave. It's a media frenzy out there."

By now, the frenzy on the streets involved more than just media. Word had spread; dozens of celebrity-stalkers and those inclined to the macabre had congregated outside the club.

New York City's finest were dealing with the facility and crowd control.

Craig had questioned Gleason himself before leaving. He seemed like a Wall Street type, and although his club might

be Goth, he was far more prone to the elegant in his manner and dress.

"I need to talk to Shaw," Craig had said.

But Shaw wasn't there. They'd heard that when he'd first
gotten up close and personal with the body, he'd screamed
like a banshee.

And Allie Benoit, John Shaw's grad student and assistant,
had told him that Shaw had spoken with the police, and then
freaked out and fled. Allie was pretty sure he'd gone to the
pub—the pub whose back wall abutted that of the old church-
turned-nightclub.

Finnegan's.

He swore, walking around the corner and reaching the pub.

The damned man just had to go to Finnegan's!

The pub had stood there almost as long as the church. It had
seen the New York draft riots during the Civil War, and the
violence of the Irish gangs that had once held huge sway in a
city where immigrants poured in daily from around the world.

The pub had witnessed so much history.

Including the recent history of the diamond heist that had
nearly cost his girlfriend her life.

"She won't be involved!" he said firmly, speaking aloud.

But before he entered, he knew, somewhere in his gut, that
the die was already cast.

Of all the pubs in the world.

Finnegan's.

CHAPTER
TWO

AS HE ENTERED THE PUB, CRAIG'S ATTENTION WAS ALL
for his search. With luck, Kieran would be at the office today
or—

But, no, she walked directly over to him.

And he couldn't do what he wanted to do—tell her that
she wasn't to have the least interaction with *anyone* connected
to the murder.

He didn't have the right to make that kind of demand.

And since she was here, she might have already served John
Shaw, and John Shaw would've talked to her...

At the moment, though, he needed Shaw. She'd understand that; he never had to explain himself or his intentions
to Kieran.

She knew what he did for a living; he knew about her professional work for Drs. Fuller and Miro. They respected each
other's professions and discussed things when they could—or
when the other might have a useful insight. Or when, as occasionally happened, they became involved in the same case.

Fuller and Miro worked with the police and the FBI. They often gave their considered opinion of a suspected criminal's state of mind or behavior.

They'd been involved, all four of them together, in a situation before—the so-called Diamond Affair.

But now...

He wanted to hold her and yet he couldn't; he was here professionally. He strode past her, his eyes on Shaw.

Even as he approached the booth where John Shaw was seated, he was still hating the fact that the church where Jeannette had been found was directly behind Finnegan's. He'd come to terms with being in love with Kieran—and the fact that she, too, dealt with criminals.

However, it was still difficult for him to accept that she was sometimes too quick to put herself in danger in defense of others.

Yes, it seemed to be a *Casablanca* moment.

Of all the old abandoned dug out holes in Manhattan, the damned catacombs just had to be close to Finnegan's!

Too close... This place was too close to where a young woman lay dead, where her body had been stashed with the bones of those long forgotten.

Craig knew John Shaw, and Shaw knew him; they'd met at the pub several times when the professor had come for his professional meetings or get-togethers—or when he just wanted to sip one of his ultra-lite beers and chill.

"Craig!" John said, looking up at him with surprise. "I— Oh, my. You're coming to see me. So I guess it should be Special Agent Frasier. Not Craig. Look, I'm not sure what else I can say to anyone. All I know is that we opened that coffin and...and there she was."

Craig slid into the booth and smiled at him. "You must be pretty rattled."

"Yes. You're here officially? The police told me not to say anything yet. They need to contact the poor girl's family. I mean, that's why you're here—coming to me and not Kieran, right?"

"Yes, John, this is official. The NYPD detectives are on the case, of course, but we're taking part, as well. We've put together a task force. This as a very high-profile murder."

John nodded, his white hair—something of a strange mullet cut—flapping beside his ears. His glasses slid down his nose with his effort, and he pushed them back with his forefinger.

"Of course. This needs to be solved fast," John said. "But…" His expression grew even more perplexed. "I don't know how I can help any more. I don't know how I can help, period. Professor Digby—Aldous Digby, one of my associates—and I were there, and three grad students. Oh, and two of the construction guys. The guys were watching—waiting to get back to work. I didn't let them touch the coffin. Nice guys, but, you know, that coffin might be two hundred years old and, well, you need to have a delicate touch. And Ms. Gilbert… The second I saw her… I have to admit I screamed. I was rattled, as you said. But I made sure everyone got out. We did and then went up to the church—the club area—to wait for the police."

"Right. So there were seven of you. I have the names," Craig said. He was certain that the meticulous Detective Mc-Bride had sent his email.

He'd also seen Jeannette Gilbert's body at the site.

He winced, the picture of her still so clear in his mind. Her lovely, pale, perfect face. The white dress. The red rose.

John nodded. "Seven of us were in there—and seven of us

got out quicker than a flash. And we were all interviewed."
He sighed loudly. "Hell of a thing for the owner of that place.
They've barely been open what, a month or two? Then they
have to stop work and close up because an engineer finds the
coffins in the dirt and then the catacombs. They bring us in,
and… Sad. So sad. By God, she was beautiful! Poor thing."

"Just to confirm, you were there yesterday, too?" Craig
asked.

"Of course. I was there as soon as the situation was reported." He paused. "Did you know that the land where the
Waldorf Astoria sits was once a potter's field? Think of how
old this city is. A number of the parks we enjoy today were
originally cemeteries. I worked the old slave cemetery they
discovered a few years back, so it was natural that I'd work
on this one, too."

"You started on the church yesterday?"

"Yes. I did. I was called yesterday morning, and I made
arrangements to get there as fast as possible."

"And then?"

"I assessed the location. I called in Digby and my assistant,
Allie Benoit. You don't pry apart ancient caskets willy-nilly.
We researched church plans, but the original architect's plan
is long gone." He shook his head. "You must be familiar with
what happened. The church sold the property to the club
people. There was an outcry, not that it made any difference.
But the building is so historic. Everyone wants to shop Fifth
Avenue, see a show, bank on Wall Street. They forget that
Wall Street *was* a wall. Canal Street was a canal—or a cesspool, really. Those are all part of our city's origins, and we
need to preserve history!"

Craig nodded, although he wasn't convinced they'd needed
to preserve the cesspool that had been Canal Street. He spoke

quickly, not wanting the academic to bluster endlessly. "What time did you get in there yesterday?"

"Let's see… They called us right around ten in the morning. I was there within the hour."

"So, who was there then?" Craig asked. "Besides you and the colleagues and workers you've mentioned."

"Oh, lots of people. Let's see, the manager and owner, Roger Gleason. He'd been working down by the construction area. They stored their booze down there—in the old crypt they knew about, I mean, with the coffins and bodies all gone now. It's a foundation, a basement. The basement—the *crypts*—were far more extensive than people realized. The wall had hidden some of the old coffins and shrouded corpses, so when some of the corpses were moved, the 'second' crypt was missed."

"Okay. Anyone else know what was going on?"

"At least two construction workers and one of the barmaids-slash-dancers. Have you seen what they do in there? She was dressed up in a little black bra and skirt and wearing some wicked makeup. The girls dance on tables when they're not handing out booze."

"So, employees, construction workers—anyone else?"

"Oh, yeah, the rep from the historic preservation group. Henry Willoughby. Loves history. He's not a scientist, but he's a great hands-on guy, ready to protect the past and help out if he can. The man loves New York and studied history and architecture. His wife passed away a while back, and now he gives all his love to the city. He stayed long enough last night to check in with us, make sure we were ready to catalog the bodies and the artifacts we found. I would've brought in more crew, but—"

"Who stayed, then? Who was actually there when you kept working?"

"Me, Digby showed up, my grad students—plus a structural engineer and a construction worker, all to see that we didn't bring down a wall, I assume." He cleared his throat. "Of course, after I initially went in yesterday, the construction guys created a kind of door for us."

"How long were you there yesterday?"

"It was almost midnight before I left. I didn't touch or open anything. I stepped over the hole—where the wall broke when they were working on the foundations—into the crypt beyond. Digby and my grad students and I were there. We make drawings and assessments and plan before we start the actual work, so, yes, I'd say it was midnight. By then, of course, the vampire dancers were gone and all the club people had been told to go home. Once they made the find—the second crypt—they closed down, of course, but people were hanging around. It's...it's history being reclaimed! Roger Gleason, the owner, seems like a nice guy. He has a conscience and some perspective on what's important. We didn't have to get court orders or anything. He simply agreed to close for a few days. They had patrol officers covering the place, making sure that once the news about the crypt got out, some Goth freak or necrophilia-pursuing creep didn't try to break in."

Craig nodded. He knew the answers to most of what he was asking; he just wanted it from Shaw and he wanted to ensure that their facts were straight.

"Yesterday," Shaw said, "you understand, was *discovery* day. I planned where to put some lights. I judged the space for people and decided on equipment. I did all the assessments, got my ducks in a row, you know what I mean?"

Craig nodded again. "This morning when you arrived—were things exactly as you'd left them?"

"What?"

"Had anything you'd done been changed? Were tools missing, anything like that?"

Shaw frowned. "I…I don't think so. I don't get it. I'd roped off different areas in the basement for my people. We had our little brushes and chisels and…no, I'm positive that our work tables were the way we'd left them," he said. He leaned forward. "Didn't Ms. Gilbert disappear about two weeks ago? She didn't look as if she'd just been killed. She…she was beautiful as she lay there, but decay had set in. I guess down there, with the cool temperature, natural decay wouldn't be what it would up here." He briefly closed his eyes. "If she was embalmed, she wasn't embalmed well, but she was dressed up. As if she'd been prepared for a viewing. Seeing her gave me chills! Chills! And I work with the dead all the time. When did she die?"

"The medical examiner is estimating her death to have been between one and two weeks ago. He'll tell us more definitively when he's done the autopsy."

"So, you think that—"

"I don't think anything yet," Craig said. "We need more information from the experts before I can even speculate. Go on, please, tell me about this morning."

"Okay," John said. "This morning." He looked longingly at his scotch glass.

It was empty.

"You want another?" Craig asked.

"Yeah," John said huskily. "Yeah. The long dead are one thing. Fresh corpses…or not so fresh corpses…"

Craig knew what he meant.

He had seen the body.

He scanned the bar area but didn't see Kieran. Declan Finnegan, however—looking like an old-time Irish bartender as he dried a glass, decked in a white apron tied around his waist—was behind the bar.

Craig walked over to him. Declan, he knew, had been fully aware that Craig was in the pub and that he'd been talking to John Shaw.

"You want another scotch for him?" Declan asked.

Declan was the oldest of the Finnegans; he wore his sense of responsibility and dignity well. All the Finnegan family were attractive and charming people with different degrees of red in their hair, and they all had eyes in varying shades of blue. Even a casual observer had to note that they were related.

Declan tended to be the most serious in demeanor. He didn't ask questions, not of Craig; he knew he'd learn what was going on if and when it was appropriate.

"Thanks," Craig said. "Any idea where Kieran is?"

"She and Kevin were helping out before. I'm not sure where they went." He poured the scotch. "Anything for you?"

"Soda water."

Declan quickly poured him a glass from the fountain, and Craig returned to the table. *Where the hell had Kieran gone?*

She was helping out her brother today, which meant she was working here somewhere. If he was going to start worrying every time she wasn't in sight, he'd need to get a psych evaluation himself.

John Shaw took the scotch from him; it looked as if he was going to gulp it down. Craig set a hand on his. "Hey, that's prime stuff, my friend. Sip it."

"Yeah, yeah, of course," Shaw murmured.

"Okay, so, you got in today—"

"Early. Just after seven. This is an important true find. The historical value is immense."

"Of course. I understand," Craig assured him. "So, today. You haven't opened any of the other coffins in the catacomb, have you?"

"No. Some of the coffins have disintegrated, and the remains are down to bones and dust and spiderwebs. Remnants of fabric...belt buckles, shoe buckles..." John rambled, studying the amber liquid in his glass.

"But you found Ms. Gilbert in the first coffin?"

Shaw nodded glumly.

"What made you open that one first?" Craig asked.

The question seemed to confuse Shaw for a minute. "It seemed to be the best preserved." He paused, staring up at Craig. "Actually, it was at an odd angle on the shelf. As if it had been moved. Oh...that was obviously because someone had been there! They'd put her body in it!"

"Do you remember it being that way the day before?"

"No! That must've been it. There was something different!" John Shaw said. "I didn't realize it immediately. It was such a...subtle difference. The thing is, I thought I'd start with the best preserved, but so did—" He frowned at Craig. "It was definitely the best preserved. And someone else knew that, too. Her killer."

Jeannette had been dead at least a week, possibly two. But she'd been placed in that coffin in a forgotten crypt much more recently than that.

The killer had learned about the historical find, and he'd made use of it for his own designs.

"Excuse me," Craig said abruptly. "I'll be right back."

He wanted to see where Kieran was; it suddenly seemed important.

She wasn't at the bar. She wasn't on the floor.

He hurried down the hallway to the office, not bothering to knock.

Kieran was there, and Craig let out a sigh of relief.

But then he saw that she wasn't alone. She was sitting there, on the sofa in front of the desk, talking earnestly with her twin brother, Kevin.

They both looked up at him, startled—and their expressions could only be described as guilty.

Kieran jumped up, looking at Craig and then Kevin.

"Hey," she said, talking to her brother first. "You've got that audition—you better get going!"

"Yep, right," Kevin said, rising quickly. "Definitely. Craig, are you involved in the situation over at the old church? No one is supposed to know anything yet, but I think that everyone everywhere knows that the body of Jeannette Gilbert was found in an old coffin. I think someone tweeted it. So much for the 'please keep silent' request. I'm sorry. Sounds terrible. But, what is the FBI doing in on it?"

"There's a similarity to another murder, down in Virginia," Craig said. "We may be looking at a serial killer."

"Oh?" Kevin said. "So…" His gaze fell on Kieran, and his voice sounded a little sick. "You're going to be involved with the investigation?"

Craig nodded. "Lead for the FBI."

"Better get going, Kevin," Kieran said. "This is truly so horrible, but we all have to keep working."

"Yeah. I'll see you all later tonight," Kevin said, and headed out of the office.

When he was gone, Kieran looked at Craig.

"What was that all about?" he asked her.

"That—what?" she asked.

"I sometimes wonder how your brother manages to be an actor. He's a horrible liar."

"What did he lie about?"

"What are you lying about?"

She arched her brows, wishing she'd met and fallen in love with an auto mechanic, a taxi driver—anyone but an FBI agent.

"Since I haven't said anything, I haven't lied about anything, either!" she protested. He wouldn't let it be, she thought. Hell, he was an investigator. It was what he did. But what could she say? Betray a confidence?

"It's about Kevin's love life," she said. There. That was the truth. "And I'm just not— Well, you know, you can't talk to me sometimes and I can't talk to you."

It was the semitruth, but he probably wouldn't have let it go at that. Except that her cell phone started ringing and she pulled it from her jeans pocket. Caller ID quickly informed her that it was one of her two psychiatrist bosses, Dr. Fuller.

"Hey," she said, answering the phone gratefully. "Is everything all right? We did decide to close today, right?"

"We did—until about an hour ago," Dr. Fuller said, his tone regretful. "I was actually planning a day of tennis."

The man was very good at what he did; beyond being a gifted psychiatrist, he had an unbelievable wealth of knowledge in all things related to his field—his pharmaceutical awareness was nearly uncanny. He could rattle off the names of dozens of drugs, what they did for what, and who should and shouldn't take them with greater ease than most people could recite the alphabet. He could offer empathy that would crack the hardest core, and be staunch and unwavering when needed.

He also looked bizarrely like a pinup underwear model and loved his wife and the game of tennis with absolute passion.

"Oh?" Kieran said, looking over at Craig and wondering if he could or couldn't hear her employer's words as well, since he was standing so close to her.

"We've gotten a call from Assistant Director Richard Egan—Craig's boss," Fuller said.

"Oh?" she repeated, certain now from his wary expression that Craig could hear the conversation. But this was not unusual; her bosses were frequently called in as consultants by the NYPD, the FBI and other local law-enforcement agencies. As the doctors' psychologist, Kieran often worked on evaluations for those perps in custody, and with the doctors on identifying the personality type of those still at large.

"He wants us in on the old church murder. They'll have someone up from Quantico, he told me, but, for the moment, he wants us in. I'm on my way, but I'm up in Connecticut. I was thinking you might go over—it's right by Finnegan's."

"I'm at the bar now."

"Can you go over right away? I'm not sure how long they'll keep the body in situ, and I want our own photos, notes of everything you see. Can you go?"

She glanced at Craig. He was wearing a very hard expression.

"Of course," Kieran said. "Special Agent Frasier is right in front of me. He'll be happy to see that I'm accompanied over."

"Great. I'll see you as soon as traffic allows," Dr. Fuller said.

Craig groaned aloud. "I don't like this one," he said softly. "I don't like it at all. I really wish that you weren't involved."

"Craig—"

He lifted a hand to stop her. "I know. It's what you do. I just wish that it wasn't what you did on this particular case."

Because of Kevin, she'd wind up involved one way or the other. Better that she'd been asked to go in; better that she could see the victim and the surroundings before trying to understand the psyche of the person who could do such things.

She smiled. Though she was fairly tall herself, she stood on her toes to plant a quick kiss on his lips.

"Face it. You don't want me involved in any case."

"Okay. True. But, this…well, I guess you'll see for yourself. It isn't—it isn't something you should see. It isn't something anyone should see, and it's sure as hell something that never, ever should have happened. But…"

"I'm careful. I'm always careful, Craig, you know that. And I love my work with the doctors, even if it's usually in an office."

"Let's go, then," he said.

They left the office. While Craig dismissed the professor, Kieran spoke quickly with Declan, apologizing for running out, especially when the pub was now filling up. People who were never downtown were downtown that day. People who had nothing to do with architecture, churches, clubs, archaeology or anthropology. Despite police preference, Twitter had broadcast the news.

The building that had once been a place of worship and now housed Le Club Vampyre was, beyond a doubt, beautiful. It was grand and tall with flying buttresses. Gargoyles had been created for every rain gutter and more. Entrances were designed with pointed arches. Inside, she knew, the ceiling was vaulted, majestically painted with angels gracing the heights.

While Trinity and then Saint Paul's Chapel had been designed for the use of the early British settlers, by the time Saint Augustine's had been built, the city had grown. A colony had become a state in America, and that growing population had wanted to build something grand.

The church was literally in back of the pub, but they had to head out the front and come around to the parallel street entry. In doing so, they waded through a sea of media and onlookers to reach the interior of the church. Once inside, there still seemed to be a crowd.

"Seems like a lot of people at a crime scene," Kieran murmured to Craig.

"Up here, in what is the nightclub area now," Craig said, "you have a lot of cops. Some of the nightclub workers. Some historic board people. But not down below. Even before Gilbert was found, only a few people were allowed down there."

"Ah."

"Yep, lucky girl," he said drily, looking ahead.

Kieran studied her surroundings quickly.

She'd been in the church a few times when it had still been a place of worship. While she'd grown up in the Catholic Church, her parents had loved the beauty of the Episcopal house of worship so close behind their pub. It had been fantastic then, so beautifully built, and it had seemed they always had a great reverend, super music and lots of good things. It had been sad to hear of the place being sold.

But not much had really been changed, not as far as the facade went, nor even the inner structure.

The new owner had maintained the feel of great space. Where the altar had once been, there was now a long bar. To the left and the right, the smaller altar areas had now become little nooks with plush chairs and coffee tables. To the far right was a bandstand and DJ's box. Heavy red velvet drapes kept the antique feeling while allowing for the little nooks to close off for privacy. The center of the room—with the exception of a secondary bar—was empty, spacious and airy.

"There. Egan has gotten here himself, and he's with the owner," Craig said, taking her arm and walking over to a trio of men.

She knew Richard Egan, Craig's boss, head of the criminal investigation division at the FBI's New York headquarters. He looked the part; he was somewhere in his fifties, Kieran thought, with a headful of neatly cropped silver-white hair and a tall, lean, fit and extremely dignified physique. He nodded grimly as he saw them approach.

"Ms. Finnegan, thank you for coming so quickly. We have some of our people coming up, but due to the high-profile situation we have going on here, I wanted the good doctors Fuller and Miro in on it all as quickly as possible." He paused for a moment to glance at Craig. "Mike says you went to look for Shaw?"

"I did, sir. I found him, and Ms. Finnegan, of course."

"I'm grateful you were able to get here so quickly. Let me introduce you, Kieran," Egan said, and turned to the other two men with whom he'd been standing. "Henry Willoughby, Ms. Kieran Finnegan."

She quickly shook hands with the man. He was middle-aged, lean, with a trim ring of gray hair around his bald head. He was very solemn—clearly concerned with the goings-on. She'd seen him on a local news show occasionally; he had a fine way of speaking, and his enthusiasm over a museum opening or city history was contagious.

"Henry's president of a wonderful group called Preserve Our Past," Egan explained.

"Yes, of course, I've seen you on TV," she said, and offered a small smile.

He returned it grimly.

"And I'm Roger Gleason, Ms. Finnegan, owner of Le Club

Vampyre—the business and the building. Obviously, we're very distressed by what's happened here."

"Certainly," she said. Gleason was nothing like the other men. She judged him to be in his early forties. He was tall, stylish and handsome, with a sweep of blond hair that fell across his forehead. His suit, she estimated, had to have cost a month of the average workingman's wages.

"I hope you can help us," he said.

"I'm here for Drs. Fuller and Miro," Kieran said. "Dr. Fuller will be here as soon as he can possibly get through traffic."

"Yes, well, thank you, Ms. Finnegan," Gleason said. "Traffic—he could be hours."

He turned to Craig. "Do you think they can help?"

"Definitely. There's never a guarantee that profiling a perp will result in apprehending him—no two human beings are really alike. But, yes, profiling has been key in solving many cases. I'll bring Ms. Finnegan down to the crypt.

"Mike is still there?" he asked Egan.

Egan nodded. "Mike, the detective, the ME and the forensic team," he said.

Craig nodded and led her behind the main bar—the old altar area. Kieran pictured the place as it had been as a church. Naturally, yes, the crypt would be beneath the altar.

They descended marble steps into the cool dankness of what had been a crypt and now housed spirits of a different kind. Rows and rows of wine and liquor bottles now lined the walls and were neatly arranged on the concrete floor.

The basement area here looked much like it did at Finnegan's, she observed. Except, of course, at Finnegan's, the cellar had always been solely for liquor storage.

Not "storage" for the dead.

"I wonder if the staff ever feels uncomfortable down here," Kieran said.

"The dead who rested in this area are gone," Craig said. "Besides, you need to—"

"Fear the living, not the dead," Kieran said.

"Yep. They're the ones who will hurt you."

A patrolman stood to the far rear where large chunks of the wall had been knocked down and a broad opening had been created. Two women wearing jumpsuits that identified them as part of the forensic team were hunkered down over a black chest, working with samples. A photographer was snapping pictures.

She spotted Mike standing with another man who appeared grim and weary but calm.

He looked at her and nodded an acknowledgment. Kieran knew Craig's partner well and liked him very much.

"This is Detective Larry McBride, NYPD," Mike said. "Detective, this is Ms. Finnegan. She's with the psychiatrists the Bureau often uses in the city, Drs. Fuller and Miro."

The detective studied her as he offered a hand. He apparently hadn't realized that it was still gloved. He pulled off the glove and shook her hand. "Ms. Finnegan. I know Dr. Fuller. Fine man."

"You know him?"

He nodded, grimacing. "I'm a tennis player."

"Ah," Kieran said.

"Let's do this," Craig said. "Kieran, this way to the forgotten crypt."

He turned her around and led her through the broken wall.

He was stoic. To anyone else it might appear that nothing bothered him. But she knew him well enough to know the crypt did bother him. Not because of those who had died long ago, and hopefully through natural means. He was a good agent, Egan had told her once, because he had empathy. He was sorry for the victim, the woman whose body he had already seen.

She realized that she was far more squeamish than he—and she also realized that she had never been on the site of a murder before. The murder hadn't taken place here, but...

She paused for a minute, taking in what she saw.

The crypt stretched far beneath the earth. There were marble sarcophagi here and there amid the rows of what she could only think of as shelving—shelving for the dead. She thought that the rows seemed to go on endlessly, housing hundreds of interments. She'd been in the catacombs in Rome and this felt very similar, except that slabs for the dead were not just against the walls, they were in those endless rows of stone as well, one on top of the other. It was almost as if the tombs where the dead rested were many tiered bunks in a dormitory. Some of the shelving had broken marble slabs. Some had nothing, and bone peeked from rotting shrouds. Toward the front where she stood, coffins lay upon the same shelving. Most were deteriorating; all seemed to be covered with a haze of dust and cobwebs.

She pulled out her notepad and began sketching furiously, and then reached for her cell phone, taking pictures.

"Kieran?"

"Yes?" She turned.

Craig was watching her. From his expression, she knew that he was unhappy—and not because he wanted to prevent her work in any way. He just hated that she had to see this macabre place.

He tried a dry smile. "None of those is for Facebook, Twitter or any other social media?" he asked lightly.

She glared at him, refusing to answer.

He nodded. "To the left."

She tensed, knowing she was about to look at the dead woman.

When she forced herself to turn, she felt chills seize hold of her spine and her limbs.

It was surreal.

Jeannette Gilbert still lay in the coffin—much as she had been found, Kieran surmised. The ME had been to the body, but as of yet, it remained undisturbed.

And the woman…

In life Jeannette Gilbert had been truly beautiful. Long, sweeping blond hair had curled over her shoulders, her lips had been generous and beautifully shaped, her cheekbones high. Now, even in death, she looked impossibly like a princess— as if she might be awakened by love's first kiss.

And yet…

There seemed to be something out of focus. She just wasn't quite *perfect* anymore. And, staring at the corpse, Kieran knew what it was.

She was decaying. And coming closer to her, Kieran felt as if the scent of that decay suddenly began to permeate her.

She forced herself not to back away. She saw then that the ME—out beyond the broken-down wall in the basement area—had a mask hanging around his neck. No doubt he'd donned it when he had examined the corpse.

Craig, however, stood at her side unflinching, staring down at the body with sadness and regret—and something steely in his expression that said that he wouldn't stop until the killer was found.

She turned away from Craig quickly, actually taking a step closer to the corpse in the coffin as she lowered her head.

Kevin! Kevin had been the mystery man she had been dating. Had he been in love with Jeannette Gilbert? Possibly. And if so…well, she knew her twin. Jeannette would have been a nice woman; she would have cared about people. She might have been a supermodel, but she would have given to charities, cared about children, possibly visited cancer wards.

Thank God her brother wasn't here to see this.

She swallowed hard and took pictures first this time, then sketched what she saw, adding little notes to her sketch.

The terrible smell of death seemed so close.

"This is how—where—she was found?" she asked Craig.

"Just about. The coffin was on the middle shelf. It appears to be the best preserved of those down here. That's why Shaw opened it first, and, presumably, why the killer chose it."

Kieran added to her notes.

"The entry wasn't as big last night. More of the false wall was torn down to make way for Dr. Shaw and his crew and whatever historians might have been called in. He did note that the position on the shelf was a little extended, or more at an angle. Other than that, he noticed nothing that had changed in the crypt."

As she studied the corpse, Kieran felt a hand on her shoulder and nearly jumped.

"Sorry, Kieran."

It was Craig, at her side, introducing her to the ME.

"This is Dr. Anthony Andrews. One of the best MEs in the city," Craig said, his hand now discreetly at her elbow, steadying her.

"You're with the profiling people?" the ME asked.

"Yes, civilian profilers," she said.

He nodded. "I need to bring this young lady to my office

now. We've waited here a bit longer than I would have liked. Do you need more time?"

Kieran shook her head. "No, thank you. I was hoping that Dr. Fuller might make it, but…"

"Yes, traffic. He could be quite a while. I'm sure you've recorded and noted everything that can be given to him. You're not a psychiatrist?"

"Psychologist," Kieran said.

Andrews glanced at Craig and turned back to Kieran. "Well, my dear, in my mind, you might be best suited to understand the mind of such a killer. Too many psychiatrists are pill pushers. Psychologists have to work with the human creation without benefit of mind-altering drugs. Anyway, a pleasure to meet you, though I have seen you. Finnegan— you're related to the owners of the pub behind us, right?"

"I'm one of the owners," she told him. "There are four of us—my brothers, Declan, Kevin, Danny and myself. Declan manages the pub and usually tends bar."

He grinned solemnly again. "Ah, well, then, your brother may not be a psychologist, too, but he's is a heck of good listener. I've seen him talking to people at the bar. Seems to know what makes them tick. For now, if you'll excuse me… I'll get to my part in this investigation."

She nodded and returned her phone and notepad to her bag.

Craig led her out.

Andrews called to him. "I've been told this takes precedence, so autopsy in about two hours. No, let me say precisely…3:00 p.m."

"Thank you. Mike and I will be there," Craig said.

He brought Kieran back to the marble steps.

She was glad of his arm. Not only was she affected by the dead body, but she couldn't stop thinking about Kevin. That he had been Gilbert's mystery man, and that the model had alluded to her feelings for him in several interviews.

She pictured the beautiful young woman on an autopsy table, giant pincers being used to crack open her ribs...

She winced inwardly and began to worry.

There was no way someone hadn't seen something—or didn't know something. She had to talk to Kevin, and he had to talk to Craig.

News about the murder was out. Speculation was no doubt rampant already.

And her twin was going to be a suspect in the murder.

CHAPTER
THREE

CRAIG HATED ATTENDING AN AUTOPSY.

He did, however, attend whenever possible. No detail was too small when seeking a murderer.

And here, downtown, it was easy enough to get to the Office of the Chief Medical Examiner. Young and old, victim of accident or murder—or just having faced death unattended or from causes unknown—the bodies of the deceased in lower Manhattan came here. The OCME had two other locations—in Brooklyn and in Queens, serving those who died farther afield or when a death toll rose dramatically due to assaults by nature or by man.

This office was located on Twenty-Sixth Street—not far from Finnegan's and Le Club Vampyre or the NYC offices of the FBI.

"You'll have my tape for anything you might have forgotten here," Dr. Andrews said when he was finished, stepping back from the gurney and nodding to his assistant so that the man could take the body to finish the sewing-up procedure. "But it's the weirdest damned thing I've ever seen. From my findings, I believe she's been dead for most of the two weeks she's been missing. Maybe only ten days, though, which would mean that he kept her for just a few days—and has preserved her or tried to preserve her until he chose to leave her. Obviously, gentlemen, we all know that she wasn't killed in the crypt. Wherever she was killed, there has to have been a massive blood spill—she was stabbed straight in the heart. But what's so disturbing is the way that she was kept. She was not sexually assaulted, and her remains were treated tenderly."

"As if the killer regretted the murder?" McBride asked.

"I can't speak to the killer's mind. The facts of the case are this—she has been dead approximately ten days up to two weeks. There are no defensive wounds anywhere on her body. She was kept on ice, or at a very low temperature, slowing decomposition, until she was brought to the crypt. The temperature below the ground is much cooler than above, more toward the preservation side, but not enough that more decay didn't begin to set in. But, even on ice, I believe she had begun to decay before being brought to the crypt. There is no other wound on her other than the fatal jab to the heart. I'm going to suggest a strong, broad knife, one-and-one-half to two inches in breadth, five to six inches long. The fatal stab was inflicted in one smooth and determined motion."

"By someone strong? A man?" Mike asked.

"Certainly, no one feeble delivered the thrust. But, no, if the knife was sharp enough, which it was, a person of average strength could have easily done the deed. I don't know as yet what chemical compounds might have been in the body. When I receive the lab tests, I'll let you know."

"Well, we know how she died and when she died," Mc-
Bride said. "Now, if we only knew the name of the killer."

"I want to get an info board and timeline going," Craig
said. "Also, see if they came up with anything from the security cameras in the club. We'll set up in one of the conference rooms. I have a feeling our task force might get bigger,
and we'll be briefing a lot of people."

He thanked Dr. Andrews and they headed out.

It was always good to leave the morgue.

Kieran thought that she was incredibly lucky in her employment. Dr. Fuller was a truly decent man—totally unaware of his looks and completely dedicated to his field. There
wasn't a narcissistic bone in his body. He was always courteous and caring of others.

Of course, if all else should fail, she also had Finnegan's!

But her two roles converged nicely that day.

Traffic was exceptionally bad, and by the time Dr. Fuller
arrived, Jeannette Gilbert's body was long gone. Still, he
headed first to the church to view the scene of the discovery,
then he came around the corner to Finnegan's and met with
Kieran in Declan's office.

Kieran got him a scotch—he said he needed one, just one—
and ordered shepherd's pie for him. He'd been driving a long
time.

He ate quickly. He sipped his scotch as if it were nectar
from above.

She'd already texted the pictures to him; she went over her
sketches and her notes.

He sat for a minute, thoughtful.

"They're going to suspect her manager and agent, Oswald
Martin," he said.

"Yes, I know. But you don't think it was him?" Kieran asked.

"She was his meal ticket. He also worked with her for years," Fuller pointed out. "Tell me—what were your impressions?"

Kieran looked at him and then plunged in. "Organized. The killer knew what he was doing. It's likely he's killed before."

Fuller nodded. "As I understand it, the FBI's on it because a body was found similarly in another state."

Kieran continued with her assessment. "She trusted whoever killed her, so, therefore, I don't think it was a random person off the street. Also, whoever did it is meticulous in his own habits. Maybe not clinically insane, but I'd say crazy, just not visibly so. Sociopath, beyond a doubt. His own satisfaction excludes any concern for others. The usual profile would suggest a young man, late twenties to early thirties. But I think he's a little older. I also think he's got a decent income, is well educated. After all, he can definitely do some research. He found out about the crypts under the church. What puzzles me, though, is why he placed her in a coffin there. He had to have known that she'd be found quickly."

"Maybe he wanted her found," Dr. Fuller speculated. "His first victim, however, was in a mausoleum many weeks before the woman whose space she was in died. Then again, maybe that didn't please him."

"You mean that killing is like art to him?"

"Killing—and displaying the body."

Kieran nodded. "Jeannette was stunningly beautiful in life. Living art. Maybe he tried to preserve his victims, but couldn't?"

"Possibly. Buying mortuary supplies might raise a question."

Kieran gave him a brief, grim smile. "He's living his life in his own mind. Maybe he saw something in her." She thought of the original murder. "Dr. Fuller, what was the other victim like? What do you know about her?"

"Young. Her name was Cary Howell. That's all I have. Frankly, we need to get over to the FBI offices. It's just a short walk south on Broadway—I won't even have to drive again. You ready?"

"Two hundred and eighty-five miles—driving time approximately five to six hours, with a couple of pit stops, down to Virginia," Craig said. He had his board set up, having accrued more records on the Virginia case. "Victim number one—that we know of—Cary Howell, was found in a crypt when the matron of a family was about to go in." He pointed to her picture. "Killed six months ago."

Then he pointed to Jeannette's photo. "Gentlemen," he told McBride and Mike, "please note Cary and then Jeannette. I think you'll agree it's highly unlikely that we have a copycat on our hands—not when you see the details."

"A rose in her hands," Mike murmured.

"White dress," McBride said. "Let me guess—Cary Howell was stabbed in the heart?"

"She was. Of course, you'll note the decay of the body is much greater in the first case. She'd been there longer, and Virginia can be hot." He glanced at his notes and looked over them. "In fact," he said softly, "the Virginia ME bemoans the fact that the heat does what it does to bodies. The decay caused breakdowns that made certain chemical testing impossible for him."

"Still, Virginia," McBride said. "We need to find a suspect who was in Virginia when Cary Howell was killed—and here in New York when Jeannette was killed."

"Not so easy," Craig said. "The Virginia ME could only narrow down the time of death on Cary to about a week, and that week would have been six months ago. The drive to Virginia and back can be done in a day."

"Still, we can find out who has been to Virginia," McBride said. "Or if any of our suspects left the city around that time."

"Not if they took side roads," Mike noted.

"Hard to get in or out of New York City without hitting some kind of a camera," McBride said.

"True—but there are ways," Craig said. "But I don't believe that Jeannette Gilbert went off with just anyone. She knew her killer. She trusted him. That makes me believe that the killer is from or lives in New York City since, even though she traveled for work, Jeannette spent her entire life here."

"The other victim trusted her killer, too," McBride said.

"But Jeannette Gilbert was a media star. She was known. Right now, I'd like to look at this case as if it is a separate situation. We need to focus on possible suspects right here in the city, people who were close to Jeannette Gilbert."

"Sure," McBride said glumly.

"Naturally, everyone at the church-nightclub was questioned immediately, but only Gleason had actually ever met Ms. Gilbert, and that was because of an ad done at the club. He made no attempt to hide and didn't avoid any questions. He'll remain on our radar. Number one suspect—according to the tabloids—is her manager, Oswald Martin," Craig said. "I have officers out trying to find him now."

"Can't convict a man via the tabloids," McBride noted.

Mike had a sheaf of notes in front of him. "She had a row

with a photographer a while back—Leo Holt. High-fashion photographer. It was covered in the tabloids. And they lived in buildings on the same block by Central Park. However, there's nothing to link him to her disappearance."

"We really have nothing to link anyone yet. Thing is, I don't think we're going after the usual—because of Virginia. I don't think it's someone with whom she just had a petty argument. I don't think it's a scientist working at the scene, either." Craig shook his head. "But I like charts and lists, so I'll add Holt's name."

"Going in that direction, there's John Shaw himself," McBride offered. "He's creepy enough, crazy enough. My gut says no, but you could write him down, too."

Craig did. "Then," he added, "we have the owner of the club. Roger Gleason."

"Definitely slimy," Mike said.

"Can't convict on slimy," McBride put in.

"No, but we have to start somewhere," Craig said. "The first one who usually comes under suspicion is the significant other. In our case—the mystery man."

Mike cleared his throat. "We don't know who he is. That's why he's a mystery man."

"We're going to find out. We have statements from friends and associates and coworkers already, since she was listed as a missing person," Craig said. "It will come out."

"We have to add in every one of the people involved with Shaw," Mike said. "His colleague, Professor Digby. Henry Willoughby had been there, too, representing the historic preservation group. And then the grad students." He referred to his notes. "Allie Benoit, Joshua Harding and Sam Frick. All of them go to the university here, and all have worked with Dr. Shaw before."

"There's her family," McBride said. "The aunt… She's just kind of a sad sack. And the step-uncle, Tobias Green—a total asshole. Never bothered with the girl, begrudged every piece of food she put in her mouth as a kid—and threatened to sue the NYPD if we didn't find her!"

"Add the asshole step-uncle to the list," Mike said.

"I don't think you should write asshole on that board of yours. Probably against Bureau policy," McBride said wearily.

"He probably is an ass," Craig agreed, "but I'm not sure if that puts him with the kind of man we're looking for. Gilbert wouldn't have feared him, but how would he have gotten to know our other victim?"

"And you can't convict a guy for being an asshole," McBride said sadly.

"We'll still want to talk to him," Craig murmured.

"Construction workers, bar employees—we're missing people," Mike said.

"Yeah, well, we could be missing suspects that include all of Manhattan and beyond, since the news was out about the find," McBride said wearily. "What have we got off security tapes? Did Tech finish with them yet?"

"We got nothing," Craig said.

"How can you have nothing? I saw the cameras there."

"The techs studied the tapes over and over. Roger Gleason stayed late—until Professor Shaw was all set up for today. You see him and Shaw leaving together—in fact, you see Gleason setting the alarm. And, yes, the alarm company has been questioned and nothing went off last night. The cameras recorded through the night. You see no one go in and no one go out."

"That's impossible," McBride said.

"It was a church," Mike argued. "There's more than one entrance. The door to the left leads to the offices—at least what was offices when it was a church. The door to the right led outside."

"I tried it, Mike," Craig replied. "It doesn't open now. The next building is flush against it."

"There has to be another way out," Mike said. "I feel like an idiot. I went through every room at the place. I don't remember another door, but—"

"There are two side doors next to the main pointed arch entry," Craig said. "Locked from the outside, on the same alarm system. In an emergency, they open out."

"I had Forensics inspect those doors. They weren't jimmied. They weren't opened," Mike said.

"Shouldn't pass a fire code that way," McBride grumbled.

"That's just it. An alarm to the fire department goes off when they're opened," Mike said.

"Something had to have happened—a technical failure?" McBride posited. "And of course there are no alleys."

"It's Manhattan," Mike said. "Buildings wind up flush together because real estate is prime. No alleys," he added, looking at Craig.

"No. No alleys," Craig agreed.

"The cameras had to have been tampered with. Someone had to have jimmied the alarm system," McBride said. "It's looking like the owner himself might be guilty in this thing. Who the hell else could have done all that?"

Craig had to admit that it seemed the detective was right.

How had someone gotten into the church, carried the body downstairs and gotten it into the coffin without being seen?

"She was killed by a ghost," Mike muttered.

"Seems that way," McBride said, shaking his head. "But she's still a real corpse. A ghost would have had to have carried in a real corpse!"

Craig's buzzer rang then; he hit the intercom.

"Special Agent Frasier," one of the secretaries said, "Dr. Fuller and Ms. Finnegan are here. I've taken the liberty of sending someone down to get them. Do I hold them out here or send them in?"

"Send them right in," Craig said.

"Good. The shrinks can explain how ghosts work and make victims invisible, too," McBride said, his sarcasm a cover for his exasperation. "Something's wrong—film, tape, digital images. They had to be manipulated."

"We have the best techs in the world," Mike said.

"I don't care how good you are, there's always someone better," McBride argued.

That was true enough, Craig thought.

"And that would point to someone who knew Le Club Vampyre," he said aloud, glancing over at Mike.

"Or the church—when it was a church," Mike said.

"It's probably a new system. It's different being a church and a nightclub," Craig pointed out.

He was glad then to see Bentley Fuller walk in with Kieran.

"Guy looks like he's in great shape. He'd make a solid FBI guy," McBride commented beneath his breath, and he stood to greet Fuller.

Craig thanked them for coming. Kieran nodded at him and took a seat, but he picked up on her vibe right away. She looked uncomfortable. He wondered why. She hadn't appeared so miserable the first time she'd come down to the FBI headquarters, back when they barely knew one another. By now, of course, she'd been here often enough. But still, there was something off about her.

Fuller walked right up to Craig's board and stared at the image of Cary Howell.

"Wow," Fuller murmured. "Same work—as in what the killer seemed to do. Same hand, too. I would be stunned if it wasn't."

Kieran was looking at the image, too.

"But here's what different. Cary Howell was in a mausoleum. The old lady who died might have lived on for years, and Cary wouldn't have been found until then. Why hide one girl and put the other where she'd be found the next day?" Craig asked.

"He thinks he's an artist," Kieran said.

"What?" Mike asked.

"He's creating something with these women—art, in his mind. Temporary exhibits, if you will," Dr. Fuller said. "I think he realized with his first victim that no one saw the true beauty of his creation since he didn't make sure that the body was found quickly enough," Fuller explained. "I do believe that Cary Howell was his first victim—or, I hate to say it— an earlier victim. He has been experimenting and learning."

"Why put them in a coffin then, period?" Craig asked.

"Because they're dead, and the dead belong in coffins, but their beauty should be remembered, honored," Dr. Fuller said.

Craig glanced at Kieran. She was staring at his board. Her face was white.

"Kieran, are you all right?" he asked her.

"Fine," she told him. She leaned forward. "I was looking at your suspect list. And the thing is—everyone in New York knew about the historical find."

"Yes, but, everyone in New York didn't know the layout of the church or where the wall had been broken," Craig said.

"You have 'mystery lover' on the list," she said.

"Yes."

"I don't see Jeannette Gilbert dating anyone who wasn't

young, her age, say. Probably someone appealing. I don't see that as John Shaw or Henry Willoughby or..."

She paused, her voice trailing.

"Or Roger Gleason?" he asked.

"Gleason is...interesting," she admitted.

"I think most young women would find him appealing," Mike said.

"Slimy," McBride said, shaking his head.

Kieran glanced at McBride and nodded. "Some women are drawn to men like him, though. He keeps himself fit, he has a quick smile and—here's something important—he had something to offer them. He must have seen plenty of young women coming in for a job at the club."

"Rich as Croesus, he is. He owns the building," Mike pointed out. "The whole old church. Man, that's some mean property in Manhattan."

Craig looked at Dr. Fuller. "What about Miss Gilbert's manager, Oswald Martin? The man is in his late thirties. He made her rich. But she grew up, and maybe she wanted to go her own way."

"Possible, but unlikely in my mind. She was making a fortune for him. He tried to rule her life, yes, but she was getting what she wanted. She could slip away when she wanted," Fuller said. "She gave impromptu press interviews—without him around."

"He might have been furious over the mystery lover," Mike said.

"And she might have just made up the mystery lover for good press," Fuller said.

Kieran looked at him quickly. "A mystery lover is always good press," she said.

"We're all speculating now," Craig said, putting an end to

the talk. "I have agents out to find Oswald. I plan to speak with him tonight. Can you, at the moment, give us anything helpful?" he asked Fuller.

"Yes, Kieran and I have talked, but we needed to know more about his first victim, which is why we came down now, without a complete report with explanations. This is what we've got so far. This man has money. He can come and go as he pleases. He's got a respectable appearance. Normally, I would have said he was between the ages of twenty-five and thirty-five, but Kieran suggested a little older and I think she's right. He's gained the respect he receives and he's intelligent. I imagine he pulled up the original church plans. They're available online, by the way, though not even online—or in any archive—will you find a reference to the hidden crypt. Your killer listens to the news. He knew about the findings."

"And how the hell did he get in?" Mike murmured.

"There's always a way," Craig said.

"But the security footage—"

"Yes, that remains a mystery," Craig said, cutting off his partner. "What else can you tell us, Dr. Fuller?"

"The killer used a mausoleum before—a family mausoleum. He was dissatisfied. I believe he was in love with Ms. Gilbert—as he had been with Ms. Howell. Not sexually. His love is above all that. His love is for perfection, I believe. Both women were more than attractive. They were beautiful. He laid them out almost tenderly. They were...art." Fuller kept his eye on the pictures as he spoke. "I'll write up my complete report. You'll have it first thing in the morning."

Craig glanced at the clock on the wall. It was almost eight o'clock, but he knew his day would go on; he was expecting Oswald Martin at the office soon.

If the man was innocent, he'd certainly agree to be questioned. And if he was guilty? Well, he'd agree, too. He'd want to appear to be cooperating.

"Dr. Fuller, thank you for coming in."

"Well, then, I'm off. Heading to the office. I now feel the need for continued research on the minds of such men," Dr. Fuller said.

Kieran stood.

"No need to join me. You were a godsend today, Kieran. Thank you," he said. He smiled at her and then at Craig. "I'm quite certain that Special Agent Frasier will see to it that you get home safely."

Kieran looked like a deer caught in headlights.

What the hell?

"Um, sure, thank you," she said to Fuller. "Actually, I can just walk to Finnegan's. I was supposed to be helping today. It's a Friday night."

It wasn't unusual that she said she was going back to the pub. What struck Craig was the way she seemed to be so confused, unsure of what she really wanted to do.

"Someone will drive you," Craig said. "I'll meet you as soon as we're done here."

She nodded. Her smile for him was weak. She was almost out the door to the conference room when she seemed to remember Mike and McBride. She turned and bid them both goodbye, and then hurried out.

Craig didn't get a chance to wonder about her behavior. The intercom buzzed again.

Oswald Martin was there. Were they ready for him?

Hell, yes.

Kieran had been sending Kevin texts half the day.

He hadn't gotten back.

He might have gone home, but she doubted it. His audition might have run long. He might have had an instant callback.

But he should have texted her by then.

She looked at her phone as she was leaving the conference room and saw a missed text.

He was heading to the pub.

Walking out to reception, head still down over her phone, she crashed into a man coming toward the conference room.

She jumped, apologizing, as he steadied her, his hands on her shoulders.

She knew him from the tabloids.

Oswald Martin.

"Oh! I'm sorry, so sorry," she murmured. He had an escort—a blue-suited FBI agent.

"It's all right," Martin said to her.

"This way, Mr. Martin," his escort said.

"Yes," Martin said, but he was still staring down at Kieran.

"I'm Oswald Martin," he said.

"How do you do?" she murmured, not offering her name.

He kept looking at her, and then he took a card from his pocket. "If you're ever looking for work, please…just see my card." He thrust it at her and instinctively, Kieran took the card.

"Mr. Martin, if you will?" his FBI escort said firmly.

"Of course, of course," he said. "My card—"

"Mr. Martin," his escort repeated.

"Perfect!" Martin said, walking away.

CHAPTER
FOUR

OSWALD MARTIN SEEMED APPROPRIATELY GRIM, BUT COM-
fortable and at ease as he spoke in the conference room with
Craig, Mike and Detective Larry McBride.

He was horrified, a term that seemed to refer to everyone's
feeling about the discovery of Jeannette Gilbert, but he'd been
begging the police to listen to him from the time she'd failed
to respond to his call.

"The papers!" he said with disgust, waving a hand in the
air. "Internet, media—whatever! These days, everything in
the world is out there in a split-second tweet. That's how I
found out she was dead. Jeannette! A young woman—a beautiful girl I've worked with for nearly a decade—is killed, and
I see it first on social media. I told the police over and over
again that she wasn't flighty, that she didn't just take off and
that she wouldn't run away from me. But because I 'discovered' Jeannette, and because I'm older by several years, they
just have to turn it into something dirty, something wrong.
Yes, I loved her—like a big brother. And she loved me, in just

the same way. The stuff I've read is disgusting. I was 'angry' about her so-called mystery lover. What a crock. She was twenty-seven years old. She'd seen other men through the years. I could advise her, no more. Did the police really investigate? No, they were just as bad as the tabloids!"

Martin was an interesting man. Late thirties, his head clean-shaven, one gold earring and all-black attire, he looked like a modern-day Aleister Crowley. Sure, he seemed appropriately "horrified." But Craig wasn't sure that the man was appropriately *sad*.

"We're truly sorry," Mike said gently. "The people there were asked not to tweet or say anything to anyone. Apparently, asking wasn't enough."

"Yeah, well, it's a social media age, isn't it?" Martin asked. He wasn't waiting for an answer. He'd really made a statement. "I told Jeannette that all the time—that anything she did, anyone she saw, any word she uttered was up for grabs. She was a sweet kid. A truly sweet kid. The best. Her life sucked before I found her. I mean, I don't know whether or not to hate her aunt. She took Jeannette in, but she treated her as if she were an unwanted pet! Almost like Cinderella with her stepsisters, you know? She was like an indentured servant. She was worked her little tail off. But the kid was beautiful. Beautiful. Perfect, you know?"

Perfect.

To Craig the word seemed to be disturbing.

"When was the last time you saw her?" Craig asked.

Martin sighed deeply, and not without aggravation.

"I told the police!" he said. "It was two weeks ago—or now it was two weeks ago plus a day or two! I saw her at dinner. We talked about what she was doing, what she aspired to do and the contract in the offing with a major cosmetics giant.

She was going to be the new face of L'Amour, and you can only imagine… Anyway, I told her what the contract would mean. I told her that she'd really hit the big time, bigger and brighter than she'd ever been before. And I told her to quit handing out interviews, especially when it came to talking about this guy—this mystery lover—that everyone else seemed to know about. Everyone but me!"

"You talked where?" Craig asked.

"At Wine Bar Bacanalia!" Oswald Martin said. "A very public place. When we parted ways, we were in full view of every waitress, waiter, bartender and hostess in the place. You all should know this. I told everyone when I reported her missing. And I reported her missing because—due to the new contract—we had a meeting the next morning with the cosmetic company."

"So," Craig said lightly, "you reported her missing because she didn't show up for her meeting with these people?"

"What are you, an idiot?" Martin demanded, looking at Craig. He quickly appeared to regret his words. "Sorry, sorry. You can't possibly understand the importance of such a meeting!"

Yeah, what an idiot, Craig thought. He just didn't understand fame and fortune.

"Sorry, sorry, truly sorry," Martin muttered quickly. "Jeannette was a true pro. She grew up with nothing, but she was smart as a whip. She knew that the appointment we had could make the difference between her being a star who'd perhaps be forgotten as soon as a younger face came along or a supernova, shimmering in the public memory for decades. It was no publicity stunt when she didn't show up. I tried so hard to make the police believe that. And then, of course, to the tabloids, I became like a monster, a slave driver, all for my own enrichment. Was Jeannette a major cash-flow outlet for me? You bet. But I represent other acting and modeling personalities, as well. Other than what you read in the tabloids, you won't find anyone I've ever worked with who won't tell you I'm a straight shooter!"

The man stared straight at Craig as he said the last; there was passion and sincerity in his voice. It seemed to be real, but, in Craig's mind, it was far too early in the game to be certain.

"Naturally, we'll be verifying what you've told us," Craig said.

"Yep. And we'll check out the cops who worked the missing person detail," McBride said, the undertone in his voice so low Craig doubted Oswald Martin had the least idea of how deeply he had offended the officer who was there representing the City of New York.

"You travel much, Mr. Martin?" Craig asked.

"Around the USA, Europe, anywhere?" Mike added pleasantly.

"Of course. I travel all the time," Martin said. He appeared to be perplexed. "Why do you ask?"

"You do any work in Virginia?" McBride asked.

"Not much, no. Most work in the US comes out of New York, Los Angeles and sometimes Miami," Martin said, looking at them all. "Virginia? I mean, an ad campaign can take you almost anywhere, but even if Jeannette was headed to a certain location, it wouldn't mean that I'd be there with her. I tried to accompany her—every star needs a shield!—but I couldn't always, because, as I mentioned earlier, I do represent other people. Still…she was part of a shoot that was a public service announcement, encouraging people to enjoy the country. That was about six months ago. Yeah, we were in Virginia then. She filmed in Richmond and Williamsburg.

And then Charleston, South Carolina, Savannah, Georgia, and Saint Augustine, Florida. I can send the footage of the announcement, if you like."

"We would greatly appreciate it," Craig assured him. "Along with the names of your other clients."

Martin suddenly leaned forward. "You think that I'm going to balk at that? Well, you're wrong. I didn't kill Jeannette. And when that's been proved, and you all look like a pack of in-your-face asses, I'll be sitting pretty. Whatever you want, you go for it—and if I can provide it, so help me, I will. Now, are you through with me for the day?" he asked.

Craig smiled pleasantly. "Almost. Tell me. Have you ever frequented Le Club Vampyre?"

"Yeah. Hell, yeah. That place was a pile of publicity opportunities. We were at the opening, both Jeannette and me. Both openings, actually—the soft, which they had for critics and reviewers, and the hard, when they opened for the public. There are stunning pictures of Jeannette on the steps below the main arch. Her face was everywhere." He sat back, deflated, and lowered his head. "Who knew?" he added softly.

It was the first time he seemed to show real emotion, in Craig's mind.

"Are you through with me?" he asked tonelessly.

"For now," Craig told him. "We may need to call you back in the future. Because I know you're going to want to help in any way we may need. Also, we'd like a copy of your calendar for the last six months."

"Jeannette only disappeared two weeks ago."

"Yes, but knowing what she was doing prior to her disappearance may be of major importance," Craig told him.

Martin nodded dully and stood. "Gentlemen..."

"I'll see that you're escorted out," Mike said.

Craig and Larry remained in the room. When Martin was gone, the detective exploded. "He made it sound as if the NYPD is nothing but an organization of incompetents!"

"He's bitter," Craig said.

"He's damned suspicious."

That was a statement Craig didn't argue.

"It started about six months ago," Kevin told Kieran. They were seated in the office at Finnegan's again; she was behind Declan's desk while Kevin sat on the sofa by the wall. He wasn't looking at her as he spoke, but rather away, as if he were seeing the past play before him like a movie reel. "We were working on the Lilith music video." He looked over at Kieran then, his expression apologetic. "I was a shirtless hunk. She was one of the recognized beauties. The song hit the charts at number one. The video claimed awards, too."

Kieran nodded. She was proud of Kevin's achievements, even when he was playing eye candy.

"I've seen it. It's a good video. Though, honestly, I'm sorry, Kevin, I watched it for you. I didn't even notice Jeannette Gilbert."

He winced, and Kieran remembered that the dead woman had been someone he loved.

"There was a lot of filming for flashes of each beauty in the three minutes and twenty-eight seconds of the song," Kevin said. "If you saw it again..."

"Of course."

"So, we started talking on set. We just had so much in common and so much not in common. She was fascinated by our family and couldn't wait to come to Finnegan's. She has cousins and, contrary to what they write, she loves them... loved them, but..."

"But her parents died and she grew up with an aunt?"

Kevin nodded. "Her aunt had four children. Their father had passed away, too, and Jeannette's aunt was remarried to a worthless piece of trash. He couldn't see feeding another mouth. Jeannette spent her formative years hearing about being a burden and being told that she was going to have to get out on her own early, because they weren't going to feed her forever. Anyway, she wasn't a mean or bitter person. She bought her aunt a house in Brooklyn when she had the money to do so. But she loved that Declan ran this place now and that the rest of us had other work, but that we all helped out here. I guess she always wanted a real family—one where she was unconditionally welcome."

"I'm so sorry," Kieran said. Images of Jeannette Gilbert in death kept flashing before her eyes. "Kevin, how serious was your relationship? How often were you seeing one another?"

He hesitated and then shrugged. "At first? I thought it was going to be a one-night stand. Not on my part—I was like a starry-eyed kid. I couldn't believe she'd even looked at me. I tried to maintain some dignity, but I figured I might have been a novelty to her, entertainment for that one night. And she had to leave the city for a work project. Anyway, when she was back, she called me and we started seeing one another. I lived for every chance to be with her. And she wasn't keeping quiet because she was ashamed or anything like that. She wasn't even trying to pretend that she was attainable to the zillions of men and boys drooling over her. She wanted something good and private, something…normal. Then one day I couldn't reach her. But I wasn't crazy. I knew she'd come to me when she could. We both knew that we wouldn't always be able to contact one another. There were events that had to do with our professional lives. But then…then I heard…"

He stopped speaking for a minute, and she watched his eyes fill with tears.

Before they could spill over, he continued. "I didn't think that Oswald Martin had done her in, either. She didn't hate him. He didn't follow her every move. That was some writer's imaginative speculation. But I did wonder if it was some kind of a publicity thing because she was about to become the face of one of the biggest new cosmetic firms to launch in the past twenty years. This is so, so…wrong!" he finished on a breath.

Kieran wanted to hold her twin and comfort him. She was afraid that the door was going to open any minute. While she knew that Kevin loved his brothers and would happily share this with them, keeping this on a need-to-know basis was best right now.

Declan or Danny couldn't inadvertently spill information they didn't have.

"Kevin, where did you two see each other?" she asked.

"My place," he said huskily. "No one pays attention to my place. I saw her at her apartment only once. It was with a group of people. She invited me to a reading, a show that may or may not make it to Broadway."

"But you stayed after."

He shrugged. "It wasn't something anyone would have noticed. There were a number of actors there. She was friendly and nice to everyone. Her work reputation was amazing. She was never cross with a single makeup person, lighting person, cameraman…anyone."

"You're telling me that absolutely no one knows that you were seeing her, that this actually started six months ago, but no one knew?"

"That's what I'm telling you," he said.

Kieran pondered that. "Kevin, trust me, someone knew," she said. "Someone saw you together somewhere."

He shrugged. "She was with actors all the time. Posing at parties, openings, fashion shows. I don't think anyone would have noticed me over anyone else." He shook his head. "I don't know what to do."

"Kevin, I'm sorry, but I have to ask. How serious did you two get?"

"We both knew we loved our careers. Sometimes it's bad when two people are actors, or models, or in that kind of world. Egos clash. But maybe we were different enough. I really love acting. I take the underwear commercials or whatever because I see them as a stepping-stones. Jeannette didn't love it so much. She loved art and images and what a good photographer could do with her. But we also wanted to make sure that our relationship worked. We weren't making any real commitments until we'd been together at least a year. She was famous—I'm not. She wanted to make sure that I could handle that. Maybe she wanted to make sure that I didn't want to use her, either. You know, fake a real love just to use her for more exposure and better parts. If we made it a year—trusting one another, still wanting one another, ready to deal with the whirlwind as a couple—then we'd put our relationship out there." He paused. "She used to tease me. Said it would be the coolest thing in the world if we were secretly married here. At Finnegan's."

"Oh, Kevin, I'm so sorry. I can't believe that you kept all this from me. And for so long! I'm your twin."

"Well, you've kept a fair amount from me, too, at times," he reminded her.

"Sometimes I don't talk because I'm professionally not able to do so," she replied.

"What do I do?" he asked her. "Just step up now and tell the truth?"

"That's probably the best. You can talk to Craig. He'll believe you. You know that."

Kieran started, hearing the doorknob twist. Then there was a bang on the door.

"Hey, what's going on in there?"

It was Danny, the "baby" of the family, younger than Kevin and Kieran by a little more than a year. He was the wild child of the family, now a respectable tour guide for the City of New York, though, of course, he could still get into a great deal of trouble. Always with the best of intentions, of course.

Kieran stood quickly and opened the door. "Did I lock it?" she murmured.

Danny burst into the room and flipped on the TV. "This is so sad and so crazy!" he said. "Imagine, that poor girl found in Le Club Vampyre! And now... Wow! The bad boy of the silver screen stepping up and offering a huge sum of money for information on her murderer. Brent Westwood! You've got to see this news conference. It's Brent Westwood saying that he was Jeannette Gilbert's secret lover!"

It was past nine. Craig was getting ready to head home from the office, and he'd told Mike and McBride to do the same. But his office door opened.

"You might want to hold on just a minute!" Mike said, stepping back in.

"What—"

"Put the TV on. Any news channel," Mike said. He'd already gone for the remote that controlled the screen on the far wall of Craig's office.

Light and sound filled the room.

A man stood at the front of the New York field offices of the FBI, surrounded by a sea of reporters, all jockeying to get better positions with their microphones.

Craig recognized the guy; it took him a minute to know why.

Then he realized quickly that it was Brent Westwood, aging star of stage and screen. He was an exceptionally well-muscled man, an "action hero." Craig remembered that he'd halfway paid attention to a slice of life news piece recently that had talked about the beautiful people of "yesteryear" who were still working hard at their craft, even if they weren't getting the leading roles they'd once enjoyed.

The actor listened to a question from a reporter and answered it gravely.

"You had to know Jeannette to understand," he said, the right amount of pathos in his voice. "She was, at heart, a shy girl. She wanted what we had to be special. We're both public figures, but we didn't want our relationship to be public. It was something so private, of the heart."

"Weren't you worried when she disappeared?" someone shouted.

"I'll be honest. I thought it was a publicity venture, directed by those controlling her career," he said, not mentioning any names.

"But wouldn't she have told you?" another reporter asked.

"In this field, we have to be very careful. I knew that she'd tell me what was going on as soon as she felt that she could. Was I worried? Yes! But I knew that the police—New York's finest—were working on finding her. I feared their anger, really, when she surfaced. I never expected that they would find her...as they did."

He put a hand in front of his face, as if shielding himself from more questions—and as if hiding his tears, as well. "Please, I'm beside myself with grief, but I'm here to see if there is anything at all that I can do to help in the investigation into her death. This is..."

He broke down and turned away.

Mike groaned. "Great. He's coming here. And he's using this to garner publicity for himself. That girl had great taste in men." He snickered. "Maybe she was looking for a father figure."

"He was the biggest thing in action movies at one time," Craig said.

"Guess they don't know our offices actually close at night," Mike muttered. He turned to the NYPD detective. "You want to handle this?"

"He probably knows you're here, given what's going on," McBride said.

"I'm sure he knows what he's doing," Craig said. He pointed to the screen. "There he is, going for the door—and there's security. In less than a minute, someone will be calling up here."

As he spoke, the intercom buzzed.

It was one of the young agents in reception.

"Do we go get him?"

Craig didn't believe that the man pretending so much grief was Gilbert's killer.

Such a recognizable man didn't sneak around easily. Nor did he appear to be the type who would have dressed a murdered girl so carefully. Or managed to get down to Virginia to have carried out a murder there and done the same. Craig had no proof. It was only a gut feeling, but his gut feelings had served him well.

He toyed with the idea of having security send him away and tell him to come back during office hours.

But, of course, that would make the Bureau look callow. And he wouldn't do that.

"Of course, anyone with information that could lead to the solving of this heinous murder is thanked for bringing us information at any time," he said.

And so Mike sat and McBride sighed, and they waited for the actor.

The three of them—Kevin, Kieran and Danny—stared at the flat-screen television in the office, watching as Brent Westwood spoke to the press.

Kevin's expression was blank, stunned.

"I don't get it," Danny said. "Not that Westwood wasn't—isn't—a cool guy and all, but, hey, Jeannette Gilbert was a kid in comparison. Not that I'm judging. We've seen a lot of older guys with younger women and younger guys with older women who seem to be happy as larks. Love is love, right? No matter what our age, sex, race or preference. Still...I wonder if it all seems so shocking to *us* because the church—the club—is right behind us." Staring at the screen, he was unaware when Kevin looked at Kieran with a warning glance.

Let it lie. Don't let on about anything I was saying to you.

"And the whole grave thing," Danny went on. "I mean, do you know that half our city parks are built on old graveyards?" He turned and looked at Kieran. "John Shaw was in today, right?"

"Yes, he was pretty shaken," she murmured.

"I wonder... I'd love to get down into that basement sometime. Think he'll take me down there?"

"I would think," Kieran said.

"After all this, obviously. I mean, go figure. They make that kind of find, and then discover a missing starlet displayed down there. Wow. So sad. And still…"

Kieran could feel Kevin's tension. He wasn't angry with his younger brother. He was just ready to explode.

The door to the office opened and the last of their clan, Declan, stood there, looking in at the three of them. "I know you guys have other jobs, and, hey, I should be all right and well-staffed here for a Friday night. But Cody is on her honeymoon and with everything going on, those who came to gawk around the block are here now, hungry and thirsty. Mary Kathleen is running around out there like a madwoman. Don't any of you actually help anymore when you're here?" he asked.

"Hell, yeah! Sorry!" Danny said, leaping to his feet.

Kevin rose more slowly. "I'll take the bar," he said.

"No, no. Go home, Kevin," Kieran said. "I don't have real work tomorrow. It's Saturday. That okay, Declan?"

"Sure. One good body actually involved in working would be great," Declan said.

Kevin still appeared a little shaky.

"I'm so tired," he murmured.

"Then go home," Kieran said, jumping up. "I'll be a bundle of energy, Declan. I promise."

"Hey, well, you did work today, too," Declan reminded her.

She nodded. "Yeah, kind of makes me need to work now," she said, and headed out of the office. "Kevin, go home!"

"I'm going," he assured them. "Thanks," he said softly, and left.

Declan was right. Their Friday nights were often busy, even when Wall Street, the Financial District and the government offices closed and downtown became somewhat quiet.

But Finnegan's was known for bringing in great Irish bands and local talent, and people were often willing to hop on the subway or drive down for the established platform of good food, great taps and music. Also, when the club had opened around the block, many who had tired of the constant thrum of the dance music had found themselves wandering over for the more relaxed venue.

But tonight was exceptional—once again, because of the club. Not because it was opened.

Because it was closed.

And the talk among everyone had to do with poor Jeannette Gilbert.

And most of the talk was the same.

The slimy manager-agent had done it.

The mystery lover had done it. No, the mystery lover wasn't a mystery anymore, and good God, everyone knew that Brent Westwood was no killer! He stood for truth, justice and the American way.

What about the step-uncle who had raised her? The jerk! Or her aunt, or her cousins?

What about the guy who had bought Saint Augustine and turned a venerable and historic old church into a club? Hey, that guy bore some watching, too. And then there were the freaks who wandered around the city. And that history group. Everyone knew that some of the city's cling-to-the-past historians were insane. That was it! One of them had murdered her to prove the point that you needed to let the dead rest in peace!

Everyone had a theory, and Kieran heard them all.

She spoke with their regulars and also noted all the new people—those who probably hadn't been downtown in years but had come down to witness the events at Le Club Vampyre, if only from the street. She noted businessmen and construction workers. Older women, younger women. All kinds of people.

One especially attractive young woman at the bar drew Kieran's attention because she kept pulling out her phone and looking around the pub.

"Can I help you in any way?" Kieran asked her.

She smiled. "Just biding time," the woman said. "That old clock on the wall is right? My cell phone has died."

"Yes, it's the right time," Kieran told her.

"Thanks!" The woman smiled at her. "You have to be Kevin's sister," she said. "One of the Finnegan family."

"Yes, I am. You know Kevin?"

"I was in a print ad with him about a year ago. He told me about this place. First time I've had a chance to get down here. Is he here somewhere?"

"No, he went home. I'm so sorry. You could give him a call."

"Ah, well, I'm only here a few more minutes. I'll call him, though, and I'll come back." She smiled. "You're gorgeous—but then, so is Kevin!"

"Thank you. My twin has the camera charm, trust me!" Kieran said. She would have talked longer, but another patron called her and she moved on.

It was around 11:00 p.m. when Craig reached her on her cell, checking to see if she was still there. He told her he'd head into the pub, and they could go home together.

She felt her heart beating a little too quickly. She didn't have to worry that she wasn't saying anything to him about Kevin's admission. Brent Westwood had gone to Craig's office, claiming to be the mystery lover. But still…

Lying to him was so uncomfortable.

Was she really lying?

Yes, she reasoned, omitting the truth—an important truth—was a lie.

Luckily, when he arrived, he offered her a weary smile before heading to an empty bar stool. She watched him talk to Declan and order a soda. He looked tired. Despite knowing he'd have to be up for work early the next morning, he was waiting for her.

The Friday night crowd was diminishing, so Declan thanked her and told her to go on home.

She didn't argue.

"Your place or mine?" Craig asked, pointing the way to his government car, parked down the street. Thanks to his decal, parking was much easier for Craig than it was for most people in the city. "You know," he said, as they reached the car, "we don't have to be asking that question of one another all the time. Moving in would be kind of like the right move now."

"Probably," she murmured. "My place tonight?"

"As you wish."

She glanced his way. He had to be far beyond exhausted, but he was also easily able to go with the flow. She studied him for a moment; he seemed deep in thought, and, of course, she knew he was thinking about the day's events.

She winced, turning away. She really was so in love with him. What was not to love? He was a walking wall of extremely striking testosterone, masculine to the hilt, yet he never behaved rudely, and never seemed threatened in any way by another man's—or woman's—talents or abilities. He was faultlessly courteous. Oh, he had a temper, she knew, but the ability to contain it. His features offered exceptionally fine cheekbones, a strong jaw and wonderful, hazel eyes that far too often seemed to be all-seeing.

"One day soon," she murmured, finally responding to his comment about moving in together.

She was suddenly, almost irrationally, angry with her brothers. First, one of Danny's best-intended foibles had gotten him into the trouble when she'd met Craig; now Kevin's tragic romance seemed to be putting her once again in an extremely awkward situation.

That anger quickly dissipated. She felt so bad for her twin.

In minutes they reached her apartment above a sushi restaurant–karaoke bar in the Village.

Someone was warbling an Aerosmith number as they climbed the stairs. They were both so accustomed to the sometimes painful entertainment that they barely noticed.

Upstairs, she immediately headed for the shower. "Underground graves," she muttered, heading in.

He joined her.

She wasn't surprised. Or disappointed. Sharing a shower with Craig, she wouldn't have to talk to him.

But as he stepped in behind her, slipping a bar of soap from her fingers and easing it down her back, she was the one who nervously spoke.

"So, what about the mystery lover?"

"Narcissistic blowhard," he said, twirling her around, finding her lips.

His kiss was good, wonderful. Seductive. And it made her forget the day. Hot water and steam swirled around them. The soap made their naked flesh sleek and wet. They kissed and touched and stroked one another until they were certainly clean—and their sense of hunger and need was great. Then they stepped out of the shower, reached for towels, more or less forgot the concept of them and stumbled onto the bed in Kieran's near-dark room, and back into one another's arms.

Once there, they eschewed foreplay. She crawled atop him and straddled him, and he entered her, the heat of his body bursting within her. They made love, again and again, their lips locked as they climaxed each time with a ferocity that left Kieran breathless. She marveled at it, amazed that she was with him, that the world could be so good, that sex was such an amazement every time.

He pulled her down into his arms and held her and stroked her hair. The glow of aftermath and a sense of warmth and security enveloped her.

And then she realized that he was lying there awake, no doubt thinking about the day once again.

And he picked up right where he had left off.

"Liar."

"Pardon?" Warmth and serenity slipped away.

"That man. Brent Westwood. He's a liar. I can't prove it. There's no way, really. Jeannette Gilbert is dead. But, in my gut, I know it. There's no way in hell that man is the mystery lover Jeannette alluded to in her interviews. He's a liar." He smiled grimly as he stroked her face. "I will, however," he assured her, "discover the truth."

CHAPTER
FIVE

CRAIG STOOD JUST INSIDE THE DOWNED WALL IN THE
basement of Le Club Vampyre and looked around.

Techs had been studying the security footage of the club
for hours; none as yet had discovered if the footage had been
altered and, if so, how.

And if it hadn't been altered, then it seemed that Jeannette
Gilbert's killer had slipped into a cloak of invisibility that had
covered her, as well.

"We've established that the killer's not stupid," Mike said,
watching Craig's expression. "And, according to our good
docs and Kieran, he's organized, and we know that he's killed
before. According to the info we have on his first victim, he
has a vision, a way of leaving his victims. Maybe he's even
trying to learn how to preserve them. He just hasn't gotten
it right yet."

"Art," Craig murmured. "Yes." He stooped down to look
at the floor. Everyone in the city who read a paper or turned
on a computer or a television had known about the discovery

of the early graves behind a false wall in the basement of the building. Anyone would have known. But who would have known how to enter the place without being seen?

"Makes Roger Gleason a good suspect," Mike said. "He's definitely been here. He's a respectable man. He might have been meeting with Jeannette Gilbert for some kind of a publicity thing. Wasn't she part of a promotional event here?"

"Yes, I believe she was. We don't have anything on Roger Gleason—yet," Craig said.

"You hear about the find…and a day later, bring a girl down here to bury. According to the autopsy, she was dead already," Mike mused aloud.

"Yeah. He must have planned to leave her somewhere else. I wonder where," Craig said. "I still can't fathom how he got down here."

"The security footage is somehow jimmied."

Craig looked over at him. "Egan has our people working with their people. None of them can figure out how the tape was fixed. And if it wasn't fixed, there's another way in here."

"Yeah? Under the ground?" Mike asked.

"Yeah, under the ground."

Mike groaned. He was older; he actually had the seniority. But the two of them had been working together for years, and they had a great relationship.

Mike walked down the rows of tombs—those sealed and those not—muttering as he leaned over the shelves of the dead, pushing at the walls.

Craig did the same. It was eerie work; he tried not to look at the skeletal remains beneath their decaying shrouds. He thought about Shaw and the historical people.

They probably wouldn't be happy. They worked with delicate chisels and tiny brushes, and he was pushing aside nearly two-hundred-year-old remains in his attempt to find what he was looking for.

It seemed, however, that he hit nothing but the solid granite on which the city sat.

"Special Agent Frasier!"

He nearly bumped his head, startled by the uniformed officer who had come to talk to him.

"There's a rep here from the mayor's office. She's with Henry Willoughby, Aldous Digby and Roger Gleason. They're waiting to talk to you in the storage area," the officer told him.

"Yeah, of course," Craig said. He glanced at Mike and shrugged.

The body was gone. Jeannette had been taken to the morgue.

The forensic team had gone over the area with a fine-tooth comb.

It had to be opened back up to the archaeologists, anthropologists and historians who would record the find and see that the remains were reinterred in a cemetery in Brooklyn or the Bronx.

He and Mike walked back out past the broken wall to where Roger Gleason was waiting with Henry Willoughby and Aldous Digby and a young woman in a smart pin-striped business suit. Her heels were too high for the marble steps that led to an uneven basement floor, but she represented the mayor, so he figured her attire had to be proper.

"Special Agents," she said, addressing him and Mike and offering her hand in a shake. "I'm Sandra Adair from the mayor's office. Naturally, we're grateful for the federal interests here. And we're appalled about the murder of Ms. Gilbert. But, gentlemen, we've spoken with Assistant Director

Egan, and we've all agreed that it's time to let the historians get back to work. Are we all in agreement?"

"Yes, I believe it's all right for the work to continue," Craig said politely. "With Ms. Gilbert now in the tender hands of the medical examiner, Professor Shaw and Professor Digby may continue their documentation of the long dead."

He kept his voice modulated, trying to hide his irritation.

Willoughby lowered his head, smiling, no doubt aware of Craig's feelings. Sandra Adair seemed oblivious, and Roger Gleason apparently didn't care one way or another; he wasn't reopening for business yet.

"Well, then, thank you, and, naturally, we'll be anxious to hear that you've solved the murder of Ms. Gilbert," Adair said. "Mr. Willoughby, I'll leave it to you to call the experts back in. Oh, by the way, Special Agent Frasier. I don't believe your phone has been working down here. I have a message for you from Detective McBride. He wants you to call him."

"Thank you," Craig said.

She turned to head back up the old marble steps. He gritted his teeth and then stepped forward to help her. She was annoying, but he didn't want to see her flat on the ground with a broken ankle.

"We're okay?" Digby asked. He let out a sigh. "To be honest, I'm anxious to do this work, but I'm equally anxious to get in and out."

"Yes, we'll need John Shaw," Willoughby said as Craig headed up the stairs.

Craig turned back to Digby. "Professor, you were here when Ms. Gilbert was found. Is there anything in particular you noted? Anything you could tell us that might help in any way?"

Digby was thoughtful.

"The floor," he said.

"The floor?"

"People had already been in, of course. But, there's always a kind of a film—time and decay—on the floor. Now that I've had time to think, there was something a little off. It seemed to me that much of it was…too clean."

"Was that before or after the body was found?" Craig asked him.

"When we first came down, I thought it odd. The tombs, the shrouds, the coffins all had that film. But the floor seemed clean. Right at the start."

Before Craig could comment, Willoughby got down to business. "I'll call Shaw so we can get moving. This is going to take weeks."

"Yes, thank you, Mr. Willoughby," Craig said. He headed out then and didn't look back.

He heard Mike speaking with Gleason, thanking him for his concern for the city.

Then Mike headed up after him.

An officer was at the main Gothic-arched doorway, keeping watch over who entered and exited. Craig nodded and headed out to the street, aware that Mike was with him.

"Rat terrier," Mike said.

"Pardon?"

"It's not really her fault. I mean, there's no reason to stop the experts from their cataloging and corpse inspections," he said drily. "She's doing her job, that Ms. Adair. She's just nervous-looking and yappy—like a rat terrier."

Craig grinned. "Yesterday we dealt with an asshole— according to McBride—and today a rat terrier."

"Yeah, but at least you don't have to pretend to be polite to an asshole!" Mike said.

Craig took out his phone. "I've got to call McBride."

When he hung up a minute later, he told Mike, "McBride has Tobias Green down at the station."

"Lovely! Can't wait to meet the man."

Kieran didn't have to be at Finnegan's on Saturday morning.

Saturday mornings were traditionally slow. But as she walked into the pub she mumbled something about being worried that the news might cause another surge in clientele.

The truth was that she knew Kevin would head there when he could. It was a natural instinct for all of them; they headed to the family when they were in trouble.

But Kevin wasn't at the pub. He did, however, call her right away.

"I'm actually honestly working," he told her. "One line in that new cop show. I'm a detective today. Ironic, isn't it?" he asked her.

"Kevin, you have to talk to Craig. He knows that Brent Westwood is lying."

"How?"

"Instinct? I don't know. He just knows. Maybe the way Brent Westwood came across when he headed to the FBI building and they interviewed him."

"They did know each other. That much is true," Kevin said.

"Let Craig and Mike and the cops know the truth, Kevin. Don't you want them to catch her killer?"

"God, yes!"

Kieran instantly regretted her question. She quickly assured her twin that she was there for him, and that he had to make the decision to talk.

When she hung up, she noted that John Shaw was at the bar. He'd ordered one of their Saturday specials—a lobster pie—but he was picking at his food. Instead of sipping at his old ultra-lite beer, he had a scotch glass in front of him again.

Empty.

"Kieran!" he called, seeing her. "Be a love and come on over here! Would you be so kind as to get me another drink?"

She walked over to the table and shook her head. She pushed a glass of water his way as she said, "You're trying to numb your mind with shots, and it doesn't work that way. Talk to me instead."

John groaned. "So, the pub-keeper girl just has to be a psychologist. Don't go trying to fix me, Kieran. I'm not ready to be fixed."

"What happens when they call you back in—and it's barely eleven thirty in the morning and you're on your way to full-blown drunk?"

"You're way too pretty and young to sound like my mother!" John said. "I'll just call Declan over here and tell him he runs a pub and that you won't give me any alcohol!"

"Call him. This is a pub, John. In the true tradition. We're not out to make huge profits on our booze—"

"You'll be out of business soon enough!"

"No, John, listen to me—"

She broke off because his cell rang and he quickly picked it up.

Then his eyes widened and he stared at Kieran.

"Yes, yes," he said. "I'm ready!"

He hung up, staring at her. "What are you, my girl? A damned clairvoyant? That was the mayor's office. I can get back in the basement! I can go to work. Quick, Kieran, can you get me coffee?"

"That I can do," she told him.

When she returned with the coffee, he'd consumed half his lunch and half the glass of water.

"John, may I come with you?"

"Um…well, I have to get ahold of Professor Digby and my grad students. I have to make a new assessment of what we should be doing. And I'll need more pictures. Real work won't start right away. It takes a bit to get organized again, you know. But you've already been down there, you're part of the task force, or your doctors are anyway and…sure!"

"Thanks."

"Hey! You can act as my assistant until the grad students get there. How's that? I know you're an excellent note taker!"

Kieran thanked him again and told Kevin what she was doing. She thought about at least texting Craig as well, but then decided not to. He seemed to be especially agitated about this case, and there didn't seem to be any reason to get him going. Besides, she wasn't in any danger; there were still cops all around the old church.

"Anthropology and archaeology!" Shaw said as they walked toward the church. "So similar and yet, different. As you know, I am also an anthropologist—an expert in the field of comparative study of people and their social evolvement, their different cultures. Archaeology is the study of human activity in the past—largely based on the implements they used. We come together nicely, studying what foods were eaten, what diseases were suffered, how long people lived, what made some live much longer than others. Oh, I do love the study of man! No other such fascinating and varied creature exists! Well, I mean, you know the differences in psychology and psychiatry—lots more years of study and often major money-making abilities being a few. But the study of the human being in all its guises is so very, very fascinating. I'm delighted to be getting back in—"

He looked at her and broke off. "I am so sorry about Ms. Gilbert. I do hope they catch the killer quickly. It's just that…"

"It's all right," Kieran assured him. "I understand."

John Shaw produced his credentials at the arched entrance to the building. Kieran had been a little worried that an officer might not let her in, but the cop on duty at the door had apparently seen her there before. She was ushered right in along with the professor.

Nothing seemed to have changed in the club area since the day before. It was, in fact, empty. As they headed toward the bar and the marble steps behind it down to the crypts below, she heard voices.

Their footsteps must have echoed because, as they neared the stairs to the crypts, two men appeared from the offices to the left of the bar.

Roger Gleason, wearing another handsome, casual suit, and Henry Willoughby, nicely dressed as well, but just a bit heavier and not quite so dapper, stepped out to greet them.

"John, good to see you back. Professor Digby will be joining you shortly. He ran out to grab a coffee. We had a rep from the mayor's office down before. We're good to go," Willoughby said. He smiled, noting Kieran. "Good day, Miss Finnegan. You're back. You have an interest in the very old, as well?"

"I love the history of New York," she told him. "My family, you know, owns a pub that has been serving since the pre–Civil War days."

"Of course, of course," he said, but he looked at John Shaw.

"Kieran has kindly agreed to serve as something of an assistant for me while I get myself together again," John said.

"Ah, pity!" Roger Gleason said, smiling as he looked at Kieran. "I would have loved it if you were applying for a job. You know, don't you, that I also work to keep our city entertained? My bartenders and waiters and waitresses are invited to perform now and then. Helps with their tips and makes my place a bit different. First saw something like it in Vegas. Thought it was great."

"That is great. There are so many talented people in this city," Kieran said.

"And young and stunning. And a blue-eyed redhead!" Roger Gleason exclaimed, studying her.

"Very stunning," Willoughby said, appearing a bit anxious. "But, Roger, she is here to help John get going, not to apply for a job."

"Of course. There is still an officer sitting in the basement, though I'm not sure why," Gleason said. "The side doors are locked, and there is no way in except through the front. But then, we're all about preserving what we can of New York's fine history," he added.

"Let's head on down, shall we?" John Shaw suggested, trying not to sound giddy.

"Yes, yes!" Willoughby said. He led the way down the stairs.

"Enjoy, professionals," Gleason said. "I'll be in my office, planning for the business I might have again one day." He left them.

Kieran quickly followed Willoughby and John Shaw down the broad marble stairs. Neither man gave a glance to the storeroom with its racks of wine and liquor and kegs of beer.

They headed straight to the area by the broken-down wall.

"Kieran, I know you have a notepad, so jot down all this. Naturally, the original coffin is gone—I'm assuming the cops will return it when it's time. But I do want to point out that I believe the coffin was crafted and brought down here about 1830. I believe it was made of mahogany, an expensive wood. Now, remember, in the early 1800s, this was pretty far uptown and the parish had a clientele who was making good money at the time." He walked ahead, expounding as he went. "Now, toward the back where there are so many dead in shrouds, I believe they might have been victims of yellow fever or some other deadly disease to have swept through. There is a partition of sorts toward the rear that might designate a fear that the dead must be away from the others, while accorded a Christian burial to their standard of living. During times of pestilence, it took time for coffin makers to keep up. Let it also be remembered that the art of embalming did not come into popularity until the Civil War, when so many dead had to go great distances to be returned to their families. But the cool temperature down here and the structure of the granite seemed to have created something like natural mummies for us!" He walked about as he spoke, pointing things out.

Kieran tried hard to keep up with notes. The man could have definitely used a voice recorder.

Mr. Willoughby scampered behind them. "Professor Shaw, fear not! Your work will not be interrupted. Mr. Gleason might be whining about his club being closed at the moment, but he's also a very wealthy man, and happy that the place in the museum for many of the artifacts we find down here will be named for him," Willoughby said. He looked at Kieran and smiled gently. "He's really not such a bad sort, Ms. Finnegan, my dear. He just thinks that you would be a lovely addition to his crew of employees. You do have the loveliest features! Like an alabaster statue!"

"Thank you," Kieran murmured, and hurried after Shaw,

who was now halfway down the side wall, noting dates when he saw them. "Bad wood! Horrible rot," he pointed out, pausing. "And how odd. The others here are in coffins as well... and of much better quality. Look at the brass on those handles, dear. While on this... Hmm, can't even tell right off what the handles were made of. My God! That cross on that one must be twenty-four karat gold!"

Kieran kept up with Shaw's rambling, noting, however, that he seemed to be very aware of wood and brass and precious metals, even the linen used when they came to the corpses that were covered in shrouds.

She kept noting the dead.

Several of the coffins had windows at the head section—something popular in the 1800s, Shaw noted, when people feared being buried alive, and when it was in fashion to look at the coffin, and, through the window, see the face of the deceased. Of course, they weren't *buried* here. Some were entombed; some, Shaw said, were merely laid to rest. "Shelved; just like in the Roman catacombs," he said. "I have, of course, seen this before. Not common after the mid-eighteenth century, but then, our dead were here before then!"

"Don't touch anything, Ms. Finnegan," Willoughby said softly. "You never know what kind of mold or fungi might have grown down here. Once everyone is working, gloves will be a must. You have heard, of course, about the so-called curses that came with the pyramids? It's my firm belief, after a great deal of study, that every such death can be deemed a natural cause, since these microscopic killer creatures are natural."

Shaw paused to inspect one particular coffin. Willoughby, who had moved ahead, whistled softly. "Ah, they've taken pains against vampirism, even here, in the crypt of a church!"

Curious, Kieran hurried down to where he stood. He pointed.

Time had nearly made a linen shroud—aged to a peculiar yellow-white color—part of the body it had covered. She could see, just below the shroud, that there seemed to be a strange dismemberment between the skull and neck and shoulders.

"Head was removed," he told her.

"That's not just…time causing decay of the body?" she asked.

He shook his head, looking at the corpse. "No, I don't believe so. We'll discover soon enough. Oh, my dear! History is so amazing. When people died of tuberculosis, blood still sometimes showed on their mouths after death, and it was assumed that they had risen to feast on the living. There are a few other reasons for premature burial. I've seen some fantastic things! You are a scholar yourself. You must come by my office, and I can show you things that you can't believe!"

She would be glad to do so. "I'd love to see your office," she assured him.

He moved on, careful not to touch, peering closely here and there.

Kieran wasn't quite so happy to do so. In the farther reaches of the catacombs, where the shrouded dead by far outnumbered those in decaying coffins, she felt as if the weight of death was heavy. Empty eye sockets, only partially shielded by decaying shrouds, seemed to stare at her, as if she was trespassing where she should not be. In the shadows where the lights didn't reach, the dead seemed as if they could move.

Rise in their shrouds…

And walk.

"Kieran, if you will, please, help me make note here!" Shaw called.

She hurried back to him, but she didn't have to try to be his assistant much longer. Professor Aldous Digby, a tall, broad-shouldered, bald man of about fifty, arrived, and with him, Shaw's grad students, introduced to Kieran as Allie Benoit, Joshua Harding and Sam Frick. Allie was an attractive young brunette with a prominent nose and large dark eyes, Joshua looked like he ought to be out on a surfboard with his sandy hair and deep tan, and Sam Frick was very dark and lean, a wiry young man with a great handshake.

Kieran gave her notebook to Sam.

"So, my illustrious young almost-colleagues!" John Shaw said. "Today, once more, we're back to noting place and theories on time and condition. Allie, you and Sam with me. Joshua, if you will assist Professor Digby. In the next few days, we'll be joined by other experts. Such a find cannot be jealously guarded by just a few, though, I do admit, I'm delighted to be the first here. We, will, however, rest assured, work tirelessly as there is so much to be done."

Kieran stepped back. The crypt had become oppressive.

She had been eager to come.

Now, she was eager to escape.

"I will leave you experts to your work," she said.

Willoughby nodded. "Yes, of course, but my invitation was sincere. You must call me and come to my office. You'll be fascinated by the history of this city."

She smiled, refraining from telling him that she was, at the least, well aware that New York City had a fascinating history.

Escaping upstairs, she ran into Roger Gleason, who was just coming downstairs.

"Had enough of those gleefully looking over the dead?" he asked her lightly.

"It is an extraordinary find," she told him.

He nodded. "Yes, the find is fascinating. It's a pity that poor Ms. Gilbert met her death to arrive down there, as well. I have to admit, I'm glad they're getting to the study and removal of the bodies in the hidden crypt. No disrespect to the dead, but New York is also a living and vibrant city."

She was silent, musing his words, and he took her silence to heart.

"I'm sorry. I guess you're one of those New Yorkers horrified that a church has become a club."

"I think I'd be more horrified if the building were to be torn down," she told him.

"Exactly! I bought the thing when it so desperately needed the work done on the foundation, and I've poured a small fortune into it. You'd think some New Yorkers would be grateful for that fact. Ah, well, you're leaving. You must come back. Come back when we're open. We're not an evil den of iniquity. It's really quite nice. And, of course, I'm serious. If pondering the minds of sick New Yorkers fails to hold interest for you, you're invited to work here anytime."

She thanked him and fled.

Out on the streets, the odor of hot dogs and sausages cooking seemed to be strong, along with that of a few unwashed bodies and someone roasting chestnuts that had apparently burned.

New York air had never smelled so good.

She tried to reach Kevin; he didn't answer.

She saw that she had missed a call from Craig and one from Dr. Fuller. She tried Craig back and left him a message, and then called Dr. Fuller. It was Saturday, and they didn't work Saturdays unless they were in the middle of an important case.

Well, they were involved, and this was certainly an important case.

"Kieran, how are you?" he asked. "Enjoying your Saturday?"

"More or less," she told him, and then added, "I was just down in the hidden crypt with Professor Shaw."

"Interesting that you should say that."

"Really?"

"Yes, I've just come across something that may or may not have anything to do with what we're dealing with now. Want to stop by the office? No, no! What am I saying? The office? On a sunny afternoon? No, I'd love to meet you at the sushi restaurant by the park. Would that be okay?"

"Absolutely," Kieran told him.

She hoped that by the time she walked the near mile to the sushi restaurant, she'd forget that she'd spent much of the morning with the long dead.

It was surely impossible to give assholes names worse than that of assholes.

Somehow, Jeannette Gilbert's step-uncle, Tobias Green, seemed to need something far worse.

Muttering under his breath, Craig added a few more adjectives to the term.

Craig and Mike weren't in with Larry McBride and Tobias Green; they stood behind the one-way glass in the interview room and observed as Green answered every one of the detective's questions with an angry roar.

"I'm suing, I promise you. I've got an attorney already. You think my niece was famous? Wait until I finish with the NYPD! They'll be worldwide infamous!" Green said. "Worldwide fucking infamous as fucking morons! I spoke with the police when Jeannette went missing. I spoke with them and told them they'd better find her."

"Mr. Green, it's been brought to my attention that you

didn't get along at all with your niece," McBride told him calmly.

"That's rags! That's bullshit. That's garbage! Didn't she buy me and the wife a nice house? I fed that girl, I housed her and I cared for her. How dare you suggest that I'd hurt her in any way. I told you that she wouldn't just disappear."

"When was the last time you saw her?" McBride asked.

"Moron! You have your notes. Same as it's been every time I've been asked. Sunday at our house. She bought my wife a pretty scarf and brought it over."

"Neighbors said you were drunk and yelling," McBride said. "You were screaming something about her owing you and your wife better presents than scarves."

"I had a few beers, and we were fooling around." Green was a beefy man with graying dark hair and a stubble on his chin. To Craig, the man's eyes appeared to be dark and beady, but he wondered if he was predisposed to dislike the man.

He looked at Mike. "I don't think he's our murderer."

"Pity," Mike said. "Looks like the kind of guy who could benefit from being locked up."

"Did she owe me?" Green roared. "Hell, yeah, she owed me! She wasn't my kid."

"I'm sure you made her well aware of that fact," McBride said.

"She owed us, yeah, she owed us. We kept her out of foster homes or an orphanage. You think it's easy, feeding kids in this city?" Green exploded.

"I still need to know more about your whereabouts, Mr. Green," McBride said evenly.

Green leaned forward. "What, are you stupid? You're trying to accuse me of killing my niece?"

"Step-niece, another mouth to feed," McBride reminded him.

"What a fucking idiot you are—and it will come out when I sue the shit out of the NYPD for failing to act when Jeannette might have been saved. That's just it, smart guy. We do have a house. My wife did get a lousy scarf. Why the hell would I kill a girl who had the sense to know that she did have a debt to pay, even if she was stingy about it?"

McBride rose and came out of the room, joining Craig and Mike.

"Well?" he asked.

"I don't believe he's our killer," Craig said.

"Because she was a meal ticket for him now?"

"Because he's a total slob," Craig said. "Look at his clothing. He's got food all over himself. His shirt is half in and half out. According to the profile, our killer is far more refined."

McBride looked in at Green and nodded. His phone buzzed and he took the call.

At the same time, Craig felt his phone buzzing.

It was Egan.

And he was certain that he and McBride were learning the same information at the same time.

"You and Mike get in here. You with McBride?"

"Yes, we're at his station house. What's up?"

"I'm afraid we might have another corpse on our hands."

"A girl has been found?"

"No, a girl has gone missing."

Craig was silent a second. "Sir, this is New York. Our missing person reports flow in constantly. Is there a reason we suspect the worst?"

"Yes, there's a reason. She recently won a Beautify the City pageant. She was beautiful, Craig." Egan was silent for a breath. "Perfect," he added softly.

CHAPTER
SIX

"ACCORDING TO MARTHA STOUT–A PHD AND A CLINICAL psychologist who spent years teaching at Harvard, as you know—one in every twenty-five people is a sociopath," Dr. Fuller said, eyeing his plate of sushi as he spoke. "We've all read this. Of course, this means that a person is all about themselves, and we have lived through the 'me' generation." He offered Kieran a smile and then homed in perfectly on a piece of the restaurant's signature lobster roll with his chopsticks. "Now, we all know such people do not necessarily become violent. In fact, thankfully, most just go to work every day, come home, eat dinner and watch television. But...well, you and I have both worked with the other kind. Anyway, I got it into my head today to start studying killers with corpse fetishes."

Kieran had still been staring at her Boston roll and had actually gotten a piece up and dipped in her soy sauce. She set it back down.

"Ed Gein is one of the best known, but then, he was the

inspiration for a great deal of fiction, including *Psycho* and *The Texas Chainsaw Massacre* and *The Silence of the Lambs*," Kieran said. "He, however, abused corpses. He made ashtrays and lamp shades and his own outfit of human skin. Ed Kemper killed because he wanted to see what it felt like. But he, too, made things out of corpses. Jeffrey Dahmer was a cannibal, as several serial killers through the ages have been.

"And many have had tragically low IQ ratios," Dr. Fuller said. He pulled a sheet of paper from his pocket. "You have serial killers like Burke and Hare back in the day in Scotland. They wanted the bodies to sell for medical science. The past is tragic with such killing because of greed, and because of severe mental problems that don't allow for someone to be totally self-absorbed, but nonviolent. But I have found a number of sadder cases that had to do with a deeper need."

"Necrophilia?" Kieran asked. "But Jeannette Gilbert wasn't violated in death."

"No. There was a case of a Florida man who was in love with a dead woman—stole her corpse from the grave, 'married' it and lived with it for years and years before being caught. He kept preserving her. In Kansas, they caught a man who had a houseful of corpses. At first, it was women who were already dead that he dug up, but then they weren't enough and he starting killing, as well. He kept them so that they could live in the house with him. He set them up every night at the dinner table so that he wouldn't have to eat alone. He kept them beautifully. In fact, he studied embalming so that he could do so!"

Kieran had taken a full semester on serial killers before graduating. She knew most of what they were talking about. She knew as well that Dr. Fuller was aware of her training—it was important in many of the cases they worked with when they were called in by law enforcement.

"That was Louis Galleon," she said. "He was lonely. Women turned him down. He convinced himself that the dead women were in love with him. And, when he began to kill, he apparently killed women who had turned down his advances, claiming, according to his statement to the prison psychiatrist, that he'd known they were just teasing him and really wanted to be with him for eternity." She was quiet for a minute. "I do remember the description given by Dr. Jenkins, the state-appointed psychiatrist. 'He was immaculate in his hygiene habits and careful in his dress and manner.'"

Fuller nodded. He laid his printed page on the table between them and easily popped another bite of sushi into his mouth.

"This is from five years ago—a similar case in New Jersey."

Kieran picked up the printed sheet; it was a copy of an article from a Jersey paper. She glanced it over and read aloud, "'Miss Lawson's body was found on the grass at Saint Steven's Memorial Cemetery, gently laid out in a fine gown, hands arranged as if in prayer and beneath the cemetery's famed statue of the crying angel.'"

She looked over at Fuller.

"Read on," he said.

Kieran did so. "'She'd apparently been dead for several weeks. Attempts had been made to preserve the body with mortician's wax and she'd been doused heavily, according to the Office of the Chief Medical Examiner, with an expensive perfume.'"

Kieran kept reading silently and then looked up at Fuller.

"No," Dr. Fuller said softly, no doubt anticipating her silent question. "The killer was never caught. Now, this may mean something, and it may mean nothing."

"I think we should bring this to Craig right away," Kieran said.

Dr. Fuller nodded. "Yes, you must do that," he said. "I have a tennis appointment with my wife this afternoon. I figured you'd be seeing your young man." Fuller never referred to Craig as anything but "your young man." He did so pleasantly, and he had an excellent rapport with the agencies with which they worked.

He reached over and speared a piece of her Boston roll. "I see that you're not eating this," he told her. "Excellent roll. Do you mind?"

"Of course not," she murmured.

He chewed—and then stopped midchew. He swallowed and told her, "Ah, Kieran. You're looking at me as if I am one in the twenty-five. I assure you, I care deeply about people. But if I were to lose my appetite at every sad turn in my profession, well, I would starve."

Kieran smiled. "I guess I'm just not hungry," she told him. She rose and told him, "Thank you. I'm going to try to get this to Craig right away. This man may have been active for years. He might have started very slowly. But now..."

"He might be gearing up." Dr. Fuller nodded at the article. "Take that to your young man. It just might be helpful."

Kieran left him finishing up her Boston roll.

Craig stood in the conference room that had been dedicated to the task force working on the Jeannette Gilbert case.

A picture had been added to the board.

It was that of Sadie Miller, beauty queen, resident of Brooklyn, recent design-school graduate and winner of the last beauty pageant she had entered.

Craig had been through a number of pictures of the young woman; he'd chosen the one for the board because it wasn't a glossy-magazine-style pose. It was of the young woman in a natural shot, caught in a smile as she turned to speak with a friend.

He had just left his own office where he'd spoken to her best friend and roommate, Marie Livingston. Marie had been tearful—grateful, however, that the local police had spoken with her and that Sadie's disappearance was being taken very seriously, even though it had only been a night since she had disappeared.

"We had this deal," Marie had told Craig. "Sadie's dad died when she was ten and her mom just passed away two years ago. All our friends texted their parents when they were getting on a plane or going away, and so Sadie and I texted each other. I lost my folks recently, too, and I'm lucky, I have a brother and I keep in contact with him all the time, but Sadie is an only child. So, you see, if she was planning on staying out all night, she would have called or texted me. She didn't. She hasn't come home. I called our friends. None of them has seen her. I left last night at six to head to the theater district for dinner and a show with a cousin in from Nebraska. Sadie said that if she went out, it would just be down the street for dinner and that if anything major came up, she'd let me know." Tears had filled Marie's eyes. "I came home and Sadie wasn't there. No text, no call. And I dozed on and off all night, waiting. No text and no call. Sadie just isn't like that, Special Agent Frasier. She isn't!"

Now Sadie's picture smiled at him from the board. Naturally, their first thought had been that she'd left, either willingly or not, with a boyfriend. And, yes, there was a young man she'd been interested in, but he'd recently been deployed. He was in the Middle East.

That certainly left him out as a suspect.

Marie had given them a list of friends to call, and the friends were all being called. Men had now been sent out as well to scour her Brooklyn neighborhood. McBride had returned to his station to get information out to the departments in all five boroughs, and Mike was in with Egan, reporting on the nothing that they had so far.

Someone had to have seen something. Craig was convinced of that. The problem was always finding that someone and, sometimes, making them realize that they did know something or had seen something.

Craig stared at the board, at the picture of the dead women—and the missing woman. He looked at the list of suspects they'd written, those involved with Jeannette Gilbert and Le Club Vampyre and the historic find.

There had to be a connection between Jeannette and Sadie.

Somehow in their lives, they had come across the same person.

Maybe not. Maybe, with any luck, Sadie was just missing, and they would find her soon. She'd had a one-night stand and she'd lost her phone, but she'd reappear soon.

Craig had the feeling that wouldn't prove to be the case. He wrote the word *connection* with a big question mark.

Then the phone rang, and he was glad to hear that it was Kieran.

"Hey, I know you're working, but I think I have something for you," she told him.

"Yeah? And what are you doing?" he asked, disturbed that he was so quickly on the offensive with her. "Kieran, this guy is really sick and he's out there. You're not—"

"I had sushi with Dr. Fuller," she said flatly.

"Yeah, yeah, sorry, what is it?"

"He found something interesting," Kieran said. "Should I come to you?"

"He found something interesting? Why isn't he in here?"

"He isn't sure it means anything. It's just something that he found. You know Dr. Fuller. Casual reading about heinous serial killers before lunch and then a tennis date. And, Craig, really, it may not mean anything, but…"

He glanced at his watch. "You near? Can you come on up?"

"I'll walk right over."

Kieran was glad that she was welcomed now at the offices of the FBI.

The New York City FBI shared a building with a number of government agencies, including Citizenship and Immigration Services and Homeland Security.

It was a busy place.

But Kieran was accustomed to walking through security and handing over her bag, and, as usual, Craig sent someone down to get her.

When she reached his office, he'd just gotten a couple cups of coffee and hers was ready by the desk. "I don't know about you, but I need it," he said. "Thanks, Ginny," he told the young agent who had brought her in.

And then, to Kieran's surprise, he closed the office door and took her into his arms, holding her tightly for a minute.

He didn't tend to be demonstrative in his workplace.

"You okay?" she asked him.

"I'm fine. But I hate what I'm seeing with this case. We may have another victim. Or our possible victim might walk back into her apartment any minute. We're concerned. This killer made Gilbert up as if she were a beautiful life-size doll. The other victim in Virginia was the same. The woman who's missing now is a beauty queen." He rubbed his brow, and she saw the stress and how it affected him. "We just do what we have to do. Doesn't mean that it's easy. Egan told me once that he'd quit if the dead ever stopped bothering him."

Kieran nodded. "I know. I saw her in that coffin. It's hard."

He nodded, taking a long swallow of his coffee. "What does the illustrious Dr. Fuller have?"

"He was looking up killers—just because his mind constantly works, I'm pretty sure. Anyway, he was looking up killers who kept bodies. He came up with the usual cases that are well-known, such as Ed Gein and Dahmer and a few others, but they desecrated the bodies, and practiced cannibalism and necrophilia and...well, this killer is different. Dr. Fuller tried all kinds of key words on the internet, I'm sure, and then stumbled upon this."

Kieran handed Craig the printout of the New Jersey article.

Craig read it and looked over at her. "I'd say this definitely could be our man," he told her. He picked up his office phone. She listened as he called one of his favorite coworkers in the tech department, told him about the article and asked him to do a search for anything else like it. He hung up, looked at her and said, "Hang on. I want to talk to Egan for a minute. I don't want to go trampling on the Jersey police. Not 'cause I'm a nice guy. But I want the Jersey guys to believe I'm a nice guy. I want their help and we usually do fine, but now and again, you hit a guy not fond of federal interference."

"Sure."

He headed to his door and then turned back. "You're okay? You don't have to help out at Finnegan's?"

"No, I'm fine," she told him.

She idly looked around his office. Craig wasn't given to having too much around him, but he did have a few paintings on his walls; he liked views of bridges. She was also glad to see that he had her picture in a frame on his desk. That made her smile.

He walked back to the door and looked in at her. "Want to take a drive to Jersey?"

"Do I want to drive to Jersey?" she asked.

"You interested?"

"You're going to take me?"

"I like it when you're with me," he said.

She was a little disturbed by what she knew he really meant.

It wasn't so much that he wanted her working with him. It was just that bad things were going on. He didn't like her alone on the streets.

But she was interested, and she knew that come Monday, Drs. Fuller and Miro would be working with someone from the Bureau and she might as well be up to date on what was happening.

And seeing what she could on the Jersey victim would be important.

It wasn't bad, in such a big and crazy city, to have a number of friends in law enforcement.

But sometimes...

"I love being with you, too," she said sweetly.

"I just have to stack some papers up in the conference room. Come with me and you can see what I've added."

She followed him down the hall and into the conference room where, she knew, they spent time keeping order on clues and theories. Craig always kept a board; it was important to him. He was also good at staring at his boards and putting the pieces of a puzzle together.

But, that afternoon, when she stepped in and looked at his board, she gasped.

"What?" he demanded.

Kieran walked over to the board. She looked at the picture that had been added, next to those of the Fredericksburg victim, Cary Howell, and Jeannette Gilbert.

"What?" Craig demanded tensely.

Kieran turned and looked at him. "I saw her, Craig. I saw her. She was at Finnegan's last night."

Craig still meant to get to Jersey that afternoon.

But it was going to have to wait.

He arranged for Egan, McBride and Mike Dalton to meet him down at Finnegan's, while Kieran called Declan to warn him that the FBI and police were descending on the pub.

And then they headed in.

Neither Danny nor Kevin was there, but Declan's sweet Irish fiancée, Mary Kathleen, was working that afternoon, and she assured Kieran she had everything under control as Declan and Kieran headed into the office.

It was crowded with the FBI men and McBride in the small space.

Declan, while a little bewildered, was still extremely helpful. He always was; Declan was solid. Craig had liked him from the get-go.

"This young woman, Sadie, was at the bar a good hour," Declan said. "Not a heavy drinker—she had two rum and Cokes in that time. We were so busy, I didn't talk to anyone for long. But I remember she was very pleasant, said she was in the neighborhood, killing time, waiting to meet up with a friend. She asked me if it was crazy with everything going on at the church...club. Whatever."

"Did she meet up with anyone?" Craig asked.

Declan shook his head. "I have no idea. She paid her bill at about 10:45 p.m. Cash. Just left the money on the bar. I didn't actually see her leave. Did you, Kieran?"

"No, but I spoke with her. She was really nice. She wanted to know if our clock above the bar was right. I told her that it was. I'd have liked to have talked to her more, but it was just crazy."

Craig glanced curiously at Kieran. She had been so serious. When she had first seen the picture of Sadie Miller she swore she had just seen the young woman. He'd asked her if she was certain. After all, even though New York could tend to be a "neighborhood" place where people hung out in the same stretch of blocks, it was a city of eight to sixteen million people, depending on the time and the season. But Kieran had been positive that it was Sadie she had seen. And she was definitely shaken. Well, she'd seen the corpse of Jeannette Gilbert. And it was unnerving to think that this young woman she had spoken with might have met a similar fate.

"I'm pulling all my credit card receipts from last night," Declan said. "And I can make you a list of the regulars who were in here last night, but I don't think a killer or kidnapper came in here and paid with a credit card. Of course, I guess criminals aren't all super bright, so there is a possibility. And of course it's possible that someone else might have spoken with her. Bobby O'Leary was at the bar with his soda and lime. You all know Bobby. He was hurt near here during the diamond case you all worked. He's a great witness because he's always stone-cold sober."

"We'll speak with Bobby," Craig said.

"He might have come in since we've been in here," Declan

said. "There's a soccer match he wants to see, and he likes the big screen over the bar."

"I'll check," Kieran offered.

She seemed anxious to flee the office.

"I'm hoping someone might have seen something. Downtown—especially with that Le Club Vampyre closed right now—is quiet late at night, especially on the weekend, except for this place and a few others. I mean, sometimes the city streets are so busy you've seen a hundred or more people in a block." As Declan spoke, he was going through his computer, checking their card receipts. "I'll print this up," he said, keying in the function. Across the room, the printer jumped into action.

"Thanks. Give me an email copy to get to Tech, too, will you?" Craig asked.

"Absolutely," Declan promised.

A moment later, the office door opened and Bobby O'Leary stepped in.

Bobby was another good guy. Craig knew because he had been involved—being attacked and seriously injured—during their search for the diamond killers. He was the perfect older Irishman with bright blue eyes, snow-white hair and ruddy cheeks.

"You're looking for a lass, so I hear," Bobby said. "Beautiful girl! Sweet as can be. I talked to her for several minutes. I believe she thought I was the least dangerous thing at the bar."

"Bobby, thank you," Craig said. "Did she tell you where she was going? Did she mention anyone's name?"

"No, she said that she had an important meeting, and I said that I was surprised, because people don't usually have important meetings late on Friday night. She just said that it was very special to her and with busy people, you had to take

the time that they had. Let's see, we talked about sports—
she's not into real football—soccer, you know—but she loves
American football. Oh! She said she'd wanted to come down
to Finnegan's for a long time. She'd known about it, but
getting downtown wasn't always that easy. Except now she
realized it was just a hop on the subway. Charming girl, absolutely charming. And she was disappointed Kevin wasn't
here. Apparently, they worked together on some thing or another a year ago."

"She knew Kevin?" Craig asked, looking over at Kieran.

She wasn't looking at him. Rather, she kept her gaze on
Bobby.

"She did mention that," Kieran said. "That's right. But
it was so crazy, I didn't get much in the sixty seconds that
I talked to her. I think she said they did a print ad together
about a year ago, and that he'd mentioned then that the family owned a place down here. I don't believe she'd seen him
since. She said that she'd call him. Probably just to mention
that she'd been down here."

"So she wasn't looking for Kevin or looking to meet up
with him?" Craig asked.

"No," Bobby said. "Definitely not. She was meeting someone busy and special. Who the hell that was, I don't know."

"Did you see her leave?" Craig asked.

"I did, sir. She left money on the bar, looked at the clock
over the bar and told me it was lovely chatting with me. I said
that it was quite grand speaking with her. She turned and left."

"But you didn't see her on the sidewalk after she left?"

"No."

"Did anyone seem to follow her out?"

"Special Agent Frasier, that door might have been at Grand
Central Station last night, it opened and closed so many

times," Bobby said. "It was very busy. Did I see anyone give her special attention and follow her? No. When murdering-bastard diamond thieves aren't in this bar, it has an incredibly respectable clientele!" he added indignantly.

Declan arranged for the staff who'd been on duty the night before to come in one by one. Richard Egan, Mike and McBride joined Craig in the questioning. No one knew anything other than that the lovely young woman had been there, that she had been charming and polite, and—general consensus—she had left at 10:45 p.m.

Not long before Craig had arrived himself.

"I'll head back to headquarters," McBride said after they'd finished speaking with all of the staff members. "As you know, we already have all our available men searching for Ms. Miller. I'm going to post this information farther afield and make sure every man out there knows how important it is that we find this poor girl. Anything that can be done, we'll do it. I know the Bureau has agents out there, too, but the NYPD does nothing but New York City."

Craig nodded. "NYPD—finest in the world."

Kieran remained strangely silent, but when they'd finished speaking with everyone at the pub, he was still determined to get to New Jersey.

He was afraid that she was going to balk at his invitation now.

There was something up with her; he knew her too well.

But as they parted—Mike to head back to the office to see what the tech people could find, McBride to speak with his officers and Egan to follow through on his own research—Kieran gave him no problem.

First, though, she checked with her brother.

"You need me tonight?" she asked Declan.

She looked hopeful when she spoke to him.

"Ah, sister, sweet love of my life!" Declan teased. "We always need you. But we're pretty covered for tonight. It won't be as busy as last night."

She seemed disappointed.

"Take all the time you need with Craig," Declan added seriously.

And Kieran didn't look at all pleased. Her smile for her brother was definitely forced.

Craig was silent as they left, and so was Kieran.

He cursed softly—it was a resident's requirement—at the traffic they hit going through the Holland Tunnel.

He glanced over at Kieran. She didn't notice the traffic—or his words.

"You okay?" he asked her.

"What?" she said, startled as she looked at him.

He couldn't help but notice the depth of her eyes, the endless blue, and how beautifully the deep red of her hair complemented her pale skin.

Unbidden came a terrifying thought.

Beautiful women were being taken.

There were literally millions of women in the City of New York.

But not all of them were perfect.

Like Kieran.

He forced himself to shake it off.

"I asked if you were okay," he said.

"Yes, of course, I'm fine. I'm just…well, rattled. She was so nice, Craig. I mean, seriously, so sweet and nice. It's horrible to think that someone might have hurt her. Killed her."

"Right now, she's just missing. And maybe this person she met had something spectacular for her."

She looked at him drily. "Maybe."

"Hey, let's look for the good."

Though she nodded, she said, "I know you and I know the way your mind works. I know you guys are afraid that she's already dead. Because, according to the ME, Jeannette was probably killed right around the time she disappeared. This guy likes to hold on to corpses—not live bodies."

"But we don't know," he said firmly. "What I also don't know is why you didn't mention the fact that Sadie Miller knew Kevin."

"What?"

"You heard me."

"Kevin? Why would I mention that? It had nothing to do with her being at the bar. He said something to her about Finnegan's over a year ago. I probably forgot. I was so stunned to see the picture."

"You're always a lousy liar, you know."

"I'm... Why would I lie?"

"Why *would* you lie?" he demanded. He couldn't look at her; he was out of the tunnel and making his way through two giant semis on the highway.

"I don't know what you're talking about, and I'm not one of your tech support or office workers—or a suspect! Don't interrogate me."

"Don't treat me like an idiot."

"You're assuming that role."

"And don't try psychology on me. I refuse to feel guilty. I asked you a question. You were quick to say that our missing woman was someone you had seen, but you didn't mention her name, or that she was friends with Kevin."

"They're not exactly friends, and I never did get her name. I didn't know it until I was with you. The place was crazy busy last night. She and I exchanged a few words without the nicety of an introduction. As far as mentioning that she had worked with Kevin ages ago, I guess I just didn't think about it. Half the people in the pub have met at least one of the members of the Finnegan family somewhere at some time!"

There was an edge to her voice. She was trying to sound irritated.

She wasn't irritated.

He knew her.

She was afraid. And he knew, too, that Kieran's fear was seldom for herself. When she was afraid, she was usually afraid for others.

Off the highway, he pulled into a parking lot. She looked over at him, alarmed.

"What the hell is it about your twin you're not telling me?" he demanded.

CHAPTER
SEVEN

THERE IT WAS—FLAT OUT. AND SHE SUCKED AT DECEPTION because she hated lying, especially to Craig.

But it wasn't her place to share the information Kevin had given her. Especially since another man had gone on national television to announce that he'd been Jeannette Gilbert's mystery lover.

So what the hell did she say, especially with him staring at her?

"Craig, please, I don't know what you want out of me. I don't know what you suspect Kevin might have done, but you know Kevin. You know all of my family, and you know that I haven't a single sibling who would willfully hurt anyone. And beyond a doubt, no matter what the circumstances, they'd never commit a murder. So just what is it you want me to say? If you have a question, ask Kevin!"

Kieran hoped that her bravado was strong enough. She kept her eyes on Craig's, hoping that they didn't fall. She damned the fact that she was in this situation.

But she couldn't betray her brother's confidence. When she spoke to him, she could demand that he speak with Craig himself. Obviously, once Brent Westwood had stepped into it all, it had seemed a moot point to bring up Kevin's name again. Sadly, it seemed that Kevin's name was coming up no matter what.

Craig stared at her a long while.

So long that she was really, really glad that she wasn't a crook and that he wasn't really interrogating her at the moment.

Then, to her relief, he pulled out of the lot and they were on their way once more, headed out to Newark, New Jersey.

At the station they met with a detective, Donald Beck.

Kieran was glad when Craig introduced her as his "colleague."

Beck, a seasoned and experienced detective with a crinkled face to show it, was quick and pleased to greet them. "Captain called me," he told Craig, escorting the two of them to a small conference room. "For us, sad to say, the murder of Cheyenne Lawson has become a cold case. We worked every angle—boyfriend, ex-boyfriends, teachers, parents, every relation we could find." He hesitated, deep in memory. "I was lead detective on the case. I drove the medical examiner and forensic experts on our team crazy. I was so frustrated. I'll never forget seeing her body there. It was Saint Steven's Memorial Cemetery. Very old, with graves dating back to the 1700s. Grim ones, you know, like the simple tombstones with the skull and wings and grim reminders of death—*As I am now, so shall you be.* Then, you come to the Victorian graves, very ornate. Stately family mausoleums, with cherubs and angels. And then the current ones, when only the good Lord knows what you might have. A fellow was buried in a Cadillac before some of the new rules on burials went in. Thing is, the place is kept up. Family members come here, and there are burials and entombments fairly frequently."

He tapped an envelope on the table. "I emailed what I could. But these are some of the original shots at the scene when we found her body. Still haunts me. I've seen bad shit around here—pardon my French. Really bad shit, bullet holes the size of grapefruits, knife wounds that have nearly severed limbs and enough blood at a crime scene for a bath. But there was something about this, something about the perfect way she was left that was more disturbing than all the horror. Killed, stabbed, a knife to the heart—but no blood. She was all clean, pure, beautiful. Cheyenne Lawson was a local homecoming queen. And the way that she was set out there... as if she was asleep on the grass. Like she should just wake up. But, then, of course, when you went closer, you knew that she'd never wake up again, and you started to smell the rot. It was all the worse because of the smell of perfume mixing with the decay. She was found in late spring. The sun was high in the air. It was bad."

Kieran leaned forward, chilled as she looked at the photographs that Craig laid out.

The young woman, Cheyenne Lawson, had been beautiful. A wealth of curls were spread around her head and shoulders. She'd been dressed in white—a gown that might have been a wedding gown or a prom dress. Her hands were folded, as if she lay there in silent prayer. She'd been positioned beneath a gorgeous statue of a winged and weeping angel.

Close-ups showed the young woman's face—the brown spots where death was clearly showing, the sinking in of the cheeks.

"Bugs," Detective Beck said. "One of our best techs is a bug man. He could tell from eggs that had been laid and what had hatched just about how long she'd been dead. We esti-mated two weeks."

"Had she been reported missing?" Craig asked.

Beck shook his head. "Thing is, she was killed soon after high-school graduation. Everyone thought that she'd gone on a trip to Eastern Europe with a friend. Her mom had been sick, so she wasn't taking her to the airport. Cheyenne was getting an Uber. She wasn't reported missing because she'd warned her family she might not report in for a while. I guess they were going to a lot of the countries that were previously part of the Soviet Union, and they'd been warned that hos-tel internet and phone communication kind of sucked. She was an incredibly responsible young woman, and her par-ents weren't worried that she couldn't handle herself—and the friend reported in from Georgia—the country, not the state." He pushed another envelope toward Craig. "Statements from family members, friends, schoolteachers, authorities." He shook his head, clearly upset. "She was ready to go on her trip. Her parents thought she had gone. Her friend just thought she'd been stood up. Six girls were supposed to go on the trip—only three made it." He was silent a minute. "I can't tell you how hard I tried."

"Was there a suggestion anywhere that she might have been meeting up with someone?" Craig asked.

"There's the one mystery I could never solve," Beck told them. "According to the friend, Cheyenne had told her she was going to meet up with someone really exciting and her life might take a different path. If she didn't show at the air-port, no one should worry. And so no one did," he said sadly.

"Detective, do you know if her picture was in the paper at any time?" Kieran asked.

"Of course. She was homecoming queen. And she made a

national paper, too, for a history project she had done. There's a copy of the article in the file I gave Special Agent Frasier," Beck said.

Craig looked at her with a nod of encouragement. Maybe her question had been good enough to make him a little less aggravated with her.

"Do you have the time to show us where she was found?" Craig asked. "I'm sure we can find it, but—"

"I'm at your service. This is it—the case that has haunted me for years," Beck said, rising. "I'll take you there right now. Actually, you can drive. I'll direct. I go sometimes. My family is buried in the newer section. And every damn time I go and stand in front of that angel, and I wonder how heaven could have borne witness to such a tragedy as that sweet girl's death."

Kieran was quiet and thoughtful as they drove. She was in the backseat; Beck was directing Craig from the front passenger's seat. He kept up a steady stream of talk, telling them about the people he had questioned and how he had gotten nowhere. Cheyenne hadn't just been a homecoming queen; she'd been a straight A student. She'd spent her weekends with Habitat for Humanity. She loved all kinds of music, and she was a nut for museums—the more unusual the better.

Her father had adored her and had been working in Alaska on a pipeline—some good money coming in, but it would only go so far in providing for his family—when she'd gone missing and turned up dead. Her boyfriend had been in the military, joining right out of high school.

"I'd think that she'd stepped out on the street and walked into a killer who worked on opportunity," Beck said, "except for that last thing she told her friend. 'If I don't show up, don't worry. I'm looking into something that might prove to be very exciting.'"

"Did she want to model or go into acting?" Kieran asked from the back.

"I don't believe so, at least from what I know about her." He shrugged. "I couldn't let her murder go, even when new cases came in and we were told that we had to back-burner a case that led us to nothing more than dead ends. But I can't be sure what was in her heart. Who knows with young girls? Maybe. But it didn't sound like it. She was into math and science and history. She'd talked about going into medicine or teaching in a college. And she'd wanted to write a book."

"About?" Kieran asked.

"How legends came about," Beck said. "Why we do what we do, why we feel the way we do. She was fascinated with the stories like Bloody Mary and the Jersey Devil and such," Beck said.

They'd reached the cemetery, and Craig drove down the well-tended road. The cemetery was well laid out, as if an early colonial planner had known just how many people would die when.

"Park here," Beck suggested, and Craig parked.

Kieran was quickly out of the car, looking over the cemetery. She spotted the life-size weeping angel at once and walked to it. She paused, and for a moment, Craig was afraid she'd lie down on the grass where Cheyenne's body had been found.

Don't do it, don't do it! he thought, tension filling him.

She glanced at him, and he realized that she wasn't putting herself into the mind of the victim, but, rather, she was thinking as the killer.

She pointed to the trees and bushes behind them, across the roadway, right at the edge of the oldest section. "At night, no one would see you here," she said softly. "And while there is a gate around most of the cemetery, at those trees, where there are buildings right behind, there's no fence."

"Those are old warehouses. The oldest predates the cemetery," Beck said.

"He knew the cemetery. The killer knew the cemetery," Kieran said. "He knew before he came exactly where he would lay her out. He meant for her to be beautiful and to appear to be sleeping. She might have been his first. I think I read about this in that article from Dr. Fuller. I believe that he tried working with mortician's wax and other implements... but he failed. He met up with her somehow—lured her as he did the others—and he killed her to keep her. Because she was beautiful. But he couldn't maintain her beauty, and he needed to show her off before the beauty was gone, before the artistry was no longer there."

Craig watched Kieran move about, as if she could retrace the killer's steps, almost as if she could see what he had seen.

"Others? More than one?" Beck asked. "We heard about Ms. Gilbert. But..."

"Another woman in Virginia—Fredericksburg. Except she was found in another family's mausoleum when it was time for grandma to go in," Craig explained briefly.

Beck shook his head. "We didn't catch that one up here, but then, you're a Fed. The Feds are first up when a killer is hitting different states, right?"

"We have the ability to move around," Craig said lightly. "I haven't been down to see and hear what particulars I can glean from there yet, but I will go down now. I believe we are looking at a serial killer and that you had an all but impossible case before you because it was the first time the killer struck. Since then he's moved on. Virginia next, and now New York City."

"You have to stop him," Kieran murmured.

"Is he still in New York, do you think?" Beck asked.

"I think he might be," Craig said.

Kieran looked at him. "Because," she theorized thoughtfully, "New York City may actually be his home. He's respectable—living a day-to-day life where the people around him would be shocked to discover that he was a killer. He has the kind of job that would allow him or cause him to travel. He is interesting, or has ties to interesting employment."

"Photographer? Agent?" Craig murmured.

"But, according to Detective Beck, Cheyenne Lawson wasn't concerned about modeling. She was more of a scholar," Kieran said.

"She did need money. Her parents are working-class stiffs with four more children. Cheyenne knew she'd need to work her way through college. She had scholarships, but not enough to pay the whole tab of the kind of school she wanted to go to. If you suspect that there's someone out there posing as a photographer or a modeling scout, I'd say she might have been intrigued to meet with such a man. She'd have been excited, not longing to be a model herself, but seeing it as a means to an end," Beck told them.

"Do you think there's a possibility that this man now has Sadie Miller?" Kieran asked. "And that she could still be alive?"

"Yes, it's possible," Craig said.

Possible. But he didn't have a good feeling. It seemed that the young women were killed soon after they were taken.

And their bodies held.

Kieran was watching him anxiously. And he knew that she had read his thoughts. That while it was certainly *possible* that the young woman was alive, it wasn't probable. Not if she'd been taken by this killer.

He turned to Beck and thanked him for his help. The detective promised to get everything he had on the case to Craig, including his thoughts or notes at any given time.

When they returned Beck to the station and headed back to the Holland Tunnel, darkness had fallen. Silence fell over the car until Kieran's voice broke it.

"There has to be a way to find her!" she said.

"FBI agents, hundreds of cops, and all other law enforcement in the area and the country are on the alert," Craig said. "If Sadie Miller can be found, she will be found." He hesitated. "She may still reappear, you know. Maybe something came up. Maybe she went out drinking. Maybe—"

"He has her," Kieran said softly. "But I do believe there's a prayer of finding her."

"There's always a prayer." It was Saturday night; other agents were working the case. Police were working the case. But glancing at Kieran, he knew that she couldn't let it go.

Neither could he.

Before he could make any suggestions, she turned to him.

"Let's head to Finnegan's," she said. "Please."

"Okay."

He drove to the pub, not pressing Kieran. When they arrived, an Irish band was playing to a decent-size crowd, but everything seemed to be working smoothly.

Kieran disappeared almost instantly, heading into the crowd. He saw that she had woven her way through a number of happy gyrators on the floor—straight to someone.

Kevin.

Craig walked to the bar; Declan was behind it, listening to a tale an old-timer was telling.

He gave Craig a quick, welcoming smile.

Craig didn't have a chance to determine if he wanted a beer or a soda, when he heard his name called softly from the side.

"Craig."

He turned. Kieran was there—with her twin, Kevin.

"We need to speak with you," Kevin said quietly.

"Office," Kieran murmured, and she moved ahead.

Craig and Kevin followed.

Kieran perched on the sofa, indicating that Craig should take the chair behind the desk and Kevin a chair before it.

Craig was truly curious by then. Kieran didn't speak, and he waited.

"This has been eating at me, driving me crazy," Kevin said at last.

"And *this* is…?" Craig prompted.

"I don't know what this thing is with Brent Westwood," he said.

"A publicity ploy, if you ask me," Craig said.

Kevin nodded. "She didn't dislike Brent. They'd met upon occasion. But Jeannette was far from in love with the man. They weren't dating. They weren't even friends."

And suddenly, of course, Craig understood completely. Kevin was an actor. Kevin was staggeringly good-looking, even from a heterosexual-male point of view. He was also a good guy. The only trouble he'd gotten into as a kid had always had to do with standing up for the little guy. That in itself was actually an admirable quality.

There really wasn't much not to like about Kevin Finnegan.

"So you're the real mystery lover?" Craig asked quietly.

"If I'd known anything, if I'd have been able to help in any way, I would have spoken up. I loved Jeannette. Truly loved her," Kevin said softly. "And when news came out that they'd found her, dead in that coffin, I was shocked, stunned…"

Craig knew Kevin—and knew that he was telling the truth.

He wasn't, however, sure how others on the FBI or police task force might see it all.

Kevin knew Sadie Miller, the young woman who was missing.

Kevin was admitting to an affair with Jeannette Gilbert, one of the young women who'd been killed.

And since they didn't know the exact time of death, there was no way to know for certain if Kevin had been in New Jersey or Virginia when the other young women had been killed. New Jersey was a hop, skip and a jump away, except for traffic, of course. And Virginia? Easily managed there and back within twenty-four hours.

And might he have been easily trusted by the victims? Yes. Sad, but true. Beautiful, charming people easily gained trust.

"Say something, please," Kevin said earnestly.

"There's absolutely no evidence against you. But you have become a person of interest. Not only that, Kevin, but you could help a lot, tell us more about other people in Jeannette Gilbert's life," Craig said. "Tell us what she thought or knew or felt about those close to her."

Kevin lifted his hands. "Craig, I know how Jeannette felt about people, but I don't know what was or wasn't—only her perspective. I mean, Oswald might have been a creep in a way, but Jeannette cared about him."

"Her perspective might prove to be very important," Craig said.

"I'm so sorry," Kevin said. "So sorry." It was a whisper.

"You really loved her?"

Kevin nodded.

"And how did she feel about you?"

"I believe, with my whole heart, she felt the same."

"So why didn't you panic when she disappeared?" Craig asked.

Kevin looked over at Kieran, and Craig could have sworn that they exchanged words that were silent to the rest of the world.

Twins.

"Jeannette was really famous as a model, far more so than as an actress. We talked and talked about our careers," Kevin said. "And about us. We didn't want it to be an infatuation. You know, we met on a sexy music video shoot but we didn't want our relationship to be something that wasn't real. We were giving it time. We'd agreed that we wouldn't be ridiculously jealous or interfere with one another's careers. When the time was right—and I believe that would have been soon—we would have gone public. I don't know. Maybe I was insecure, too. She was world famous, and I'm just a working actor, working and making a living, but not on the covers of magazines. I wanted to know that we were…real. And I believe that Jeannette needed to know that she was really loved, too. Not because she was famous. Because she was herself. She was so hurt as a child. She was taught that she was a burden. I never met him, but she said that her step-uncle was a jerk and that her aunt was an idiot for letting him run her life and the lives of everyone around them. She cared about her cousins—she even cared about her aunt. But, she didn't buy her the house because she loved her so much. She bought her the house because she intended to pay all her debts."

Craig was thoughtful. "I don't believe the step-uncle killed her. I don't think he has the finesse to be our man. Or woman. Though I believe this killer to be a man."

Kevin wore a look of agony. "When I think of how frightened she must have been, I get ill. I want to kill—"

Kieran made a move toward her brother. "Good God, Kevin, don't go saying things like that!"

"I don't have a tape recorder going," Craig assured her. He turned back to Kevin. "Was her step-uncle ever violent? Did Jeannette tell you that he struck her or abused her?"

"No. He wasn't violent. He just treated her like a complete sack of bricks around his neck, and then, when she left, he saw her as a cash cow."

"What about Oswald Martin? You were telling us she really cared about him?"

Kevin almost smiled. "She loved Oswald. Said he was over-protective, but, after her childhood, it was nice. That's why I have to admit… I thought that Oswald planned her disappearance. He was always thinking of new things she should be doing. Younger faces were always on the horizon in Oswald's mind. But I didn't spend time with the two of them together."

"Do you know Leo Holt?"

"I do. We both worked with him on a print ad for jeans."

"And?"

"You haven't questioned him yet?"

"He's next up."

"Well…he's interesting," Kevin said.

"How so?"

"Women love him. That's probably why he's able to get such great shots. He says the words *sexy pout* and makes them all look like they're ready to crawl on top of a man. He's decent. He's tough. There's no messing around when he's working. But, still, he smiles and teases people, and he gets what he wants." Kevin hesitated a minute. "Maybe," he said softly. "But I don't see him as the killer. He's a perfectionist, but he has more problems with the ad agency people than his models. He always has a vision, and it's not always a vision that the company shares."

"I heard that Jeannette had a row with Leo Holt," Craig said.

"Row?" Kevin said, surprised. Then he shrugged. "He was angry with her one morning for looking tired."

"Were you there?"

Kevin shook his head. "Jeannette told me about it. She was giggling. It was after a night that we'd spent together. She told Leo she was tired and that being tired sometimes was part of life, and that makeup could fix a few dark shadows beneath her eyes. Anyway, Leo told her that she wasn't to go out again on a night before he was shooting. And, of course, she laughed at him, and he said that he wouldn't hire her again. She told him he was full of it. He'd hire her again because she was good, and she was one of his favorite models."

"You know this how?"

"Because I've worked with him on several projects. He has her pictures everywhere. He says she's one of the best in the business, and that she can portray any emotion at the drop of a hat." He smiled suddenly. "She was gorgeous, and she was getting better and better. Who knows how great she would have been?" Sadness filled his eyes.

Craig knew that Kevin hadn't killed Jeannette. He knew Kevin. If they'd lived in the mid-1800s—when New York City had been filled with Irish street gangs—Kevin would have been trying to keep the peace. If he ever killed, it would be in self-defense, or to protect someone he loved. There were no real explanations as to how he could be so certain; he didn't have Kieran's degree in psychology. He'd just been in law enforcement a long time. He had instinct.

"I'm still going to need you to come in to the station," he told Kevin.

"Tonight?"

"Tomorrow."

"I'm supposed to be singing with a choir group near Saint Patrick's in the morning. But I can beg off."

"You cannot. It will hurt you career-wise," Kieran said firmly.

"This is about Jeannette," Kevin said.

"I don't want you in the morning anyway," Craig told him. "We're questioning Leo Holt then." He leaned forward. "Kevin, do you know how bad this is, how serious?"

"I do," Kevin said softly. "I'm not sure if you do. She's dead. Horribly murdered. And I loved her."

The emotion in Kevin's voice was tragically sincere. Of course, the man was an actor; it was what he did for a living. What he loved.

Craig knew him better.

Other men did not.

"I'll be in my office tomorrow," Craig told him. "Whenever you finish with the choir, give me a call and come on over."

"Can I get into that office on a Sunday?"

"Oh, yes, trust me," Craig assured him. "We'll get you in."

Kieran had risen. Kevin seemed to take a cue from his sister; he rose, as well.

Kieran walked over to him and hugged him tightly. She looked at him then and said, "Honestly, Kevin, I am so sorry. I know how badly you're hurting."

Craig looked at them, and he almost smiled. Finnegan siblings. They'd stand together like a brick wall, and, he believed, they'd go down together like a brick wall, chip by chip.

He stood himself.

"Kieran, you ready to go home?" he asked pleasantly.

"Sure. Let me just check on Declan," she said.

She headed out before them. Craig paused to shake Kevin's hand and then embrace him briefly. "I do know how you're hurting. But we need the truth out there—at least in law-enforcement circles."

"Of course. I was talking to Kieran first… Honestly, if I'd thought that my speaking up could have helped in any way…"

"I believe you," Craig said.

He followed Kevin out but couldn't find Kieran. She wasn't at the bar, talking to her older brother.

He was surprised by the unease that seized him. When he turned, he saw that she was standing at one of the tables that ran to the side of the bar, just in from the entry.

And he saw why.

John Shaw was there with the trio of grad students, Henry Willoughby and the owner of Le Club Vampyre, Roger Gleason.

Gleason seemed a little too sophisticated for the company of the academics, but he seemed to be smiling affably at whatever was going on.

He looked up as Craig approached the table. "Special Agent Frasier. When I saw the lovely Ms. Finnegan, I didn't think that you'd be far behind. Any progress?"

"We like to think of every day as some kind of progress," Craig said. "Have we made an arrest? No?"

"And you won't, most likely," Shaw said glumly, his smile at whatever had been said previously fading. "There are some rumors on Twitter saying that New York City has a serial killer loose on the streets. And it might turn into a Green River or Zodiac case—and the killer might never be caught. A serial killer! Is that true?"

Craig maintained his calm. "Are we looking at other situations? Yes. But, sir, our best analysts tell us that there may be as many as twenty to two hundred serial killers at work at any given time. Terrifying statistics, I know. Have we decided this is the work of one killer and wish to announce a serial killer? That's a bit premature."

Gleason laughed softly. "I think that means he's not allowed to give out that kind of information. We'll only find out if there's a press conference."

"But we are back to work in the old Saint Augustine's crypt!" Willoughby said. "Please, please, don't take that the wrong way. A woman's life is certainly of the greatest value. But there is nothing we can do to change what has been done."

"Ah, yes, the city's history is for the ages," Craig murmured. "You've all just finished work for the day?"

"It's not work when you love what you're doing," Shaw said.

"I guess you'll see a lot of this crew here," Gleason told Craig drily. "Salute!" he said, lifting his glass of beer.

"Good for Finnegan's business!" Shaw said.

"Oh, I think Finnegan's is going to survive just fine. After all, the pub has its own history," Craig said.

"And a wonderful new generation to carry on with Irish hospitality!" Allie Benoit announced, raising her glass, as well. "Truly, it's great to come here. Great food, great music, just the right amount of noise. Great all way around."

"Thank you," Kieran murmured. She looked over at Craig. "Declan is fine. Shall we go?"

"Don't forget—give me a call and come on by," Willoughby told her.

"I'll be delighted," Kieran said. She waved a hand in the air. "Good night, then."

She seemed eager to escape.

Craig was glad; he wanted to be alone, as well.

As they left the pub, he glanced back quickly. The students and John Shaw were busy talking. Kevin had joined the table; he was looking at Craig as Henry Willoughby went on about something or another.

Roger Gleason was watching them leave, too.

Gleason had also known Jeannette Gilbert, Craig thought. Gleason was fastidious and smooth and rich.

The man lifted a glass to Craig.

Craig waved and set a hand on Kieran's waist.

And he was glad when he had hurried her to the door, and they stepped outside. The night sky above them seemed benign; the sounds of distant horns and the bustle of the city were somehow good and reassuring.

But, still, he knew that something was off-kilter.

In the pub?

Between him and Kieran? She'd lied to him. She'd covered up for her brother. And it was almost as if she had made it a point to show him that they were united, the Finnegan four, and they would always stand together, even when it meant they'd stand against him.

"You don't have to be with me," she said softly. "I know you're angry."

"I do have to be with you," he said, and managed a grim smile, shaking his head. "We have to be together, especially because I am angry."

And he was. But, somehow, it seemed that a cloud covered the moon and the stars and shadows—menacing shadows—suddenly seemed to abound.

And anger—even if righteous—didn't seem right.

Far too much danger lurked in the night.

Yes, he was angry. Because logical or not, right or not, he was afraid.

CHAPTER
EIGHT

THE SILENCE IN THE CAR WAS DEAFENING. KIERAN'S VOICE broke through it like water crashing through a dam, her words flooding the car. "We both have ethics, codes...what's right and what's wrong, and I knew it was wrong for Kevin not to speak, but I had to get him to be the one to tell you what he'd been doing, that he'd known Jeannette Gilbert and that he for one minute didn't believe that she was seeing Brent Westwood." She looked over at Craig.

"You can't tell me everything, when it comes to work," she said.

He looked her way. "Kevin is your brother—not your work."

"And he came to you. He told you the truth."

"We wasted time with Westwood."

"The man held a press conference. You can't lay that on Kevin."

Craig kept driving in silence.

"I am sorry. I couldn't change anything," she said. "It's the same as if I were counseling someone who had committed a crime. I'm really sorry, I just..."

She was surprised when he turned to her, a half smile on his lips. "Yeah," he said, his tone husky. "I got that."

"But you don't forgive me."

"Yes, I do."

"Really?"

"Really. I do understand." He was quiet for a minute. "He's not just your brother. He's your twin."

"I love all my brothers equally."

"Yep. Got that, too."

He was smiling; he'd forgiven her. There was still something about him that didn't seem right.

She'd put her brother before the truth. Before honesty. Before him.

A silence fell between them again.

Moments later she once again was the first to speak. "What's your feeling after New Jersey?" she asked. "And...tonight."

He was thoughtful for a minute and then glanced over at her. "I don't believe your brother is a killer, if that's what you're asking."

"I didn't think for a minute that you'd suspect Kevin. I know that others will see him as questionable, though."

"I can't speak for them. But I can tell you what I know at this point. We definitely have a serial killer on our hands. I believe the New Jersey victim was his first. We don't know if there are others around the country, though I do believe that we'll discover that sooner now. When there was the one incident in Jersey and the one in Virginia, I don't believe it was enough to code similarities in all the law-enforcement systems. Now we're looking."

He checked his rearview and side mirrors and changed lanes before he continued. "I do believe, however, that the killer is a New Yorker or spends most of his time in New

York. Northern Virginia is a farther drive, but it's still a do-able drive from New York City—back and forth—in less than a day. You and the good doctors Fuller and Miro know more than I do. What makes a man like that tick? He's not going to be a common laborer. This killer wants perfection. He's clean and neat. He stabs his victims in the heart, which has to be very messy—where he finds places to do that, I don't know—but then he cleans them up to display them in an or-ganized manner."

He shook his head as he glanced over her. "There's one thing I'm curious about. The discovery of the bodies in the crypt came after Jeannette Gilbert had disappeared and, we believe, when she was actually killed. Our guy had been hold-ing her, or her body, at least. How could he have known that such a discovery as the crypt would be made, giving him a place for the display of Jeannette Gilbert's corpse?"

"I don't think he did know," Kieran said. "I think he had other plans. But what they were, I'd like to know. All the old churches in the city still have graves in crypts or they have small graveyards, as in Trinity and Saint Paul's Chapel and others. And there's a great old graveyard up in Washington Heights. Brooklyn has newer cemeteries…and Woodlawn up in the Bronx is extraordinary. I mean, as far as making a cemetery a lovely place to visit, if such a thing can be."

"They show movies at that cemetery in Hollywood, and they have all kinds of concerts there, too. Nice concept, re-ally. Death is a natural part of life. Remembering the dead with a way of living…not bad, really."

Craig had found parking in the Village. He paused before getting out of the car. "It's not going to be easy for Kevin. He's going to have to answer to other people."

"I know."

He was still for another minute and then got out. They were about a block from Kieran's place. He took her arm as they walked.

"Watch your curiosity on this one," he said softly.

"Craig—"

"I know. I know that we both respect what the other does for a living. Just be careful, huh?"

"I will meet no one alone, I promise."

But as they walked up the stairs over the karaoke bar— that night, a really good soprano was doing a great version of "Memories"—Kieran was mulling the situation in her mind. She knew that Dr. Fuller hadn't let it go. When he hadn't been playing tennis or entertaining his wife and kids, he'd been investigating similar murders and looking through his files.

But she wasn't due into work until Monday.

That gave her Sunday to do a little investigating on her own.

"What are you thinking?" Craig asked her.

"Just pondering," she murmured, fitting her key into the door.

"Pondering what? Sounds dangerous," he told her.

Inside, she turned to him, slipping her arms around his neck. "Pondering how you keep that fantastic and entirely seductive bronze tan going when we live in New York and I've yet to see you at a tanning salon. Pondering how you manage to have the coolest kneecaps this side of the Mississippi. Pondering the length of your fingers, and the soap you use and—"

"Kneecaps?" he asked.

"Kneecaps," she said solemnly.

He started to laugh.

"You are giving me such a pile of…rubbish, shall we say? Man, you are trying hard to suck up for lying to me."

"I didn't lie. And I'm not sucking up."

"It's okay. I think you should suck up."

She smiled. "I'm doing all right at it, then?"

"Sure. Keep going."

"Toes! You have really fantastic toes. And you're rugged, sensual, incredibly proportioned…"

"Really excellent suck-up," he told her.

Her gaze turned serious then. "I'm pondering what it is about a specific person that is so incredible that you can't bear being away from him, why his flesh is so amazing, why his touch is so erotic, why—"

She kissed him.

The kiss deepened. As they kissed, lips locked together warmly, they moved inside.

In the bedroom, he managed to remove his Glock and set it on the nightstand, never breaking the kiss.

They began to shed their clothing, trying to rid themselves of shirts and shoes and aid the other at the same time. Their clothing wound up tangled around them, then they strewed some in a pile on the floor.

They'd never really fought so it wasn't exactly make-up sex, but it was incredible sex.

She lay next to him, touched him, felt his touch. Felt his lips. Felt liquid kisses and softness and hardness, tenderness and passion. And, running her fingers down his torso and over his abdomen and below, she wondered if it could always be like this, if she could want him so desperately, love him so much, feel such a climax each time they made love.

Later, as they lay curled together and she was almost sleeping, he rolled over and came up on an elbow to speak with her.

"This one makes me really nervous," he told her.

"I saw her in that coffin," Kieran said. "I understand."

"You—"

She stopped him with a finger to his lips. "I'll be careful. Really careful. I promise. I won't be alone."

He fell silent, holding her.

And she meant to be careful. But the question of where Jeannette Gilbert might have lain right after she'd been killed was troubling her, and she needed to know more, so much more.

She'd keep her word. She wouldn't be alone.

But she did have brothers. Declan would be at the pub. Kevin would be at the church, working with the choral group. Danny was a fantastic tour director, and he probably had tours scheduled. But tomorrow was Sunday. Sunday was a great day to go to church and then explore the city.

And she knew she could make Danny accommodate her schedule.

Craig's first order of business when he arrived at his office that Sunday morning was to follow through with every agency and find out if the police, the FBI or any of the informed law-enforcement agencies had discovered anything new regarding Sadie Miller.

They had not.

Sadie had walked out the door to Finnegan's pub on Broadway and somehow walked into thin air, or so it seemed at the moment.

That meant, Craig figured, that she'd walked out and— assuming she'd been taken by this individual—she'd walked right into the arms of her abductor.

Detective McBride sounded down when Craig spoke to

him. "I've had every patrolman in the city on the lookout. I've talked with Jersey. I've talked with counterparts upstate and into Connecticut. Everyone is looking for her."

"I'll okay it with my director," Craig told McBride, "and then I think we'll get her picture out there on the news. You never know—someone might have seen her and we just haven't hit that right someone yet. The longer she's gone…"

"Yeah. The bleaker it gets," McBride agreed. "I'll see you in a few hours."

"Yeah," Craig said, and hung up. McBride would be in when they interviewed Kevin.

Mike tapped on his door and told him that they'd brought in Leo Holt, the fashion photographer.

"How is he?" Craig asked him.

Mike shrugged. "Amiable. And smart. He knows he's not under arrest, and he has nothing against talking to us."

"What kind of a vibe are you getting?"

Mike shrugged. "I don't see this guy is the violent type. A little on the oily side, but he's solid and not the kind who would have to troll for dates. Does he sleep with a lot of models? Probably. Would he kill? I don't think so, but, hell, I've been fooled before."

"Okay. I'll talk. You watch?"

"It's a plan," Mike said. "Down the hall. He's got coffee. We're keeping it casual." He hesitated, clearing his throat. "Kevin is coming in about noon?"

Craig nodded. He'd already talked to both Richard Egan and Mike as well as Larry McBride about his conversation with Kieran's brother. They were all eager to hear what Kevin had to say.

Neither Mike nor Richard Egan had reacted much.

"Couldn't see it myself, so, I'm not surprised," Egan said. "I mean, a woman like Jeannette Gilbert with Westwood, even if he did have his heyday. And Kieran's brother, well, he is a decent guy with looks to kill. Bad way to put it, I guess. But I just don't see that, either. McBride might feel differently. We'll see during the interview. Wish he'd come in sooner. He could give us something."

"I wonder if he was as shocked by Westwood's press conference as the rest of us," Craig said.

"Could be."

Kevin's interview was to come. For the moment, the concentration was going in a different direction.

Leo Holt, Craig decided, had just the right look for his chosen profession.

He was dark-haired and dark-eyed, lean and wiry, with a nicely sculpted face with clean, sharp features. He might have been cast as a Renaissance poet or a French aristocrat, and he was probably perfect in the New York fashion world.

He sat in one of the interrogation rooms, fully aware that he'd been asked in because he was a suspect, or person of interest. But he appeared to be fine with the proceedings.

"I knew I'd be called in," he told Craig, his long fingers idly drumming the table. "I worked with Jeannette frequently. And, yes, we had a thing a few weeks back. She came in looking like holy hell, hadn't slept the night before. I knew she was seeing someone. She was young and beautiful. She should have been seeing someone. I was happy for her because she seemed to be so happy. She was dating an actor—I knew that. Didn't know it was that Brent Westwood, and I surely don't see it! I mean, nothing wrong with the guy and older actors date younger women all the time. Guess they need it for their egos because that's the thing with modeling or being an actor—there's always a younger, more beautiful face, stronger, more perfect body, in the offing. But, in this instance, I still can't see how Jeannette could have been so crazy about him. I mean, her eyes would glow when she talked about the guy she was secretly dating."

He shrugged and switched gears, back to the row in question. "Anyway, yeah, I yelled at her that day. Yeah, she yelled back. And in the end, I made her promise that when she was working with me, whatever her schedule, she'd get sleep the night before. It shows. I mean, makeup is great. And hell, yeah, there's no model out there who isn't Photoshopped to some degree. When you take beauty and just improve it, well…you have improved beauty. I wish there was something that I could tell you. I honestly do."

"Your building is just a block down from hers," Craig said. "You never saw her coming or going? You never saw her with Brent Westwood—or anyone else?"

Holt glared at him. "Have you missed something? This is New York City. A million people pass you by every day."

"Yeah, but you usually notice the ones you know."

"I never saw her with a guy. I mean, yes, we were friends. I did a lot of work with her. She was my favorite model to shoot. But you got to remember—we worked for other people. I could ask for her when I thought she'd be perfect, but a lot of clothing and makeup lines have a specific model in mind, often a young, beautiful actress."

He fell silent, frowning. Then he shrugged.

"What?" Craig asked.

"I was just thinking. Jeannette knew she wasn't much of an actress. She said that her mystery man—and that's what she called him, by the way, her mystery man—was helping her. That he was good, and he understood all kinds of techniques and that she felt she was already on the way to being a better actress as well as model. She wanted to become a *real* actress. Not a movie star or a persona, but an actress. Jeannette was never a fool. She knew that beauty faded with age. And she wanted to stay on top." He paused a moment. Then he shook his head. "I was just thinking... Funny, because I never really thought of Westwood as being a good actor. I mean, he's good at action stuff, but he's not really an actor, if you know what I mean."

Craig nodded.

"And it wasn't just acting," Holt said. "She wanted the world. Not in the material sense, though she liked having money. Never had it as a kid. She was pleased at what she made, all right. But she felt that she lost out on more than money. She wanted to know things. She wanted to know about the world. Every time she traveled, she told me that she wished she knew more about people and places and things, what made people different, how they saw the world and felt about everything. Not just to become a better actress, but to become a better person. She was bright." He fell silent again. "She was an amazing person, like a star—and she should have shined brightly so many more years."

"Tell me, Mr. Holt, have you had work in Virginia recently?"

"Virginia? Yes, and Jeannette Gilbert was on that shoot. What does the state of Virginia have to do with any of this?" he asked.

"There was a shoot down there, right? Whereabouts were you?"

"Fredericksburg. We were shooting at one of the battlefields there for Misty Mystique. It's a perfume. It was one of those things where the ghosts rose up to follow the woman, she was so sensual. Jeannette was beautiful, not just in a still.

When she walked with that little smile of hers, she probably could have woken the dead." He fell silent for a moment. "And now she is dead," he said softly, shaking his head.

"And when was that shoot?"

"Six, seven weeks ago? I can have my assistant check the calendar and call you," Holt said.

"I'd appreciate that."

Holt leaned forward. "I can't tell you how many people weren't just horrified because of the sensationalism. Jeannette was the real deal. She'd been through hell and still came out of it as a sweet girl. If I can do anything, I really will."

"Thank you. We'll be in touch," Craig said.

Holt nodded grimly and rose to leave. Craig rose with him. He met with Mike behind the glass, from where he'd been watching. Egan was there, too.

"Readily admits he was in Virginia," Egan noted.

"I don't think that would be enough for a conviction," Mike murmured.

"Wiseass," Egan said, shooting him a look. Then he turned back to Craig. "Let's grab some coffee, and then you can tell me everything you know and everything you think. And, yes, after we talk to Kevin Finnegan today, I'll arrange for a press conference. We need to get Sadie Miller's face out there, and we need other young women in the city to be on the lookout. In fact, we need to make sure it all goes national."

"Yes, sir," Craig said.

He headed down to the conference room where he had his board with facts and faces set up, and as he stared at it, he found himself worried again.

Perfect. The women were perfect.

And, in his mind, there was another woman who was certainly perfect, too.

Kieran.

He dialed her number. He was almost surprised when she answered in a whisper.

"Kieran? You okay? Where are you?"

"Church," she told him.

"Oh. Okay."

"Don't worry about me. I'm with Danny. I'll be with him, and I'll be at the pub. And…"

"And?"

"Take care of Kevin for me when he's in, okay?"

"Will do," he said.

He hung up.

And he turned to stare at his board.

As he did so, he hoped that all those who studied the human mind were right, that they could let go of the blowhards and braggarts and assholes.

Because this killer wouldn't have such a manner. He'd be finicky and refined.

That's what Dr. Fuller thought; that's what Kieran believed, as well.

And still, they needed to narrow down the field.

He started to scratch out notes to himself.

Refined.

Not step-uncle. Not crazy mugger off the street. Someone smart and savvy, respectable, with something to offer that lured the women in.

That could well be Leo Holt. Or Roger Gleason, billionaire owner of the club where Jeannette had been found. Or…

A man of science? John Shaw, Aldous Digby, Henry Willoughby, one of the students?

As he pondered the question, Egan walked into the room.

"Kevin is here early. Let's head straight to the conference room. McBride is already on his way."

★ ★ ★

As long as she could remember, Kieran had loved Trinity Church, and, down the street, Saint Paul's Chapel. There was something that spoke so keenly of history at both of them, down to the near past when Saint Paul's had been covered in the wreckage and soot of the Twin Towers after 9/11.

She coerced Danny into attending services at Trinity. They'd been brought up Roman Catholic, but Kieran had always loved her father's view on religion: "It's mostly all good stuff. It's what men do with religions that can be very, very bad."

She felt perfectly comfortable attending the service, and the music was beautiful.

It wasn't until after that Danny demanded to know why they'd gone to church at Trinity.

"Well, it's old," Kieran said.

They stood outside, in the old graveyard.

Danny looked at her suspiciously. "Um, yes. The original Trinity Church—circa 1698—was destroyed in the Great New York City fire of 1776. It was a major blaze that swept across the city, destroying about five hundred buildings. But, with the British coming in to occupy the city after a few Continental losses, much of the congregation headed north—in the footsteps of Washington, who had fled to save what he had left of a ragtag army. Head up to Saint Paul's Chapel, of course, and you can see right where Washington worshipped!"

"Yeah, I know that much," Kieran said.

Danny grinned. "In 1788, construction began on a new Trinity, consecrated in 1790, but snows weakened what was, I assume, not the best construction. The church standing here now was begun in 1839 and finished in 1846." He pointed north and continued, "Saint Paul's Chapel—just up the street—was built in 1766 to accommodate the Episco-pal congregation living north of what was the main city at the time, and it still contains something like eight hundred gravestones and thirty or so vaults in the graveyard and under the chapel. Alexander Hamilton is buried at Trinity. The famed actor George Frederick Cooke is buried in the Saint Paul's Chapel graveyard. There's a story out there that George Cooke's skull was stolen from his grave and used by Edwin Booth during his production of Hamlet. Whether that's true or not, no one really knows, and I don't believe that the city or the powers that be at Trinity will allow anyone to go dig-ging to find out if the skull is indeed in the grave or not."

"Creepy," Kieran said.

"Seems like things are only creepy when we know about them. Every day people walk over graves they know noth-ing about."

"True." Kieran nodded. "Tell me more."

"Happy to oblige!" Danny told her. He was just her ju-nior by a year, and, as the youngest, he'd had a habit of get-ting into the most trouble. But Danny had found his calling as a tour guide. He loved stories—so much the better when those stories were the truth.

Kieran remembered a trip to Ireland when they'd all kissed the Blarney Stone. Seemed Danny had taken the gift of gab to heart.

"So," he continued, "in the early 1800s, laws were passed that forbade burials south of Canal Street. And, with everyone running out of space, the dead had to be buried up and away, so Trinity Cemetery was designed up in Washington Heights. Good thing, you know. Yellow fever, typhoid, cholera—best to get the bodies away."

"So, there's a graveyard here at Trinity, a graveyard at Saint Paul's and another graveyard up at Washington Heights…"

"Ah, yes. And there was Old Saint John's Burial Ground, which is now James J. Walker Park, between Leroy, Hudson and Clarkson streets. Only one stone remains—a memorial to firefighters from about a hundred and fifty years ago. Anyway, the stones themselves were pretty much buried, and very few of the dead were reinterred."

"Interesting," Kieran murmured, feeling overwhelmed. Her idea of trying to find where Jeannette's killer had originally intended to leave her body now seemed foolish. And, even if she found a place or *the* place, would it help catch the killer?

"When there were stones there, it was a place of genius inspiration. Imagine. Edgar Allan Poe used to wander there when he lived on Carmine Street." Danny seemed to relish the idea. "Maybe I should become a writer," he added.

"Go for it," she told him.

"Wow, amazing encouragement," he said. Danny looked at her, worried. "Okay, so I gave up a tour this morning to be with you. Weekends are big, you know."

"I'm sorry."

"It's okay. I'm doing really well with the company. I'm lucky. People seem to love my tour, and they actually write it up on Trip Advisor. But it's you I'm worried about. You were good this morning, but now you seem depressed. And I thought it was a damned nice and really upbeat sermon!"

Kieran laughed softly. "It was. The service was beautiful, Trinity is beautiful and I love looking out over this graveyard."

"So," he said softly. "We're actually at church trying to figure out who might have killed Jeannette Gilbert, since we both know it wasn't our brother."

"Kevin talked to you about Jeannette?" she asked him, trying not to show her surprise.

He shook his head. "Kevin called both me and Declan last night. He wanted us to know what had gone on, and what was happening now."

"Of course," Kieran murmured.

"What are you looking for exactly, Kieran?"

She sighed. "I don't know exactly. But Jeannette Gilbert disappeared and was killed before they discovered the old graves in the walled-up crypt. I think the killer had to have other plans for Jeannette's body."

"Ohh," Danny said. "Not far from here, you have the Marble Cemetery—established 1830—and, unrelated, but near, you have the New York City Marble Cemetery. Lots of people are actually buried all over, even though many interments were moved out as the city grew and grew. You also have a single grave, a monument to a child who died around 1797, and then on West Eleventh Street, between Fifth and Sixth Avenues, you have a tiny graveyard with about thirty graves. Peter Stuyvesant is buried at Saint Mark's in-the-Bowery, and there are graves under and around the church. Not to mention some of the older, bigger ones when you move up northward on Manhattan or out in Brooklyn, the Bronx and Queens. Bay Ridge has a Revolutionary War cemetery and... Kieran, its New York. Tons of people, hundreds of years."

"Needle in a haystack," she murmured. Then she looked at him. "Maybe not so much. Can you think of anything near here? Not so touristy as Trinity or Saint Paul's. Maybe something that had been hidden, or something like a cemetery for a single child, like you were talking about that's, say, between here and Finnegan's or between here and the old Saint Augustine's?"

"Yeah. Actually, I can." He grimaced. "It's private property, though. Owned by a Brit. I know about it because my boss—Cindy, you know her—was bitching and moaning about it. There's an old place about a block or so south of Saint Augustine's, or, now, Le Club Vampyre, that's in dire need of repair. It's actually on the historic register, and they were talking about going in. The building there now is from about 1840, but before that, there was an Old Dutch farmstead. Imagine—a farmstead in lower Manhattan! Anyway, there was a tiny family cemetery, and when they built over what had fallen apart, they put a covered carriage way—now the end of a driveway— over the old graves. You can still see about five tombstones, and there are steps leading to an underground crypt."

"Show me."

"You're kidding me. I told you, it's private property. You're always telling me that I have to shape up and fly right and follow the law."

"Danny, you stole a diamond."

"Borrowed!"

She ignored his word choice. "I only want to do a tiny bit of trespassing. There's a difference!"

"We can end up in jail. And then Craig will be mad at me!"

"Danny, I need to see this place. Please."

He stared at her for a moment, then let out a sound of sheer aggravation and started walking north on Broadway.

Kieran followed his quick pace until they came to Saint Paul's Chapel and she slowed. She saw that the graveyard had been roped off.

"Wait up!" she called to Danny.

Kieran saw a woman working in the graveyard, patting down soil, and called out softly to her.

"Morning!"

"Morning," the woman called back.

"Excuse me. Do you have a minute to answer a couple of questions?" she asked.

The woman rose and walked over to her, wiping her forehead. "I have a minute."

"If someone were to die and want to be buried here now, would that be possible?" Kieran asked.

The woman smiled. "Planning ahead?" she asked.

Danny groaned.

"No, I was curious. I love Trinity and Saint Paul's," Kieran said.

"First, you'd have to be a parishioner. I don't think you could be interred here, but it might be possible at Trinity. You'd have to speak with the Trinity people. If you head north, you'll find the Trinity cemetery. It's quite lovely." She hesitated and shrugged, looking at Kieran as if she might be a bit of a ghoul. "If you're just interested in history, there are also wonderful little hidden cemeteries in the area. There's one not far away. It was a family cemetery, and it's still on private land, so… Well, you can kind of see it from the street. Don't trespass. It's against the law."

Kieran thanked her, and the woman went back to her seeding.

Danny turned to Kieran immediately. "What do you think we're looking for? From what I've understood of what's going on, this guy crawled into a dusty old crypt to display his victim. Do you think that he left you a calling card, a map somewhere? Honestly, Kieran, we should be looking at someplace big and maybe something that's charming and lovely. Where he could go maybe at night and not be seen. What do you think? This guy is like a ghoul, too? A cemetery aficionado?" Danny asked. "If so, we could go up to where it's legal to be!"

"Take me to this little hidden cemetery," Kieran said.

He turned and walked hard; she had to scamper to keep up with him.

He cut off behind Broadway, and they were just about a block or so away from Le Club Vampyre.

And then he stopped.

Kieran crashed into his back. She steadied herself and stared.

The building appeared to be older than it probably was. No care had been taken for a while, and it stood on a little sliver of land with an actual spit of lawn before it—almost unheard-of where they were. To the side was a driveway or car park covered with carved wood, probably well over 150 years old.

Peering through the high gates, Kieran could see crooked stones in the back, beyond the gravel of the car park.

She pushed at the gate. To her amazement, the lock fell open.

"Kieran!" Danny warned.

"You stay here."

"Hell, no! I'm going with you. You think I'd let you fall down a gutter or a—"

"Grave?"

She pushed the iron gate open and hurried in, not sure why she was so determined.

When she made it to the back, she was disappointed. All she saw were five or six crooked headstones in a mass of over-grown weeds.

"What did you expect?" Danny demanded.

"I don't know," Kieran said. She looked about and started around the graves. She walked to one and knelt, trying to read the weatherworn words inscribed on the stone.

She leaned forward.

And as she did so, the earth gave way beneath her and she fell...and fell.

Deep into a dark, dank pit in the earth.

CHAPTER
NINE

CRAIG REMOVED HIMSELF FROM THE INTERVIEW BY CHOOS-
ing the farthest chair. Since Mike had become friends with
the entire Finnegan family when Craig and Kieran had begun
seeing one another, he, too, made a point of being an observer.

That left Richard Egan and Detective Larry McBride at
the table facing Kevin.

Egan had been at Finnegan's on Broadway often enough.
But he didn't choose to excuse himself from the interview,
considering himself a customer of the bar, not a friend of the
family.

Kevin basically came to tell them a story that might have
had the kind of fairy-tale ending that would have made any
romantic smile—had Jeannette Gilbert lived. It was the typical boy and girl meet, catch one another's eyes in the midst of
work, feel the brush of one another's touch, a certain breath-
lessness, adrenaline rush...

The hope that the other person might feel the same.

So now Kevin merely repeated the story as he'd told others

when asked. He hadn't really looked at anyone when he spoke. He was just reciting the events. His features were taut and pained, and Craig thought that he'd seen just a look before. It was when someone didn't care anymore what happened to them.

The worst has already happened.

"Why didn't you come forward immediately?" Egan demanded. "When she was missing—when you heard that she was dead? That's very suspicious behavior, you know."

Kevin lifted his hands and let them fall, shaking his head slightly. "When she disappeared, I thought it was part of a publicity stunt. I kept thinking I'd hear from her. She talked about Oswald Martin a lot. She thought he was brilliant. He'd certainly managed a stellar career for her. But she also thought he was crazy. She loved when he'd arrange for her to bring presents to hospitals. To kids, especially underprivileged kids. You really... you really should have known her," he said softly. "She came from so much that was rotten and bad, but she was never mean or bitter. She just wanted to make things better for other people."

There was no catch in his voice; there was no gulping sound that escaped him. Instead, tears just dripped down his face.

Richard Egan glanced over at Craig.

McBride cleared his throat and asked, "I still don't understand why you didn't come forward."

"I planned to come forward. But then, I saw Brent Westwood on television. Jeannette worked with him. She had a small part in a movie with him about a year and a half ago. But if she saw him as anything, she saw him as a father figure. And the thing is...well, old-timer or not, Westwood is something of a legend. If I came forward... I don't even really know how to explain this. I don't want the papers turning this into the old-timer said and the upstart said... I don't want Jeannette's name in the rag magazines, not now…not when she's gone. She was truly fine. She didn't do drugs, she didn't sleep around…and I'll be damned if I know why Westwood did what he did other than for publicity."

"Mr. Finnegan," McBride said, "don't you understand that you might be able to help us in some way? Or, indeed, that in cases like these, we look first at the wife, the husband, the significant other or—in your case—the mystery lover?"

Kevin looked up then, staring hard at McBride. "I'd have never hurt Jeannette. I loved her," he said simply, and then added with passion, "Don't you think that if there were anything I could say or do that would help catch her killer I would speak right up? I hadn't seen her—the last conversation we had together was her laughing and telling me that Oswald Martin has something up his sleeve that she thought was crazy but fun. She told me to watch for it and tell her what I thought."

"And that's why you weren't worried when she disappeared?" McBride asked.

Kevin nodded. "I can tell you that she did hate her stepuncle. She didn't hate Oswald, even though he was controlling and pissed her off now and then. And while she believed that he could be a taskmaster, Leo Holt was an amazing photographer. I don't know much about other people she was working with." His eyes widened. "Roger Gleason. We were both at the opening of Le Club Vampyre—separately, of course. But, she managed to whisper to me that Gleason was a very rich sleaze, and that she was glad she never had to worry about money because she would always make her personal choices herself."

"So, Roger Gleason was interested in her?" McBride asked.

"Yes, but I don't see that as unusual. She was beautiful. Everyone was interested in her. There was a light about her, a glow. She wasn't just amazing to see, she was full of life, charming. People came to her because she was just so…vital."

Silence fell in the room again. Then Egan cleared his throat.

"A tragic and senseless loss," he said. "But I believe you also know the missing woman—Sadie Miller." He opened the folder he had on the table and produced a glossy photo, pushing it toward Kevin. "Print ad for Michael Malone jeans. That's you in the jeans, and Ms. Miller right behind you."

"Yes, of course, I worked with Sadie," Kevin said.

"And you don't think it's unusual that you knew both women?" McBride asked.

Kevin stared at him, apparently both confused and a little irritated. "I model and act. Both these women modeled and acted. Although, actually, Sadie had told me that she wanted to go back to school. She wanted to get a degree in archaeology. Maybe she knew John Shaw. Maybe she knew Aldous Digby. I don't know. Maybe she never pursued any of her desires." He shook his head. "I worked with her a year ago. I told her to drop into Finnegan's sometime. She thought it was cool that my family owned a place that was so old."

"But she never came by, not until the other night?" Egan asked.

"I didn't even know about it. I wasn't there when she came by."

"And you don't think we should be suspicious of you?" McBride said.

"Maybe you should be. I don't know. I'm not a cop—or an agent. There are, yes, thousands of actors in New York City. But it's not that unusual that you know people in the field. Even if you don't work with them, you've probably sat in a crowded audition venue with them somewhere at some time. We're a giant city, but there are small worlds within it."

"You remain a person of interest, Mr. Finnegan," McBride said.

"And that's fine. Just don't waste too much time concentrating on me, because I didn't kill Jeannette. And Sadie is a fine person, and not to be crude, but if there's the slightest chance she's still alive, you ought to have your asses out on the street and be looking for her," Kevin said flatly. "Whatever you do to me, it doesn't matter."

Mike, apparently, couldn't stand it any longer.

He leaned forward and said, "Kevin, we have to ask these questions."

"Yes, I know."

"Kevin, your cell phone—is it the same one you've had?" Craig asked.

Kevin nodded and reached into his pocket, sliding it across the table.

"We'll get it back to you," Egan told him.

"Sure," Kevin said. He managed a small smile. "I was about to say that I don't care. But there are pictures in there, so…"

There was silence around the table.

"Where do I go from here?" Kevin asked, the sound of his voice throaty.

Craig wasn't sure if he was asking about what he should do for the police or the FBI, or what he should do with his life, now that Jeannette was gone.

"I think we should let that press conference stand, don't give out any more information right now and just follow where it might lead," Egan said.

"Your call," McBride said.

Egan nodded. "I don't want to feed the rags, either. I do believe that another interview with Mr. Westwood is in order." Egan stood. The others followed suit.

"Kevin, we do, of course, know where to find you. And, I'm sure, as this goes on, we'll need to speak again. If there is anything at all that occurs to you—no matter how small— you're to let us know immediately. No reacting to anything else you see—you get with one of us immediately."

Kevin nodded gravely. "Of course."

The cell phone he had placed on the table began to ring. Craig glanced down and saw on the caller ID that it was Danny Finnegan calling his brother.

Danny had been spending the day with Kieran.

Craig went to get the phone, but Kevin was closer and he did so by rote.

"My brother," he said. "May I take it? I'll give it right back."

"Of course," Egan told him.

Kevin lowered his head and listened and said, "Yes," and then a minute later, "Yes," again, and then, "Sure, all set here."

He quickly set the phone back on the conference table and said, "Thanks. So, I'm on my way. And you do know where to find me, and I will call if there's anything else," he added softly.

A junior agent was waiting to escort him out of the building. Kevin greeted her politely, and they started out.

"Sir, I'm going to follow him," Craig told Egan. "Mike, will you—"

"Get the phone to Tech, find anything pertinent to Jeannette Gilbert, yep," Mike said.

Craig didn't wait for questions from McBride. He hurried after Kevin.

The man was already out on the street—he had long legs, had lived in New York all his life and could speed walk with agility.

Craig quickened his own pace.

At some point, Kevin must have known that he was being

followed because he glanced back. He didn't acknowledge that he saw Craig. He just started moving quickly again.

Craig caught up with him in front of a Chinese Laundromat, catching him by the shoulder and turning him.

Kevin let out a sigh. "Yeah, okay, you're following me."

"Where are we going?"

"Ah, come on, Craig. Danny is going to kill me."

"Danny should have been told that you were at the FBI building."

"Now, that's the truth," Kevin said, sighing again and shaking his head. "Anyway, I've really got to go."

"We've got to go. Where?" Craig said.

Kevin shook his head again and turned and started walking, aware that Craig was dogging his footsteps.

"They're not far...but..."

"But what?" Craig demanded.

"They were trespassing."

"Trespassing?"

"Private property. An old family cemetery at a historic property. Absentee landowner, so Danny said. We're supposed to be getting Kieran out and off the property before anyone knows."

"Out of what?"

Kevin kept walking as he answered. "A hole in the ground," he said. "If you're coming, we've got to hurry. No car. It's close enough that it's faster on foot—just about a block or so from Finnegan's and Le Club Vampyre." He looked at Craig at last. "Sounds to me like she's fallen into a crypt—you know, into some kind of a vault or mausoleum. You know, for the dead."

Kieran wasn't hurt; she was startled and the breath had been knocked out of her.

She knew that quickly. She'd really made more of a slide

than a fall, and, groping about to try to stop herself, she knew that her arms and legs were functioning.

She was simply down in a hole in the dirt, covered with dirt. But she didn't land on dirt, but rather, something hard.

"Kieran!" Danny called to her desperately.

"I'm all right!" she called back. "Hey, you don't happen to have a flashlight on you, do you?" she called up to him.

"A flashlight? We need a damned ladder!" Danny called back. "But, here, take this! Watch out below, coming down. It's a laser light on my key chain. I'm going to find something to get you out. Or maybe there's stairs somewhere. You must be in a tomb of some kind."

Kieran shivered fiercely. It was cold down here. She heard the clink as Danny's key chain hit the ground near her, which smelled musky and earthy.

Something moved nearby. A chittering sound came to her. *Rats.*

Well, rats were the least of it. She had to get out of here.

She reached around the cold ground for Danny's key chain and found it at last. Switching on the light, she saw that she was in a narrow shaft. Cobwebs seemed to be everywhere; rats indeed had found a home. One skittered away from the little ray of laser light.

She got to her feet and realized that she was in something like a small catacomb. At least here, the dead had been entombed behind what seemed to be marble slabs.

Danny had suggested stairs. Yes, if it was an underground burial chamber for the family, there had to be stairs down to it.

Time might have made more of the roof collapse, but maybe not. She started to turn and realized that there were a few sarcophagus-like tombs on the floor here, as well. The one she stood by had the Masonic symbol at the top. Running the laser over the tomb, she saw that it read, "Reginald Vincent Huntington III, departed this life September 5, year of our Lord, 1827."

She called up to Danny. "Yeah, it's a crypt! You find a ladder?"

He didn't answer right away. He'd gone away from the hole, hopefully seeking a way to get her out.

Kieran began to move around, Danny's tiny laser affording decent light. To her right, the crypt seemed to come to an abrupt end. There were marble slabs with names and dates, but they were the end of the line. She turned to go in the other direction, figuring that there were forty to fifty interments in the place, along the walls, and in the line of sarcophagi that was similar to that beneath the old Saint Augustine's.

Except that Saint Augustine's was much bigger.

The next sarcophagus belonged to Reginald Vincent Huntington II, who had died in 1818.

The marble tombs were simple and beautiful.

She kept heading out carefully. The floor seemed to have been clear enough, enjoyed only by the rats and insects until she'd caused the cave-in. There had to be other breaks in either the wall or the roof, though, to provide for the abundance of rodents and spiderwebs and insects. Maybe there were stairs down here, and maybe someone had even come down in the last decade or so.

She moved forward; there was another sarcophagus ahead of her, and it seemed to have some kind of a marble effigy on its top.

Kieran moved closer, the little laser light held high in her hand.

She was almost upon it before she stopped, an eerie sensation of ice-cold horror spearing down her spine.

It wasn't an effigy.

And it wasn't marble.

It was human.

Or had been human.

A woman lay there, down to mummified skin and bone. The skeletal face had all but lost the jaw, and she appeared to be screaming in silence.

She'd been dressed in white, a white now turning beige with time and decay and the stain of the body as it both rotted and became partially mummified.

Her hands were folded on her chest. A dead flower was grasped within them.

The laser light and key chain fell from Kieran's fingers. Onto the corpse. The hideous contortion of the stretched-skin face was caught and highlighted in that glow, creating a macabre sense that the corpse itself might rise.

For a moment, Kieran was frozen. And then she backed away.

And she began to scream. And scream.

She turned, blindly racing toward the end of the tomb. To her amazement, she crashed into another body.

Maddened, she began to shake, longing to beat her fists against something.

The killer! The killer was here. The killer had been here. Because that body had not been on that marble slab since the 1800s. It had lain there a year perhaps, no more.

"Kieran! Kieran!"

Somehow, the sound of her name finally penetrated through the wall of raw panic that surrounded her. She stood still. She looked through the shadows cast by the laser light, and she realized that it was Craig.

Impossibly, it was Craig. And his hands were on her shoulders. She knew the scent of him and the feel of him, and her screams caught in her throat as she stared at him, feeling the terror in her heart slowly subside.

To her amazement, she was able to speak. It was a hushed whisper, but she managed to speak.

"The Jersey victim…she might have been first, but I think he followed up more quickly with another kill than we had thought. Craig…there's another. There…there, behind me, in the light!"

"We'll get you out of here," he said.

"I'm fine," she lied.

But she had no problem following him.

There were stairs. And they led up to a tiny metal hatch door just ten feet from the carriage entry to the house.

She didn't let go of his arm, afraid that she would fall when she first saw the daylight again, grateful as never before as the sun fell down upon her.

Craig wanted Kieran to go to the hospital for a checkup; she'd fallen a good ten to twelve feet into the crypt. It was hard to tell if she was injured, of course, because she was covered in dirt and spiderwebs.

She insisted that she was not hurt, nor would she go to the hospital to be checked out. She was fine. The day was warm enough, but she did sit at the end of the rescue vehicle, a blanket around her shoulders, hot coffee in her hands, and she spoke clearly and evenly, only shivering now and then.

"I didn't think… I wasn't expecting to find a new corpse. Well, she isn't new, but she isn't old. As in eighteenth-century old," she told Craig, Egan and McBride. The other two men had made it quickly to the site. "I don't really know what I was thinking, except that we know this man has killed before."

"We all knew he'd killed before, and you weren't expecting a corpse?" McBride asked. "What the hell were you doing here? This is private property!"

"I was thinking about old cemeteries. This man likes old cemeteries. And, the thing is, you can reach old cemeteries more easily than you might think," Kieran said.

"If you're a descendant of a person down in the Marble Cemetery, you can still be interred there," Danny offered. "Or at Trinity, or other old cemeteries in the city."

"I'm trying to get inside the killer's mind," Kieran said. "I just wanted to get a feel for more of the cemeteries and crypts and... I didn't think I'd fall through a hole. I just meant to get a look and get back out and maybe see a few more places..."

Her voice faded.

"How long has she been dead?" she asked in a whisper. "That's not— I mean, it can't be Sadie Miller, right?"

"No, it's not Sadie Miller," Craig said. He looked over at Kevin and Danny. "You two! You let her do this. Danny, you were with her."

"Have you ever tried to stop Kieran?" Danny asked him. "And you should be grateful! She stumbled upon another murder. This girl Kieran found... Her family might have wondered for years and years and now, at the least, they'll know. I mean, who the hell else would have ever come here and made this discovery?"

Danny had a point, and he knew it.

McBride said sternly, "There's still a matter of this being private property and the two of you trespassing."

It was really a moot point. They all knew by now that the place was owned by a Brit, an absentee landowner, who was—from a distance—involved in a legal haggle with the city's historic boards and code department.

"How many do you think there are?" Kieran whispered softly. "And how long dead, and is there any kind of a prayer for Sadie Miller?"

"We don't know about Sadie, Kieran," Craig told her. "But we are looking for her. McBride has men out, and he's spoken with his counterparts everywhere nearby. Yes, there's hope. There's always hope."

Egan walked off to meet with Dr. Anthony Andrews, the ME, who was just coming up out of the crypt. Egan had specifically asked for Andrews; he believed that having one ME on these remains was crucial to determining if this was the work of a serial killer, what methods he used, and how and if he was evolving.

"Excuse me," Craig murmured, turning to join them. He paused, looking back at Kieran and her brothers. "And don't you move!" he warned.

They all stared back at him in grim silence.

"Well?" Egan asked.

Andrews nodded an acknowledgment to Craig. "I wish I could tell you that I could give you something exact when I get her on the table. The conditions underground caused a certain amount of preservation, but, as you saw...I'd say she's been down here at least a couple of years."

"Are we looking at the same killer?" Craig asked.

"Same method of death. Hard for me to say right now, but I didn't find any indication of defensive wounds," Andrews said. "Who knows? The forensic teams might find something on this, though I'm willing to bet that this killer wears gloves. Maybe we'll get something, who knows? Anyway, I will be able to get it down to a month or so once we've had the autopsy." Andrews hesitated, looking at Craig. "This city is filled with the dead. Yeah, bodies have been moved, but

there are little places like this, church graveyards and crypts…
Who knows how long he's been at it?"

Statistically, about thirteen thousand people were reported
missing in New York each year, Craig knew. Some were
found; some were runaways. Some were the very old suffering from Alzheimer's or dementia, some suffered from other
diseases and many were children.

Many were young women, as well.

He wondered how many young women might have met
this fate.

Andrews looked at Craig. "Anything on Sadie Miller?"
he asked.

Craig shook his head. "Finding out exactly what was happening with our other victims is difficult," Craig said. "This
young woman…we don't even know who she is, yet. But with
Jeannette Gilbert, we do have a timeline. Do you think that
there's a chance Sadie Miller is still alive?"

Andrews hesitated. "I really can't pinpoint exact time of
death," he said. "Might she be alive? Yes. But, if so, I doubt
that she'll be alive for long. I just sent you a report, by the
way. I'm guessing that you've been too busy right now to get
to your email. Jeannette Gilbert did have a sedative in her
body. Lorazepam. It's usually for anxiety, for people who can't
sleep. It can help with those who have seizures and it can also
cause pretty acute short-term memory loss if it's taken in high
doses. Combined with that, she had Rohypnol in her blood."

Roofie. The date rape drug.

"So she was drugged before she was killed," Craig said.

"Yes, but there were no signs of sexual assault. Rohypnol also inhibits memory. You're still looking for someone
Jeannette trusted. He had to get close enough to her to get
the drugs into her. I believe that it was swallowed—put into

a drink or perhaps into food. Anyway, if it had been forced into her, there would have been a needle mark somewhere, and Jeannette Gilbert would have shown bruising. I couldn't find anything on the body that suggested she'd fought anyone in any way."

"Thank you," Craig told him. "I think that means that the killer did keep her alive for a day or so at least. That means there may be hope for Sadie Miller."

"Then I pray you find her fast," the ME said. "Now if you'll excuse me, they're going to bring this victim up, and I'm going to head into autopsy as soon as possible."

Craig nodded.

He'd heard the doctor's words and took them to heart. He knew the work of law enforcement wasn't only to find justice for the victims of crime.

Their work was to save the living.

"Press conference—now," Egan said. "We'll do it in front of our office. We'll have you and McBride do the speaking. There will be no mention of Kevin and Jeannette Gilbert—not until we've had a discussion with Mr. Westwood again." He already had his phone out to make arrangements with the media.

Craig nodded his understanding and headed to the back of the ambulance.

For once, Kieran had listened to him. She remained at the back of the rescue vehicle, flanked on either side by one of her brothers.

"You *should* go to the hospital," he said.

"But I'm really all right. And hospitals need room for people who are not all right. I'll go to the pub, Craig. We'll all be there. Danny canceled his tours for today. Kevin is finished with his choral commitment and his appointment with you.

We'll be there, all three of us. And Declan. And you know that the pub is always filled with off-duty police."

"Go on, then," he told her. "McBride has your statements, right?" he asked, looking at Danny.

He nodded. "Yes. And if anyone is prosecuted, it was all my fault."

"Danny, you weren't at fault at all!" Kieran said.

"I'm a tour guide, Kieran. Your job needs you to be squeaky clean and—"

"Oh, give it a rest, both of you," Craig said. "There isn't going to be a prosecution. Go to the pub. I'll see you there later."

"Wait," Kieran called to him.

He turned back.

"I have to go home, please! I've got to shower," Kieran said.

"You two—you're with her, right?" Craig asked.

Kevin and Danny nodded solemnly.

"Why am I even asking that?" he muttered. "It's like the blind leading the blind!"

"Straight to Kieran's, then straight to the pub," Danny said.

"No more graveyards and no more trespassing!"

"You have our solemn vow," Kevin told him.

He left them at last.

The good thing was, he knew, for that day at least the three of them would do exactly as he had said.

They might have their faults, as did all living, breathing souls.

But a solemn vow from a Finnegan was as good as solid gold.

CHAPTER
TEN

THERE WAS ACTUALLY AN EVENING RUSH AT THE PUB, AND Kieran could tell that Declan was glad to have all three of his siblings on the floor helping out, or running below to the cellar when backup supplies were needed.

Since, in the last year or so, Kevin, Danny and Kieran had spent fewer and fewer hours at the pub, Declan's fiancée, Mary Kathleen, had taken over as floor manager.

That worked for everyone.

Mary Kathleen was, in Kieran's opinion, the very best of all things that tended to make up an Irish personality. She was a little beauty with bright blue eyes and hair that was nearly pitch-black. She was a bundle of energy; she spoke her mind in no uncertain terms, but her mood tended toward the positive and cheerful, and patrons loved her. Many of the old-timers spoke about how, in the future, the pub would be like it had been in the past when Kieran's parents had worked it together, as had many couples before them, all the way back before the Civil War.

Declan and Mary Kathleen would surely carry on that tradition. It was a good thing. Such a good thing in a world that was ever changing, and most certainly not very often for the better.

Kieran got along beautifully with the young woman who would one day be her sister-in-law. Mary Kathleen was great with responsibility and easily gave directions to the staff.

Kieran loved her work with Drs. Fuller and Miro and wanted no responsibility at the pub. Neither was she great at giving any kind of orders.

Mary Kathleen was sweet, thanking the three of them for their help tonight, as always. She gave them stations as the popular dinner hours came and went. After all, it was Sunday, crowded for the very traditional roast their clientele loved.

It was good to work; movement was good.

The more Kieran moved, the less she remembered seeing the corpse.

The less she worried, pondered or mulled over the situation.

And yet, she couldn't really stop.

Kevin's loss of the woman he had loved so dearly was heart-wrenching.

People tended to grieve for what was terrible and hurt with those who suffered, even when the suffering was far away. But this loss was so close. Her twin's loss. She knew his world had been changed. Life itself had become something different. Just waking each morning would be a process of learning to go on.

She was sorry for Kevin and all those who had known and loved Jeannette.

And she was sorry for the family of Cary Howell, killed in Virginia, and for the family of Cheyenne Lawson, killed in New Jersey.

She was so sorry for those who had loved the young woman she had stumbled upon that day. They would just be learning that there was no hope left for them.

And yet, nothing could be done for her.

She couldn't help but wonder about Sadie Miller, who had just disappeared. Had the killer already taken his knife to her? Was he sitting with her body, mulling on the work he had done in the past, trying to determine how best to display her, whether to hide her or whether to leave her in the open?

What, she wondered, made the killer choose how he was going to do what?

She was mulling the question and wiping a table when Kevin came up to her. "Come in the office. Your lad is on the television."

She hurried after him to the office. She saw that they'd missed the original broadcast, but the local news stations were showing the press conference over and over again.

Craig was an excellent speaker. He carried an easy air of authority while not appearing to be in the least unapproachable.

He talked about the Jeannette Gilbert case, informing the public there were certain things that he couldn't say yet, not in an ongoing investigation. Because of her death, murder investigations in other states were now being compared, and law enforcement wanted to alert the populace that a serial killer was at work.

Young women, especially, needed to be exceptionally vigilant. They should stay in crowds when they were out, spend time with known friends and family. Because, they believed, the victims had been lured by someone trustworthy, Craig begged women to take great care in embarking on any promised lure of employment, entertainment or special interest.

A dozen reporters asked questions; Craig fielded all of them well, stopping them before they could come at him in a barrage.

"We're asking for the public's help. A young woman has now been missing two days and, because she fits the victim profile, we're seeking any aid the public can possibly give us to find her. If anyone has any information at all regarding Sadie Miller, we ask that you call our dedicated number."

A picture of Sadie appeared on the screen. She was smiling in the photograph—smiling beautifully.

Larry McBride stepped forward for the NYPD, reiterating some of what Craig had said and asking that anyone aware of suspicious behavior to please inform the authorities immediately.

Then the question came up about that afternoon.

Witnesses had reported a commotion at the old Huntington mansion; they'd seen forensic teams and rescue vehicles.

"We believe, yes, that we have found a previous victim of the same killer. As of yet, however, we've little information, and none that we'll share before discovery of the victim's identity and notification of her next of kin," Craig said, stepping forward.

A flurry of questions then was halted by Egan, who stepped forward to end the press conference.

"We don't want the city in a panic. We do want the city aware and alert. Thank you all very much. Again, all and any help is greatly appreciated."

The scene switched to that of a pretty female news anchor, commenting on the news conference and asking all those in the city to please take the warnings to heart.

"Well, there you have it," Kevin murmured. "They have to catch this guy!" he said passionately. "And Sadie is out there. Still out there."

He didn't ask if Kieran thought she was alive or dead. He just let the words hang on the air.

Kieran set her hands on his shoulders. "They'll find Sadie. They're very good at what they do."

"Not good enough," Kevin said, and turned to head out of the office. Kieran followed him.

The press conference had taken place hours ago, so she figured Craig should be arriving at the pub soon.

It had quieted down; the dinner hour was over.

But the pub was far from empty. And seated at the side tables before the bar—as seemed to be their habit—was John Shaw. He was accompanied by Roger Gleason, Henry Willoughby and a number of his minions, Allie Benoit, Joshua Harding and Sam Frick.

"Ah! Here she is!" John Shaw announced. "You were there, right? You were at the old Huntington mansion. You know what happened there. My God! Another cache beneath the ground. It's amazing what lies underfoot, eh?"

Kieran frowned, walking up to join the table. Allie Benoit met her gaze and rolled her eyes apologetically.

Roger Gleason smiled at her. "They've been hoping to see you."

Willoughby sighed. "John has been hoping to see you. I may be a historian, but, sometimes, we really need to let the dead rest."

"Except that you found another murdered girl, right?" John Shaw said. "My God, we do have a most unusual serial killer on our hands. One I imagine of great interest. I mean, not a butcher, but a fastidious man. What does he want? What does he get out of what he's doing? It does seem so strange. It's as if he's conflicted. He does and he doesn't want his kills to be seen."

"John, really," Willoughby murmured.

"Ms. Finnegan," Sam Frick said, "the young woman who was found… I'm so sorry. Had she been dead long? I mean, they know it's not the missing woman, right?"

"No, she's not the missing woman," Kieran said. "Listen, I don't really know anything. I'm sorry. I've seen the same information you have."

"We just saw it. We were working all day," Willoughby said. He shook his head. "John is right about one thing—you just have no idea how much lies beneath the streets of New York. Time changes things, you know? I mean, finding history here, well…it's not always easy. And the Huntington mansion has always been privately held, though I, myself, have been appalled to see how poorly our absentee landowner has seen to it."

"But another hidden vault!" Shaw said.

"A privately owned vault," Henry Willoughby reminded him strongly, rolling his eyes. "Hey, no one loves old New York more than me—and no one is more aware of the law."

"Oh, the Brit who owns it can't care about another family that's been dead a hundred years," John Shaw said. "From what I've heard, he only bought it for the investment. But, hey, what do I know?"

Roger Gleason cleared his throat. "Gentlemen, there will be no more work on any other site until you've finished with my place. I do intend to reopen. Obviously, I can't keep the club closed for an endless amount of time. We'll just close off the entire basement during opening hours."

Kieran saw that Craig had finally come in. She was glad; all she wanted to do was go home.

"Excuse me!" she said quickly, and she fled toward the entrance, eager to stop Craig before the Le Club Vampyre crew involved him in conversation.

"May we just leave?" she asked, rushing up to him.

"Yeah," he said, holding her steady against him. "You want to tell your brothers goodbye?"

What she wanted was to just run out the door. But her purse was back in the office, and she did need to let Declan and the others know that she was leaving.

By the time she'd run to the office and stopped quickly by the bar, Craig had been reined in by the group at the table.

"A serial killer—trying to prove what?" Shaw was saying when she returned.

"I don't think that serial killers are trying to prove anything. They kill for their own pleasure, and they don't have any empathy for their victims," Allie Benoit said. She shivered. "Those poor girls. Do you know how long this has been going on?" she asked Craig.

He shrugged easily. "Open investigation," he said quietly. "I can't really talk about it."

"But aren't we part of this investigation?" Henry Willoughby asked, perplexed. "Roger Gleason was the one to report the hidden crypt as soon as his construction men found it. I was called to see that history was preserved. John Shaw actually found poor Ms. Gilbert, and Allie, Josh and Sam were working with him and Professor Digby."

"Where is Professor Digby?"

Shaw sniffed. "Some scientist. He can't wait to get out of the dust and grime at night. He shouldn't even notice. After all, knowledge is everything. Says he needs to shower as soon as possible, even before a bite and a drink!" Shaw told him. "Ah, I'm not being fair. I've worked with Digby forever. He's a good man. Never thought a scientist could get freaked out, though. But, hey. This is the first time we found a person re-cently deceased when we were working. I can't blame him."

"Poor guy," Allie Benoit noted.

"I think it freaked out all of us," Joshua Harding said. He looked at Craig glumly. "Freaked me out! But," he added, glancing at John Shaw, "I'm on scholarship. I can't afford to be too freaked out." He turned and smiled at Kieran. "Thank-fully, we get to come here at the end of the day. Warm and cozy and good food."

"Thanks," she murmured, glancing at her watch. "Gotta run. We'll see you all." She slipped her arm through Craig's.

He got the hint.

They left.

"So Digby is freaked out," Craig murmured as they stepped outside.

"Yes," Kieran said, following his lead since she'd no idea where he'd managed to park the car. "And it makes you won-der. Can you imagine anyone being excited about an appoint-ment with Digby? I mean, poor Digby is just not exciting."

"Not Digby, but maybe he was a doorway to something that was exciting for someone who wanted to move into a life working with history or archaeology," Craig said.

She knew they were talking about Sadie Miller. "There's been nothing on Sadie?" she asked softly.

He shook his head. "Cops have been everywhere—her place of work, the coffee shops she hangs out, the dinner spots, the clubs…nothing. They have posters up, and we have the press conference on the air. If anyone knows anything, they're not speaking yet."

"The more time that goes by—"

"Yes. Thing is, she might have been killed right when she went missing," Craig said. "There's really not anything more

we can do to find her. There's an army on the street looking
for her already."

But was it the right army? Kieran wondered. The cops
were good, but would they think to look in unusual places?

Ridiculous and bad thought on her part, she decided. If
she or anyone else knew the right unusual places to look,
they'd be doing so.

Then again, look where she had found another murder
victim today.

If only she'd found a live woman instead!

They reached her place and went up the stairs. That night,
ironically, or so it seemed to Kieran, someone was warbling
out a decent rendition of Alice Cooper's "The Man Behind
the Mask."

At her place, Craig headed straight into the shower. Kieran
crawled into bed and waited up for him.

But the shower was on a long time.

When it stopped, Craig still didn't come out.

She got up and headed to the bathroom door and tapped
at it.

"Come in."

She walked in and she had to smile. He was a good agent
because he was always thinking.

He was a good man because he always cared.

He'd been writing on the mirror, making notes in the
steam. He did it now and then, looking like a big kid.

He turned to her, his hair and body still damp from the
shower. "Sorry."

She stepped toward him and looked at his notes as he spoke.

"Right now, we have Cheyenne Lawson, left on the grass
of the cemetery in New Jersey. We have the victim you found
today, unidentified as yet. I think we'll discover that she's

been down there a few years. Six months ago, Cary Howell was killed in Virginia. Now Jeannette Gilbert. And Sadie
Miller is missing."

"You think there were others in between?" Kieran asked.

"I don't know. Based on what I know about serial killers, sometimes the need speeds up. Maybe it was one a year,
then one every six months, and now…I don't know. I'm sure
it's something Dr. Fuller has had on his mind. They'll have
a consultation with him and our specialists in the morning.
We do have people coming in on this."

She nodded. She slipped her arms around his naked torso
and rested her cheek on the dampness of his back. "I'd like
to believe that we can find Sadie alive," she said.

"And maybe we will. However, you really need to stay out
of graveyards."

"Hey! Wasn't my fault time caused the earth and the roof
of the crypt to give in."

"You could have been hurt."

"You could be hurt or killed every day."

"We've been through this, Kieran."

"That's right, we have," she said. "Hey, not to worry! I
have a full workday at the office tomorrow," she told him.

He was still thoughtful, turning to hold her, smoothing
down her hair. "I'm thinking about a drive to Virginia. Tomorrow night or Tuesday. There are some things I need to do
tomorrow. I'm going to have a talk again with Professor Aldous Digby, because he did have opportunity and is a suspect."

"I can't see Digby being a killer."

"I can't, either. But I've been fooled before. And I'm checking in with a number of religious leaders in the area and cemetery directors. We need them to check out their catacombs

and/or crypts. I really need to get them all working—before I find you in another crypt."

"Not fair. I fell in."

"Because you were trespassing in the graveyard."

"I had an idea—a vague idea. It seemed right at the time."

"Ah, and there's the problem! You get an idea and walk right into danger."

"What about going to Virginia?" she asked. "You think it can really help? Don't you have all the police files?"

"If we can't really figure out what he's doing with his display, it's best to know everything we can about the victims."

"Yes."

She pulled back. "Are you thinking about me going on your trip to Virginia?"

"I am. You and your training—and your gut—may be of great help."

"And that will keep me off the streets, right?"

"A two-pronged win," he told her.

"Craig…"

"Ah, well, it's night now, and there's nothing we can do but try to relieve some of the tension," he said, his fingers moving over her cheek, over her throat and down to her breast.

"Tension, huh? I'll show you tension," she said softly, and she moved against him. She meant to tease and torment him, her touch running intimately down his abdomen. But as she teased, he suddenly made a move, lifting her high above him, then bringing her down slowly against him.

She laughed and kissed him and whispered softly, "You know, one of us will wind up bruised to pieces if we try—"

"I have no intention of trying anything with a hard sink and slippery tile," he assured her, holding her to him as he walked back out to the bedroom with her, her legs curled about his waist, her arms around his shoulders. He eased her down to the bed, slid his damp form next to hers, caught her fingers within his and drew them above her head. He kissed her then, and she felt the force of his body and the rise of his erection against her flesh, and for a few moments, she forgot about the world. She loved his body, everything about him, and loved the way he moved when she touched him, loved the intake of his breath and, maybe most of all, she loved the look in his eyes when they came together at last, when he thrust into her, and it seemed that they were all but one.

The day had been long, offering so much that was ugly in the world.

But the night was long as well, offering a great deal of what was beautiful.

A young employee named Marty Wallace was Craig's favorite tech. Barely into his twenties, Marty had a way with video footage, computer cryptology, cell phones and more that made him an indispensable asset, in Craig's mind.

Mike perched on Marty's desk; Craig stood by as Marty opened his computer screen to show him the calls that Kevin Finnegan had made from his cell phone.

"There—that would be Jeannette Gilbert's private number," he said. "Calls to and from Kevin Finnegan start about six months ago and end the day before her disappearance was announced. I've got transcripts of the voice messages she left him. Last message is right here. 'Love you, Irish. Miss you every time we're apart. We've made the six months mark—six to go, and I guess we're the real deal. Listen, if something good comes up in the next few weeks, take it. Oswald has a cool idea for publicity. I may be really busy. Know that I'm thinking of you.'" He paused a minute and looked up, flushing.

"There's more?" Mike asked.

"Yeah."

"Well, then, go on," Craig said.

Marty flushed, sighed and turned back to his computer screen.

"'I'll be thinking of you hot and wet and naked...and thinking of how hot and wet I'm going to be when we meet up again. Okay, that was to tantalize. I do love you, Irish.'"

"Poor Kevin," Mike murmured.

"So, that Westwood guy was full of it, huh?" Marty asked.

"I'm thinking so," Mike said.

"I mean, unless she was into a lot of guys," Marty said. "She never gave that impression, though. You know how so many pop stars faked... Well, you know, that thing what's her name did on that music awards show that was so slutty and dirty. Kids watch that stuff, and she got down and kind of grossly sexual. Jeannette wouldn't have done that. Gotta admit, I go to a lot of movies and music venues and...yeah, I read the entertainment mags. You never got anything like that about Jeannette Gilbert. She was sensual, you know? But classy. That's how she came across. Man, you fell in love with her."

"I'm sure that's what you were thinking," Mike teased.

Marty flushed again. He was a nerd, a great one, but very shy, and he didn't date often.

"You're missing the point. You really did kind of fall in love with her in a more ethereal way. To be crude, hell, yeah, most guys would want to bang her. That doesn't sound right for the office, but...best way I can explain it. But with her... you kind of admired her, too. You'd want to bang her and then bring her home to Mom."

"I guess that's a little more charming," Mike said.

"What about Sadie Miller?" Craig asked. "Any calls on Kevin's phone to her?"

"Nope. A ton to Finnegan's, to his siblings, to his agent, to a music director, to his actor friends. That's it."

"Seems like Kevin is telling the truth and nothing but the truth," Mike said.

"Give me a printout, will you, Marty? I want to make sure that Larry McBride has this. I don't want him to think that anyone in the office is protecting anyone in the Finnegan family," Craig said.

"You got it," Marty promised him.

Craig pulled his phone, and Mike lifted an eyebrow to him.

"I'm calling Oswald Martin. I want to know just what his publicity plan had been—whatever it was that Jeannette was talking about when she called and left that message for Kevin."

"I can really get them back? You think that I can really get my children back?" Susie Grace said, a smile beaming across her entire face.

The worn-looking young woman had been seeing Kieran for six weeks.

The man with whom she'd been involved would remain locked up for at least a year on a drug charge.

Susie had been in a rehab facility. The court had determined—through her medical doctor and therapy—that Susie deserved another chance. She'd failed at beating her addiction because she'd fallen for the man who'd supplied her and made sure to give her a push back down every time she'd gotten clean.

Susie had thought she'd met a great guy—a doctor, a man to adore her eight-year-old twins and a man who took her to nice places for dinner. No one knew the real man, until his ex-wife told them his sexual tastes had included a few prac-

tices considered deviant by most. Susie hadn't been aware of
what he did to her once he'd drugged her to sleep, not until
she'd screamed in a waking haze and one of her daughters
had dialed 9-1-1.

She was a sweet woman whose husband had died while
serving in the military. After losing him she'd been like a babe
in the woods, susceptible and easily manipulated.

It really could be an ugly world. Of course, Kieran realized,
she had chosen to work with ugliness when she had signed
on with Fuller and Miro, with their work on criminal cases.

But there were good things in this kind of work, too—
like seeing Susie's face when she said, "You're really going
to get your kids back. Dr. Miro spoke with your caseworker
at Child Services this morning. You know the terms of your
probation. You have to remember to go to your meetings,
and you have to see me once a week for the next six months.
You're going to be able to do that, right?" Kieran asked her.

"Oh, Kieran, no problem, no problem whatsoever!" Susie
promised. She fell silent. "And…I really don't hear voices
anymore."

The drugs in her body had caused Susie to believe that she
was hearing the furniture talk to her.

"I'm glad. You know that you were never crazy. Hearing
voices can be the result of many of the drugs he had you on."

"I know," Susie said. She shivered suddenly. Then she
laughed. "Well, I am a scaredy-cat. I got it in my head to
better myself and get to know the city better during my time
of seeing you and straightening out. I took a tour of the East
Village."

"Nice. I live there. I love the East Village."

"Oh, I know! It's the way you talk about it that made me
want to go. You made it sound so artsy. I know that you live

there, but did you know that the East Village was once a farm that had been deeded to Peter Stuyvesant?"

Kieran did know, but Susie's enthusiasm was great, and she let her keep talking.

"It was also known as Little Germany at one time. I learned so much cool old history. And new history. Can you have new history? I guess today is history tomorrow. But, anyway, I did love the tour. It was so interesting. Writers and artists flocked there and..." Susie's voice suddenly faded, and a worried frown set into her brow.

"And?"

Susie lifted her shoulders and grimaced. "I took a ghost tour—shouldn't have. It included stories about Stuyvesant, Joe Papp, Washington Irving and Edgar Allan Poe. By the time I left, I thought I heard someone moaning at one point!" She shivered. "Oh, I shouldn't have told you that! Really, I'm not hearing voices. I just creeped myself out."

"Don't worry, Susie, you should tell me everything and anything," Kieran said. "And don't worry. I've turned the wind into moans in a few places, too. And I live above a karaoke bar. Talk about moaning."

Susie managed a real smile.

"Honestly," Kieran continued, "I know how much you love your children. I don't believe you'd even want them home with you again if you weren't ready." She stood up from her desk. "A ghost tour is one thing, Susie. If you hear voices in your head when you're having your morning coffee, call me right away."

"I will, I promise."

Susie hugged her fiercely, and Kieran returned the embrace but quickly told her, "Hey, I'm just the therapist. Thank Dr. Miro. She's the one who decided that you're really ready."

With tears in her eyes, Susie nodded and headed out of the office. She caught Dr. Fuller in the hallway, coming to Kieran's office.

He hadn't been her doctor, but she hugged him anyway and he wished her well.

He walked into Kieran's office, smiling. "Susie loves you, Kieran. She really loves you."

"She loves you, too," Kieran said.

He grinned and took the chair in front of the Kieran's desk that Susie had just vacated. "We're really so happy to have you, you know."

"I'm happy to be here."

"You have another appointment?"

"Paperwork for the state. Our assessments on three cases."

"Oh, good." He settled in as if that meant she had no work.

"I just keep thinking," he said. "Well, we're going to have a meeting this afternoon with the Feds. They've sent a behavioral scientist up from Quantico to go over our notes with us. I think that Assistant Director Egan was afraid we'd be offended. Of course, we're not. Just as you need every cop and agent out there, you can use every scientific mind available. Oh, sorry. I'm talking the Jeannette Gilbert case, of course."

"Of course."

"How did you stumble upon that other victim?" Dr. Fuller asked her.

"You just said it. I stumbled."

"But...how did you know where to go?"

"I didn't. I was looking at cemeteries and graveyards. Danny is a tour guide. He told me about the Huntington mansion, and that, actually, there are grave sites all over the city we don't really know much about."

"And tons that we do know about," Dr. Fuller said.

"They're asking all the religious heads around the city to check their catacombs, crypts and graveyards," Kieran told him. "And the groundskeepers and directors at all the non-denominational cemeteries and grave sites."

"Good, I think it's going to be important. What's disturbing me now is...well, that poor young woman who's missing. The more time that passes, the less chance she has of being alive. If only we knew... You don't know more than I do, right?" he asked.

"About what in particular?"

"The dead women. Do they know if they were killed right when they disappeared?"

She shook her head. "I only know that the medical examiner believed Jeannette Gilbert to have been dead ten days to two weeks before she was found. The most recent victim— the young woman from yesterday—was almost mummified in a strange way. I doubt they'll be able to pinpoint the exact time of death."

"I just can't stop thinking about this case," he said. "Of course, every other minute now, a station is showing the life of Jeannette Gilbert. The girl was famous before, but now... well, she'll always be young and beautiful, right? What's so sad, too, is that it seemed she was lovely in every way, kind and generous. I've read the files on the other two known victims. Kind, compassionate, smart young women, as well. Not that you want anything so horrible to happen to anyone, but it's truly tragic that such wonderful people should be lost so young. Well, anyway, Dr. Miro and I are headed over to the FBI offices soon. I keep feeling that I should be able to put my finger on something—identify what this person is after with a clearer picture. There's something at the back of my mind I just can't clearly define. Well, we'll see. Three heads will be better than one. Oh, listen, we won't be back in. And with all you went through this weekend, feel free to leave after your last appointment."

He smiled and left her office.

Kieran turned to her paperwork. She should be happy. It seemed she had made someone's life better.

She couldn't stop thinking about Sadie Miller.

CHAPTER
ELEVEN

"I DON'T *MIND* IT, PER SE—THIS PROFILING. I MEAN, HELL, bring on the mediums and the séance people. Whatever works. I'm just not a big believer in criminal profiling. The FBI helped us once years back, told us the killer would be a white male of a certain age and of a certain intelligence, probably a blue-collar worker. Turned out a jealous woman was stabbing her friends," Larry McBride said, shrugging. "Now, Ms. Finnegan, I don't mind her around. Or, for that matter, that Dr. Fuller."

"It's just another tool, and, honestly, it often helps," Craig told him.

"As I said, maybe," McBride said. He was sitting across the table from Craig and Mike as they awaited the arrival of Professor Digby. "Gut—it's what cops have worked on forever. And you'd be a liar if you were to tell me anything different. Besides, so far, I can't see how they've told us anything we hadn't figured already. Obviously, no grease monkey is doing this—the girls are too clean. They're quickly killed.

They're laid out gently." He shook his head. "I can already imagine what they're going to tell us. He's between the ages of twenty-four and thirty-eight. He lives alone—or with an incapacitated parent or someone he looks after. He probably has access to his own basement. Where else would he hide girls once he's taken them until he's laid them out?"

Craig was only half listening to McBride.

The detective was frustrated. So were they all.

The case was going nowhere.

True to his word, Oswald Martin had sent over his notes on his upcoming plan for Jeannette Gilbert. There had been nothing in it about a disappearance. Oswald had been making arrangements for Jeannette to start a reading program at a number of hospitals in the tristate area. He wanted to show her as a leader in the community, in a different light as she used her celebrity to make a positive impact. There would have been little time for her to do anything else in the busy days he'd booked, and she'd no doubt have had the press dogging her all the way—which was, of course, the plan. But until it happened, Oswald Martin had been keeping it secret.

Kevin Finnegan hadn't lied; Oswald Martin hadn't lied. When the complete plan had arrived in Craig's email, he'd had Marty verify every appearance that had been planned.

There was no way out of it. Finding this killer could take days, months, years.

The thing was, a young woman was still missing.

And they'd take any help they could get to track her would-be killer. Including profilers.

Craig rose when he saw a young agent escorting Digby into the room. He appeared to be bewildered.

But, then, Digby often appeared to be bewildered. Maybe it was simply the way he looked.

"Thank you for coming down, Professor," he said.

Mike and McBride had risen, as well.

"Well, sure," the professor said, taking the chair they indicated for them. "You fellows should have just come to the site. Other folks who might remember things are there all the time. Roger Gleason must think an old pair of nerdy professors are suddenly going to go off with his fine wines or something, because he's there every day. Willoughby is a historian—he has things in his head that would never occur to me. A virtual volume of information, he is. And John Shaw, of course. John found Ms. Gilbert. Even the grad students. Pretty good crew we've got working on this." He offered a weak half grin to them. "Don't make a lot of money, you know, investigating the past, documenting the dead and old death practices."

"Sometimes it's good to have you all together. Sometimes it's good to see if you can remember things that aren't in the collective mind," Craig said. "I'm just curious as to why the place bothers you so much. You do go into work every day, right? But we see the others chilling out with a beer or a drink or having some food at Finnegan's. They say you head right home."

"Yes, I do," Digby said solemnly. "Maybe it's the rats. Maybe it's the walls themselves. Maybe it's still the idea that poor Ms. Gilbert was there. I don't know. I don't like the place. I know that every day Gleason is up there in his office. I know that Willoughby comes and goes. He has meetings with all his uptown blue bloods now and then, which is a good thing. Without some money going into it, no one would care about our precious past. But as for me…"

"What?" McBride asked.

"You can't go telling the others. I'll be a laughingstock," Digby said.

"This is for this office, for our ears only," Craig assured him.

"Like I said, I hear things all day down there. The crypt is a big one, stretches out pretty far. There are rows in it of what is basically shelving or something like bookcases for the dead. And you have the tombs that line the floor, back walls and side walls. When I'm moving down the lines or that shelving, recording data, I don't like it. You know that thing people say—you get a shiver when someone is walking over your grave? I feel that way when I'm down there."

"I visited the catacombs in Paris," McBride told him. "My wife wanted to go. Me? I see enough dead. But I know what you mean."

"Except that I'm always in places like the catacombs of Paris, and I'm usually fine," Digby said.

"Where have you traveled most recently, Professor? Have you been in the country for the last year or so?" Mike asked, making it sound more like an interested, work-related question than one that would be voiced in an interrogation.

Digby's face lit up. "No, funny that Detective McBride mentioned Paris. The university sent me out there to investigate an unbelievable site—the discovery of what we believe to be old bones and artifacts from the Hundred Years' War. Carbon testing is still going on, but it was unbelievable! Story has it that one side or the other massacred a whole village. History! It's told by the victors, so they say, and it's for us to tell the truth."

"Sounds wonderful, Professor," Craig said. "How long were you there?"

"Almost a year. Just made it back about a month ago," Digby told them. "The university was wonderful about it, but then, of course, the prestige of having a professor involved in such a find is quite something in the academic field—not to mention, of course, what I'll publish when the results are in."

"That's wonderful," Mike said, trying to keep the enthusiasm in his voice.

And of course they were all thinking the same thing: they'd verify what Digby was telling them, but if he'd been in Paris for a year, it was hardly likely that he'd hopped back to kill a girl in Virginia.

"You mentioned something about the floor to me when we were talking before," Craig told him. "That it was too clean, that it didn't seem to have the film on it that very old things usually seemed to have."

"Yes, I did say that. I don't know how to explain it... Maybe it's just an older man's mind on a place he doesn't much like." He shrugged and offered them another crooked smile. "Maybe a Victorian maid was down there at some point!"

He laughed at his own joke.

They all laughed with him.

They thanked him for coming, and he was escorted out.

"Well, one down, at least," McBride said. He looked over at Craig and Mike.

Craig leaned forward and hit the intercom, asking that Dr. Anthony Andrews be called. Soon, the ME's voice came over the speaker system.

"What did you find? Any ID on the body yet?" Craig asked.

"Not yet. She wasn't in any fingerprint system. We're looking at dental charts now."

"What did you find about cause of death?"

"Same situation, gentlemen. A quick stab to the heart. She was killed elsewhere, cleaned up, dressed up and laid out."

"How the bloody hell does someone walk down a city

street and get a body down into an unknown crypt without
being seen?" McBride muttered.

"Downtown can be quiet," Mike said. "Especially in the
dead of night. You know that thing about New York City
never sleeping? Not true—it's actually not easy to find an
all-night diner."

"There's one near Penn Station and one near Lexington,"
McBride offered in response to Mike's remark. Then he went
back to what he was saying. "What was I thinking? Hell,
there's a shoot-out in the street in broad daylight and no one
sees a damned thing. Why was I expecting someone to notice a guy walking around with a corpse?"

Craig brought the conversation back to the point of his
call to the ME. "Dr. Andrews, how long had she been down
there? When did she die?"

"Four years, gentlemen, give or take a few months. From
what you've told me, our young lady in Jersey was killed
about five years ago. You have a woman who died in Virginia six months ago...and now Ms. Gilbert. And now a
missing woman."

"He's speeding up," Craig said, and he stood restlessly. "We
have to find this guy. We have to find him and stop him."

"If he's speeding up, he'll make a mistake. He'll make a
mistake, and we'll get him," Mike said.

"Yes, I believe we will, but...how many will die first?"
Craig asked.

Mike didn't answer.

There was a tap at the door. Craig glanced over to see that
one of their new young associates was hovering there.

He had brought Brent Westwood in.

"Mr. Westwood," Craig said, ushering him into the room.

"I came in right away. I told you about Jeannette. I told you about working on a movie when she disappeared. I—I don't have anything else to say," the actor told them.

When they'd first met him, he'd been full of emotion and bravado. Now he looked uncomfortable.

"Sit down, Mr. Westwood. We have reason to believe that you lied to us," Craig said.

"Yes, sit," Mike told him, and smiled.

Westwood looked flushed—and guilty. "I told you about the movie. You can check with the director. I was upstate—with no chance of coming back down here. I loved Jeannette—"

"But Jeannette didn't love you," Craig said.

"What? She—she did! How could you know Jeannette's feelings? I'm telling you—"

"Do you know, Mr. Westwood, your lie could lead us to prosecuting you for hindering an investigation?" Mike asked.

"She did care about me!" Westwood protested.

"No. You weren't the man she was referring to when she spoke about her mystery lover," Mike said.

"How dare you!" Westwood blustered.

"I say we arrest him now," Craig said.

"Arrest me!"

"He could tell the truth," Mike said.

"You can't know her feelings—" Westwood began.

"You never slept with her," Craig said quietly.

Westwood's mouth worked; his eyes flicked to the side. He didn't know what they knew—and didn't know what science might have told them. Of course, they had no way of knowing if Westwood had ever had intimate relations with Jeannette Gilbert. But Westwood apparently didn't know that.

"Our relationship was far higher than such graphic intimacy. You don't understand. We talked. I didn't take advantage of her—"

"And you weren't her mystery lover," Craig said. "She was a young woman, Westwood. When she was truly in love with someone, it meant physical love for her, as well."

"You didn't know her!" Westwood said.

"Ah, but we know people who did. People who knew her very well."

Westwood looked away again. "There might have been someone else in her life."

"I'm going to get some coffee, Mr. Westwood," Craig said. "Would you like some?" He smiled. "You're going to be here for a while."

Kieran had worked through the lunch hour and was just perusing the take-out menus they kept in the office when she was startled by a buzz on her intercom from their receptionist and bookkeeper.

"You have a visitor."

"Who is it? Send him on back."

"He's already on his way. It's your brother."

She looked up. Danny was in the doorway. He walked in and plopped down in the chair in front of her desk.

"Hey, sis. We can go and eat real food, you know," he said, glancing at the menus.

"You came to eat lunch with me?" she asked him.

"I just finished with a tour," he told her. "I was kind of in the neighborhood. Well, not really. But you got me thinking."

"How nice."

He grinned at her. "About old graveyards and the forgotten dead in the city."

"I see."

Kieran arched a brow at him. She'd kind of promised Craig

that she wouldn't go prowling around graveyards and crypts anymore.

But there was still a missing woman out there.

She leaned toward her brother. "Okay, so…"

"I know of a few other places."

"And we can tell Craig about them."

"Yes, we could. Meanwhile, I'm feeling the need for a beer. A dark beer."

"We carry plenty at Finnegan's."

"Yeah, well, I was thinking of a subway jaunt down to the East Village. McSorley's."

McSorley's Old Ale House had a claim to being the oldest Irish tavern in New York. None of the Finnegans had ever decided to contest that fact, more because they had always operated as a true pub—with an extensive food menu. McSorley's had also had the motto "Good ale, raw onions and no ladies!" until a 1970 ruling decided the "no ladies" part had to go. While Kieran knew there had been years when there had been "the ladies room" at Finnegan's, they'd always been a more family-oriented institution.

She loved McSorley's; it was one of the few remnants of Civil War–era New York still in business.

"Okay, so what's in the East Village, Danny?" she asked, wise to her brother.

"Just come to lunch with me," Danny said, and grinned. "That way, we're both innocent!"

Kieran rose, sliding the menus into her desk. "Let's go."

They hopped the subway and headed to the East Village. As Danny quickly led the way, Kieran hurried to follow after him.

"Where are you really taking me?" she asked him. "The Marble Cemeteries are both down here, I know, but—"

"Lunch, Kieran, lunch! I'm starving!" Danny said.

True to his word, Danny took her to McSorley's. He got a dark beer; Kieran opted for water. He chose the hash and she opted for the cheese plate—just cheese and a packet of crackers along with onions.

Onions came with just about everything at McSorley's.

The place was a dive bar, and nothing had been taken from the walls since the early twentieth century. There was a pair of Houdini's handcuffs at the bar. Kieran had liked to come with friends and imagine those who had come before—soldiers heading off to wars, early businessmen deliberating deals and the advent of the 1970s and the first women to grace the tables.

"This is real New York!" Danny said. "You know that Poe lived and worked here, right?"

"Yes, Danny."

"Well, he had a bit of a rivalry going with a poor fellow who was only published in any major way long after he was dead, back in the 1950s. Typical story. Great writer named Dirk Der Vere. Old Dutch, I'm guessing. Anyway, the fellow wrote tragic, haunting tales, but he was a major laudanum freak and alcoholic. Fought with every publisher everywhere—and so most of his work wound up in family chests that only came to light in the last century."

"Sad, very sad. And?" Kieran asked.

"His family was wealthy, which, I supposed, led to the man's ability to wallow in his addictions. Anyway, he died young."

"Again, very sad."

"He died about two blocks from here, and there's a tiny graveyard that's about a four-by-ten sliver of dead grass at the back side of the house."

"And you want to trespass?"

"You can see it from the street."

"We're going to see a gravestone from the street?"

Danny shrugged. "I thought I should get you out of the office. And I did want to come to McSorley's—and I didn't want to come alone."

"Okay." Kieran fell silent. She knew that Danny had finally realized that he was actually in love with her oldest friend— and family friend—Julie Benton. But Julie had gone through a horrible divorce, not to mention a part in the diamonds heists a ways back, and had taken off to spend time with her family in Maine. Danny was not the kind of man to look elsewhere when his heart was in Maine. Kieran wasn't sure that he'd admitted his feelings to himself, and she was sure he'd never said anything to Julie.

But that did leave his big sister as his best possible companion. So she went along with him.

"Funny, really," Kieran said.

"What's that?"

"One of our patients who was just in the office said she went on a ghost tour down here and loved it—but scared herself into hearing things."

"Easy to do. I wouldn't mind leading ghost tours here. The area is really great," Danny said. "There are all kinds of tales about Houdini and Poe from around here. A good guide or storyteller could certainly make a few people see ghosts. The little graveyard, though, that's sad to me."

"Let's go see it," she said.

They paid their bill at McSorley's Old Ale House and headed down Seventh Street. Then Danny made a few twists and turns and they were there. Many of the buildings in the area were Civil War vintage, but the one Danny walked her by stood out among the rest. It still had a tiny front lawn and steps that led up to a Victorian-era porch. The sign above the door, however, read Braden and Sons, Fine and Vintage Photography.

"I think I'll just ask if we can take a peak," Kieran said.

"Go ahead. Ruin all the fun!" Danny said.

She ignored him and headed inside to a desk where a man in a bow tie, vest and rolled-up sleeves was speaking with a woman before the old-fashioned counter. She was obviously pleased with her purchase, oohing and aahing about the wonderful way her son looked in a Yankee drummer boy uniform. Obviously, in this studio, people were photographed in historic costumes.

Kieran waited patiently. When it was her turn, the clerk greeted her with a smile. "Hi! Let's see…you could be a great Rose O'Neal Greenhow! Or better yet, my personal favorite, Pauline Cushman! She was really beautiful. Honestly, I'm not sucking up or anything, but I can just imagine you in a fine Victorian dress… Cushman worked her way into being such a fine spy by giving a toast to Jefferson Davis. She was an actress, and I'll bet she was excellent!"

"No, no, I'm not here for a picture."

"Why not?" Danny said. "You'd be great!"

"And you, sir? Will you be in it? Is this a romantic trip to New York City for you both? Oh, God, no—sorry! Look at you. You two are related, right?" the clerk asked.

"Brother and sister," Kieran said. "And really we're—"

"We're both huge history buffs," Danny interjected, then he turned to his sister. "Go for it, Kieran!"

She glared at him. "Only if you do, too, brother dear!"

Danny grinned and turned to the clerk. "Irish Brigade, of course, my good man!"

"Come, then! My dad started this business back in 1970—

his dad bought the place in 1946, right after World War II. Nice when you keep a family business going. I'm Nat Braden, by the way."

Nat led them to the back where there were scores of costumes to choose from. As he and Danny went enthusiastically into choosing the right outfit for her, Kieran's cell began to ring.

It was Craig.

She winced. She thought about not answering, but she had to.

"Hey," she said. "Anything new?"

"Digby is innocent."

"I didn't know he was a suspect."

"Everyone is a suspect."

Danny let out a whoop of pleasure at something he was being shown.

"Where are you?" Craig asked.

"Uh, in the East Village. Danny wanted to eat at McSorley's."

"Are you still eating? I'll join you."

"No, actually we were just walking and..."

"Sixty-Ninth New York State Militia," Nat said, and Danny let out another whoop.

"Where are you, Kieran?" Craig asked, no doubt having heard the voices.

"We got it into our heads to have period pictures made," she said.

"Which shop?"

Wincing, she told him and hung up.

Danny looked at her.

"Craig's on his way," she said.

"Oh. Oh, well, we are just having pictures made," Danny said.

Nat Braden frowned. "What else were you up to?"

"To be honest," Danny said, "I was just going to show my sister the old gravestone at the back side of the property."

"Oh, well, we'll finish up the pictures, and I'll take you out there!" Nat said, smiling again.

"Great," Kieran murmured.

By the time she was dressed up—and Danny and Nat had helped her choose the appropriate ridiculously large and flowered hat—Craig had arrived.

Naturally, suspicion was written all over his face. And then, of course, as he looked at Kieran, confusion took over.

"Fuller and Miro are down at the office," Craig said to Kieran. "But…I thought this was a workday for you."

"Lunch," she said.

"Which would have been about two hours ago." His eyes raked her. "I had no clue that you were into vintage photography," he said.

Nat Braden came around from the picture set and looked at Craig. "Joshua Chamberlain—young and dashing and the hero of Gettysburg! Oh, sorry—are you from the South?"

"No, thanks, I'm not here for a Civil War picture."

"How about a mobster?" Nat said enthusiastically.

Craig lowered his head, actually grinning. "No, I'm just here to catch up with these two."

"So you want to see the grave, too!" Nat said. "Sure, my pleasure."

Craig turned his gaze on Kieran, who held up her hands. "We were just going to walk by to see the stone," she said.

"Sad story," Danny began. "It's like that grave for that poor little kid who died at the end of the 1700s, only this one is later, around 1840, or something like that. New York is strange like that—odd little graves here and there with great historical stories to go with them."

"Ah," Craig murmured.

"I'll show you as soon as we've finished up here," Nat said.

"Waiting with bated breath," Craig said quietly.

And so, Nat began to shoot pictures.

Kieran felt the heat waves of anger washing off Craig as he watched. She posed quickly and demurred quickly when Nat offered to shoot more in other costumes for free.

Next up was Danny.

She stood next to Craig. He felt like an inferno, and he made no move to touch her.

Finally, the shoot was done. Nat called to his brother, Hank, in the back, and told him they were heading out to the yard.

It was truly just a sliver of ground. A large marble stone was there, with the remnants of a smaller stone encased in the marble and a little historic plaque beneath the old headstone: "Here lie the earthly remains of Dirk Der Vere, poet, author, passed this life on March 3, 1841, at the age of 27 years, 3 months and 5 days. The Der Vere family owned the property for nearly two centuries, becoming British when New Amsterdam became New York, and Patriots at the time of the American Revolution."

"It's just a stone, a memorial," Danny said.

"I wonder if the guide told your story about the poor author who wasn't published until he'd been dead forever," Kieran murmured. She looked at Craig and shrugged. "I do counseling with a young woman who just took the ghost tour down here. She was convinced that she heard moaning."

Craig stared at her and frowned. "Moaning?"

"She was on a ghost tour, and I don't even know exactly where, though I assume that the guides would come by here," Kieran said.

"Sure, they go by here," Nat said. "It's an old place with a lots of history. But moaning? I've heard people shriek on those ghost tours."

Craig wasn't amused. He turned to Nat. "Is there a crypt here?"

"Um, not that I know about," Nat told them. "There's a basement," he offered brightly.

"Could we see the basement?" Craig asked.

"Oh, well, I mean, we may have more business now, and my brother and I run this place together, and it's not a big deal to come out in the yard—if you can call this a yard—but..."

His voice trailed off, till Craig showed his badge.

"FBI!" Nat said, his eyes widening. "What would the FBI— Oh! Oh, this is about the dead girls. I don't have any dead girls in the basement, I swear it! I swear on my mother's life!"

"Mr. Braden, I don't think you have a dead body in your basement, but I would love to see it," Craig told him.

"Okay," Nat said slowly. "But why?"

"The family owned this property for over two centuries. Dirk Der Vere is buried here. I'm thinking there might also be an underground crypt, long forgotten," Craig said.

"Of course, of course, if it could help...yeah, but it's just a basement. Come on, follow me!"

Nat headed back in. They went around the front of the shop—where Hank now stood, a slightly older version of Nat—and through to the kitchen. The stairs to the basement were there.

Nat turned on lights.

It was a finished basement, filled with photography equipment and trunks of costumes and props. Craig walked around the whole of it.

"See, just a basement," Nat said.

Hank chose that moment to come down the stairs. "What the hell is going on?" he demanded.

While Danny explained to Hank, Craig walked to the wall closest to the sliver of grass that held the grave marker. He pulled boxes from the area to discover a two-by-four-foot rusted grate in the ground.

"Where does that lead?" he demanded, looking at Nat.

"Hell if I know. It's a grate. I thought it was ventilation or whatever," Nat said.

Craig glared across the room at Hank, who shook his head, now wide-eyed with wonder. "I don't know. We've never had need to touch it. There are always boxes piled up there. Even when my dad and granddad were alive. It's just a grate. Who opens a grate into the ground?"

"Someone," Craig said softly. He reached for the grate. It pulled out easily into his hands and led to what appeared to be a tunnel in the earth.

"You got a good flashlight?" he asked Nat.

"Yeah, yeah, we got a flashlight," Nat said.

He and Hank turned into one another in their efforts to procure a flashlight.

As they scurried about, Craig asked, "Is there any other entrance to the basement?"

"A delivery door, just there, at the end toward the back," Nat said, stopping.

Kieran walked over to the area Nat had indicated. She could see a fold-up ladder and latch opening to the back of the yard.

She turned back as Craig was heading into the tunnel. She started to follow him. He stopped, cracking his head where he'd bent to enter the shaft that could only be accessed by bending over.

"No. You stay!"

She let out a breath and nodded. He was FBI; she was not.

They all waited—her, Danny, Nat and Hank—as Craig disappeared.

"I don't believe this," Hank whispered. "All these years..."

"It's possible that it's just a hole in the earth," Nat said. "Or, maybe we have a historic find right here! That will help business. I mean, we're doing all right, but...wow! How cool would historic photos be at a place where a real historic find occurred?"

Both brothers looked hopeful for a minute.

But then they heard Craig's voice, shouting from the tunnel. "Help me!"

"Craig! Are you all right?" Kieran called.

Craig's voice came to them again. "Dial 9-1-1! Get an ambulance—fast!"

Kieran fumbled for her phone and dialed 9-1-1. As she did, Danny hurried forward to help Craig.

He was awkwardly emerging from the tunnel, bent over and moving with difficulty.

He was bringing with him the dirt-covered body of a young woman.

Sadie Miller? Had they found Sadie Miller?

"Is she...d-dead?" Nat asked in horror.

CHAPTER
TWELVE

"LORAZEPAM," DR. FREDERICK DAVIES SAID. "AND ROHYP-
nol. High dosages were found in her system. She's going to
pull through. Quite a miracle when you consider that the
young woman was underground for several days, deprived
of food and water. She's come around a bit here and there as
we've treated her."

Lorazepam. And Rohypnol.

The same substances Andrews had found in the body of
Jeannette Gilbert.

"And is she conscious now?" Craig asked anxiously. He'd
waited outside the emergency room doors for what seemed
like endless hours, but had been less than a full sixty minutes. He'd wanted to burst his way into the ER where she
was being treated, praying that she'd say something.

But there were few people fiercer than those in health care
when they were desperate to save a life. And, of course, she'd
been out cold when they'd gotten to the hospital.

He had been allowed in the ambulance, behind the EMT.

The whole way there each traffic snarl had weighed on his nerves; he'd wanted to get out of the ambulance and punch the drivers of a few nonmoving vehicles.

He'd gotten hold of Egan and Mike while in the ambulance. They'd assured him that a forensic team had been sent to the shop, but they'd gone in quietly, and while Craig knew that the news would be out that Sadie Miller had been found, he was hoping that Egan had managed to keep the where and the how of their discovery away from the media for the time being.

"Hey," Mike said quietly, patiently, placing a hand on his shoulder.

Mike had set things into motion at the photography shop, warning the brothers to keep quiet, unless, of course, they wanted to wind up suspects themselves.

He'd left the forensic crew working and come to hospital.

Kieran and Danny had followed in a taxi as quickly as possible; the two were in the waiting room, sipping bad coffee.

He'd wanted them to go home; but the simple fact was that Sadie Miller wouldn't have been found if Kieran and Danny hadn't gone exploring, if Kieran's words about her therapy patient hadn't sparked something in his mind.

They deserved to be there.

He reined in his thoughts and focused on what Dr. Davies was saying. "The patient is sleeping heavily, in what we consider a good sleep. She's not in a coma. But what I'm trying to warn you is that she was dosed with a sedative known for causing short-term memory loss."

"Yes, I've heard that the drug can cause memory loss."

"We can get lucky. She might know what happened…she might not. And dogging her with questions won't change that."

"Dr. Davies," Mike said, "my partner and I have been at

this for a while. We understand fully that a woman's life and well-being are of the utmost importance."

"Yes," Craig said. "We understand. But may I sit with her?"

"You may. Right now she's being transferred to ICU."

"Thank you, Doctor," Craig said.

He turned. Kieran and Danny had risen and come to him. "I'll be here awhile," he said quietly.

Wide-eyed and solemn, Kieran nodded. "Of course. You'll call me right away when she wakes up, right?"

He nodded.

He prayed that by some miracle, the doctor was wrong, that Sadie Miller would wake up with a perfect memory and she would immediately give him the name of her abductor.

In a perfect world...

Perfect.

He looked at Kieran with her finely honed features, huge blue eyes and wealth of auburn hair. She'd been dressed for work, but somehow the pin-striped and skirted business suit she wore seemed to do nothing but complement her willowy form.

He lowered his head, not wanting her to see the look in his eyes.

New York had tons of beautiful woman. There was no reason to fear for her in particular. She wasn't a fool; she wouldn't head out to meet with someone when she knew that the victims had been tricked. The killer didn't come in with guns blazing; he somehow finessed his victims to his will.

Her hand fell gently on his arm. "We'll head to Finnegan's."

"Yes, and if you're here late, I'll stay with Kieran," Danny told him. "At her place."

"Thanks," he said.

"I'm going to head in and call McBride. We'll get an officer on duty outside the ICU," Mike said.

Craig nodded.

Good call. It was entirely possible the killer would start checking hospitals, wanting to come back and finish her off before she could talk.

"She has to be in here under a different name," he told Mike. "And we should let 'slip' that she's at a different hospital, somewhere in Brooklyn or the Bronx."

"I'll see to it," Mike promised. He turned to Kieran and Danny. "I have a car here. Wait a few more minutes, and I'll drop you at Finnegan's."

"Excellent," Danny said.

Craig looked at Kieran one more time. She offered him a semismile, and her voice was soft when she spoke. "She's alive, Craig. She's going to make it."

He allowed himself a smile in return. "Yes, but..."

"But?"

"I asked you to avoid graveyards."

"Hey, I had lunch with my brother, and it was actually my neighborhood. I didn't go into a crypt—you did. And she's alive, Craig."

"Yes, and I'm grateful and it's a damned good day. But..."

"But what?"

"If something were to happen to you, none of it would matter to me."

He turned before she could reply. Dr. Davies was waiting for him. He followed the physician as he led the way to intensive care.

Once he was in the room, a nurse gave him a chair. She was a small, young woman with a fierce attitude, and she warned Craig that she could see him through the glass from the desk. "Call me when the young lady wakes up. Do not barrage her with questions."

"Yes," Craig said simply.

The nurse smiled at him. "I heard you saved her life."

"Not me—a number of people in the right place at the right time," he said.

She left him to sit and watch over Sadie Miller.

Sadie had an IV going into her system. Her face was pale; even her lips were a chalky color. Still, she presented a picture as beautiful as could be imagined.

Perfect.

The word haunted him.

He was still watching her an hour later when he felt the vibration of his phone. He stepped out and told the nurse he was going to the hallway.

It was Mike calling him.

"The newspaper called with what we all believe is a real missive from our killer," Mike said.

"Oh?"

"He wrote a letter—old-fashioned letter. It's written on common paper bought at any drugstore, grocery store or other around the country. Naturally, forensic teams are on it now, hoping against hope for saliva on the envelope, fingerprints... Anyway, want to hear what's written?"

"Mike, yes, dammit—"

"'Death, that hath suck'd the honey of thy breath, hath had no power yet upon thy beauty: Thou art not conquer'd; beauty's ensign yet is crimson in thy lips and in thy cheeks, and death's pale flag is not advanced there.'" Mike paused, then asked, "Do you know what that is?"

"Sounds like Shakespeare."

"It is. From *Romeo and Juliet*," Mike said. "Gotta admit, I wouldn't have known, but we have some romantics around here who have seen the movie. God bless Netflix! It's Romeo speaking, when he finds Juliet seemingly dead."

Craig had seen the play as a boy. Both of his parents had thought it was important to see some Shakespeare.

And, of course, the two protagonists had died—died young and beautiful.

"Are they certain it came from the killer?"

"We have Isabel Dunn from the Bureau here now. She and the good doctors Fuller and Miro both believe it's authentic."

"Based on those lines?"

"The envelope was addressed to the paper with the words *Attention Editor* and *An Explanation: a kindness done* written on it," Mike explained. "Of course, they could be wrong, but it seems like it just might be our guy."

Maybe, Craig thought, the killer actually wanted them to know—to understand why he took the lives of these women.

He was trying to preserve what was young and beautiful.

Craig let out a long breath. "Was Egan able to keep the newspaper from publishing what they got?"

"He did some bargaining," Mike said.

"Great. Thanks."

"Nothing yet, right?"

"No, nothing," Craig said, but, as he spoke, he turned to see the young nurse approaching him. "Special Agent Frasier, Ms. Miller is awake."

"Gotta go, Mike. Call you right back."

He turned and hurried after the nurse.

"Even his citizens called him Peg-Leg Stuyvesant!" Henry Willoughby told Kieran.

Willoughby had come into Finnegan's alone and chosen one of the tables where the "crypt keepers"—as Declan had

coined them—always sat after their days at work. He'd given
Kieran a huge smile of pleasure when he'd seen her and coerced her to sit with him for a spell. She'd asked him how the
work was going, and he'd rolled his eyes and told her, "Shaw
is slower than dripping molasses. Good man, though. Knows
his stuff. But me…I can't do it hour after hour, day after day.
I'm surprised his grad students haven't revolted on him. The
hours that man can put in!"

She'd mentioned how they were lucky that they had people
like him to preserve history, and the next thing she knew, she
was seated next to him, sipping coffee, receiving a lecture.

"Now, Stuyvesant! That man was so important to New
York City!" Willoughby said. "Now, there's no descendants
left with his name. They say that's because the poor fellow
was charged with losing New Amsterdam to the British. But
what was the man to do? There were British warships in the
harbor and not a man in the Dutch colony seemed to feel like
fighting. Stuyvesant had no choice but to surrender the city.
They say he was a mean son of a bitch. Hard as nails and very
strict. The Dutch West India Company had to step in a few
times. Ah, but then the Brits came. But, thing is, he stayed
on. So much of lower Manhattan was his farmland. And he's
buried at Saint Mark's in-the-Bowery. You knew that, right?"

Kieran had known it. It didn't matter. Willoughby kept
talking. She thought that he must have been a lonely man,
having lost his wife, and, apparently, having loved her so
much. It was okay to just let him talk.

"Beautiful church, Saint Mark's! Stuyvesant purchased land
from the Dutch West India Company in 1651 for a farm—
or *bowery*, which, of course, is why the area is still called the
Bowery! Ask most schoolkids—they have no idea. But then,
they have no idea of much else, eh? Anyway, the first chapel

was for the family. Stuyvesant's great-grandson sold it to the Episcopal Church for a dollar in 1793, and the church we see now was started in 1795 and consecrated in 1799. Fabulous old place! Stuyvesant is still there, of course, he was buried in a vault beneath the church. Wouldn't John Shaw like to get in there! Ah! But Saint Mark's is still a practicing house of worship. With a whole city massively grown up on what was a farm. Then again, we are the New World! Ah, my lass, as they say here in Finnegan's! History is a sad, sad thing to lose. There's so much downtown—so much aboveground and underground. New York! Such a wonderful place. Thank God for people like those grad students! Another generation rising up to preserve!"

Kieran smiled at him and looked at her phone.

No call yet from Craig.

"Alexander Hamilton!"

"Pardon?" she said, turning back to Willoughby.

"I said that Alexander Hamilton helped with all the legal machinations to make Saint Mark's independent of Trinity!"

"Really?" Kieran murmured. She smiled. She actually liked Willoughby; the man was a font of information. He'd been a little shy with her at first, but now he'd let down his guard.

"I love this city!" he told her.

She smiled. She was anxious to get away for the moment, but she didn't want to appear to be rude.

More than anything, she wanted to be alone with her thoughts. No matter what she did, she couldn't stop thinking of the killer.

Kieran believed that the killer had a lair—one lair where he brought his victims, and where he killed them and prepared them. It was someplace extremely well hidden. A place where he could clean up his victim and himself. A place where the pool of blood from a wound to the heart wouldn't be found. She'd read that in London, Jack the Ripper had been able to walk through the streets with blood on himself or his clothing because so many people in the East End were butchers or worked in slaughterhouses.

That wasn't modern-day New York City. People might just step over the homeless in the street, but they'd note a man covered in blood.

Henry Willoughby knew the city; he could probably bore dozens of people to death because he could go off on tangents, but he was a good man to know.

"Hamilton! Fascinating man, too!" Willoughby said.

"That Alexander, he was a busy man!" she agreed.

"And by the way, the musical is fantastic," Kevin said, swooping in at the table to rescue her. "Excuse us, Mr. Willoughby, Kieran has a phone call in the office."

"Excuse us," Kieran reiterated, eagerly following her brother to the office.

The business phone was on the hook. She looked at her twin.

"No phone call. I was rescuing you," he said.

She smiled and thanked him. "I didn't even know you were here," she said.

"Slipped by you a few minutes ago. Danny brought me up to date on what's been going on." He smiled at her and reached out to smooth a stray lock of hair from her forehead. "I'm so glad you found Sadie Miller alive," he told her.

Kieran felt a pang in her heart. Kevin was glad. She knew, however, that her brother couldn't help but wish that it might have been Jeannette who had been found alive.

"Have you seen the news about this afternoon?" he asked.

"No, not yet," she told him.

He switched on the TV. The news came up midstory.

"Don't worry, it will repeat," Kevin said.

As Kieran watched, a dignified reporter faced the camera, saying Sadie Miller, missing since Friday, had been found. At the moment, they had no details on her condition, but she had been taken to a hospital somewhere in the city.

The scene switched to a press conference given by Richard Egan. He informed the public that they believed that Sadie Miller had been taken by the serial killer, that they were grateful she was alive and that women in the city needed to be vigilant.

A barrage of questions followed.

Egan was good at fielding them. He had a stern way of saying "this is a case still under investigation," that almost shamed someone for pushing him.

"Doesn't she know who did this? Wouldn't she know?" a reporter called out.

"Ms. Miller has suffered incredible pain and trauma. We ask for the moment that you let her do a little recuperating. When there is more that we can give you, I promise we will get the information out as quickly as possible."

"Where was she found?" someone else demanded.

Egan had already left the podium.

The scene turned back to the original reporter, who wrapped up the story. "We will be pursuing this information here for you, so please, stay tuned."

"They don't even know she was found at the photography shop?" Kieran said, incredulous. "There was an ambulance. And then a forensic team had to have come... I didn't see them, of course. Danny and I were in a cab following behind right away. But..."

"Ambulances are always on the streets—it's a big city. You guys were out of there quickly, and the cops didn't arrive with sirens blaring. They want it on the hush-hush for now, I guess. Maybe a way to lure the killer out? I don't know. Hell, I'm an actor, not law enforcement. But, I suppose, until they've investigated further and something is known, the police and FBI must be protecting the brothers who own the shop. With all this going on, you could get a crazy vigilante out there who believes that they were in on it, and they might suffer some violence themselves. People can get crazy. They weren't—weren't in on it in anyway, were they?"

"Oh, I really don't think so. I mean, anything is possible, but I read people fairly well, and it would be hard to fake them crashing into one another and their amazement—and fear—at what was found," Kieran said.

Her phone rang and Kieran started, looking down at it. "Craig!" she told Kevin.

"Hey," she said into the phone. "Did she wake up?"

"She did, and she's so sweet, so grateful." He was silent a minute. "You know, your patient really saved the day."

"My patient?"

"Yes, the woman who told you she had heard moaning during the ghost tour. Sadie said she actually remembered kind of waking and thinking that she was dreaming. And she heard something in her dream—moaning. She thinks that what she heard was her own moaning."

"Craig, did she say who—"

"She has no idea. She can't remember. She doesn't even remember that she was at Finnegan's the night that she was taken," he said. "The last thing she can recall is a Sunday morning, and getting ready for church."

"Could her memory come back?"

"Maybe. But she suffered severe trauma. The brain, according to her doctor, protects the body—and sanity, I suppose—

by blocking out what was so horrible. This drug she was given in high doses, lorazepam, also causes the same effect."

"I spoke with her that night in Finnegan's. What if I were to see her now? Talk to her?" Kieran asked. "Such things can jog a memory."

"We can try," he told her.

"I'll come back to the hospital."

"No, she's sleeping again, and I've been asked not to waken her. Her roommate—and best friend—is here. We'll let them sleep and start fresh in the morning."

He sounded weary. Bone weary. But, still, there was relief in his voice.

"We're taking a drive tomorrow," he reminded her. "Right after the hospital. There's got to be something else we can discover about this killer. Maybe it's in Virginia."

"You should head home, then. Your place. I can meet you there."

"No. I'll come to Finnegan's. You sit tight. I'll be there soon. In fact, I'd love a shepherd's pie if you can finagle some help from the kitchen."

"I can do that. I know people here," she told him.

The minute she hung up her brother Danny burst into the office. "They're all here again. That whole crazy scientist crowd. And you know what? I know why kids wind up hating history. Those guys spew out dates and facts, and kids are supposed to remember them without any of the human touch. I get it with grad students—they have to be hard-core academics. But I've seen Gleason hanging with them on some nights. What the hell is a guy like Gleason doing with them? He has to be going crazy."

What was Gleason doing with the academics? The guy was an entrepreneur.

Before she had a chance to answer Danny, Declan appeared, poking his head into the office. "Hey, could one of you run down for a couple of bottles of Jameson's? Mary Kathleen let most of the servers go, and we're suddenly short of whiskey."

"I got it," Kieran said.

"I'll go," Danny offered.

"It's two bottles. I can handle that!" Kieran told him. "Kevin, Craig's on his way. Can you send an order for shepherd's pie back to the kitchen?"

"Mary Kathleen will see to it."

Kieran left the office and headed to the basement. She reached for the Jameson's and then paused, looking around their storage area.

No one had ever died there.

No one—not in known history, at least—had ever been buried there. And Declan kept the place well lit, so there was nothing creepy about this basement.

And yet she found herself thinking about the street, and where the basement would line up with the back of the building, and the hidden crypts at the old Saint Augustine's.

She walked to the basement wall, where there were shelves of vodka and gin. She slammed a hand against the wall and winced. Solid.

And still…

She knew that the crypts were beyond that wall.

Shrugging off the uneasy sensation, she hurried back up the stairs. As she headed to the bar, she saw that both Henry Willoughby and John Shaw were at the table, holding sway over the table of grad students.

She hurried to the bar with the Irish whiskey and then walked toward their table.

"The word *sarcophagus* comes from the Greek," Willoughby

was saying. "*Sarx*, meaning flesh, and *phagein*, meaning to eat. It's from the Greek phrase *lithos sarkophagos*, which literally means flesh-eating stone. *Lithos* is stone. We all know about cremation. Well, in a way, a sarcophagus under the sun can do the same thing—the heat can literally 'eat' the flesh. Now, of course, the Egyptians were keen on preserving the body, the Peruvians had their way, and throughout history, many societies have tried to preserve the body. Different factors can be important—cold, for one. And, of course, the right chemicals in the body. Embalming. Ah, sad, is it not? All this time, and we've really not managed to preserve the flesh!"

"What does it matter?" Allie Benoit asked. "It's just housing."

"For the soul?" Joshua Harding teased her. "You're a scientist, and you still believe in an afterlife?"

"Ah, well, the Egyptians—masters of embalming—believed that the old body was needed in the new life," Willoughby said.

"I'm not so sure I'd want this old body," John Shaw said. "A new body—ah, that would be lovely!"

"You know, this conversation would be considered strange in most circles," Allie Benoit said, shaking her head as Kieran arrived. "The funerary practices that took place a couple of hundred years ago. Actually, though, it's pretty interesting. You should come back down into the crypt sometime, Kieran."

"I'll do that," Kieran said. "What? No Roger Gleason tonight?"

"He's back up on Park Avenue, making plans. He's going to reopen the club in the next couple of days. Most of our work is in the day, and we can close off—or at least, rope off—the area between the bar storage and the find. He'll pay for a city guard," Shaw explained, "in case people who know about the find try to sneak down to see it."

"And we can't have that," Willoughby told her. "No, we can't have that. I haven't wanted the club reopened for that very reason. Can't get people into museums sometimes, but offer them something creepy and they're right there." He shook his head. "But Gleason's been decent. And if he'll pay to protect the find, that's great."

"Did you see the news?" John Shaw asked Kieran. "They found the missing young woman! Of course, you know the police and the FBI. None of us knows if she's really okay or not, but they found her and she's alive."

"Yes, and that's great," Kieran murmured.

"Ah! She knows more than she's telling us," Willoughby said.

"Well, of course, she does. Kieran is with that Special Agent Frasier."

"Craig's work is separate from our lives," she said, wishing she hadn't approached the table.

"Do you know where they found her?" Allie asked.

"I really don't know anything," Kieran lied. To her relief, she saw that Craig was coming in the door. "Excuse me," she said.

"Hey, he's here! The special agent himself!" John said with pleasure, rising to flag down Craig.

She groaned inwardly, thinking of the way this crew would pounce on him for answers. But she needn't have worried.

When he came to the table, Craig silenced all the questions that had been hurled at him. "Sorry, folks, I'm not at liberty to say anything at this time. When we do let out information, I'll be happy to talk to you."

Kieran lowered her head, smiling. Craig could handle himself.

"Want dinner here or to go?" she asked him.

"To go would be great," he told her.

She packed up his shepherd's pie, kissed Declan on the cheek, waved to Danny and Kevin, who stood by the bar, and linked her arm in Craig's to leave.

Craig had his car again.

"We can go to your place," she said.

"No, I've got more stuff at your place right now," he said. "It's all right."

She was quiet for a minute. "And...you're really not angry tonight, right? I mean, I wasn't crawling around any unknown tombs. We just went to lunch and to see the grave."

He considered her words for a minute. Then he looked over at her. "You found a young woman alive."

"You found her."

"I found her because of you and Danny. Guess that means I ought to be sucking up to you."

"Really? I like it!" she said.

A warble of an Ella Fitzgerald number followed them up the stairs to Kieran's apartment. Craig ate his dinner and headed to the shower.

Kieran followed him, slipping in beside him, sliding her hands around his waist.

"I'm ready for my suck up now," she told him.

"Elbows," he said.

"What?"

"Elbows. You have beautiful elbows."

He turned, catching her arms, lifting one to kiss a drop of water off her elbow.

"I'm so glad you noticed," she said a little breathlessly. The water was hot; the sleekness of his body was evocative.

The way he touched her was incredibly arousing.

"I work very hard to keep beautiful elbows," she said breathlessly.

"Really?" he asked.

"No. But I'm glad you like them."

"Heels," he said softly.

"Of course. I have exquisite heels," she said. "And if you try to kiss one here…"

He laughed and swept her off her feet. She squealed, warning him they could slip in the sudsy tub.

But he kissed her lips and carried her from the shower to the bed. He lay over her, still wet, and he looked down at her and said, "I will never slip with you."

She curled her arms around his neck and her legs around his waist.

"A little slippage here and there isn't such a bad thing," she murmured.

He smiled and they made love, and she slept deeply, curled into his arms. It had been a really good day. A young woman had been found alive.

When Kieran opened her eyes again, she was sure that it was barely light out.

"Hey there," Craig said.

He was already up and dressed.

"We have to get to the hospital. And pack a little bag. Depending on schedules with the ME and the detectives on the case, we may be spending a night in Virginia."

"But maybe Sadie will be able to tell us something today," Kieran said.

Craig didn't seem hopeful. "Pack your bag anyway," he said.

CHAPTER
THIRTEEN

AS THEY'D REQUESTED, THERE WAS A POLICE GUARD AT
the hospital, just outside the ICU.

There had been no incident during the night. Craig
thanked the officer, and he and Kieran were allowed entry.

Marie Livingston leaped to her feet as she saw Craig and
Kieran arrive.

She didn't know Kieran, of course, but she smiled at her as
she said, "All Sadie's vital signs are good, so they're going to
move her to a regular room today. She's still sleeping so much,
but the doctor said that's natural. She's doing really well!"

"I'm glad to hear that," Craig said, introducing her to
Kieran. "Has she remembered anything else?"

"No, not the last time we talked," Marie said. "But she
hasn't woken up yet this morning. Did you find anything?
Were there fingerprints— Oh, I guess if there was anything,
everyone would know. I'm sorry I'm babbling."

"It's all right," Craig assured her. "Has a doctor been in?"

"Oh, yes, they're wonderful here. There was a night man

on and he was great, and then I guess her main doctor was in—the fellow who saw her yesterday."

"Dr. Frederick Davies?" Craig asked.

"Yes, that was him. He said that she was doing really well."

"Excellent," Kieran murmured.

Marie let out a breath and smiled shyly at Kieran again. "Well, while you're here, I guess I can run down for something to eat in the cafeteria. Is that all right? I don't want to leave Sadie alone."

"That's fine, Marie. Take your time," Craig told her.

The woman grabbed her bag, hesitated and then left.

Kieran stood by the side of the bed looking down at Sadie. She glanced over at Craig. "She seems to be sleeping so sweetly and peacefully."

Craig nodded. "There's a chair over there. You might as well sit down." He glanced through the glass to the nurses' station, at the nurse who was looking in at them dourly, a tall heavyset woman this morning. "We'll just have to wait until she wakes up. I should have asked Marie to bring coffee back to us."

Craig pulled up another chair and made himself comfortable. They might be in for a long wait.

But he had just settled when Kieran said softly, "Craig."

He looked quickly over at Sadie on her bed. She blinked, and then her eyes opened and she was staring up at the ceiling.

"Sadie," he said gently.

She turned to him and frowned for a moment, deep in thought. Then her face lit up. "I remember."

"What do you remember?" Craig asked her.

"You. You found me...in the dark. You brought me here. And your name is...Frasier. Yes, you're Frasier..."

"Craig Frasier," he told her.

"Yes, sorry, it's still so hard…"

"Sadie, I brought someone to see you. You saw Ms. Finnegan the night you disappeared."

"I disappeared?" Sadie asked, and then she winced and said, "Yes, yes, I disappeared. And I remember darkness and thinking I heard someone crying, and I was afraid and then… Finnegan? I do know a Finnegan. It's a him, not a her. Kevin. I worked with Kevin, a long time ago. He's a great guy to work with…a great guy."

"Kevin is my brother, Sadie," Kieran said, moving forward so that she could reach over the bar on the hospital bed and take Sadie's hand. "We all own the pub together, though our older brother, Declan, runs it. Kevin is actually my twin."

Sadie looked at Kieran. Absolutely no sign of recognition showed in her eyes.

"You do look like your brother. Only way prettier. Oh, that came out wrong. Kevin is gorgeous—he's just a guy, you know?"

"Sadie, you don't remember coming to Finnegan's?" Kieran asked her.

The woman looked at her with clear green eyes and shook her head. "I'm sorry. I'm so sorry!"

"No, please, don't be upset. None of this is your fault. I'll tell you about Finnegan's, though. There's an entry with beautiful old glass in the doors. You come by a row of side tables—high-tops—before you get to the bar. The bar is old wood, really nice. There are posters for Irish fairs and Irish bands, and Guinness, of course! What's a pub without a few Guinness posters, huh? Oh, there's actually one of me. When I was younger, I did Irish dancing. My parents loved Irish dance, and they couldn't get the boys going, so they picked on me. Funny, because Kevin did wind up taking dance in school—acting major, you know?"

"Yes, I had to take all kinds of dance classes," Sadie said. She smiled as she looked at Kieran. "I wish I did remember you. I was polite, I hope?"

"You were lovely—not to worry."

Something seemed to flicker in Sadie's eyes. "I almost feel that I do know you... Actually, I haven't even seen Kevin since I worked with him last." She closed her eyes and blinked when she tried to open them again. "I'm so tired..."

"Go to sleep, Sadie. I'll come back tomorrow. We'll talk more. Maybe you'll remember something then."

Sadie nodded, her eyes already closed.

"Maybe...your face, your voice...they're so familiar."

Craig started to speak, but Kieran shook her head. She rose and came over to his side of the bed. She seemed pleased. "I'll try again tomorrow. Little by little. If we just nudge really gently, she may begin to get more memory back. I don't want her to close down."

He nodded. "Yeah, all right."

They waited a few minutes more, till Marie Livingston returned.

"Did she wake up?" Marie asked.

"Just for a minute," Kieran said.

"Did she...?"

"No, but we'll be back," Kieran said. Then she paused. "Hey, are you all right? Are you staying here with her?"

"I am," Marie said firmly. "In the hospital, everyone needs a friend. I will not leave her."

"You have my card, right?" Craig asked her. He'd given it to her the night before.

"Yes, Special Agent Frasier, I do, and I'm so grateful. If anything, I'll call you."

"I'll plan on seeing you tomorrow," Craig told her. "I'll have my partner, Mike, stop by sometime today, and you may see a cop named McBride, but don't worry. None of us will put any pressure on Sadie, okay?"

"Oh, I wish she could remember," Marie said. "That monster! Thank God. He seems to like to terrify his victims, drug them and then— I'm so grateful that you found Sadie!"

"You're a good friend," Craig assured her. Then he and Kieran bid Marie goodbye.

Craig stopped in at the nurses' station and received much the same report he'd gotten from Marie. When they headed out, a new officer was on guard duty. He solemnly told Craig he'd watch everyone and anyone coming and going from ICU.

Traffic out of the city was painful, but then, traffic always was. Still, when they were on the highway, heading south through New Jersey, he found that his mood was fairly bright.

Except this was the kind of case that you couldn't let go.

Neither, he thought, could Kieran.

He glanced over at her as he drove. She had a book out on her lap.

"My company must be really great," he told her.

She flashed him a smile. "I'm reading about death through the ages—and New York City."

"Cheerful. You are a bundle of fun."

"No, no, honestly, it's interesting. It tells about funerary art. Death's heads and simple stones were popular in the 1600s. People had a very grim look at life. And, say, back in the European countryside—where there was space—everyone was buried in the churchyard or entombed in the church itself. New York was big on cemeteries because it's always been a moneyed city. You couldn't let prime real estate go to the dead, not when the space was needed for the living, for housing, shops and things. And you should see all the different types of headstones and tombs, entombment and interments. Mausoleums, Greek, Roman, Gothic. And, of course, I'm not sure if you heard Willoughby last night—I think it was before you came in—but he was talking about the word *sarcophagus* or the plural, *sarcophagi*. Means flesh-eating. I'm reading it here, in this book, too. Oh, by the way, I didn't realize it myself until this morning, but while this book is by a George Hatfield, it has a forward by our esteemed John Shaw."

"Great reading. I think I should have gotten an audiobook. I do have music in the car, you know. Lots of it."

She grinned at him, but the smile didn't reach her eyes. "I don't know, Craig. There's something about this case that's driving me crazy."

"Something? Everything about this case is driving me crazy."

"I'm trying to get into the mind of the killer. He leaves Cheyenne Lawson out on the grass, but beneath an angel. Our as-yet-unidentified victim went into an unknown vault. Jeannette Gilbert was left where he had to know she'd be found immediately. Wherever he's left them, they've been dressed and tended to as if they were dearly loved—cherished." She turned to him. "Say Cheyenne Lawson was his first. He was trying to do something special, but he thought that he failed. Next, our victim in the private crypt that I stumbled into. Did he feel that he failed with her, too, and that he just wasn't ready? Or he hadn't achieved what he wanted? Then, he had Sadie down in that crypt at the Braden photography studio. But, so far, he hadn't killed his victims in the crypts or cemeteries where they were found. So why did he have her down there? And wasn't he taking a terrible chance? Someone might have heard her."

"He probably believed that she was completely drugged, which was just about the truth."

"Forensics hasn't found anything yet? Not a single print?"

He shook his head. "We believe that he's wearing gloves."

"And where's the blood? Killing all those women…there has to be blood! I just feel that there's something I should put my finger on that I haven't gotten yet."

"Here's what I can't figure. Sadie Miller left Finnegan's to meet with someone. We know that, even if Sadie doesn't. How did she walk out onto the street and just disappear? She had to have gone with her would-be killer. He didn't just throw a rag over her nose, knock her out and drag her off. He got her somewhere, and once she was there, he dosed her drink or something he managed to get her to eat. And the dosage he gave her must have been huge. He had to have known the drug, too—the effect that it would have had. Short-term memory loss. Once she was drugged the way he was doing it, he was safe even he didn't get to carry through his plan for her."

"I wonder why he was waiting. And that, of course, sends you back to the question of what makes his mind tick. What is he trying to do?"

"I've interviewed a number of serial killers, Kieran. I re-member one guy I interviewed. I asked him why he did what he did. He just looked at me and told me that it was fun. He enjoyed watching the light go out of a victim's eyes. Fun. He killed for kicks. Sometimes we may put too much into it. Sometimes, I think, these guys are just bad. And that's it."

Kieran smiled at him. "Ah, but you're missing what's important. We try to figure out what makes them tick and who they are because that helps to find them."

"Finding them. I won't argue with you there. Finding them is what matters."

"There's a whole section in here about the old church Saint Augustine's. It was built in 1782 and burials took place there until the laws forbid further burials south of Canal—except for certain circumstances. I guess a major politician, a religious leader—or a really rich man—can get in where he wants. Anyway, there had been a small graveyard to the side of the church, and there were known catacombs below the altar."

"Yep, and they were all just moved."

"The bodies in the graveyard were reinterred in Brooklyn soon after the law was passed, and the church sold the land that had been the graveyard as the city grew. So, at first, it paid to be rich or prestigious and buried in the church. But, then, as you said, when the church was deconsecrated, all the known people went on out to Brooklyn, too."

"There's just no guarantee for a body, huh?"

Kieran grinned. "Cremation—and scattering at sea. That's probably pretty permanent. Anyway, here's what's so odd. The whole section of catacombs that was just found—when foundations were set to be shored up last week—had to have existed before the law came into being, so they've been there since the late 1700s. But you have all these historians and scholars involved, and no one knew they were there. They were literally just discovered—after well over two hundred years. So, anyone could have heard on the news that the old crypt or catacombs had been discovered. But, whoever it was also had to know the layout of the church and how to rig security footage and alarms and all the rest. And he has to be fairly agile to carry a body around. This should really limit the suspects."

"Well, it would."

"It would if?"

"If we knew what other people knew."

She was silent a minute. "Gleason," she said quietly. "Roger Gleason. He knew the church. He controlled the alarm and the security cameras. Who the hell else could it have been? Unless…"

"Unless what?"

"What if there is another way into the church? I went down to get whiskey for Declan last night. I looked around the basement. It almost abuts the church."

"And you found a secret entrance?" he asked skeptically.

"No," she admitted. "I guess my point is that much of underground or subterranean New York has been lost. There was a fire that wiped out almost everything. The British were here, Patriots fled, the British ruled, the Patriots came back. Fire, construction, opposing factions. Records were lost all over the city," Kieran said.

"Which is why no one knew about the crypts."

"I think someone did," she said, turning to him. "I think someone already knew that they were there, and I think our killer did want Jeannette found. He still hadn't gotten it down right. She didn't stay as beautiful and perfect as he wanted. He felt the need to keep going. But he also wanted his work seen before it all went too badly. So, she's put in a coffin that John Shaw is sure to look into first thing."

"You could be right," he told her. With his eyes still on the road, he reached over and took the book from her and tossed it into the backseat.

"Craig, what…?"

"The sun is shining. It's a perfect day. You're supposed to let go of things so that you can look at them again with fresh eyes," he said.

She nodded. "A bit ironic, don't you think? We're on our way to find out about another victim."

"And we have a few hours to go." He started humming as he went to switch on music. He paused.

"What is it?" she asked.

"Something we're keeping quiet about for now. Our FBI analyst and Drs. Fullers and Miro think that the newspaper received a real communication from the killer."

"What? And you didn't tell me?"

"Hey! I was more worried about Sadie."

"What was the communication?"

"Words from Shakespeare's *Romeo and Juliet*. Romeo in the crypt."

"Not a love theme?"

"No, 'Death…hath had no power yet upon thy beauty,' or something like that. He sent just a few lines.'"

"Craig, that's really important. That's the key. This guy is trying to find beauty—perfect beauty—and preserve it. And he keeps failing."

"So he does."

"Why didn't you tell me about this?"

"Egan wants to get a handle on the killer. He's trying to keep the story from the papers and from the general public."

"I'm the general public?"

"No! But, of course, you and Danny and your family have been asked to keep confidence about yesterday, as well." He glanced at her. "And we all know that the Finnegan siblings can keep secrets."

"Oh, low blow!"

"Sorry. Couldn't help myself. But, seriously, it's better this way, Kieran. Not everyone can keep quiet. And at the moment, he doesn't want any information out about where Sadie Miller was found. Partially to protect the Braden brothers, Hank and Nat."

"And he thinks they won't say anything?"

"From what I understand, they're happy to keep quiet. They're not sure if the fact that a kidnapped girl was under their feet for a couple of days will make the shop more popular—or make it an anathema."

Kieran nodded. "Right. So the killer wants perfection. But he knows that youth fades with age. Craig, he doesn't want them to get old. He wants them to be beautiful and young and smart forever."

"He ought to leave history alone and study mortuary science," Craig said.

"Maybe. Maybe he's trying—in his own way."

"Maybe I will turn the radio on."

Kieran grinned and leaned back. A minute later, they were listening to the band Bastille.

They really did need to do something to shake the case.

Hard when they were both obsessed, when they were on their way to study an earlier victim—and hard when Le Club Vampyre—the old Saint Augustine's—was right behind Finnegan's pub.

The lead detective on the case in Virginia was a woman named Rebecca Owens. She looked to be in her midforties, a serious woman with short, prematurely graying hair and a wiry build and an easy, solid manner. Craig introduced Kieran as a colleague, a psychologist, which, of course, she was. It still felt a little strange. Sometimes she still couldn't help feeling a little like a schoolgirl playing at being a grown-up.

Detective Owens led them into her office and wasted no time getting down to business. "We let the Bureau know about this case, even though it was one murder, because it was so bizarre," she said, passing Craig a folder. "We went through all the usual—boyfriend, family, past teachers… It was a sad case. It's haunted me since. I'm glad the Bureau is involved. I'm not glad, of course, that it seems the killer's moved on from here, but if you all have new leads or fresh clues, I couldn't be happier," she told them.

"We believe that your victim wasn't his first or his last, I'm afraid," Craig told her.

"I saw in the news that you found a girl alive," Detective Owens said.

Craig nodded. "We were very grateful to have found her alive."

"In an old tomb."

"Yes," Craig told her.

Rebecca Owens dragged her fingers through her short hair. "I pray we don't find any more young women down here. We've got lots of battlefields, and, God help us, enough cemeteries with vaults and mausoleums, and old churches, too."

"If I'm right, he came back to the New York area. That seems to be his real stomping ground. Along with a foray over to Jersey."

"What do you think I can do for you, Special Agent Frasier?" Owens asked. "I've sent copies of all our files to the Bureau."

"I know, and we appreciate that. I'm interested in firsthand knowledge of the site where she was found, and anything you can tell me about the victim herself," Craig said.

"I'll take you out to the cemetery," Owens said. "And as for Cary Howell... I didn't know her personally, though I came to feel that I did. There was such an outpouring of grief over her, first when she was reported missing, and then when she was found. She was young, eager, beautiful and bright. And nice! She would help anyone. Her dad told me that she volunteered at one of the senior living facilities. The old-timers would talk about the past and she would listen and, apparently, really be enthralled. She loved the world. The world loved her," she finished sadly.

"So she was perfect," Kieran said softly.

"Just about—if anyone can be perfect. Strange, but true. When you look at a person who is that kind and nice, it makes them more beautiful, don't you think?" Owens asked her.

"I do," Kieran agreed.

"I called one of her girlfriends, a young woman named Janet Harlow," Owens said. "She'll meet us out at the cemetery."

"She doesn't have to meet us there. Isn't that kind of hard on a friend?"

"Not really," Owens said. "This friend, Janet Harlow, goes out to the cemetery just about every day. You see, Cary Howell is there now—in her own family's tomb. Janet brings flowers out every few days. Makes her feel better, and, hey, if anything makes someone feel better, I say go for it."

They passed beautiful country as they drove from Fredericksburg out to the cemetery. Rebecca Owens, doing the driving, talked about the city.

"You had two battles at Fredericksburg," Owens told them as they drove, "and nearby, you had Spotsylvania and the

Wilderness and the Chancellorsville Campaign. We're really beautiful. You have to come when you can enjoy the country."

Craig agreed. There were grass and trees. Not that New York City didn't have grass and trees. After all, Central Park was huge.

And still…

Not like this.

Owens drove through a massive Victorian gatehouse and then along a trail. The cemetery had certainly seen a heyday during the Victorian era; there were all manners of mausoleums, large tombs, angels, cherubs and crosses. Owens pointed out the Catholic area and the Jewish area of the cemetery. "Cary Howell was found among the Protestants," she told them.

She parked the car. The cemetery was well tended. Flowers adorned many of the graves.

They got out of the car and headed toward a massive old mausoleum combining Greek and Gothic styles.

A large iron door guarded the entrance.

A chain with a padlock wrapped around the gate.

The family name of Boone was inscribed in large letters above the entrance.

"Obviously, the family now keeps it securely locked," Owens told them. "Gladys Boone died six months ago. The funeral removed the marble slab to receive her coffin. That was when they found Cary Howell. I can only imagine what it was like for those in attendance the next morning. Poor family—burying Mom and finding a murder victim where she should have been gently laid for her eternal rest."

"There are no underground crypts here?" Craig asked.

Owens frowned. "Not right here. There's a small old family grave site not too far from here, though. I believe that they have a large underground vault. I don't think, however, that anyone has been entombed in there since…I don't know, maybe the early 1900s."

"Where is Cary buried now?" Craig asked.

Owens pointed. "Close," she said softly. She started walking. Craig was tempted to take Kieran's hand as they walked across the grass.

He didn't.

They arrived at Cary Howell's family tomb. It was of a darker stone, older looking, and offered more of a Gothic appearance.

As they reached it, Craig saw that the door into the mausoleum was open.

"Janet is waiting, I believe," Owens said. "It's a large mausoleum. The Howell family is big, and they've been in the area a long time. I believe the mausoleum is from around 1820. I guess they intended to stay for a few generations."

He stepped back to allow the two women to enter. He was glad that Detective Owens wasn't offended. He liked her. She was sure of herself and her position, and didn't feel that she had to assert herself or be insulted by simple courtesy.

"She is here," Owens said very softly, pointing.

The mausoleum looked like a chapel, complete with an altar at the far end and above it a beautiful stained glass window picturing a pair of doves. The window let in a stunning array of light, illuminating four rows of short pews that allowed for a visitor to sit before the altar in reflection.

As beautiful as it was, there was still an essence of sadness.

A young woman with long dark hair, wearing jeans and a flannel shirt, stood at the far end, in front of the altar. She turned as she heard them coming.

She smiled and walked around the pews to greet them,

offering them her hand in a firm shake. "I'm Janet Harlow. Rebecca—Detective Owens—asked that I speak with you. About Cary." She turned and indicated one of the tombs. "Cary is there now," she said softly. "I know she isn't really there but...I still like to bring flowers. Actually, I grew up with her, so I knew her whole family." She gestured to the tombs. Then she seemed to realize she was speaking quickly and flushed. "I'm sorry. I loved Cary. And I hope this awful man is caught and gets the death penalty. It's a federal case now, too, so he just might, right? I'm not mean and vengeful, really. It's just that...well, you can't imagine how wonderful Cary was." She paused and looked from Craig to Kieran with wide eyes that seemed to pray they weren't judging her.

"I'm so sorry for your loss," Kieran said, stepping toward Janet and linking arms with her to lead her to the front pew. "I didn't know any of the other women we believe the same man has killed. My brother did. I understand your feelings. This man has targeted people who grace the world with their smiles and actions. The people who are not just beautiful on the outside, but on the inside, too."

"Are you a cop?" she asked.

"Psychologist," Kieran said.

Janet seemed to withdraw from her, wary. "You think you can fix this man? You want to find him to talk to him, to get him off for being crazy?"

"No. I don't believe I can fix anyone," Kieran assured her. "I want to understand him, the better to apprehend him so that he can be brought to justice."

Janet spoke cautiously. "You're not going to go on and on about how he's sick and needs help, right?"

"Far beyond my pay grade. I swear to you, my entire mission is to see that this man is brought to justice—and to stop him. No matter what, we can't bring Cary back. But if she was the person I understand her to have been, she wouldn't have wanted more women killed. Please, help me—help us. We have to get him off the streets."

Janet studied her a minute longer and then nodded. "You're right. Cary would do anything that she could. How can I help?"

"Just talk about her."

Detective Owens started to move forward; Craig caught her gently by the shoulder and shook his head.

Owens nodded.

And they listened.

Janet talked about Cary, with Kieran's encouragement. She told Kieran about their days at school, growing up, their first dates and parties.

Owens moved impatiently. Craig set a hand on her shoulder again.

"I can see how great she was," Kieran said. "Always kind to the unpopular kids, helpful to those with any kind of a handicap, and loved because she had the determination to do things, whether others accepted her or not. She changed those around her. Janet, she was brilliant, too, right?"

"So smart—a dozen colleges had wanted her!"

"What did she really love? What did she really want to do?" Kieran asked her.

"I think she wanted to write—nonfiction. Oh, she loved novels. But she had a tendency to love stories that were about history. Especially about this area. Or biographies. She had dozens of them, from the Russian royal family to Abe Lincoln. And generals—she loved Robert E. Lee. And she wanted to write a good book on the whole John Brown thing in Harpers Ferry. She wanted to write a book that explained that his motives had been pure, but the man had been a cold-blooded killer. She never saw things from one side. She was so smart and so fair."

"She sounds incredibly bright. Janet, I'm sorry, this may seem like a strange question, but was she fond of cemeteries and churchyards?" Kieran asked.

Janet's eyes widened. "Yes! She loved them. She said that history was to be found in church records, graveyards and cemeteries. Not just facts and figures, but how people felt about life and death."

"Do you know any of her favorite haunts?"

"Um…well, she liked to go to the old rectory."

"The old rectory?"

Janet nodded. "Just outside the city. There was a church there once. They say it burned down when sparks flew during the Battle of the Wilderness. The rectory still stands, though. It's locked up, of course, and the roads are bad. It belongs to the state—they keep planning to make some kind of a tourist monument out there, but funding just hasn't come up. It's posted 'no trespassing,' but—" Janet paused and looked back at Rebecca Owens apologetically "—but we ignored the signs. There are all kinds of gravestones around it. Some tombs above the ground are all overgrown with weeds. She meant to write about it one day, too."

"Thank you, Janet," Kieran said sincerely, her hands on Janet's. "Thank you so much."

"You're going to catch him?"

Kieran smiled at her. "I believe that people like Special Agent Frasier and Detective Owens will catch him, and everything you've told us will help. And when he is caught, you'll be told immediately. I can make you that promise."

Janet nodded and wiped at her eyes. "Thank you. I—I

have to go. I have a sister still in high school. It's my day off, so I'm supposed to be picking her up…giving her sage older sister advice."

"You've been great."

Janet stood. Kieran remained on the bench, looking at the marble plaque that covered Cary Howell's interment.

Janet came to where Craig and Rebecca Owens were standing by the door. She hugged Rebecca, and then, impulsively, she hugged Craig. After his initial surprise, he hugged her back and watched as she hurried to her car. He turned and looked back at Kieran. She was standing by the place where Cary Howell lay, enclosed by marble.

"It would have been a great book about the old rectory, if you'd had a chance to write it. I'm sure that anything you set your mind to would have been just great," she said softly, touching the stone. Then she turned to them.

"You made Janet feel good, Ms. Finnegan," Owens said. "I'm grateful for that. But I'm not sure what you've gotten out of this."

Kieran looked at Craig.

He nodded grimly and turned to Owens. "We need to get out to that old rectory and graveyard."

Owens sighed. "Cary Howell spent hours in DC and loved to drive down to Richmond and head out to Hollywood Cemetery there, too. Honestly, Special Agent—"

"The rectory and graveyard. Please, Detective," he said.

"Sure. All right. Anything for the Feds," Owens said.

Kieran was actually surprised that some politician somewhere along the line hadn't ordered the demolition of the rectory.

Once, it had been a fine little house, serving, she imagined, the Episcopalian ministers who had tended their flocks at Saint Mary's in the Forest, as the little church that had burned to the ground had been called.

Walking around the piles of rubbish on the floor, Kieran imagined a time when cozy wingback chairs had sat before the fireplace and, perhaps, a reverend had sipped tea and counseled a distraught parishioner.

Kids—or perhaps the homeless—had apparently broken in to stay. Twenty-first century cigarette butts and beer cans were strewed about in abundance. An old mattress had been dragged into the living room. Tattered blankets lay about.

But it wasn't really the house that interested Kieran.

"The graveyard is out back?" she asked.

"Yes. Out back and to the side."

Kieran was already heading for the rear of the little house. The back door was still on its hinges, but it was broken out in many places. She opened it and looked out.

The graveyard gave new meaning to the term *overgrown*. Long grasses and weeds were in abundance; trees had grown through many of the gravestones.

She spun, hearing a crunch of leaves. Craig was already behind her. His eyes were intent on the ground. "Someone came through here," he murmured.

She saw that he was already walking around a few aboveground tombs, broken stones and wingless angels. And she saw what he saw—that the long grass and weeds were bent or flattened, as if someone had dragged something along the trail.

She followed him to an aboveground tomb, dedicated to Malachi Fitzpatrick.

Craig brushed leaves off the tomb.

"Revolutionary War hero," he murmured. And then he looked at Kieran. "And his wife—and three of their children."

"Memorials are often to more than one person," Owens called, coming after them.

"Yes, but they wouldn't all fit in that stone box, would they?" Craig asked her. He looked at Kieran. "Which means there's a vault beneath or some kind of receptacle that allowed for all those bodies."

"Maybe, but—"

"Grab an end," Craig said.

"Special Agent Frasier, that thing has been sealed for over a hundred years. You're going to need men and a crowbar, and I don't even know what other equipment," Owens said, dismayed.

Kieran met Craig's gaze and smiled. He'd understood exactly what she'd heard when Janet had talked and talked.

And now, she understood him.

The killer might have lured Cary Howell here, knowing how she loved the place.

And if this had been his killing ground, they wouldn't need any equipment. The top slab of stone would easily slide off the tomb.

"Oh, God! Do you think there's another body?" Owens asked.

"Not another body," Craig said. He shifted almost too hard. His end of the tomb slid to the left and Kieran barely maintained her hold on it, but she did so enough to keep it from hitting the ground hard.

She and Craig stood back, looking down at steps into the tomb. Something brown and crusty covered them along with the leaves and infiltration of dirt.

"I think we found the place where our killer met Cary Howell," Craig said. He hunkered down, touching one of the dried brown spots. He glanced at Kieran and then turned back to Owens. "We need a forensic unit out here. I believe you'll find these spots to be blood. And once we head down those steps, we'll find more blood. Maybe a receiving table for the coffins before final interment. I believe it's where the killer drugged Cary, where he killed her, where he cleaned her and dressed her. It's where he gave in to his particular brand of depravity—before he brought her to the tomb."

CHAPTER
FOURTEEN

SOMEHOW, KIERAN REALIZED, THEY'D GONE THE ENTIRE
day and into half the night without thinking about a meal.

Now they were finally about to eat.

Maybe, *not* thinking about food had been a normal human
reaction to the strangeness of the day. Kieran knew that Victorian cemeteries had been planned so that loved ones might
actually come and visit—and picnic.

Didn't work for her. So, she hadn't been hungry during
the day.

Now, though, it was late.

Rebecca Owens had called in the discovery at the graveyard. A forensic team and other detectives had arrived. With
gloves and booties, they'd headed down to the scene themselves. There had been a receiving table—a place for a coffin to lie while its final interment was prepared. The stone
table had borne remnants of blood. And, Kieran suspected,
the pile of bloodied clothing they'd found stashed in a corner
had belonged to Cary Howell.

And one intrepid forensic worker had made quite a find. Caught between a piece of stone and earth was a bit of fabric. It was a clothing label. It hadn't come off the clothing in the corner. From its white threads, they reasoned it had come from the white gown Cary had been dressed in.

The label was ripped. Only a bit of the end of it remained, and all they could read was a curlicue *"elli."*

While Craig had left Rebecca Owens and the state of Virginia to secure the site and handle the evidence, Kieran had taken picture after picture with her phone.

Afterward, Owens had driven them to their hotel; they'd showered and changed quickly to find that the diner was open with home-style food after ten, and so there they were.

"Hmm. Something that ends with *'elli,'*" Kieran said, studying the picture of the label on her phone.

"You sent those photos to the office, right?" Craig asked.

She looked up at him. "Colleague," she said lightly, "when have I ever failed in my professional duties?"

"You haven't," he told her, studying her. "I mean, for a civilian I met during a diamond heist, you're pretty darned astute."

"Ah, but I was already working with Dr. Fuller and Dr. Miro," she reminded him.

"Yep." Craig took a long swallow of the draft beer he was drinking, his eyes on her. "And they took on the criminal investigation part of the work."

"Hey, you're the first one who ever sent me out to Rikers Island," she reminded.

"You weren't quite so into getting down in the fray back then. My God. I created a—"

"Monster?" she asked.

He smiled and shook his head, and then his expression

became serious. "You were right on today, Kieran. A lot of guys—and women—in the Bureau believe in high tech and pounding the pavement. You have a people touch. A great people touch. You had her talking—of course, what she said had to do a lot with your graveyard obsession of late."

"It's not my obsession!" Kieran protested. "It's *his* obsession."

"You're right. Owens didn't find the killing ground, neither did the Jersey cops or us in New York City. You have been dogged on visiting this cemetery and that churchyard—and you've been right on. But we never would have gotten there if you hadn't talked to Janet. And Sadie owes her life to you."

Kieran flushed, uncomfortable with such high praise.

"Sadie really owes her life to Daniel and our patient—and to you. You're the one who started digging."

"I wouldn't have known where to dig if it weren't for you."

"We've got to hand that one to Danny," she said.

He nodded, still solemn and thoughtful as he looked over at her. "Danny knows the city," he agreed.

"I keep thinking, Craig. Roger Gleason. He owns the club. He set the camera. He set the alarm. He knew Jeannette."

He hesitated and then told her, "He's been watched since Jeannette Gilbert was found. Egan has had surveillance on him since Saturday."

"Saturday. Jeannette Gilbert was found on Friday—and Sadie Miller was taken Friday night. And we found her still alive. Can't they bring him in and hold him for twenty-four hours or whatever it is that the law says? He's…"

"Slimy?" Craig suggested.

She counted off on her fingers. "He knew the venue, better than anyone else. He owns the venue. Someone did get in and out of that crypt, not on any cameras, and the alarm didn't go off. Jeannette had been to the club. He could have lured her there easily. She might have even believed that he was part of a publicity campaign if Oswald Martin hadn't really explained it to her."

"We'll talk to him again tomorrow," Craig said. He glanced at his watch and then glanced up.

They were being joined by Detective Rebecca Owens. She slid into the booth at Frankie's Roadside Diner next to Kieran, who sat across from Craig.

She looked at Craig and said, "I thought I'd tried every angle. I looked high and low, and we interviewed well over a hundred people. And you come down and find the right hole to dig in one day," she said, shaking her head. "I'm grateful, of course. Really grateful. But I do have to admit I'm feeling on the lame side right now."

"You shouldn't," Craig told her. "We've just been dealing with the fact that this guy seems to like the underground world. And we haven't found his workplace or his kill zone in New York City. I think we just got lucky here. Well, I got lucky. Kieran managed to get just what we didn't even know we needed from Janet."

Owens nodded. She reached across the table for Craig's beer and swigged it down in a very long swallow. "Sorry. I'll get you another. Well, so, we've found where he killed Cary. How do we find him? The forensic team may come up with something. But forensic teams went over the site where Cary was found with a fine-tooth comb. He wears gloves. He's careful. He didn't leave so much as a cell of evidence. But maybe they'll get lucky down there."

Kieran had her phone out, studying the pictures she had taken, already sent to Craig's office, and, as far as she knew, already being studied by Craig's favorite tech, Marty.

"E-L-L-I," she said, reading off the letters on the bit of label. She looked up at Craig. "Something— Craig, I think I know where this label comes from!"

"You do? Well, of course you do," Owens said, flagging down the server and ordering a beer and asking to replace Craig's, as well. "And the meat loaf, Raoul, if you have any left!"

"Kieran?" Craig pressed.

She smiled. "I've shopped there. It's a little clothing boutique off Houston Street. The owner's a really attractive older woman with an accent. French, I think, though I know one of the clerks is Italian. It's a bit pricey—I don't shop there often—but she has beautiful things...like...like beautiful white dresses. The place is called Chic-er-elli."

"There was a different label on the dress found on Jeannette Gilbert," Craig said. "It came from Saks." He had his phone out, keyed into his notes. "No trace of a label on the dress Cary was wearing when she was found."

"So, the other part of this label is somewhere," Owens said.

"And there were two different major chain labels found on Jane Doe and Cheyenne," Craig said.

"He's careful and smart," Owens muttered bitterly. "I wonder if he knows the label ripped. Maybe he doesn't care. Maybe he thinks we're all running around blind. Oh, wait. We are."

"This is a small boutique. A salesperson might remember to whom she sold a white dress," Kieran said.

"He bought it six or seven months ago," Owens said glumly. "The place may not even have the same employees."

"We'll find out tomorrow," Craig said. "Kieran, you sure that's the place?"

She looked at him. "My little black dress," she said. "I love it. I do know the label."

Raoul, the server, arrived at the table, delivering their drinks, Kieran's fish and the meat loaf that Craig and Rebecca Owens had both ordered. The man hovered at the table.

"What are you doing, Raoul?" Owens asked. "The meat loaf is great, as always. I eat here a lot," she told Craig and Kieran. "Not that many places open after ten in this immediate area."

"You're working with Detective Owens, right? On Cary's case?" Raoul asked Craig.

The FBI agent nodded.

Raoul still hovered.

"They're Feds," Owens told the server. "You can put my meal on their tab tonight." She shrugged. "Bigger organization, bigger budget."

Craig grinned at that. "Bet you can't guess which fleabag motel our federal budget has us staying in!"

Owens enjoyed that.

Raoul still looked anxious.

"I just wanted to say…find him. Find who did this, please."

"We won't stop looking until we do," Craig promised him.

"Thank you. Cary was special. She knew everyone, loved everyone. She was beautiful, she was nice, she was…perfect."

He turned and walked away.

"Close-knit community down here, especially once you're on the edges of town," Owens said quietly. "And, please… you have to keep that promise." She sounded a little emotional, and she quickly turned away and then said gruffly, "The taxpayers are saving on this one, huh? The two of you are a couple? Only one room at the fleabag motel? She is your girlfriend, right?"

"Yes," Craig told her. But he smiled at Kieran across the table. "And my colleague," he added firmly.

Kieran smiled. The fish was delicious, she was famished. And, later, the "fleabag" motel was just fine.

When they lay in bed together, Kieran rolled to Craig and said, "That felt good."

"I haven't really touched you. Yet."

"Actually, your touch does feel good—even before you even touch me. Chemicals in the brain and all. It's anticipation, you know. Very seductive and titillating. But that's not what I meant," Kieran said.

"Oh?"

"What you said to Owens. That, yes, we were a couple. But, yes, we were colleagues. That was really nice."

He smiled and pulled her naked body to his.

"Guess that means it's your night to suck up to me."

"Hmm, hope I haven't run out of body parts," she murmured, speaking against his throat and moving her lips down to his collarbone and shoulders.

"I can help you find some," he promised.

"'The past and present collide!'" Dr. Miro read. "'VIP re-opening of Le Club Vampyre tonight!'"

Miro read with a certain flair, placing the paper on the end of their small conference-room table, leaning toward Bentley Fuller on the one side, and then Kieran on the other. She did so dramatically—being a little on the dramatic side. At five feet and ninety-five pounds, Allison Miro was sheer vitality.

Kieran had loved her from their first interview, and her respect for the woman, and for Dr. Fuller, had only grown as their caseload had grown.

The finest thing about both doctors was their serious care

for others. They donated a fair amount of their proceeds every year to charities—after they had been checked out to assure that the majority of the donation went to the charity and not to overhead.

Like them, Kieran's first love was helping people.

Her work included sessions with those who had testified, those who had been accused, those who were witnesses and, sometimes, young adults who just might be saved from becoming career criminals. Battered wives, two battered husbands, addicts and people who had been damaged by life. She loved talking with them, helping them see the root of their problems and helping them improve their own lives. There was nothing as good as a day when she saw a real breakthrough in a patient's eyes—a wife who realized that she was suffering from battered woman syndrome, an addict who realized that adding a depressant to being depressed was not a solution or a young adult who found the world of backstage theater work to be far more fun than working as a prankster, thief or vandal.

She really was in an ideal world for work. Her employers also loved her family pub, and they saw no conflict at all in her relationship with Craig Frasier. They simply saw more opportunities.

She glanced at the two doctors at the conference table, grateful for their faith in her abilities.

And grateful she'd gotten into work at a reasonable hour that morning.

There had been no way out of traffic that morning when they'd driven out of Virginia and done their best to avoid the DC mess heading north, even when they'd left just after 5:00 a.m. It was amazing just how many people in the nation's capital were up and about at that time.

They'd still made the drive in just about five hours. She hadn't gone home; Craig had dropped her straight at work before heading in himself. However, on the way, he'd been in touch with Egan and Mike and Detective McBride.

She'd just finished briefing her employers on the trip to Virginia, and how they had found the vault where the killer had lured his victim, stabbed her, cleaned her and redressed her. Both doctors had been grave, no doubt realizing there must be such a site in New Jersey, as well. And, of course, one in New York.

Finding the site might well send the killer into a tailspin.

"I think more and more about this man," Dr. Fuller had said.

"He's definitely obsessed with the underground," Kieran had added.

"And beauty and perfection and youth," Dr. Miro had finished—right before presenting the paper and doing her dramatic reading.

"So Roger Gleason plans on reopening Le Club Vampyre tonight?" Kieran asked. If the FBI or police had managed to find him, Gleason would be at the FBI offices as they spoke, being interrogated again.

"Yes, why?"

She wasn't sure that Craig would want her mentioning the fact that Gleason had become more of a person of interest than ever. So she came up with a phony reason.

"It's Wednesday," she said. "I'd have thought he'd have opted for a Friday night, a time when he could really make a big deal out of it. A weekend."

"Ah, my dear Kieran! You are usually far better at listen-ing!" Dr. Miro said, smiling. "VIP opening tonight. Invitation only. There's a short list here of some of those invited, including the mayor."

Kieran shrugged. "I'd still have thought he'd have gone for the weekend. What if all his major VIPs have early-morning meetings tomorrow?"

"VIPs can probably change their schedules," Dr. Fuller noted. "And, of course, they'll want to be there early, at any rate."

"Yes, Gleason has managed to get press all over the place. I'm thinking he might see this as a dual opportunity—huge night tonight, huge nights on Friday and Saturday," Dr. Miro said. "However, I do think that we should show up."

Kieran laughed. "I don't think I'm on the VIP list."

"Oh, but you are! We all are," Dr. Miro said. "The email invite popped into my box first thing this morning. And, under the circumstances, we think you should go."

"Oh," Kieran said, waiting.

"You'll be my date for the evening," Dr. Fuller said.

"Though I'm sure your young man will be there. I don't see the FBI letting that venue open again unless they have a presence there," Dr. Miro said.

"My wife and I can't both be out," Dr. Fuller explained. "My daughter has a school play tonight. She's going to be a spring flower. Bad enough that one of us misses it."

"Okay," Kieran said. She smiled.

"Where would you like me to get you?" Dr. Fuller asked.

"Finnegan's," she told him. "It may be difficult to find parking, Dr. Fuller. If I'm at the pub, we can just walk around the block and we'll be there."

"Fine. Eight o'clock?"

"Eight o'clock," she agreed. She glanced at her watch; it was already midafternoon, and she believed that Craig also meant to pick her up and return to the hospital to try speaking with Sadie Miller again.

"You're free to leave whenever you need to do so. It is a dressy occasion," Dr. Fuller told her.

She smiled. She thought she made a fairly presentable appearance when she came to work. But, apparently, Dr. Fuller was a little worried she might not be up to snuff for a gala event.

"Yes, sir!" she said, and she fled from the conference room.

Back in the privacy of her own office, she tried Craig's number. No answer. She thought about calling the hospital and inquiring about Sadie Miller's condition.

But, of course, the hospital would deny that Sadie Miller was there. And she couldn't just drop in on the young woman—not without one of the agents in charge of the case.

She rose impulsively and grabbed her bag; she'd been given leave to go.

Dr. Fuller doubted her ability to dress well for the evening? Well, she'd do her best to see to it that she was gowned appropriately.

She knew a lovely little boutique not far from Finnegan's. Craig, of course, had reported to Egan, and she was sure someone from the FBI had been out at Chic-er-elli.

But, she had the sudden urge to stop in herself.

"Do I need my attorney?" Roger Gleason asked, staring at Craig across the table. "I was 'asked' in. I'm sure I'd be here now whether I had agreed or not."

"You're not under arrest," Craig told him. "But…okay, the best technical experts in the world have been over your video surveillance footage. No one came in or out of your club the night before Jeannette Gilbert was found. You know the layout of the building. You arranged with the Episcopal Church for the bodies beneath the altar to be moved appropriately out to the cemetery. You knew Jeannette Gilbert."

"You're grasping at straws!" Gleason said, running his fingers through his hair. He looked distressed at last.

Distressed—but guilty?

"I knew Jeannette. I own the place. But I'm sure you've had me watched. I'm sure you've checked into my past. There's nothing anywhere to suggest that I could be guilty of such a thing! I liked Jeannette. She'd been good for my club. And these other girls... I like women, Special Agent Frasier. In the normal way! And I know you hear this often enough, but I don't need to lure them. My vanity isn't so great that I believe they want to be with me more than any other man, but I am incredibly wealthy. I did not commit these horrible deeds."

"We're just working hard on trying to figure any other way that the alarm didn't go off, and that the footage shows nothing. Absolutely nothing."

"Search my house," Gleason said. "You're welcome to do so. Search anywhere you like—with my blessing. I'm not guilty of these horrible crimes."

He sounded like a man deeply perplexed himself—worried, and frustrated.

"I know I set the alarm," he said. "I know that I did. And how someone got in without being picked up by the security cameras, I don't know. I don't have an answer."

"And that scares you."

"That I don't have an answer? Yes, it does."

"You really have nothing to say."

Gleason was thoughtful. "My concierge. Elton Jennings. He started at ten the night before Jeannette was found. He can tell you that I came in right around eleven at night. And

Joe Perkins came on at six in the morning. He saw me when I left at seven."

Craig already knew that; Egan had checked the schedules of their multitude of suspects and had agents verify their whereabouts whenever possible.

"What, do I look like Spider-Man?" Gleason asked, frustrated. "There's no other way in or out of the building unless you pass the concierge. There's no fire escape from the penthouse."

"People lie," Craig told him. "Especially if they're paid to lie."

He thought that Gleason would get mad. Sometimes, it was good to get a suspect mad.

But Gleason didn't rise to anger. "They're both good men. They have good jobs. Neither has a sick child or a reason to be bribed, Special Agent Frasier. You're being offensive to the two of them right now. I didn't pay them off to say that I'd never left. I never left. I didn't need to try to pay anyone a bribe." He leaned back. "I'll do anything the FBI asks to help with this, but if you're not going to arrest me now, let me go. Please. I'm reopening the club tonight to a special VIP list. Of course, you're invited. You and any of the FBI you'd like to have there. And the cops—McBride. Anyone you want. We've already extended an evite here. I'm sure you know that already. And we've invited those shrinks you work with and Ms. Finnegan. Invite anyone you want, Frasier. But for now please. Arrest me or let me go."

"You invited the FBI?" Craig asked.

"Well, okay, so yours isn't exactly an invitation. It's an announcement saying that while I've hired private security, due to the circumstances, anyone the Bureau sees as important is more than welcome to be there."

Craig sat back. Egan hadn't said anything to him, and Egan was watching the interview from behind the glass.

"Excuse me," he told Gleason.

He rose and left the room. Mike and Egan met him in the hallway.

"Evite came in while you were talking," Egan said.

"Think it's because we brought him in?" Mike asked.

"He hasn't had his phone out," Egan said.

"And he didn't send any messages or emails when I picked him up," Mike said thoughtfully, "so, at the least, he did extend the announcement before you talked to him. Of course, under the circumstances, he had to have known we considered him a viable suspect."

"What do you think?" Egan asked Craig.

"I think we should let him go. And definitely attend tonight," Craig said. "Anything yet on the boutique—that Chicer-elli?" He knew that they'd had an agent in that morning. The owner hadn't been in, and the sales attendant on duty didn't recognize any of the people in the pictures that were shown to her. The clerk had left a message for the owner. One of the other salespeople had been due in after two, and one woman was off for the next two days. She was being tracked down.

"We have agents going back there soon," Egan told him. "Nothing yet."

"Does seem like a place where Roger Gleason might shop for a female friend," Egan told him.

"Let's let him go and keep up the surveillance on him. And we'll attend tonight." Craig looked over at Mike. "Mike and I can head back down to the boutique ourselves," he told Egan.

"All right. What about Ms. Miller?"

"I'll bring Kieran by to see her right after we head to the boutique. She just might trigger something in Sadie's mind."

Craig headed back into the room where Roger Gleason was waiting. "You're free to go," he told him.

"Free. Right." Gleason grimaced. "You can tell those guys watching me that they're welcome to come on in. They can't drink on duty, but our bartenders make some really good nonalcoholic drinks. Expensive, of course, but we do try to cater to everyone."

"Thanks. I'll let them know," Craig said.

No sense in denying what the man had obviously seen.

He walked back out of the room himself, leaving Gleason to wait for an escort out of the office.

"Where are you?"

Craig's words came to Kieran over the phone as she left the subway and hurried down the street.

She was so tempted to lie.

"On the street," she said. That was the truth.

"On the street where?"

"Downtown."

"Almost at Finnegan's? They let you out of work already? Nice job."

"I'll be working tonight. I'm going to be Dr. Fuller's date this evening. I'm sure you've heard. Gleason is opening the club back up tonight."

"Yes, I've heard. You're Dr. Fuller's date?"

"His daughter is in a play—she's a butterfly or a snowflake or something," Kieran told him.

"Okay. Well, I'll get you at Finnegan's in about an hour. I'm stopping by that boutique—Chic-er-elli. Then I'll get you and we'll drop in on Sadie."

Kieran paused. She was standing right in front of the shop with the artistic sign that read Chic-er-elli.

"Oh, you know what? I'm right by the shop. How about I head there and meet you?"

"How about it?" she heard—but not over the phone.

And then she winced. Because she turned, and Craig was headed down the street toward her. He was just about ten feet away.

She closed her phone. "I needed a dress for tonight," she told him.

"Oh, yeah. Saks was too inconvenient? And this place is surely right in your price range."

She wasn't sure if he was angry, but he was definitely being sarcastic.

"I told you, I'd been here before. That's how I knew the label. Aren't you glad I knew the label? *Colleague?*" she asked him.

He stepped up to the shop and opened the door and looked back at her. "Our *colleagues* Drs. Fuller and Miro come into the office or speak with people at their offices. They don't go out hunting dangerous criminals."

"This is a boutique in broad daylight on a busy New York street," she whispered, sailing in past him.

Craig followed.

The boutique was really charming; it was done up with Victorian-era red love seats and chairs, models on podiums in sexy lingerie and elegant gowns. The walls were covered with fine wallpaper and handsomely framed scenes of New York City.

Craig paused to look around. Kieran waited.

Then they headed to the counter.

A very pretty young redhead was behind it. "Can I help you?" she asked.

"Yes, thank you. I need to ask you some questions," Craig said pleasantly, producing his credentials. He glanced down at Kieran. "She needs to buy a dress."

"Oh, yes. Liz told me that someone would be in. And Mrs. Chantelle—the owner—is aware, too. She's in Boston, but she's on her way back to the city. She's spoken with some-one…but, um, you really need a dress?" the salesclerk said, turning to Kieran and looking confused. "I'm here alone at the moment. Um, well—"

"Start with the pictures," Kieran suggested. She heard the little bell over the door sound. She didn't need to turn to know that Mike had been right behind Craig.

"With you in a moment, sir," the salesclerk said.

"It's okay. I'm with them."

"I'm Special Agent Craig Frasier, that's Special Agent Mike Dalton and this is Kieran Finnegan," Craig told the young woman. She still looked flustered.

"I'm Nancy Collins," she murmured.

Chic-er-elli was a high-end boutique; customers seemed to be few, allowing for one salesclerk at a time, so it seemed.

Craig glanced at Kieran as he reached into his pocket. She knew they were thinking the same thing.

When he displayed the array of pictures—prints, newspa-per clippings, Facebook printouts—before Nancy Collins, she studied them.

The grad students were first—Allie Benoit, Joshua Harding and Sam Frick. They were followed by Oswald Martin, Leo Holt, a scruffy-looking man Kieran hadn't seen and didn't know, and then John Shaw and Professor Digby. He laid them all out on the counter, watching the woman's face. Then he

added in pictures of Henry Willoughby, Roger Gleason—
and Kevin.

Kieran tried not to react. She'd believed that Kevin was
no longer a suspect.

"Take your time, please, really look at them," Craig said.

The woman did so. "You see so many people day after day,
that faces begin to blur before you."

"Yes, but look closely. Have you seen any of these faces in
the shop?"

She pointed to a picture. "Him, I've seen his face."

She was pointing at Leo Holt.

"I mean, I think he's been here."

"Do you think that you might have sold him a white
dress?" Craig asked.

"We pulled all the sales slips for the last year," she said, distracted. "We sold over a hundred white dresses in that time.
Mrs. Chantelle deals with a designer in Italy who specializes
in white dresses because of all the young women going for
confirmation in Italy, and then, of course, she creates them
for young women who have *quinceañeras* and so on... I believe that we had charge slips for sixty of them. The others
were paid with cash."

"Who the hell uses cash these days?" Mike murmured.
"Other than..."

He didn't say "criminals" or "killers." He just let his statement fade ominously on the air.

"Wait a minute. I've seen this guy," Nancy Collins said,
pointing to the picture of Kevin. "Oh, wait, no—not in the
shop. I've seen him in a magazine...maybe on television." She
looked up suddenly at Kieran.

She appeared seriously confused. "That's not...you? I mean,

you didn't have a sex change or anything, did you? Not that there's anything wrong with it, but…"

"No, that's not me," Kieran said. She glanced at Craig. Even under the circumstances, he was smirking.

"You're sure you saw him in a magazine or TV and not in the store?"

"Oh, I'm sure. I would remember if I'd met him in the flesh!" she said.

Kieran smiled pleasantly at Craig.

"It's very, very important, Ms. Collins. Please keep studying the photos," Craig implored solemnly.

And she did so. "Maybe him," she said. She pointed to the picture of Roger Gleason.

Kieran felt the tension that seemed to shoot into Craig.

But then the young salesclerk said, "No, no—I saw his picture in the newspaper this morning. Oh, yeah, I know who he is. He owns that club. I'm going one night. I'm going to save up to go! How cool, I mean, in an old church with creepy graves beneath and— Oh!" She looked up, her face filled with guilt and remorse. "Oh, yeah, I'm so sorry. It's where Jeannette Gilbert was found."

No one spoke.

"Anyway, I don't think that he's been in here," she said.

"Anything else?"

"This guy or this guy—maybe," she said. She was pointing to pictures of Henry Willoughby and Professor Digby. "Maybe not. They kind of look familiar, but then, they look like each other, don't they? This guy—him I'd remember!" she added, pointing to John Shaw. "I mean, he looks like he got his finger stuck in a wall socket."

John Shaw did have something of that look about him with his wild white hair.

Kieran looked more closely at the pictures of Professor Aldous Digby and Henry Willoughby. They were similar. Both men were bald. Both were tall and straight and dignified in appearance.

"Do you think you saw one of these men? Did you sell them a white dress?" Craig asked.

Nancy Collins shook her head, looking seriously distressed. "I'm so sorry. Even the girl looks familiar to me. I just don't know. Mrs. Chantelle said she'd be in here by seven, ready to speak with whoever needs her. I only work three afternoons a week."

"Thank you," Craig said, hiding his disappointment.

Nancy Collins turned her eyes to Kieran. "We have a white dress that would look fabulous on you. And it's on sale. There's only one left. It's a six. Want to see it?"

Kieran thought about Jeannette Gilbert in her white dress lying in the coffin.

She smiled. "Thank you. I'm more into the little black dress thing, you know what I mean."

She was startled when Craig said, "I'd like to see that white dress."

"Um, sure. I can show you the white—and something in black."

She disappeared into the back and then reappeared.

She showed them the black dress first; it was an elegant, simple little piece, fitted with a V neck, cold-shoulder sleeves and elegant little crystals along the neckline.

Kieran wished she could afford it; a glance at the tag assured her she could not.

"You should definitely buy it," Mike told her, grinning.

She showed him the tag. He winced.

"It would have been nice," he whispered.

"How about the white?" Craig asked.

"Oh, yes!"

It was a lovely gown as well, and quite different. The neckline was high; the sleeves were covered with lace. It would have been a truly breathtaking gown on a young woman.

It was…virginal. Pure.

"That's really not our Kieran," Mike noted.

Kieran shot him a frown and looked at the tag.

"Wow. It's really discounted!" she said.

"Why is it discounted so much?" Craig asked.

"It might have been on hold and never picked up. We don't buy many of any one item. We try to offer unique clothing. But when all sizes are gone and a garment remains too long, it goes on discount. I can check the books and see, if you like," Nancy said.

"If you would," Craig told her.

She went back behind the counter. "Oh, yes, here it is. It was supposed to be picked up the other day, but there's a cancel notice next to it—deposit forfeited," Nancy read, looking on her computer screen. "I guess the buyer let it go."

"Who was the buyer? There must be a name," Craig said.

"There is. Joe Smith," Nancy said, pleased to be offering something.

The bell above the door made its tinkling sound. An older woman in an elegant little hat and fox stole entered.

"Um, may I help that lady?" she asked. "It's Mrs. Bolton— very wealthy. And we work on commission."

"Of course," Craig said. "And thank you. Here's my card. And Special Agent Dalton will give you a card, and, of course, we'll be back, but if you should think of anything…"

He collected the photographs on the counter.

"Of course," Nancy said, accepting the business cards and

starting toward the newcomer in the shop. She paused. "It's a no on the black dress?"

"Yes, unless you can switch the tags on the white and the black?" Mike teased.

Nancy didn't do well with teasing.

"I— Is the FBI requesting such a thing?" she asked.

"The FBI is completely joking!" Craig said flatly. With a hand on Kieran's back, he ushered them all out of the boutique.

CHAPTER
FIFTEEN

"THE DOCTOR SAID THAT I COULD EVEN GO HOME TOMOR-
row!" Sadie Miller said happily, smiling as Craig and Kieran
entered her room.

As usual, Marie Livingston was there, too. "I've taken a
week off work so I'll be able to be her nurse. Well, I mean,
I don't qualify as a nurse, but I can fetch things and order
Sadie to stay put."

"I've told her that it's completely unnecessary. I'm really so
much better," Sadie said. "Marie has a boyfriend. Poor guy,
she's barely seen him."

"Assistant Director Egan asked that I be the only friend up
here with Sadie," Marie explained. "But Lance is a great guy,
and he totally understands."

"Sadie, I know you want to be out of here. I know you
want your life back," Craig said. "But I'd really appreciate it
if you'd stay just a few more days."

"Stay in the hospital? But—"

"I think we're close to catching the killer," he said.

Kieran glanced at him. She knew it was a bald-faced lie. They'd found one of his lairs; they'd found a dress label that didn't seem to be getting them anywhere. They suspected Roger Gleason but had nothing tangible. And in his gut, he wasn't sure.

"How can this help?" Sadie asked him.

He was surprised when Kieran answered gently for him. "Sadie, God, I hate to say this, but we're afraid that he'll come for you again. He knows you're alive. He doesn't know where you are right now. If you go home, if anyone finds out…"

"It's easier to keep a guard on you here," Craig told her. "We're afraid he'll think that you've remembered something."

"But I still don't remember. I am so sorry!"

"So, I figure maybe we'll talk again," Kieran said.

"If you think that will help," Sadie said, gnawing on her lower lip. "The terror!" she said softly. "That's what I remember. Waking up, unable to move…everything pitch-black."

"So, I'll tell you what I know about the night," Kieran said cheerfully, taking a seat on the hospital bed at Sadie's side. "Finnegan's was so busy. You were at the bar. You were sitting next to a friend of mine, Bobby O'Leary. Old gruff Irishman. Nice as hell, though. He has big blue eyes and super-ruddy cheeks. He's always a little grizzled-looking. Doesn't shave that often so he has a white-stubble thing going on. So, you were by Bobby, and you talked to him. You probably thought he was safe, which he is. I mean, he wasn't trying to pick you up. I was there, running around like a chicken without a head. But I stopped to talk to you, and you said right away that I looked a lot like Kevin."

"You do," Sadie said. "You really do. And your brother is a good guy. A lot like you."

"Thanks," Kieran told her. "Okay, I'll describe Finnegan's. Maybe the setting will jar something in your memory."

Craig stood silently and watched and listened. Kieran did a great job with the description, her voice pleasant and easy. Sadie spoke a few words now and then, asked a few questions. But nothing sounded familiar.

"I feel that I do know you now," Sadie said. "I wish so badly that I did remember!"

"It's okay," Kieran told her. "It's okay." She glanced up at Craig. "We'll try again tomorrow?" she asked.

"We'll try again tomorrow," he said. "And, Sadie, we'll speak with the doctor. For your health, for many reasons, we'd like to keep you here a little longer."

"For her life!" Marie said flatly.

Craig didn't correct her.

Kieran rose to join him to leave the hospital. "Just keep getting better and better," she told Sadie.

They were halfway out the door when Sadie suddenly spoke again.

"Soda. Soda with lime."

"What?" Craig asked, spinning.

Sadie looked at them. "I—I remember an old white-haired guy with a brogue. He ordered a soda with lime. Is that right? Is it a real memory?" she asked.

It was.

Bobby O'Leary was an alcoholic in recovery; he still sat at the bar at Finnegan's every day.

Ordering soda with lime.

Craig turned back into the room, and Kieran walked back to her side. She sat at the bed again and took Sadie's hand into her own.

"You are remembering. You just remembered my friend, Bobby O'Leary."

Tears stung Sadie's eyes.

"But…I still can't remember you!" she told Kieran. "And I can't…I can't remember going there, or leaving there—or why I was even there!"

Kieran smoothed her hair back. "Sadie, it's all right. It's wonderful. You've made a start. Now…relax. Get some sleep. Watch a movie on television, think about good things to come. Let it be an easy thing. You'll remember. Just give it some time."

"We should be feeling pretty good about all this," Mike said, standing with Craig inside Le Club Vampyre and adjusting his tie. "Okay, we don't have the guy yet. But we stopped him. A girl is alive. Alive, Craig. You found her alive. And now you've found one of his lairs. We're close on his trail and, if you think about it, pretty damned quickly."

"Has to be quick—when we hope a killer is holding someone alive and we hope to keep it that way," Craig said.

He looked around the club. Kieran and Dr. Fuller had yet to arrive. The party, however, was already in full swing. Craig saw a number of Broadway performers he'd seen on stage several times, and one of the newest singing sensations to hit the charts was on the stage with a band composed of well-known New York musicians.

The bold and the beautiful of the city were out en masse.

Many were posing for the famed photographer Leo Holt.

And then, of course, there were the nerds. Gleason had graciously provided for those working most closely on the crypt to come. Willoughby, of course, looked fine. He was accustomed to public appearances.

Digby kept working at his tie.

John Shaw was gaping.

The grad students were enjoying the open bar.

"I feel great that we found Sadie," Craig said. "But I still don't like it. I don't like tonight. I have an uncomfortable feeling about something very bad that we're missing."

"Egan headed out to find a judge after Gleason left," Mike reminded him. "There will be a thorough search of this place *and* his home."

"The killer doesn't work in his home, Mike. He works underground somewhere. Another old crypt, a deserted subway platform, hell, I don't know where. But not in his home."

"He'd still have to have some kind of blood-soaked clothing, something on a pair of shoes or boots… Craig, there's always something. And…"

"And what?"

"It might not be Gleason. He has the property, the access, the everything, but it may not be Gleason. And I don't think you believe that Gleason is the killer."

Craig hesitated, looking at his partner. "Everything does point to him," he said.

But Mike was right. Craig wasn't convinced. Smooth, suave—slimy—Gleason still had an amazing business prowess that seemed to be formed on blunt honesty. He wasn't a nice guy; he seemed to be a this-is-what-it-is guy. He hadn't closed the club to honor the ages or Jeannette Gilbert. He hadn't even closed it to appease the police. He had done it because if he didn't, he'd be condemned in the media. Bad for business.

Being seen as perfectly cooperative and helpful in a murder investigation was a good thing. Reopening—with care taken that a historical find was safeguarded—made him look great in the media, too.

He was smart.

"Hey! Wow!"

Mike nudged Craig, and he turned and looked to the door. Kieran had just arrived with Dr. Fuller—and another man.

Kevin was at her side, in a tux, looking like the hero from an action flick.

Dr. Fuller, of course, looked like he'd walked off a magazine page.

But they paled in comparison to Kieran in a little black dress.

It might not have come from Chic-er-elli, but it looked like a million bucks. No, she looked like a million bucks. The sleeveless dress fell just short of her knees and hugged every curve. Her hair fell around her shoulders in a rich auburn wave; the color was picked up by the lights in the club and seemed to shimmer like dancing fire.

Craig wasn't surprised when he saw a surge toward the Gothic entry of the club, photographers, all snapping away, thinking they were catching unknown performing sensations.

"You are one lucky guy," Mike said. "You should take care not to forget it."

"I don't forget it."

"Not that you're chopped liver yourself," Mike told him.

Craig grinned. "It's all right. You don't need to wax so eloquently for my ego," he assured his partner.

"Want to go say hi?" Mike asked him. "Maybe show people she's really with you?"

"No. I want to watch who else wants to go say hi," Craig told him. He realized that his level of tension had grown since Kieran had walked in.

But why? He was right here.

She had come in with her employer, a man Craig knew

well and trusted, and her brother, a man who would die before he let anything happen to her.

But the level of tension he felt rose even higher when he saw
Roger Gleason head toward the door to greet the beautiful—
perfect—trio.

The place was actually dazzling. Kieran was delighted that
she'd called Gleason to ask him if Kevin might accompany
them. This was the kind of event that Kevin needed to attend. All kinds of "the right" people for an actor to meet
were here tonight. Not that Kieran knew who they were,
but Kevin would.

Except that he seemed as stiff as a board when they entered.

Because, she realized now, that there was no way Jeannette Gilbert would not be a topic of conversation tonight.
And while the police and the FBI had chosen to let the lie
that Brent Westwood had told stand as far as the public went,
both the older actor and Kevin knew the truth themselves.
And, she noted, Brent Westwood was in attendance, holding
court with a number of people over at the bar.

Roger Gleason arrived at the door to greet them.

She was glad to see that he was especially cordial to
Kevin, assuring him that he was more than welcome and
that he should have been on an invite list with everyone from
Finnegan's.

"Everyone at that pub has been great to me and the crew
of folks who has been working here," he said. Then Gleason looked at Dr. Fuller anxiously. "Will you…know a type?
Know who the killer might be if you run into him here?"

Gleason, Kieran realized, was serious, tense and anxious.

Because circumstantial evidence had suggested that he was
the killer?

Or…because he was the killer?

"Mr. Gleason, if only it were that easy," Dr. Fuller said. "Sometimes, people do give themselves away in conversation. Sometimes, a killer has to gloat—or say something. Then again, sir, is there a reason you suspect that the killer might be here tonight?"

"The killer knows me and knows this club," Gleason said, his tone gruff. "And he's managed to put this at my door. Yeah, I think he's here tonight. Come on, please, come up to the bar. Let me introduce you to a few people."

Kieran looked around as they headed to the bar. She saw a popular fashion designer holding court in one little area, a rising politician in another. Stars of stage and screen seemed to have gathered at the bar.

Naturally, she looked for Craig and Mike.

And they were there.

They were standing at the far end of the main bar, near the entrance to the steps to the crypt. Just when she caught Craig's eye, a giggling young blonde woman tripped into him. Craig steadied her, giving her his attention. He looked up at Kieran then, and she loved the expression in his eyes. He just wasn't a flirt. The expression looked a lot more like, "Help!"

He was an FBI agent. He'd have to manage on his own. She smiled and shrugged, and he shook his head and then listened to whatever the young woman was saying.

Roger Gleason was introducing Kevin to a producer at the bar. Dr. Fuller had engaged in conversation with Leo Holt, who was telling them that he—like Kieran—had missed great professions as models. Kieran told him that he was sweet as she kept looking around.

When she saw the huddle of academics in the corner—

rejoined by the grad students, all holding drinks in elegant glasses—she smiled and walked over to greet them.

"Professor Digby, John! Joshua, Sam, Allie—hey! And Mr. Willoughby, nice to see you."

"You, too, dear," John Shaw said. He shook his head. "This is amazing."

"So odd to be here when it's like this," Willoughby said. "I mean, not that I haven't attended a black-tie affair here and there, but…this! This is something."

"So cool," Joshua said.

"Free booze," Sam agreed.

"They're such children. Can't take them anywhere," Allie added.

"Hey, it is a glittering night of celebrities," Kieran said. "But I see, John, that you keep looking toward the stairs. I'm sure they have tons of security, and that the crypt is safe. Not to mention the two FBI agents hovering near the stairs."

"I suppose it's like having a child—no one can look over a find quite the way you can yourself," John told her. "But I am enjoying myself—among the living. I am. I really am."

"Of course, he's really much more of an extrovert among the mummies and all," Digby teased, and laughed at his own joke.

"Digby! You should talk!" John Shaw said.

"I never claimed to be comfortable among living people," Digby said, a bit indignant now that the tables had been turned.

"Well, my friends, if you look around, I'm sure the dead are, in truth, far more interesting than some of the poster-people attending tonight," Willoughby said. "That new designer queen…Tatia, or whatever she goes by. The woman has hardly moved. She's kept her expression as bland as a pancake. And that petite little model over there—she hasn't even spoken. All she does is pose. So, perhaps, the dead are not so bad, eh?" He turned to Allie Benoit and smiled.

"Let me think," Allie said. "Nope. Excuse me. I'm going to go find someone among the living to speak with tonight."

"I guess we should split up and mingle," John murmured. "I mean, we do spend way too many hours together."

"I'm out of here," Allie said. "Hey, want to join me?" she asked Kieran. "Never mind—I forgot. You're with ruggedly handsome and deadly serious over there. Okay, I'm off on my own to flirt with the rich and famous!"

"Maybe one of us can make the little model smile," Joshua suggested to Sam.

"I should join you," John Shaw said.

"No offense, sir, but we won't get anywhere if she thinks we're dragging our grandpa along," Joshua told him. He smiled at Kieran and hurried off, followed closely by Sam.

"Hey, Kieran, you don't have to stand here with a trio of old-timers," John Shaw said. "I think we've been appropriately put in our places."

"Among the dead!" Digby said, and sighed. "Almost old enough," he added cheerfully.

"Speak for yourself," John Shaw told him.

Willoughby wasn't smiling. He was looking toward the stairs to the crypt below.

Two young women scantily clad in tuxedo-like uniforms with fishnet stockings had just gone running down them.

"Mr. Willoughby, I'm sure that the site is protected. The bartenders and other employees have to go down to the storage area for supplies," Kieran told him.

He gave her a weak smile. "Somehow, it doesn't seem right, does it? I mean boxes of booze where bodies used to lie."

"Well," Shaw said, testing his sense of humor again, "there were spirits—and now there are spirits!"

He was so pleased with his joke. Kieran smiled, as well.

"I can't take it. I just really can't take it," Willoughby said. He started around the corner of the bar.

"Mr. Willoughby?" Kieran said, following him.

Though Craig and Mike had been standing by the stairs, they were apparently mingling elsewhere now.

However, a security officer was there.

"No one goes down unless you're an employee," he said sternly.

"I'm Henry Willoughby! I'm in charge of the historic area," Willoughby said, speaking with authority. "Let me pass, sir. I intend to see that history is preserved against this onslaught of elite partiers!"

The guard stepped aside. Kieran followed Willoughby down the marble stairs.

One of the pretty tuxedo-clad women was just coming up with a bottle of rum. She stopped and looked at them. "Oh, Mr. Willoughby!" she said. She gave a serious shudder. "Checking up on things? I don't see how you do it—all those decaying old corpses! I can't stand being down there!"

"No one should be down there," Willoughby said. He was distracted. Kieran gave the server a sympathetic smile and kept walking downstairs with Willoughby.

The second young tuxedo-clad woman passed them on the stairs as she came back up, as well. She caught Kieran's eye and shuddered slightly.

"Mr. Willoughby," Kieran said. "They're just working."

"Gleason is rich enough," Willoughby said. "He could have kept the club closed a little longer. It's not even a full week since they found Jeannette Gilbert."

They reached the bottom of the stairs. To the right, as always, the shelves of wine and beer and alcohol remained. To the left, another security guard stood by the area of the broken-down wall—and all the graves beyond.

"No one allowed down here, sir," the security guard said.

"I'm Henry Willoughby—entrusted by the City of New York to see that this area stays safe!"

"I'm watching it, sir," the guard said.

But, just after he spoke, a strange rustling sound came from the far reaches of the crypt.

"Sir!" Willoughby said, indignant. "What, did a horny guy bribe you, you idiot, to get back there with a girl? Some people!"

"No one went back there," the guard protested.

"There's something going on," Willoughby announced, heading into the area filled with the old tombs.

"Sir, if it's dangerous…" the guard protested.

Kieran quickly read his name tag. "Mr. Gillian, please—there are a pair of FBI agents upstairs. Frasier and Dalton. Please find them, get them down here."

He nodded to her and hurried for the stairs.

Willoughby was already gone. Kieran hurried after him.

She passed by the first row; most of the bodies here were in coffins. As she came toward the back, she called out to him. "Mr. Willoughby?"

There was no reply. The crypt seemed eerily silent; if she listened carefully, she could detect the music from above as if it were far, far away, barely a hint of sound.

She couldn't hear Willoughby; he didn't answer her.

Kieran looked at the row of tombs and sarcophagi in the middle between the first and second rows of catacomb shelving. Nothing.

She started down the second row of tombs.

There were no marble slabs—broken or intact—on the second row of bodies. Shrouds covered them, some as if melted into the bodies, some disintegrating so badly that skulls—disarticulated from the rest of the form—seemed to be staring at her.

Bony fingers protruded from one, almost as if they reached out in an attempt to help the body crawl from the slab on which it lay.

The lighting—focused near the broken wall—paled here.

And Kieran realized she was afraid.

She heard someone moving along the next aisle of bodies. "Mr. Willoughby?"

There was no answer.

She froze dead where she was.

Someone was down there. Someone who was now trying to move around the other row and come toward her. There was an eerie menace to the slow, careful sound of the steps.

Kieran took a breath and started to run.

She heard her pursuer give up the attempt at silence and rush into her wake.

Craig was startled when he saw the security officer looking through the crowd, apparently anxious to get to him.

The flirtatious blonde woman—who had known them for agents—had first tried to get Craig and Mike to take her downstairs. Everyone wanted to see the old crypt.

He'd firmly refused, but she'd continued to talk, telling him that she was being managed by Oswald Martin and would love it—love, love, love, it!—if they'd go over with her to where Oswald Martin was speaking with Leo Holt. She felt awkward going over alone, but with two handsome men at her side, well, it would just be great!

Martin had had an answer for everything Craig had thrown at him, and in his own way, he had cared about Jeannette Gilbert, Craig thought. But Leo Holt was with him, and Craig relished another chance to talk to the photographer.

But they had barely started a conversation—with the girl saying how she'd love, love, love a nice shot with two special agents—when Craig saw the officer and excused himself. Naturally, Mike followed.

"Mr. Willoughby heard something down in the crypt and took off. He was there with a young woman who asked that I get you. Now, I don't know what he could have heard. I was at that wall all night. I looked away for about two seconds when one of the girls working this thing needed help with a box. There's been a guy at the stairs…but there are people everywhere!" The guard looked aggravated—and guilty.

Craig wondered how much time he might have spent helping one of the beauties in the scanty tuxedo costumes.

But there was no time for recrimination.

He headed for the stairs and hurried down them.

As he did so, all the lights in the place suddenly went out.

Upstairs, auxiliary lighting came on amid the startled cries of those present and the whine of the band's instruments.

Down in the crypts…

It was pitch-black.

It had been dim before; now Kieran could see nothing at all.

The eerie silence seemed to envelope her; the musty smell of the long dead wrapped around her.

It wasn't the dead she need fear.

Someone was following her.

She needed to get back to the entrance to the forgotten crypt. If the lights were out, she was certain they were out on purpose.

She thought she heard someone speaking; she couldn't tell where it was coming from. It was soft—so soft. But then she began to recognize the words.

"'Thou art not conquer'd…Kieran.'"

Softly spoken, her name, so softly said. She had to wonder if she'd really heard it.

She barely dared draw in a breath. Had she imagined it?

She wasn't imagining the whispering. There was no doubt about the soft, raspy voice.

"'Beauty's ensign yet is crimson in thy lips and in thy cheeks…'"

She heard it clearly, but she didn't know from where. Sound seemed to bounce off the stone of the catacombs, catch in the shrouded and entombed bodies.

"Come, come to me. I will love you, keep you…perfect."

Terror filled her; she fought it desperately.

Fear was a good thing, she knew. It made a person alert and wary. But terror led to panic and panic was no good, and she wasn't a person who panicked…

Not usually. She was damned close to it, though!

The sound, the invitation, had come from a bit of a distance. Someone was quoting Shakespeare—the same passage that had been sent to the newspaper.

Only the killer knew what they had written.

If she stayed right where she was…

"Kieran!"

This time, she heard her name called loudly, in a deep, rich and very masculine voice.

She almost cried out in answer.

She refrained.

Then, she heard the unmistakable sound of a shot fired. And then another, and a volley of several more.

Next to her, a corpse exploded.

She dropped to the ground, willing herself to silence, trying hard not to move.

Then, light blazed into her face. She blinked.

"Kieran!"

It was Craig. She jumped up and into his arms.

"You're okay? You're okay?" he asked anxiously.

"I'm fine. I don't know who is shooting. It's so dark, I have no idea what's happening."

"What the hell were you doing down here?" Craig demanded.

"I was trying to keep Henry Willoughby from coming down," she said. "Ask the guard. He just took off. I couldn't reach him. Craig, I have to tell you—"

"Where the hell is Willoughby?" She heard someone else shout. It was one of the security guards, she thought. Probably the man who had tried to stop them from entering.

With good reason.

And yet...

The killer had been in the crypt. She was certain of it.

And then another shout came to them. "I found Willoughby. Oh, God!"

"What's wrong?" Craig shouted.

"Willoughby. He's here, but...someone needs to call an ambulance!"

CHAPTER
SIXTEEN

THE POLICE WERE OUT EN MASSE.

Naturally at first, it was chaos at the club and below the club.

The beautiful people all went rushing into the night, afraid and confused. The police took information from them and then urged them all to go home.

But the confusion in the crypt went on and on.

The ambulance arrived quickly.

Henry Willoughby was, thank God, alive, but bewildered, as he came to.

He didn't know what had happened to him. He didn't remember being struck by anyone, or finding anyone. But, of course, the crypt was big.

The rows of the dead went on and on.

A pile of bones was found where he lay. He might have cracked his head against the stone of the crypt, something might have fallen on him—or, whoever the hell it was who had gotten down into the crypts might have smacked him hard on the head with a rock or bone.

He just didn't know.

He had come to while the EMTs were rushing to help him. Kieran and Craig were by his side as he shook his head in fear, disgust and anger. "I knew the place shouldn't reopen! Things were just still… I don't know. Too fresh? But I can tell you this—there was someone down here. Kieran was here. Kieran knows. Yes, right? I'm not just a crazy old man!"

"There was someone down here," she agreed. "He was quoting Shakespeare, and he spoke directly to me."

"Spoke to you?" Craig asked.

Kieran nodded. "Yes, I know someone was down here," she told him.

"Did you hear someone speaking?" he asked Willoughby.

"I don't know what I heard," Willoughby said. "I know somebody else was there."

"Somebody with a gun," Craig said harshly, looking at Kieran.

But she was looking at Willoughby again.

One thought kept repeating in her mind. The killer had been down there. The killer had spoken.

To her.

"They're going to ruin it all," Willoughby said sadly, looking up as a crew of forensic experts arrived. "They're going to look for bullets and evidence…and they just won't know how to deal with things as old and delicate as these bodies in the crypt."

"Mr. Willoughby, you're alive," Kieran told him.

"Yes, yes, of course. And I'm grateful," he said.

Then, the EMTs were there, warning them that they needed to get Willoughby to the hospital and find out the extent of his head injury. Craig knew they were right, but he was frustrated. He wanted more from the man.

Willoughby argued at first. Surely he was fine. But then he tried to rise and fell back, and, in the end, he agreed to go to the hospital.

Kieran was covered in crypt dust. Her little black dress was an odd white color—as were her hair and much of her flesh.

"A corpse exploded right by me," she said, wincing. "God, I'd love a shower!"

"I need a statement from you," he told her. "Actually, you should give it to Mike."

"Sure. Of course," she murmured.

He looked over at his partner, who nodded. Kieran—just a little shaky—walked over to Mike, who pulled out a pad and listened to her gravely.

Craig moved carefully through the rows of the dead. Most of the crypts seemed undisturbed; here and there, pieces of bone or bits of a disintegrating shroud had fallen to the hard stone floor. He looked for signs of a shooter.

He could find none.

One of the techs came up to him, a bullet in her gloved hand. "Smashed, but 9 mm, if I know my ammunition. The fellows working here are licensed through the security company with permits to carry on duty here. They've all got Glocks, similar to what the NYPD use."

"It's easy enough to acquire those firearms personally, too."

"We're going to have to do more investigation to figure out who shot what where," the tech said. "I talked to one of the security guys. He'd found you and then run back down, and he swears that he was fired at first in the crypt, and then returned fire. The thing is, once the lights went out, there was something of a panic upstairs and down. No one seems able to say for certain where they were or what happened where."

"So, the killer—or the shooter in the crypt—might not

even have existed? You're saying that Willoughby might have just cracked his head himself somehow?" Craig asked. "And something *sounded* like a gun so the security personnel just shot in response?"

Police lights now flooded the place. The light should have made it all less creepy, less eerie. Somehow, the garish, unshielded lights seemed to make it all the sadder.

"I don't know what happened yet. This is going to take some time," she said, and shaking her head slightly, she turned back to work.

"Craig!" Kieran called softly.

He turned to her. Her deep blue eyes with their hint of green seemed enormous in her face.

"Yeah?"

"The killer *was* here, definitely here," she said. "He was speaking. None of that was let out to the media—I mean, none of the information about the note he wrote to the newspaper with the Shakespeare?"

"They've kept a lid on it so far," he told her.

"I figure whatever I say down here now isn't for the media, so… I heard whispering. Quoting Shakespeare. Someone was reciting lines from *Romeo and Juliet*."

He didn't want to believe her. He told himself there was so much going on. It was dark; it was a crypt. Maybe, just maybe, she'd let her imagination run wild.

"You heard that? You're certain?" he demanded.

"'Beauty's ensign yet is crimson in thy lips…'"

He was an agent; well trained, secure in his competence. They'd met with many strange cases in his years with the Bureau. But he didn't like the feeling that washed over him now. It was as if a phantom existed, one who came and went like a breath of air.

"Dammit, yes, I know it!"

There were a half dozen forensic techs down there with them and at least as many officers. The crypt was big—covering about half a block, he reckoned—but they had plenty of people searching it.

Maybe too many.

Mike walked up to them. "No one," Mike said. "There's no one here."

"But there was. I'm certain," Kieran said.

"Well, sure you were down here, and Willoughby was down here, and the guards were down here…and someone panicked when it went dark," Mike said. He smiled, shrugging with a grimace. "There was so much going on, Kieran. I think you need time to think, though. Maybe you were feeling a little panic, too."

"Don't get me wrong, I was scared as hell, but I didn't panic. There had to have been someone here!"

"Shots were definitely fired. You know that. You and I rushed in together," Craig told Mike. "That's what I mean. Someone down here apparently did panic—one of the security guys. But who fired first and at what—that's what we've got to figure out."

"Listen to me, dammit! Believe me, there was someone else in the basement," Kieran said flatly.

"Two of the security guards fired. They swear they were fired at first," Mike said. "And in the rush and in the darkness, no one can be certain that someone didn't get up or down the stairs and wasn't seen."

"Okay, so he got back up the stairs somehow. Or he disappeared—with his gun—into thin air. But I don't care what the forensic teams find. I know that there was someone else," Kieran said, her tone aggravated.

"The forensic teams are going to be down here all night," Mike said. He looked at Kieran, nodding as if he believed her. Craig looked over at Mike and arched a brow slightly.

Mike looked back at him. He didn't speak out loud. Craig knew what he was thinking.

Yes, it's Kieran, she doesn't lie, and she's been through a lot, and she's smart and she doesn't panic.

Maybe the killer had fired blindly and gotten out of the crypt in the confusion of darkness.

And Kieran could have been killed.

He set his hands on Kieran's shoulders, feeling torn between his duty as an agent and his love for this woman. He didn't want her away from him, but he had hours of work ahead of him down here.

He simply had to learn to trust other people to care for her.

"I don't want you to be alone. We'll get an officer to see you home, and a cop will stay with you. One I know. One we trust," Craig said.

"I don't need a cop in my apartment," Kieran protested.

"He'll be in the hallway. We'll have shifts if we need them," Craig told her. "Your brother will stay with you, right? Wouldn't hurt for you *not* to be alone."

"My brother and Dr. Fuller!" Kieran exclaimed. "Where are they now?"

"They were with the crowd upstairs, ushered out with the blackout when all the panic began," Craig told her. "I can't leave here until we've sifted through everything, but let's head up and you can get ahold of your brother. Cell phones don't work very well down here."

The club seemed strangely empty and just as eerie as the crypts below; it was as if the population of the world had just suddenly disappeared, evaporated into space. The expanse of the great old Gothic church was vast. With everyone out, each little sound echoed.

Kieran called her brother; he was over at Finnegan's and waiting anxiously to hear from her. He was upset; Craig could hear every word of their exchange.

"Danny, Declan and me. We're sitting here worried sick," Kevin said, his voice strong enough to resonate through the cell phone. "Though, at least, some cop told me you were fine and with the cops and agents."

"I'm fine. You guys knew that I would be with Craig. You worry too easily," Kieran said, glancing at Craig.

"A blackout and shooting…yeah, silly me. I worry," Kevin said. "Tell her I'm right, Craig—I'm figuring you're there close?"

"He's right, Kieran," Craig said.

"I'm sorry," she told them, "and tell Declan and Danny I'm just fine. I don't want to come into Finnegan's, though. I really need a shower."

"A shower?" Kevin said.

"Corpse exploded," she explained briefly.

"Of course," Kevin muttered. "But…"

They heard Kevin speaking to Danny and Declan. And over the phone, they could hear the strains of a violin playing an old Irish tune. Craig recognized the sounds of the local Irish band they had both enjoyed many times.

Not tonight.

Danny and Declan were apparently mollified by the plan. An officer would escort Kieran to the pub, pick up Kevin and take her home.

Kevin assured Craig that he would stay with his sister through the night. He'd be damned if he'd leave her.

Craig confirmed that the police officer would stay, too, guarding the hallway over the karaoke bar.

But before he could let her go, Craig pulled Kieran to the side to speak with her. "This is scary as hell, you know. You were down there—the killer was down there. Or a man we assume to be the killer. He knows you."

"You do believe me."

"Of course, I believe you. That's what I'm worried about."

She looked away uncomfortably.

"Hey, I'm smart enough to be alert, aware and wary," she assured him. "And my brothers are great—they won't let me be alone, Craig. You know that."

"I'll be there as soon as I can. It will be late."

"It's okay," she said, cupping his face with her palms. "This is what you do, Craig." She smiled. "You're not deserting me. I'm fine."

He nodded after a moment and let her go.

Mike walked over to him. "If we can be certain that it was the killer down in the crypts—though it might not have been—we can definitely scratch Oswald Martin, Leo Holt, Brent Westwood *and* Kevin Finnegan off our list of suspects. I saw all of them right before we started down."

"It was definitely the killer," Craig told him.

"You know that because...?"

"Because he was quoting."

"Quoting, yes, that's what Kieran said."

"*Romeo and Juliet.* Mike, who the hell else would taunt someone he might turn into a victim with that?"

"And you're sure she didn't imagine it?"

"She doesn't imagine things."

"If that's true, the killer was down there. I mean, assuming all the profilers and experts are right. Kieran—you think he was after Kieran? How could he have known that she would walk into the crypt?" Mike asked.

"No one could have known. She might not have been his specific target. I can't figure this out right now. But I believe Kieran, and it would be just too coincidental for someone to have sent in a letter with a passage from Shakespeare—and then have someone downstairs, where Jeannette Gilbert was found, quoting lines from the same play. We just don't know how he got down there."

"But you did tell Kieran about the letter to the papers, though, right?" Mike asked.

"Yes, I told her."

"She heard this in a pitch-black crypt—she might have been in a suggestible frame of mind. Hey, even I get the creeps in a crypt in the pitch-dark!"

"She didn't imagine it. I believe the killer—whoever the hell he is—was down here. There was a security guard on duty but he admitted that he went to help one of the servers with the boxes. So this guy was in the tomb when Willoughby went down with Kieran. Willoughby heard him there. Maybe the killer just slipped back upstairs to join the party—and maybe it was planned that way. It was even pitch-black in the club for a few seconds when the lights first went out." He followed his line of thinking to the next question. "As you said, we know that Oswald Martin, Leo Holt and Brent Westwood were right here. Did you see Gleason, John Shaw or Digby up here, or the grad students?"

"The grad students were together in a group near the backup bar. But," he added quietly, "I didn't see Digby, Shaw or Gleason."

"Where is Gleason now?" Craig asked. "Has anyone seen him since this all started?"

"I haven't seen him, but I've been with you."

"Put out a search for him."

"Right away," Mike said. "I'll find McBride, get the cops moving."

They found McBride interviewing a guest just outside the arched entrance.

McBride quickly marshaled a number of officers, and a search was begun.

Dozens of officers, in the club, out on the streets.

Down in the crypt.

Roger Gleason was nowhere to be found.

"Whoa!" Kevin said, getting into the police car next to his sister. "You were in the cellar? That must have been terrifying. They forced us out. I didn't know where you were, Kieran."

"I'm fine, really, honestly," Kieran promised. "Kevin, please, I'm sorry you went through that, but I'm fine."

"Here I am thinking first that I'm where…where Jeannette was found. And then I'm actually being given cards by several producers and directors. And then the lights go out, and I realize that you're not there, everyone is being rushed out—"

"Which producers?" she asked, pouncing on the good news.

He looked at her, a worried half smile on his lips. "I don't remember right now. I have their cards. You're missing the point. You really have to lie low until they find this guy."

"I was always close to law enforcement," she said. It wasn't really a lie. It depended on how one chose to define the word *close*.

"I do thank God you're with Craig," he told her.

"I worry about Craig. His work is dangerous."

"Yeah, his work is dangerous, but he's trained to handle

it. I worry about you. You get into these things all on your own—even without Danny's help," Kevin told her.

The officer driving them cleared his throat.

"I believe this is it," the officer said pleasantly. "But I'm staying. Have to go around to find parking—even for a cop car."

A minute later, he found a spot. Shutting off the car, he ran around to open the car door for them, but Kevin was already out and helping Kieran.

They both thanked him. "Nice neighborhood," he told Kieran. "I'd love to live in the Village."

"Took a long time to find the apartment," Kieran assured him.

It was late but, as usual, the karaoke bar was still going strong. Japanese Country Western Night! the sign in front advised. Someone with an excellent deep Johnny Cash–like voice was singing a great version of "Folsom Prison Blues."

"Not bad," Kevin commented.

"Yep, the guy is pretty good," the officer agreed.

"Did you want to head into the karaoke?" Kieran asked them both, smiling.

"Not tonight," the officer said.

"Have you seen yourself?" Kevin asked Kieran. "You look like one of those ghost dolls. Think we should head on up. But one night we'll have to drag Craig in there. I wonder if there are karaoke loving G-men? Maybe Mike—he's pretty good at cracking a smile now and then!"

"Craig smiles and you know it," Kieran said.

"I'll be out there. Sleep soundly," the officer told her when he'd checked out the apartment and let them in.

"I feel badly, having you just stand guard out here," Kieran replied.

"Overtime!" he told her cheerfully.

They both thanked him.

As soon as they were alone, Kevin plopped on the sofa and turned on the television. He flicked around until he found local news.

"Is Le Club Vampyre as doomed as those creatures upon whom the name is based?" a dramatic reporter asked. "Tonight, there was a major power surge and outage in the middle of an elite party filled with the who's who of the entertainment industry and the political scene! Not even a week ago, the body of actress Jeannette Gilbert was found in a secret crypt below the venue opened by famed billionaire Roger Gleason. While no one knows as yet what caused the exodus following the power outage, there's a rumor that shots were fired—rather than served. Stay tuned and we'll bring you the latest!"

Kieran watched her brother's face as they'd flashed an image of Jeannette Gilbert on the screen.

Kevin's expression was pained and dark.

She kissed the top of his head. "I'm going to take a shower," she told him.

"A very good idea."

When she emerged twenty minutes later, Kevin had opted to change the channel, watching bits of the Broadway shows that were currently available. Her brother truly loved the theater, whether working in it or going to it. She was sure the evening had been ironic for him—filled with opportunity, yet, hauntingly painful.

"Kevin?"

He didn't answer her. She walked over and saw that he had fallen asleep.

Kieran drew a blanket over her brother and headed into her bedroom.

She was far too restless to sleep herself. Turning on the television did no good. No movie or show would capture her attention at the moment.

She headed to the bookcases wedged between the window and her dresser and finally found something called *A Complete and Comprehensive History of New York City*.

The book was about a thousand pages long, and yet, she thought, no one could really do a complete and comprehensive history of a three-hundred-year-old city in that kind of space. And still, she remembered that she loved the quirky voice of the historian who had written the book, so she picked it up, carrying it into bed with her.

Kieran glanced at the clock. Past midnight. She had work in the morning. She should sleep.

She couldn't.

She was waiting for Craig to come, and there was no hope for sleep until he returned.

She might as well learn more about the City of New York.

In the crypt a top-notch forensic team was busy trying to put the pieces together.

"I have to tell you, this is like the impossible task," Lynda Gomez, head of the forensic team for the FBI, told Craig. "We've located seven bullet casings, all 9 mm caliber. Thing is—of course, we'll have to test—but I think they all came from the security guys who were working there. They've all got legal firearms—the guards for the night were all off-duty cops, permitted to carry through the security company. I'm just trying to figure out what they thought they were firing at, because I haven't found anything that might have been fired at them. You didn't fire, right?" she asked Craig.

"No."

"You?" she asked Mike.

"I did not," he said.

"I'm still looking. But...there are hundreds of *corpses* down here. Only way to really do a thorough search is to pull every corpse apart, and, oh, boy...the legal that goes with that!"

"Thanks, Gomez," Craig told her. "Fingerprints, shoe prints...anything? Anything out of the ordinary?"

"What's ordinary in a crypt?" she asked, shaking her head. "We're taking everything we can find. Anything and everything."

Egan stood silently by Craig, grim as he watched the action. His phone apparently vibrated in his jacket. He answered it, listened briefly.

Then he turned to Craig.

"We've got the search warrant. It's pretty inclusive. Just came through. ADA Birney found Judge Monahan out at a party and...I don't think he believes a man as rich and powerful as Gleason could have done any of this, but, with all that's circumstantial..." He paused and shrugged. "No one ever wants the rich and powerful to be guilty. Maybe they just don't want to go after them, I don't know."

"They searched for Gleason. No one could find him," Craig said. "Which might... Hell, I guess that all things point in his direction."

McBride came down the stairs then.

"Did they find Gleason yet?" Craig asked him.

"Officers were looking over half the city—and we found him in his office. Said he was out talking to guests, telling them he'd get it together over whatever was going on here or close the place down."

"Truth or lie?" Egan murmured. "Anyway, a deputy is on the way with the physical warrant. Figure you can go ahead and tell Gleason—the warrant will be here before he has time to destroy any evidence or do anything."

Craig nodded and turned to Mike. "All right, then."

"Serve the warrant together," Egan said, nodding toward McBride. "I want everyone knowing that the city and the federal government are in on this together."

"You got it, sir," McBride assured Egan.

Gleason had—until he'd disappeared that night—been accessible, open and decent with the police.

Had it all been an act?

Craig sure as hell couldn't pinpoint the lie, if there was one. And yet, circumstances pointed to the man.

Gleason's place.

His security footage.

His alarm system.

Darkness, chaos and shots fired—and in the midst of it, he had been nowhere to be seen.

Craig, Mike and McBride headed up the stairs. "Okay, so we have people down here. We'll need a small army for the club and his office. What about his home?"

"I have a team in place, set to go," Egan assured him. "We've been waiting for the call. Still, I'd like to have that warrant in hand."

"I'll go to the entrance and wait," Mike said. "It should be a matter of minutes. You two go and make sure Gleason is still in his office."

Mike headed toward the door; Craig, with McBride in

tow, headed to Gleason's office. He tapped on the door and Gleason called out, "Come on in."

Craig and McBride entered the office. Gleason leaned back in his chair, looking at them with surprise at first.

Then he knew.

"Well, I guess it's about time," he said. "Especially since I was, according to the officer I spoke with a few minutes ago, missing during the blackout."

"Where were you?" Craig asked him.

"With the crowd. Everyone was shoving and pushing. I was afraid someone was going to get hurt in it all. Liability, of course, and I guess you don't believe it at the moment, but I don't like it when people are hurt."

"No one saw you," McBride informed him.

"No one? Who is the 'no one' you're speaking about? I talked to Mark Thresher, producer of *Prime Time in Paris*, and William Arrow— Hey! I even spoke with Leo Holt. He suggested that with all my other enterprises, I give up on this place."

Craig nodded. "We'll check that out, of course. In the meantime, I'm sorry, but we have a search warrant to serve. Naturally, you're welcome to call your attorney, but the search will go on."

Gleason nodded and rose. "Well. Yes, I suppose, under the circumstances, I understand. Gentlemen, you didn't need a warrant. You were welcome to search anything of mine any-where at any time."

"Thanks, Mr. Gleason," Craig said. "Your cooperation is—and has been—deeply appreciated."

"Yeah, sure, whatever," Gleason said. "Knock yourselves out. I'll be…staring at the Gothic features in the club area. Don't worry—there are a dozen cops out there. I'm sure they'll make sure that I don't go anywhere. Come get me if you need me."

Gleason left his office. Craig headed for the desk. McBride headed for a file cabinet.

He never even opened the cabinet.

"Frasier!" McBride said.

"What?"

The detective turned to Craig. "I'm no expert, but I've been around a long time. If this isn't blood on the cabinet, I'll be damned."

Craig frowned and quickly strode across the room to look.

And McBride was right.

On the handsome wood face of the cabinet, right beneath one of the brass pull rings, was a darker splotch of color.

He'd be damned himself if it wasn't blood.

CHAPTER
SEVENTEEN

KIERAN'S PHONE RANG AT 7:00 A.M.

She'd slept, but not until very late, and even as she recognized Craig's ringtone, she spread a hand out over his side of the bed.

He'd never come in last night.

"Good morning," she said.

"Morning to you, too. Everything okay with you?" he asked her.

"Fine. I was reading most of the night, barely slept. I was waiting for you… I don't mean in a bad way. I mean in a good way. I knew after everything that went on you'd be late or working through the night. You must be exhausted."

"It just hit about an hour ago," he told her.

"Well, in a way, I think I might have figured something out," she told him. "First of all, you have to remember that the city—especially downtown—is old. It has been occupied by European settlers for nearly four hundred years. The Dutch came first, and they were really run by the Dutch West

India Company because of wars with the Spanish Empire, so much so that there was no one to fight the English, and the city was surrendered and then became English. Okay, so the English were building over the Dutch. You had Broadway and Wall Street. You had Trinity. You had the Revolutionary War, British occupation and a fire that destroyed huge portions of what existed."

"Kieran," he said quietly over the phone.

"Craig, wait, listen and hear me out. Then, the Americans came in and Washington was inaugurated president. Everything was a shambles, everything needed to be rebuilt. Everyone was rebuilding, blasting—creating foundations, since they weren't just slapping up wooden structures. They were creating storehouses, cold places beneath the earth…places beneath the earth that weren't necessarily catacombs or crypts," Kieran told him. "Do you understand?"

"Basements and foundations? Pretty much so. Yes, Finnegan's has a basement and a foundation dating from the 1800s," Craig said. "And almost every building has a deep foundation and a basement. We're on a really nice big pile of rock here. But—"

"A big pile of rock that people have been digging into and blasting into forever. People need water. Water needs pipes to travel. Some electric is underground—and then, there's the subway!" she said triumphantly. "And really the subway is the point."

"The point of…?"

"How the killer is getting into and out of the crypt without being seen. Somewhere, somehow, there's another basement, forgotten subway tunnel, some other *underground* venue that attaches to the crypt."

"Kieran, we've looked for another entrance. And all we've found in the crypt is rows and rows of bodies."

"All the bodies haven't been moved."

"Kieran, a forensic team was down there for hours, searching—even through the bodies—for bullets. So far, no one can even tell who was firing at whom and from where. Everything found seems to be from the security detail's firearms. It's going to take time for our forensic teams to go through everything, especially when no one can understand what happened down there as of yet."

"I'm telling you what happened down there. The killer gets in from somewhere else beneath the ground. A building with a basement or an abandoned subway tunnel or some kind of a utilities access."

"Kieran, I believe that could have been a really logical answer. But, had it been, not even the FBI has the power, the resources or the know-how to go ripping up all the buildings in the area. And," he added softly, "the question doesn't exist anymore."

"What are you talking about?" she asked him.

"We arrested Roger Gleason last night. Or early this morning."

"Gleason!" she exclaimed.

"We knew he had the access and controlled his alarm and the cameras, but last night cinched it. He disappeared during everything going on, and the blackout was planned, caused by a disruption in the main breaker system. And there was blood in his office. The DNA isn't back on it yet, but they're expecting to find that the blood belonged to Jeannette Gilbert."

"But isn't that all circumstantial? Is that enough to...to..."

"Convict him? I don't know. Egan made the call to go

ahead and bring him in. He'll be arraigned in federal court in a few hours."

"Oh," Kieran said.

He didn't reply right away.

"That's all—oh?"

"I guess I'm surprised. Maybe I shouldn't be. I don't know why. With what evidence there was, I suppose it was one of those instances when the obvious should have been obvious. He could turn off the alarm and his cameras. But..."

"But what?"

"I thought that the FBI techs said that the footage hadn't been rigged."

"They couldn't find how it had been rigged. Not the same thing."

"Has he confessed?"

"He emphatically denies that he had anything to do with Jeannette Gilbert's death or the deaths of any other young women. He lawyered up pretty quickly."

"Of course. And you feel that this is...right?"

"If the DNA comes back as a match to Jeannette Gilbert, I don't think there will be much choice."

"Maybe not. But he couldn't have killed her in his office. There would be a blood spill a mile wide."

"No, she wasn't killed in the office. But it could be a blood transfer. He might still have had it on his hands or clothing. There's a whole team still in there, ripping things to shreds. And his home."

"They won't find anything," Kieran said.

"Because you're sure he had a work area—underground— as he did in Virginia."

"Yes."

"Well, maybe he'll talk eventually. I interviewed him at

length," Craig said. "Four of us, playing interrogation tag—me, Egan, McBride and Mike. For hours. He held to his story, and in the end, said he wanted a lawyer. We couldn't trip him up on anything. Once he's arraigned...well, he may want to make a deal. New York has no death penalty, but federal charges can carry a death penalty. However, we need to connect him to the other murders." He was quiet for a minute. "And find out if there are more bodies out there we haven't discovered yet."

"Let's hope not."

"Anyway, he's been arrested, he'll be arraigned. And I doubt that even he will manage to get out on bail, though I never try to outthink a judge on the bench. I've got to get some sleep. There's a new officer on duty out in your hall. Change of shift about an hour ago. He'll see you to work."

"If they've arrested Gleason, I should be fine."

"Humor me for today."

"Okay."

"Kevin still there? Why am I asking? Of course he is. He's your brother."

"Yes. He's out on the sofa."

"Good. You can bring him up to speed. I'm sure the media will get wind of this soon. It will be all over the news. I'll call you later this afternoon."

"Sure. Get some rest."

She sat in bed awhile after they finished their conversation. Pity, she was sure that one of the buildings near the old church had a basement that somehow led to the forgotten crypt. She'd thought she could find a way to provide some necessary answers.

Apparently not.

But then again...

Finding the killer's murder hideaway in the city might mean the difference between a conviction and a killer going free.

She hesitated, looking at her phone. Then she quickly put in a call to Dr. Fuller.

He was anxious about her; she felt guilty, remembering that he'd been led out while she was still inside and, like Kevin, he'd had to go on the assurance of an unknown officer that she was all right.

"Truly, I'm fine, just a little tired. I was wondering if I could take a few hours—"

"Of course, Kieran. We may have nine-to-five official hours, but you know that our hours are anything but official. We all work many more than that, and besides, after last night, you really should take the day. I got a call from Richard Egan. I know they arrested Gleason. That will be a relief for so many people, but..."

"But?"

"I'd like to speak with the man. Find out what made him tick. According to Egan, he's in complete denial. So much so that I'm wondering if there might be a case of split identities. And I can tell you this—they can find expert witnesses to speak for this man. Everything they have is circumstantial. Unless, of course, there's a witness against him. Perhaps Sadie Miller will regain her memory." He was silent for a minute. "I think we should go to see Ms. Miller. If Gleason has been arrested, I'm assuming they plan on letting Sadie go home."

"I'll find out," Kieran said.

"Thank you. Call me right back. You have been through a great deal with this case. As I said, you are welcome to take the day. You don't have any interviews scheduled that I know about."

Kieran didn't need the day; in truth, she didn't even need the hours. She just wanted them. There was a difference.

"I'll ask Craig about Sadie Miller and call you right back," she told Fuller.

"I can, of course, call Assistant Director Egan," Dr. Fuller said.

"Of course, that's fine, if you prefer."

"I'll do that. I'll call you right back."

Kieran thanked Dr. Fuller, trying to make plans in her head. She hadn't thought about Sadie Miller, though she knew that the police and the agents would. If Sadie Miller could identify Roger Gleason, it would make everything easier for everyone.

Hurrying out to the living room, she found that Kevin was already up; he'd made coffee.

"They arrested Roger Gleason," she said.

He'd been stirring cream into his coffee; he stopped dead, staring at her.

"Gleason?"

"Craig thinks it will be out in the news soon. There was..."

Her voice trailed. She didn't want to say the word *blood* to him. It wasn't a stranger's blood or a victim's blood to him— it was Jeannette's.

"There was what?"

"Evidence in Roger Gleason's office."

"What kind of evidence?" Kevin asked.

No choice.

"Blood," she said softly.

He picked up his mug. Kieran thought the heavy ceramic was going to crush in his hands. "And I talked to that man. I shook his hand," he said.

"Oh, Kevin," she murmured.

He lowered his head. "At least, maybe, they'll release her

body. She can have a funeral." He looked up at her. "Have a coffin all her own," he said bitterly.

"She'll have justice, as will the other young women."

He nodded. "Yeah, I'm sorry."

"Kevin..."

She let it go. She knew her twin. He had to mourn in his own way. And, at the moment, he needed to be left alone.

She poured herself coffee.

"Need me to see you into work?" he asked her.

She decided that, at the moment, she didn't want to tell Kevin her intention for the day.

She nodded toward the door. "The cop can take me in. Actually, I'm waiting to hear from Dr. Fuller. We can take you—"

"I'd signed up for a workshop at nine," Kevin said. "On Forty-Second Street."

"We'll get you there. Then the officer can drive me wherever Dr. Fuller needs me," she said. Of course, Dr. Fuller hadn't said anything about needing her. But Sadie had known that Bobby O'Leary drank nothing but soda water with lime. Logically, Sadie's next step might be remembering what happened next.

Her phone rang as she hurried back to the bedroom. Dr. Fuller informed her that Sadie was still in the hospital, there until Gleason was arraigned. "I'm going to go speak with Sadie. It would be great if you could come with me. She's met you. I believe that your being there will be a good thing."

Kieran agreed. In the living room, she cautiously opened the door to the hallway. A young officer in uniform was there, seated on a small folding chair, reading the *New York Times*.

"Good morning, Miss Finnegan."

"Good morning. Coffee?"

"Can't say I couldn't use more!"

When she brought him his coffee, she asked him if he'd mind dropping Kevin Midtown and then taking her to the hospital. He was happy to oblige.

Kevin was quiet on the way. She knew that he was thinking about Jeannette. She didn't try to draw him out. When they reached his destination, he kissed her on the cheek. "Old family pub tonight, sis? I feel the need for a little company."

"I'll be there," she promised.

Twenty minutes later, the officer dropped her in front of the hospital. Kieran hurried to the entry. Dr. Fuller was already there.

They headed up to Sadie Miller's room. The young woman was there alone, packing up her things. She greeted Kieran with a hug and shook Dr. Fuller's hand as they met.

"I'm going home," Sadie told them. "I'm excited and I'm scared. Mostly, I'm excited," she said. "They told me that they caught the man who killed Jeannette, who took me and drugged me. They said that it was a man named Roger Gleason. The guy who owned the place where Jeannette Gilbert was found."

"Do you know Roger Gleason? Do you remember meeting him?" Kieran asked.

"Ms. Miller, take your time," Dr. Fuller said. "In fact, this might help. Sit down, and let me bring you back. You were heading out to meet someone. And you were excited. You went to Finnegan's pub. You had a few drinks, just biding a little time. You were going somewhere."

She listened to the tone of his voice. Dr. Fuller could be so easy and relaxing. He wasn't hypnotizing Sadie, but his words were so soft and gentle, he might have been doing so.

"I guess I wanted to go to the club," she said. "I mean,

I'd heard about Le Club Vampyre. Everyone in the city was talking about it."

"Did you have a special in with someone? Did you, perhaps, meet Roger Gleason somewhere—and perhaps he asked to meet up with you?" Dr. Fuller asked. He pulled a notepad from his pocket and flipped through it, producing a four-by-seven picture of Roger Gleason. "Do you know him? Perhaps seeing him, you'll remember. Was he the man you were to meet?"

Sadie studied the picture. She looked at Dr. Fuller. "I know who he is. He's Roger Gleason."

"So, you were going to meet him?" Dr. Fuller asked.

"I've never met him—not that I know of," Sadie said.

"You said you recognized him," Fuller said, disappointed.

"Oh, yes, of course. His picture has been in the papers a zillion times. So, I guess it was him. I mean, the police arrested him, right?" Sadie asked.

"But you don't remember him?" Kieran asked softly. "You don't remember him from that night?"

Sadie shook her head. "I keep thinking that I remember you now," she said softly. "But I don't know if I remember you from that night, or because I've seen you now. I can't tell you how sorry I am, truly. So sorry!"

Dr. Fuller set a hand on her shoulder. "It's okay. You were given Rohypnol and lorazepam. Part of the popularity of Rohypnol as a date rape drug is that no one remembers what happened to them—not that you were sexually assaulted. It's not your fault at all, and there is no reason for you to be sorry in any way. In fact, you have been brave and wonderful and helpful."

Marie Livingston arrived as they were leaving. She was ecstatic that Sadie was allowed to go home and Roger Gleason had been arrested.

"I hope they throw the entire book at him. I hope he rots forever. No, I hope they charge him with federal counts of murder and that he's given the death penalty! If they connect him with the other women… I know that Virginia has the death penalty. I hope they kill him twice!" Marie said.

"Marie, stop. We've got to move on," Sadie told her.

Kieran and Dr. Fuller bid them goodbye. Fuller told Kieran he was going down to have a discourse with Roger Gleason. He was hopeful that the FBI, Gleason and Gleason's attorney would allow it.

Kieran wished she could get into the crypt below Le Club Vampyre. She didn't know if the forensic team had finished down there. Nor did she know if the historical crew had been allowed back in to work.

It was frustrating. She was convinced that there was an entrance and exit to the place that no one had discovered yet.

Maybe going at it from the other direction was the best approach—something she'd thought more and more about as she had been reading through the night.

If John Shaw, Aldous Digby and Henry Willoughby were hoping to get back in, they just might be at Finnegan's, close enough to the FBI building that she and Dr. Fuller might share a cab.

She arrived just at lunchtime.

None of the historians was seated at their usual tables; the pub, however, was crowded.

She headed to the bar where her brother Declan was moving like lightning. "Kieran! What's up? Everything all right? They arrested Gleason. Why aren't you at work?"

"I just left Dr. Fuller. I—"

"Man, you came to help out? Thank God! Mary Kathleen

has been going crazy. She'll give you a section. Thank you!"
Declan said, beaming as he looked at her.

"Ah...sure!" she said.

Lunch at Finnegan's was insane, of course.

All the wide-screen TVs that usually showed soccer matches
and sporting events were turned to the news.

The image of Roger Gleason being walked out of the club
in handcuffs showed over and over again. Every station had a
news team discussing the events with different specialists in
various fields of criminology.

Not one of them seemed in the least surprised that a man
like Gleason—sophisticated, a player, a billionaire—might
be guilty.

Everyone was talking.

"I knew it had to be that slimeball!" one woman was saying
as Kieran delivered fish and chips. "I knew it from the moment
they found Jeannette Gilbert in that place. That guy thought he
could buy just about anything. Who would suspect him? Imagine! And they saved that one girl, Sadie What's-Her-Name. He
could have killed and killed and filled his own crypt!"

Finally, it all died down. Kieran set her serving tray on the
bar, worn-out.

The day hadn't gone at all as she had planned.

And it was almost over. Looking at the clock above the bar,
she saw that it was after three.

She found Mary Kathleen, who thanked her profusely, and
then she found Declan, who thanked her, as well.

"I'm going to head out for a bit. I'll be back, though. I think
Kevin is heading here, and he wants to be with his family,"
she told Declan.

"See you later, then. And, really, you couldn't have come
to help at a better time!" he told her.

She smiled. He was so happy. There was no reason to tell him that she'd come by without the least intention of helping out.

She got her handbag and checked her phone; Craig hadn't called yet. He was probably still sleeping. The night had been very long for him.

She headed to the door. As she did so, John Shaw walked in.

"Kieran!" he said, smiling broadly.

"John. How's it going?" she asked.

He beamed at her. "I think all is going well. They arrested Gleason! My God, I never figured it!" He shuddered. "We worked with that man every day. Every day. He was so polite. We all knew that he was a businessman, and yet he was willing to let the work go on. Can't figure him, really. Unless it all had to do with whatever sickness plagued him."

"Ego," Kieran murmured, thinking clinically. "Sometimes, men with egos have to have their work seen and appreciated."

"Work...such as murder?" Shaw asked.

She nodded. "I believe he was arraigned this morning. Of course, they have yet to prove his guilt in court."

Shaw waved a hand in the air. "As long as they keep him locked up for now! We get to go back in, Kieran. Willoughby spoke with the mayor, the mayor spoke with the FBI and the police and the forensic units, and we're back in! It's going to be such a mess, of course. There'll be the disaster left by the forensic team. We'll have to sift through everything with a fine-tooth comb and try to restore what was, but at least we're going back in. It'll just be a few hours. I'm waiting for the final call."

"Good for you."

"Join me for a drink?" he asked Kieran.

"Sure," she told him.

"Take me back to my lite beer," he told her. "Got to keep my senses sharp."

"Okay."

She walked back to the bar.

"You didn't leave," Kevin noted, pulling clean glasses from the sanitizer. He'd arrived when she was talking with the professor.

"I'm leaving now. I'm just going to grab a drink with John Shaw. He's back to lite beer. And just give me a soda water, lime, please."

"You got it," Kevin said. "You want anything else?" he asked, inclining his head toward the side tables. "The Ghoul Crew seems to be moving back in."

Kieran turned. Willoughby had arrived along with the grad students. Professor Digby was just coming in the front door.

"I'll see what they want," Kieran said.

She hurried over and asked them what they'd like.

"A celebration!" Digby said. "A killer has been arrested— and once again, our find is back in our hands. Hallelujah and Hail Mary! This time, we should be really on our way!"

"And what would you like to celebrate with?" Kieran asked. "On the house."

"On the house?" Allie Benoit asked. She laughed. "We should have Long Island ice teas—get in the free booze while we can."

"Children!" Henry Willoughby protested. "You must drink responsibly."

"Champagne?" Kieran suggested.

"Lovely," Digby said.

She hurried back to the bar and got glasses and a cooler, and a couple of bottles of decent but not too expensive champagne and brought them to the table.

She poured, and they all raised a glass in a toast.

Kieran wasn't interested in drinking, however. She set her

glass down. Willoughby noticed, and handed the champagne back to her, quietly saying, "It's bad luck not to drink after a toast, you know." She smiled and took a quick sip, and then she turned to draw the men into conversation about the past— and the buildings on their block.

"Next to old Saint Augustine's—Le Club Vampyre, or whatever it will become now," Digby said thoughtfully, "is the Auburn Building. Circa 1848."

"Now it's offices," Kieran said.

"Retail on the first floor, offices above."

"What about the basement?" she asked.

"Storage, of course. It's a basement," Digby said. "Beautiful old building. It has gargoyles and nice moldings and all kinds of architectural detail. Maybe the builder thought he needed to go medieval, being next to a Gothic church and all."

"The other side is an office building, too. But modern. Well, more modern. There was a residence there for years, and then a tenement building. Now it's the Lamont Build-ing, circa 1930—legal and medical offices. I think you can even have your outpatient oral surgery there," Willoughby said. "Anyway, the old place was torn down when it was con-demned. Once upon a time, right after the church was built, it was a rectory."

"They have a basement, too?" Kieran asked. "Of course, foundations. All buildings like that pretty much have to have them, I assume. I mean, I'm not an engineer."

"There's a food court down there," John Shaw said. "I've eaten there—not as charming as this place, but great when you need a quick meal when you're working."

"Nice," Kieran said. She smiled at the group. "I think I'll take a walk down there."

"Kieran, trust me—the food is better here," Joshua Harding told her.

"What are you looking for?" John Shaw asked her. "It's obvious you're looking for something."

"I don't even know," she said.

Henry Willoughby sighed and stood up. "I'll walk you over. John, call me the second you hear that we've got the go-ahead."

"Will do," John promised.

"Okay, Kieran, let's go. I'll tell you what I know about the place on the way."

He started to the door. Kieran waved to the others. As she left, she turned back. Mary Kathleen had come to the table to pick up. She looked at Kieran and pointed to her glass. Kieran hadn't taken more than a sip of her champagne.

Kieran shook her head; she didn't want anything to drink.

She wanted to concentrate on what she was doing—whatever that was. She couldn't go into a food court and demand to know if there were secret tunnels somewhere in the building.

She hurried after Willoughby. He had long legs and long strides. And he was already talking, as if she were right by his side.

"...not long after the church was built. There was a grave-yard back then, of course, that extended between the church and the rectory. Money! Life is always money. Here's the thing—the dead were on prime real estate. The dead don't pay—the living pay. All the dead had to go."

They walked around the block.

"Careful looking up. Everyone will think you're a tourist," Willoughby teased her.

She smiled at him. "The city is so remarkable. So many

people—so many years. Lives on top of lives. I think people forget when they come here that we were the first capital of the country."

"So much is forgotten. The world always belongs to the young, right? Well, there she is, Kieran. The Lamont building. You want to see the food court. Okay. I'm afraid there's nothing left of the past, though. But, hey, there's one of those great chain coffee shops. Want some coffee?"

"Sure," she told him.

The Lamont building was still a handsome piece of architecture. The lobby had marble floors and giant pillars and carefully placed, huge pictures of bridges.

"Over there," Willoughby said, pointing to an escalator going downward. A sign in front of it advertised Starbucks.

"Told you," he said.

"Okay, so I'm in the mood for a mocha," she said.

She was startled to trip as she stepped onto the escalator; she was normally coordinated.

"Are you okay?" Willoughby asked, catching her arm.

"Fine," she told him. "Sorry. I must be anxious for coffee!"

"Coffee is good stuff," he said.

The food court reminded her of the food court at Grand Central Station. It was big and sprawling; there were many choices and it was busy, people running here and there and everywhere.

"Actually, there's a more local vendor over here," Willoughby said, pointing toward the far wall. "Excellent brews. They show you the coffees they have from all over the world. Hawaiian, South American... I love it."

"Well, then, let's head there," Kieran said.

They did so. It was far quieter at the end of the long expanse. There was a young man working the drip presses and he smiled when he saw Willoughby. "Hi, Mr. Willoughby. What will it be today? Kona blend?"

"Kona sounds great," Willoughby said. "And for my friend, Ms. Finnegan...?"

"Kona sounds great to me, too," Kieran said. She couldn't help notice that there was an entrance to a supply room to the right of the counter as she looked at it.

They were at the far right of the building. That meant that next door was Le Club Vampyre, and next door to the basement...

The crypts.

"Oh, my God!"

Kieran heard the words spoken loudly by a woman at the next food stand to the coffee bar.

The woman was staring up at the TV. The news was on.

Kieran stepped back to see what was going on.

"They let the bastard go!" the woman said, her voice still shrill. "Money really can buy anything," she muttered with disgust.

Kieran stared at the screen; she couldn't hear what the re-porter was saying.

She could see Roger Gleason, his attorney at his side and a group of police holding back the crowd as Gleason hur-ried out.

"Doesn't that just beat all!" Willoughby said at her side. "They let Gleason go! I'm going to have to call Digby and see what that means for us. Dammit! He could stop us from going back down to the crypts. No, the mayor won't let that happen."

What it meant, Kieran thought, was that they really had to find the killer's New York City underground lair.

"Did you hear, Kieran?"

"Yes, Mr. Willoughby. I heard."

She wasn't looking at him; she was suddenly determined.

Could she ask the young man if she could see their supply room? He wouldn't let her. But she could come back with Craig, if she could convince him that there had to be something somewhere.

"What is it?" Willoughby asked her.

"I was looking at the back there. That basement area must just about attach to the crypts."

"I suppose."

"How well do you know this guy? Well enough to ask a favor?" Kieran asked.

Willoughby stared at her and shrugged. "One can only try," he said. He paid for the coffee, leaving a generous tip. He started to speak, but then he didn't. He spent a moment adding cream and sugar to both cups, then brought them over and ushered Kieran toward a chair by the supply-room door.

"You didn't ask him."

"If we sit here a minute, we can just kind of slip in."

"Okay."

"How do you like the Kona?"

She took a swig of the coffee. "Delicious. Hot, but delicious."

They watched the young man as he puttered behind the counter.

"There! Now—he's gone out to clean the tables on the other side," Willoughby said.

Kieran jumped to her feet; she did so quickly. For a moment, she felt dizzy.

"Are you okay?" Willoughby asked anxiously.

"Fine. Let's go," she said.

And she did so, sprinting to the open doorway, hurrying to the back.

There were typical racks back there, filled with huge burlap sacks of coffee. There were all kinds of mugs, boxes of sugar substitute and sugar. Other racks held rows of boxed pastries, power bars and other light snack items.

It wasn't dark, dank or dirty.

For a moment, Kieran was disappointed. And then she looked at the wall.

It appeared to be old stone, boulders set together. Perhaps the new building had made use of some of the old foundations. After all, such rock could last a millennium or more.

"What?" Willoughby asked in a whisper. "Kieran, we need to hurry."

She walked quickly to the area of the bare wall, toward the irregular stones that she had seen.

"I'm hurrying," she told him.

As she reached the wall, it seemed that her knees were giving out, that black spots were appearing before her. She was weak...

She fought the sensation.

She reached the wall and slammed against it.

And then she began to slip down, the darkness coming in waves.

"Kieran! Kieran! What's wrong? I'm going to get help!"

Drugged! She'd been drugged. When? The coffee... The champagne...

And Roger Gleason was back on the streets.

"Help! Help!" Henry Willoughby called. "Damn that young fellow, where the hell is he? Don't worry—I will get help!"

Willoughby's voice faded.

Kieran couldn't think or feel anymore. She merely slipped into a deep abyss where there was nothing but black.

CHAPTER
EIGHTEEN

CRAIG HEARD HIS PHONE RINGING FROM FAR AWAY—AS IF he were underwater.

Then he sprang up, searching his bed for the phone. As deeply as he'd been asleep, he was suddenly wide-awake.

Outside his window, he saw it was already growing dark. Damn, he'd slept long. But, then, he'd not made it back to his apartment until almost nine, and he hadn't fallen into his bed until ten.

It was Egan on the other end.

"He's out."

"What?"

"Gleason is back out on the street, Craig. I don't know how the hell he managed it. The man is charged with one murder but suspected of being a serial killer and yet Gleason's attorney managed to get bail for him. Of all the stupid damned judges!"

As Egan went on, Craig's mind raced. Even if he was innocent, it was bad for Gleason that he was out; anything that happened would be on his head.

And if he was guilty…

Well, all the young and perfect women in Manhattan were in danger again.

"Sir," Craig said, interrupting Egan's rampage, "we need to get an officer to Sadie Miller. She left the hospital. If Gleason is afraid that she might recognize him, she could be in extreme danger. And Kieran, too. I'm up and moving. I'm going to head to Finnegan's. She's sure she heard the killer in the crypt last night. He might believe that she could recognize him, too."

"Get going. I'll have McBride find the closest officers and get them to Finnegan's now. Go. I'm on it—and Sadie Miller."

Craig jumped out of bed, looking for his clothing as he speed dialed Kieran.

She didn't answer.

He glanced at his watch. She might have left the offices of Fuller and Miro and headed to the pub already; if so, she might have been helping out. Her phone would be in her purse.

He called the pub. Declan answered after a number of rings.

"Hey, Declan, can you put Kieran on?"

"She's not here," Declan told him. "She was, but she went out. She was here with the Ghoul Crew from next door, but they're all gone now."

A startled scream suddenly sounded through Craig's phone line. He heard Declan's voice, deep with alarm.

"What the bloody hell?"

The bar phone dropped.

Craig had no idea what happened at Finnegan's; neither did he have time to figure it out.

Barely dressed, he headed out. He dialed Kieran again and again, to no avail, as he raced for his car.

He called Egan and was told officers were almost at the pub.

Then he dialed Declan again. That scream from earlier was still echoing in his mind. What was it all about? Kieran?

This time, the phone was answered. It wasn't Declan, but rather Kevin.

"What's going on there?"

"Mary Kathleen—she just passed out. One of the other girls told me that she'd said something about being overwhelmingly sleepy. And she's out cold. One of our customers—a doctor—checked her out; her vitals are fine but…we're trying to figure out what happened."

"Where's Kieran?"

"She was here…"

"But where did she go?"

"No one knows. She was talking to the whole historic crew from next door—and then she was gone, and they were all gone. Oh, my God! Craig. They let Gleason out! It's all over the news. And Kieran was here and she's gone and Mary Kathleen…it's like she was drugged!"

Kieran woke up feeling as if she'd been hit by a sledgehammer.

She had no clue as to where she was.

And she couldn't see anything. She was somewhere in total darkness. On something hard, something very hard. Stone.

She eased herself up. She was uninjured, but there was something worse…

She didn't remember how she'd gotten where she was.

She took a careful step, reaching out in the darkness and touching more stone.

She closed her eyes for a moment, wishing that she smoked. If she smoked, she might have a lighter in her jacket.

"Oh!" She said the word aloud.

She did have a light in her jacket—she had a matchbook that advertised Finnegan's. Letting out a sigh of relief, she dug out the matches and lit them.

And a scream tore from her lips.

She dropped the match at the gruesome sight.

She'd come face-to-face with a grinning skull, bits of scalp and hair remaining.

Crypts. She was in the crypts somewhere…but, where? Light of some kind would surely be back on in the hidden crypts beneath Saint Augustine's.

She fumbled for another match and lit it.

Wherever she was, it was just like the crypts at Saint Augustine's. Perhaps an extension of them?

Rows and rows of the dead rested in dark silence; there were no coffins at all, just decaying bodies in decaying shrouds, sarcophagi here and there dispersed beneath the rows and…

The slab. The slab she'd lain on. It was strangely shadowed and colored.

Her match went out.

She lit another.

She brought it close to the slab where she had lain. Yes, it was darkly stained…and the stain seemed to go all the way to the ground.

Match out; light another. At least it was a full pack. She figured she had about twenty-five matches to go.

She hunkered down, studying the floor. The stain extended here.

Her match went out. As it did, she felt a chill sweep through her.

She knew what the stain was.

It was blood.

The blood, most probably, of Jeannette Gilbert.

Her mind raced with questions. Why was she here? How had she gotten here?

More importantly, how in the hell did she get out?

She lit another match, raising it high, looking at the rows and rows of chalky white, decaying skeletons, rows and rows of shrouds…

Wait. One looked a little bit different. She hurried to that stone slab, and then she realized why.

There was no body there. Just a dress. A white dress, and atop the dress, a rose.

She inhaled and swallowed hard. Her fingers suddenly burned, and she dropped the match and quickly lit another.

She had to get out. Get away. She hurried to the next row of the dead, anxious to be far from the slab. She lit a match, trying to see if there was an end. The match went out. When it did, she thought that she saw the faintest glow.

A light was coming from somewhere. She headed toward it.

She wasn't sure why she was moving silently or carefully. But then she heard whispering.

And then words that sent a shiver up her spine.

"'Death, that hath suck'd the honey of thy breath, hath had no power yet upon thy beauty.' Ah, yes, death comes to the most beautiful, the most perfect! Lucky are those who die young, before life's ravishes ruin all that is glorious and perfect! Ah, yes, for the lucky…'death's pale flag is not advanced there!'"

For a moment, Kieran stood entirely frozen.

Panicked.

And then she remembered something.

She didn't panic. She recalled telling Mike that before. That day…that day she had gone to see Sadie Miller. With

Dr. Fuller. Then…then she had gone to the pub. She had been looking for…

What she had found—the killer's work lair.

"'Crimson in thy lips and in thy cheeks…'"

She looked at the pale, pale light that seemed to trickle in from far away. She moved toward it, carefully—listening all the while.

Then she heard a hoarse shout of surprise.

"No, no! Where are you? Where are you, Kieran? You should have finished drinking… Kieran, it shouldn't be hard, shouldn't be painful…oh, Kieran. I will find you!"

Craig rushed into the pub. Declan was there, not working the bar. He was waiting for Craig at the door.

"Officers are here, and an ambulance… Danny and Kevin are already over at the old church, searching the entire place for the people Kieran was talking to. Old Dr. Mayo was in here when Mary Kathleen collapsed. One of the girls working the floor told me that she'd had champagne… Apparently she drank Kieran's champagne rather than waste it. I have to get to the hospital… Mary Kathleen… But my sister is out there! Craig…"

The anguish in Declan's face sent greater spirals of fear shooting through Craig.

Kieran had been with the historians.

And Roger Gleason was out… He'd had time to get to his club…

But time to somehow slip into the pub unseen and spike champagne?

"We'll find her, Declan. I swear it," Craig vowed.

He turned and ran down the street—nearly knocking an old woman aside.

He'd have to apologize later.

He was afraid that the doors below the great Gothic entrance to the church-club would be locked, but no, the historians had come here.

The doors were open.

He burst in. The great expanse was empty.

"Kieran!" He shouted her name loudly.

At first, the sound of his voice echoed and echoed.

Then he heard something; not Kieran, but Kevin. And Kevin came racing up the stairs.

"Craig, they say that she was with them, but she wanted to see a building by here. Something about being certain there was a connection. Allie heard that the building had been the rectory. They say she left with Willoughby. But Willoughby called in a panic to tell them that she passed out there in the basement, but when he went screaming for help, she disappeared."

"Where's Willoughby now?" Craig demanded.

"I don't know... I saw him before...searching!"

"What about Gleason?"

"I have no idea. I know nothing except that he got out, and he called Digby and said that he wasn't going to stop history because of his own troubles—and that he was innocent. Craig, where the hell do we start looking?"

Mike burst in, not bothering to close the double, carved wood doors at the entrance. He shouted his name as he came hurrying in. "Craig! I just heard!"

Craig swung around. "Get next door, Mike. She passed out there—in the basement." He looked back at Kevin. "Where exactly?" he demanded.

Kevin shook his head. "Willoughby didn't say. The basement—there's a food court."

"I'll find it," Mike said. "There should have been an alarm tripped somewhere; hopefully, someone will know."

He turned and was gone.

Kevin stared at Craig. "Why are you standing here? We should go. We should follow him. My sister is missing!"

Craig hurried down the stairs. "It's through here, Kevin. It's through here somewhere."

"What?"

Craig waited until he reached the crypts.

"Hey, all of you!" he shouted.

The spotlights used for work in the crypts were on; the immediate area by the broken wall was alive with light.

The light naturally faded deeper into the crypts.

"The far end! The far left end of the crypts!" Craig said. "Get back there and break anything you need to and check the walls. There's an entrance that goes to the next basement or foundations here somewhere. Help! Please, help. It's Kieran's only chance."

They turned, white-faced, to do as he instructed. But Craig raced past them.

And he imagined Kieran, unconscious, lying on a tomb or a slab...

He reached the far left wall. He pushed past corpses, ignored skulls, created huge drafts of bone dust...

The picture had frozen in his mind.

Kieran, lying vulnerable. And the killer staring down at her, ready to stab her in the heart. Ready to keep her perfect for all time to come.

Kieran crept slowly through the rows of the dead, careful not to brush past the skeletal fingers that protruded here and there, afraid that they would break and fall—and give away her position.

She could barely see, making it difficult.

"Death will have no power on your beauty."

She held still for a minute; she couldn't see, but neither could the killer. All she had to do was keep moving…

Light suddenly shone a bit of a distance away. She winced and shrunk down; the killer was in another row. She was safe so far.

The glow allowed her to see that she was next to the skeleton of what she assumed to have been a very big man. The bones had disarticulated. She glanced toward the light and willed herself to be as silent as possible.

She said a silent prayer and begged the dead man's forgiveness.

Then she carefully curled her fingers around the femur.

She held it tightly and inched forward.

"I have light now, my lovely, I have light! Oh, my dear girl! Had you only finished drinking. I didn't wish to cause you fear! I never scared my beautiful girls. Well, poor Sadie! But she just didn't finish her drink, either. Sadie… I must go for Sadie. The human mind is so…strange. She might never remember, but…then again, she might."

Kieran kept moving. She realized that the killer was walking quickly now.

He had the advantage of his light.

Suddenly, another flashlight blazed, and she heard a booming voice.

"Stop! Stop where you are, you bastard!"

Two lights gleamed.

And Kieran realized that she was caught between them.

So close… She'd been so close, nearly to the place where

light seemed to glow—or had glowed, until the bold lights flared.

"Stop!" the newcomer called out again.

"Run, Kieran!" she heard then. "It's Gleason! It's Roger Gleason!"

"Kieran, it is Roger Gleason. But I'm not a killer! The bastard down here is the killer!"

She had no sense of direction. She couldn't tell whether Gleason's voice was coming from where she had been...

Or coming from where she was going.

"Let her alone!" Gleason called out again.

"What? You're going to kill her—and me?"

Kieran heard someone rushing up behind her. She turned and swung hard with the femur, as hard as she could.

At the same moment she came in contact, hands reached for her, ready to pull her down.

"Kieran!"

She heard her name called again, and this time, she knew the voice.

Craig.

Then the skeleton at her side suddenly began to move—as if it reached out for her, as well. As if it tried to embrace her with decayed and crippled fingers...

The skeleton fell to the floor, and bone dust rose around her in a cloud.

Craig rolled through onto the interment slab in the wake of the dead; he quickly hopped to his feet by her side.

His gun was raised.

Kieran saw that Roger Gleason was just a few feet to her left.

And Henry Willoughby was to her right.

Craig looked at Gleason.

Then he turned in the other direction. "Henry Willoughby, you are under arrest for the murders of Jeannette Gilbert, Cheyenne Lawson, Cary Howell and the kidnapping of Sadie Miller. Sir—"

He never went further. Willoughby rose with a howl of rage that seemed to echo through the crypts as if a thousand lions roared.

He had a huge knife raised high in his hand, and he was aiming for Kieran's heart.

She couldn't stop the scream that tore from her throat.

And she screamed and screamed as Craig fired his Glock and Willoughby fell against her, the knife wrenched out of his hand just before it reached her chest.

"She knew. Kieran knew all along somehow that it had to do with New York's underbelly. Well, that, and a very sick man," Kevin said.

He was sitting with Craig at Finnegan's, in a back booth. It was Friday evening; they'd both spent the day in Craig's FBI office.

Kieran had been an intended victim.

Craig had fired his weapon—and killed Willoughby.

There was no question that he'd had no choice; paperwork just came with the situation.

And, of course, there was the untangling of it all.

"I wonder if we would have found her if Mary Kathleen hadn't decided that it was ridiculous to let a glass of good champagne go down the drain," Kevin murmured. Then he leaned forward. "How did you know, though? I was furious at first that you didn't want to run straight to the building where she'd been when she disappeared. How did you know?"

"Kieran knew. She kept saying that the killer was getting

in and out through an adjacent building. We just had to find out where the connection was, deep in the crypts. Shaw's team helped, and Roger Gleason. He knew that he was innocent and that someone had framed him with that splotch of blood in his office."

"Why?" Kevin asked. "What made Willoughby a killer?"

"I don't know. We'll have to leave it to the experts to figure it out. What I've gotten so far—now that his house has been searched—is that Willoughby lost his wife about a decade ago. She'd been consumed by cancer. She'd been a beautiful woman. In his warped, sick mind, Willoughby wanted to find women as perfect as she had once been—and let them stay perfect. But, of course, they kept decaying on him. I don't know—maybe we'll never know—what he was really trying to do. Maybe he even wanted to get caught. But if we'd served a search warrant on him instead of Gleason, we might have known right away."

"How?" Kevin asked him.

"He had a well-worn copy of *Romeo and Juliet* on his desk. Maybe he was somehow able to see himself as a young man again, trying to find the right Juliet. We'll never have all the answers."

Kieran came by their back booth then, flopping into it.

She looked no worse for wear. Since they'd arrived, she'd been in a flurry.

She didn't really need to help out; Danny had taken over the bar, and they had a number of employees working the floor.

She'd been determined to do so.

Mary Kathleen was fine, but she and Declan were home. They'd needed the night.

Craig looked her. She smiled. She seemed especially vibrant.

"Not phased," Craig murmured. "You know, most people might consider what you went through last night to be a bit traumatic."

"I'm fine," she said. "I just felt the need to help out and…" She paused and glanced at Kevin, and Craig realized that it had just been one—incredibly eventful, but one—week since John Shaw had found the body of Jeannette Gilbert.

"You don't need to tiptoe around my feelings," Kevin said. He smiled at his sister. "We've lost before. We made it together. I know that I will weather this. I'm going to mourn Jeannette. She was wonderful, and I shouldn't forget her, nor should the world. But I'm all right." He grinned. "In fact, Miss Ball-of-Energy, I have a meeting in a few minutes." He made a face. "A director I met at the party, go figure. He's putting on a revival show—*Godspell.*"

"And he thinks you'd be a good—"

"Christ. Yep, go figure."

"I think you'd be wonderful," Kieran told him.

"We'll see," Kevin said. "I probably still have to go through an audition and all."

"Break a leg," Craig told him. "I'm not so sure I should say that in this family, but…"

"Hey. No one broke anything," Kieran said.

"Technically," Kevin said, "you did break a leg. You broke a leg all over Henry Willoughby. I guess I shouldn't be so flippant. The man is dead. I can't be sorry." He seemed to give himself a mental shake. "Anyway, as much as I respect you, Special Agent Frasier, and as a much as I love you, sister-lass-Kieran, you're at my booth and I have a meeting."

Kieran smiled and rose and grabbed Craig's hand.

"We're going," Craig said, rising with her.

They waved to Danny behind the bar; he seemed to be in his element. The talk that day was about everything that had happened.

Danny, of course, had eyewitness accounts of parts of the action.

Finnegan's was booming.

Of course, Le Club Vampyre would reopen soon; Roger Gleason has been proved completely innocent of all charges. In fact, the club would wind up being incredibly popular.

There was already talk of a movie being filmed there.

In the car, Craig turned to Kieran. "You're sure you're all right? You don't want some time, some sessions with…with your employers?"

She smiled. "You saved my life."

"Ah, but we've established the fact that you are my life," he told her.

She smiled at that.

"My turn to suck up," she told him.

"Oh?"

"Your hair…your great hair," she said.

"Thank you."

"And what a nose."

"I hear it's quite classic."

"Totally lovely," she told him.

He frowned. "I don't think that 'totally lovely' sounds very macho," he said.

"Let's get to my place. I feel the need for a shower. And, of course, if you want me to go on, I'll need a little refresher on all that I might appreciate."

They reached her apartment. They showered.

Kieran found more to appreciate.

And, of course, Craig informed her that he'd have to *show* her macho, since she was determined on using the word *lovely*.

And still, deep in the night, after they'd both shown one another several times just how much they really needed one another, Craig held her and asked her, "Are you sure? You're really all right?"

She rose above him and told him, "Always. I'm with a crack FBI agent, you know. Safe and secure."

"And loved."

"And loved. Best part of all," she said.

He smiled. And he wondered how the hell he could ever figure out how to keep her out of trouble in the future.

It couldn't be solved that night. So he just held her.

Grateful that she was alive.

Absolutely perfect.

Alive.

And with him.

★ ★ ★ ★ ★

35674050735746